CATRIONA MCPHERSON

Dandy Gilver
and a Bothersome
Number of Corpses

HODDER

First published in Great Britain in 2012 by Hodder & Stoughton
An Hachette UK company

First published in paperback in 2013

1

A CIP catalogue record for this title is available from the British Library.

Paperback ISBN 978 1 444 73187 3
eBook ISBN 978 1 444 73186 6

Typeset in Plantin by Palimpsest Book Production Ltd, Falkirk, Stirlingshire.

Printed and bound in Great Britain by Clays Ltd, St Ives plc.

Hodder & Stoughton policy is to use papers that are natural, renewable and
recyclable products and made from wood grown in sustainable forests.
The logging and manufacturing processes are expected to conform to the
environmental regulations of the country of origin.

Hodder & Stoughton Ltd
338 Euston Road
London NW1 3BH

www.hodder.co.uk

For Sarah Rizzo
with love and thanks

I would like to thank:

Dave and Sarah Rizzo and Celia and Toni too and Harry, of
course, for the granny flat, the piano accompaniment (Celia), the
daily runway show (Toni), the inter-species welcome (Harry) and
the answers to a thousand questions while I worked on this book.

Connie and Sheldon Berkowitz, Dick Hoenisch and Deborah
Golino, Carla Thomas, Karin, Takao and Phoebe Kasuga, and all
the faculty and staff of the Plant Pathology Department of UC
Davis for their friendly support.

Spring Warren and Eileen Rendahl for their entertaining and
outrageous take on life, their understanding and their instant
friendship. Sally Madden for fortitude in the face of technology.
To these three and also to Stella Ruiz and Katie Howard – thank
you for your names.

My family and friends in Scotland for being so patient while I
got my act together.

Lisa Moylett, Wonder Agent, for her steady hand on the tiller.

Bronwen Salter-Murison for the Dandy Gilver website – above
and beyond.

Suzie Dooré (aka Editrix Lestrange) for the best edit ever –
practically co-authoring this time. Francine Toon for her cheerful
and organised way with things and for her title-generating skills.
Imogen Olsen for a copy-edit that started with a shovel and
ended with a scalpel. You have saved my bacon once again.

Marcia Markland, Bridget Hartzler and Kat Brzozowski for
inducting me kindly but firmly into the ways of US publishing.

Neil McRoberts. Still. Kind of. No, really.

And thanks again, because once wasn't enough, to Sarah Rizzo.

Prologue

It was three o'clock in the morning and the moon was a sliver of ice in an ink-blue sky; not a stroke of light in the west to show that the sun had ever set there, nor a hint of dawn in the east where a bank of clouds was gathering, so the darkness was as perfect as midwinter.

The sea had come in silently, waves unrolling like bolts of silk across the sands, and now it was still and full, waiting for the turn, lapping only a little as it slid gently up and down against the base of the cliffs. And so when she reached the break in the rock, a natural cove where men had built a harbour, there was no current to wash her into the welcome of its broad stone arms.

She had always loved the water; a quick swimmer, strong and sure in the warm salty tides, quick and supple like a fish escaping a net. So when she had entered the sea for the last time in her life – when, hours ago now, she had plummeted off the crumbling edge of the headland and come up choking – she had simply flicked her hair out of her eyes, kicked off her shoes and trodden water, looking around, sweeping her arms wide, letting the shock pass through her and her breaths grow calm again. When she was steady, she shrugged out of her jacket and let it float away. She tried for a moment to open her buttons, hoping to get her corset untied and let her lungs fill to the top before she started swimming, but the water was cold and, as she fumbled, twice she felt her chin sink under the surface and had to paddle her arms again.

That was the first fearful moment – as late as that. That was the first time she thought to use her lungs to cry for help and not to power her strong swim back to the shore. Two sheep at the edge of a field raised their bony heads and stared down at her, still chewing, then turned away. She scanned the line where the rock-face met the green pasture and could see nothing, not a house, not a track, not even a gate in the fence to show that the shepherd might pass by, going home at the end of his day.

Then she raised her legs in front of her and let her head drop back, feeling the coldness fill her ears. Perhaps she would find, if she let herself, that she would float to the shore, to the narrow band of boulders at the bottom of the drop, the boulders she might have fallen onto were not God Himself trying so hard to save her that He put His hand under her tumbling body and laid her gently down into His safe blue sea.

But she was floating away. Those sheep were smaller now. So she drove her legs downwards and lifted them behind her, feeling the second flutter of panic at the weight of her skirts and petticoats against the backs of her calves. Then she breathed in hard, the bones of her corset creaking against her ribs, picked a dark patch of gorse on the face of the cliff to fix her gaze upon and set off with a long, sculling stroke which seemed to push five yards of cold water behind her.

A hundred strokes later, when she took a rest, she knew the patch of gorse was no closer, but could not bear to believe it was further away.

A thousand strokes later, when she had stopped looking for the gorse, had stopped looking at the shore at all, terrified to see how distant it had become, she rested again and then turned outwards, thinking about the fishing boats, the way they fanned out of the harbour mouth each morning, blossoming over the sea, and the way they gathered homewards each evening, from every corner of the horizon, as if the boats themselves were drawing the night in after them. One of them would pass her, close enough to hear her cries.

She practised calling, and that was the third pulse of fear. Her voice was ragged, the croak of a crow; it barely reached her own ears even in the stillness this evening. She told herself that if she trod water she would not need to breathe so hard. If she breathed through her nose and kept her mouth closed her throat would soften again and her voice would be clear and loud when she used it, when the fishing boat came.

But waiting was lonely and she was cold, and so later when her mother called out to her and told her to come home, to eat her broth and bread, to take off her wet clothes, get into her warm bed and sleep, she wanted to call back that she was coming, that she would be there soon, but she kept treading water and looking for boats and she saved her voice for the fishermen.

And when her mother scolded her and told her not to shout out to strange men like a gypsy girl, told her to come home this instant, that the broth was hot and the bread was fresh, and there was an extra blanket on her bed and she could sleep until noon, could sleep the clock round, could sleep for ever if she would only come home, at last she answered – just a whisper – that she was coming. She turned her shoulder into the black cradle of the sea and rested and she felt no pain as the water covered her.

I

Hearing her name down the telephone line twitched me away into the past as swiftly as the hook in the cheek of a trout will pluck it out of water into air and leave it gasping. Fleur Lipscott, sweet little Fleur. Husband, children, decades of humdrum adult life were quite gone and there I was again in that first golden summer at Pereford where for ten long lazy weeks the sun rose over the hills, smiled down upon us all day and then sank with a sigh into the warm sea each evening. We paddled and bathed at the little cove, drifted around the lake in a little boat, meandered the cloistered Somerset lanes behind a slow, clopping pony of gentle nature in a cart full of cushions. I could smell the lavender scent of the linen cushion-slips still.

There were three sweet golden Lipscott girls – Pearl, Aurora and little Fleur – each with a silky mass of flaxen curls and a pink rose in each cheek, and had Pereford been a house full of men or of mirrors I might have resented my straight black hair and sallow complexion, being just old enough at eighteen to know that flax and roses were better currency in the business for which we girls had been trained. But 'the Major' as his wife and daughters always called him (with inverted commas and capital letter clearly pronounced) had died when Fleur was a baby; and Mamma-dearest (with no inverted commas at all; the endearment was unselfconscious), Batty Aunt Lilah (often addressed just like that, in full) and the three girls themselves lived with a kind of gentle delight in their home and each other, which spread over all their friends. It was most effective at stopping such churlish feelings as envy taking hold, and was not even half as annoying as it sounds.

The Major had spent a great deal of time at his Highland lodge, even when alive, and so was not much missed when he died. His death was one of glory at Spion Kop, on that fatal night of pass the parcel, gamely taking command for half an hour or so after the last available colonel perished before handing on to the next major in line; but from the easy circumstances of his widow and orphans, tucked up in that cosy old house of theirs with loyal servants all around, one would have thought he had expired at eighty after six months' advice from good lawyers about his arrangements. Of course, none of this occurred to me that summer, not at eighteen; it was my husband Hugh – much later, when George at the club had regaled him with news of Aurora's engagement – who spent a bitter evening mulling over the settlements of these three girls and lamenting that not even Fleur was young enough ever to make a lucrative wife for one of our sons.

'Oh Hugh, for goodness' sake!' I said at last. 'The boys are two and one. They're babies!'

'And she's fourteen,' said Hugh, misunderstanding completely. 'I know. By the time Donald is twenty-one she'll be thirty-three. It would cause comment. No, I'm afraid I can't see my way clear, Dandy. You shall just have to put it out of your mind.'

'I give up,' I said. 'I really do.'

'Although if this Aurora one is your sort of age, they obviously don't marry young.'

For a moment, I almost wished that I had taken Nanny's gentle hints about how nice it would be for Mother to have nursery tea with the boys now they were sitting up in high chairs and using spoons since, although they were noisy and messy as dining companions go, they had not yet developed a capacity for active rudeness. I glared at Hugh and consoled myself with a sip of wine and a mouthful of devilled mushroom (Nanny would never admit either of these treats to her nursery, I knew).

He had, however, made a point worth making. Aurora, newly betrothed to Drew Forrester, was twenty-nine, and even Pearl had held out much longer than I should have dared, only

6

succumbing at almost twenty-five, and what with their dowries and their beauty, the world at large was puzzled by the delay. I was not, knowing that had I lived in that house with Mamma-dearest and Batty Aunt Lilah I should have been in no hurry to leave it either.

For it was a house without horsehair, without porridge, a house where carbolic soap was unknown and dinner gongs went unstruck. At Pereford, we slept on featherbeds and breakfasted on peaches. The maids scooped great handfuls of pink salts into our bathwater and dinner was heralded with a carillon upon a little glockenspiel of the sweetest tone.

Furthermore, Mamma-dearest's greatest delight was to lie in a hammock strung between two plum trees and spin tales for her girls, never forgetting me, and so a good part of what I remembered of Pereford was not Pereford at all but pictures from my mind's eye of her girlhood in Haryana where her hammock was hung from banyan trees and her linen was scented with patchouli mint; pictures of the endless fairy tale she wove of our delightful futures, of heroic suitors and the balls at which they would sweep us up in their arms and tell of their love, and all with the dappled sunlight winking through the leaves of the plum tree and the hammock strings creaking like the rigging of a clipper as she rocked to and fro.

I was only ever there in the summertime, starting with that first summer on the way home from Paris where I had met Pearl and made friends with her. In winter it might have been different, I suppose, but I doubt it, for the fireplaces – filled with flowers in July – were enormous and the white muslin curtains which billowed at the open windows, wafting the scent of roses into the rooms, were hung from mahogany curtain rods as thick as telegraph poles which hinted at a high measure of velvety sumptuousness in the colder months of the year. Then, in an attic where we went to play hide-and-seek (humouring Fleur, although we were much too old for it), there was the clincher: great squashy bales of calico – the sumptuous curtains stitched up tight for the summer against the moth – stacked on top of log-piles of rolled Turkey carpets and, all around, a veritable souk of coal scuttles, log baskets and peat barrels.

'Heavens, what a lot you've got,' I said to Pearl.

'One for each fireplace,' she said, and began counting: 'The outside hall, the inside hall, the upstairs landing. The far end of the drawing room, the near end of the drawing room. This little one is for Mamma-dear's bathroom and isn't it lovely. She always has cherry logs in there and the time it took her to teach the fire boy to tell the difference!'

'You have a boy just for that?' I could not help boggling, having been brought up in a house where the maids set the fires in the morning and one held off and held off lighting them since to ring for more coal was such extravagance that we often found ourselves going to bed just to avoid it, cursing that reckless moment at seven o'clock when we had thought we were cold, which we now knew was nothing compared to the shivering that set in at eleven when the embers were growing grey.

'Mahmout,' Pearl said. 'Dearest Mamma-darling brought him home with her. He was the son of her ayah and she says he's the perfect fire boy because he's always trying to get Pereford as warm as Haryana.'

'He'll set the place alight or die trying,' said Batty Aunt Lilah, who was playing with us, or at any rate was pattering around in nearby rooms while we played, not ever getting quite to grips with the rules.

'I haven't noticed him about,' I said, feeling sure that an Indian in a white loincloth (for thus I had imagined him) would have stuck out enough to be noticed in Somerset.

'Oh, no, he's not here now,' Aurora said. 'He's on his summer holidays. Mamma-dearest sends him to London every year where he has some family connections. She says he'd go into a decline if he didn't get to speak Hindustani and eat spices for a while.'

Mrs Lipscott, it will be understood, was never likely to suffer from 'the servant problem'. My own mother did not even allow her daughter to go to London every year, never mind her servant boys.

'He sits in the palm house at Kew,' said Lilah. 'Warming his bones.' Then she let herself fall backwards onto one of the stitched-up calico bundles of winter curtains, landing with a pouf! and lying there staring up at the joists of the ceiling.

'You'll have to find a better hiding place than that, Batty Aunt,' said Aurora. 'I can hear Fleur coming already.'

'Throw a sheet over me and if she looks my way I'll freeze,' said Lilah. Then the rest of us huddled behind the enormous log boxes, breathing in quietly the scent of cherry wood and that of the resinous green pine branches used for kindling.

'Once upon a time,' Fleur said, opening the attic door and coming inside, 'there was a beautiful little girl named Flower or Flora or Fleur. And she lived in a fairy castle with her two beautiful sisters, Aurora or Sunrise or Dawn and Pearl . . .' The three of us held our breaths, trying not to giggle. Fleur's Fairy Tales were held in high regard in the Lipscott family, even against the general background of delighted appreciation of absolutely anything, and they were the reason we all hid together (lest one of us miss something).

'. . . Pearl,' Fleur said again, 'or Grit or Dirty Oyster.' At this Batty Aunt Lilah snorted and Fleur lifted the sheet and pounced on her.

'You forgot all about me, you little brigand,' Lilah said, tickling Fleur. 'What about the beautiful aunt?'

'There isn't an aunt,' Fleur said. 'But help me look for the others and I might add you in.'

'And what about that other girl?' said Lilah. She always referred to me this way.

'Oh, she's in it,' said Fleur. She was unbuckling the straps of a wicker hamper to look inside. 'She's the dark queen. Dandy or . . . Actually, she can't be called Dandy if she's a dark queen.'

Crouched there behind my log basket I could only agree: Pearl, Fleur and Aurora seemed the most elegant, graceful names imaginable to me (until years later when Hugh cut through my enthralment by saying it sounded as though their parents did not have full use of their tongues and wanted to make life easy).

9

The thought of Hugh now cut just as decisively through my reverie and I returned, blinking, to the present, with the telephone chattering in my hand.

'So on three counts, Dandy,' Pearl was saying as I put the telephone to my ear again, 'you are an angel sent from heaven for me. Well, four, if we're to count how much I adore you and always have and always shall.'

'And the other three?' I asked. Either the Lipscott Delight had increased in intensity in the two decades since that summer or my nature had soured, because what had enchanted me then was pretty sickening now.

'Well, first, of course, Fleur always loved you like a sister.'

'Hm,' I said. This might well have been true but Fleur Lipscott had two real sisters whom she presumably loved like sisters too, and I could not see why I should be at the head of the queue.

'And then there's the fact that you're up there. Right on the spot.'

'I am?' I said. 'Where is she?'

'Scotland,' said Pearl with all the complacency of one who has seldom been there and has no conception of the vast empty stretches of it nor the scarcity and inadequacy of the roads. She, no doubt, thought of Scotland as a dark blur outside a sleeper carriage, which revealed itself to be a grouse moor in the morning.

'Whereabouts in "Scotland"?' I asked her.

'Place called Portpatrick,' Pearl supplied. 'Or was it St Patrick? It sounded wonderful, that I do know.'

'Hm,' I said again. With a name like that it had to be some-where round the western edges and getting to it might be nasty.

'So I rang up Daisy Esslemont and she said your name straight away.'

'No doubt,' I replied. 'Despite the fact that Daisy is "up here" too and she and Fleur know one another rather well, don't they?' I was sure they did and, although I could not quite reach the memory, something about it troubled me; no more than a whisper of unease like a strand of hair on one's face that one can blow away with a breath, but still it was there.

'And she told me your marvellous news. You are brave and clever and wonderful and—'

'What news?' I asked, cutting in. One of my sons' most revolting habits (from a very strong field) was the making of sick-noises in response to uncalled-for sentiment but I felt a quick tug just then towards making some of my own.

'Gilver and Osborne!' said Pearl. 'A detective agency! I could hardly believe my ears. I always thought of you as such a placid soul. So unconcerned and untroubled by life's slings and brickbats.'

'Arrows,' I said. 'And you make me sound positively bovine.'

'Exactly!' said Pearl. 'Now, if any of us were going to be a detective, I'd have thought Aurora was the one. So foxy and quick and such a spark of intelligence.'

At this, I took the earpiece away from my head and stared at it. Aurora Lipscott had spent that entire Pereford summer wearing daisy chains in her hair and was famous in the family for her inability to swim underwater, being so plump that even with Pearl and me pushing her down and little Fleur actually sitting on top of her she would bob to the surface in seconds like a doughnut in hot oil. *Foxy* was not a word one would ever have used of the girl. Of course, I had not seen much of the woman she had become, but I would have bet my own money that nothing much had changed and it was the Lipscott Delight that was behind her sister's testimonial.

'Intelligent or not,' I said, but provoked no murmur, 'I have somehow managed to carve out a place for myself in the field, it's true.'

'And with a very dashing business partner too,' Pearl went on. '"Leonine and glowing", Daisy said. "Roseate, aflame".'

'She never did, you big fibber,' I said.

'She did!' said Pearl. '"A red-haired young man who worships the ground you walk upon". I'm quoting her directly.'

I rolled my eyes at Bunty, who was lying stretched on the hearthrug of my sitting room and staring at me with wrinkled brow. Dalmatians are not known for their foxiness either and at thirteen years old she was past new tricks, so I had abandoned hope that she would ever understand telephones and stop assuming that each time I started talking in a room where she and I were alone I must be addressing her. It induced great guilt in me that I must appear to be speaking to her in such an un-doggy monotone and using not a one of her favourite words.

'We get along very well as colleagues,' I said to Pearl, squashing any notions of adoration. Bunty groaned and resettled herself facing away from me, just one ear still cocked my way.

'And it's marvellous of darling Hugh to embrace his horizons expanding into such lightness and . . .' Here Pearl lost hold of the metaphor and let it float away. 'Daisy said he and the young golden god are true friends, that the three of you together are—'

'No, Pearl, she didn't,' I said. 'Hugh and Alec get along perfectly nicely. And Hugh is quite happy about my detecting because I've made a lot of money at it. I keep a fair bit of this place going these days.'

'Oh Dandy,' Pearl said. 'You poor thing. You never used to let such dull thoughts darken your heart.'

Now this was beyond cheek, because when Pearl had 'finally married at almost twenty-five' it was to a man many years older than she, who spoke of nothing but golf and the gold standard, but was as rich as a sheik from refrigerated shipping.

'Well, nothing darkens the heart like the dull thought of selling up and moving to a bungalow, so I'll just struggle on,' I said. 'Am I to understand then that you're telling me about Fleur in my professional capacity?'

'Sort of,' said Pearl. 'Not exactly. Yes and no. I mean, a detective is practically legal. I'm appealing to you as a . . . wise woman.' I forbore from telling her that I had a flat rate, never mind whether she wanted wisdom or the law. 'It's just that something's wrong with Fleur and I'm terribly worried about her. She's made such gargantuan strides – Amazonian really – since that dreadful time but now, from her letters, I find myself wondering if some sort of the old trouble might not be rearing its head again.'

'What time?' I said. 'What trouble?'

'Ah, well,' said Pearl. 'Much better to lift our eyes to the hills and look forward to a better future.' I said nothing. 'But I suppose, to give you an idea . . . Fleur did have a rather unsettled patch, at the end of the war and just after.'

That was it! The hook twitched in my cheek once more and I was gone. Not so far this time; only to 1918 and Daisy and Silas's first Armistice Ball, which was repeated year after year on its anniversary (and which started my detecting career, in a round-about sort of way). Fleur, Pearl and Aurora were all there, of course, Aurora sitting out the dances in a loose-fitting gown. Even at that her mother-in-law sniped the evening away about the scandal of her appearing at all in her condition, until at last Pearl and I took pity and made up a bridge four with both of them. Pearl was more than happy not to be on the floor since a life of refrigerated shipping (she had found) makes for a wonderful provider but a poor dancing partner. Hugh of course was delighted at my taking myself away. He bowed, looked at his pocket watch and headed off towards the billiards room like a dog who smelled a bone.

And so, because I was at a card table with her sisters, I saw quite a bit of Fleur that night. Otherwise I should not have had more than a glimpse: a glittering figure dancing like a dervish; a tinkling laugh on the terrace after supper when we all trooped out to watch fireworks (an ill-advised form of celebration, which left more than one young officer white and sweating). I might not even have recognised her in the crowd. For the sweet girl of my remembered perfect summer was grown up now, her straggling ringlets coiled flat against her head, her freckles gone or at least hidden by face powder of a deathly white, like chalk dust, and as well as these inevitable if unfortunate badges of womanhood – such were the fashions of the time – changes had been wrought in Fleur that might have seen me pass her on the street without blinking.

'She got in with a bad lot,' Pearl was saying down the telephone line. 'Too wild for a girl like Fleur, and whenever they were all together she became just like them.'

Only that was not quite the whole story, because that night, Armistice night, Fleur was at a party in the house of a family friend and she had come with her sisters and their husbands, yet she was the wildest thing in the room, a sparkling little tornado of kisses and giggles, sweeping up a tail of enchanted men around her as she spun. I noticed, however, that quite a few of them made the effort to break away, shaking their heads and laughing, ignoring the piping voice that pleaded with them to come back. In fact, I witnessed two getting free of her pull at once and saw the look they shared, of amusement and scorn. It made me hurt for her, with her ringlets, sitting on her sister's broad back in the shallow salt water of the cove.

And when she visited our table as the rubber wore its weary path to the final tally (Aurora's mother-in-law, Mrs Forrester, was the very worst kind of bridge player, both impetuous and deadly slow), as well as hanging over her sisters, wrapping her arms around their necks and swapping the endless Lipscott endearments, she also offered up a series of sharp little digs about the house and the other guests which I had to work at not countering with digs of my own.

Aurora and Pearl only tittered.

'Now really, Floribunda,' Pearl said. 'Play prettily with the other children or Nanny will take you home.'

'But honestly, Oysie,' Fleur was saying (this nickname had stuck, as one of the many), 'what a place. It's like a barracks. Not right for a party at all.'

'It's a tower house,' I said. Fleur turned dreamily towards me, blinking as though the movement of her head had made her dizzy. 'A fort, rather than a barracks, actually.'

'Although,' she said, 'come to think of it, I've been to some marvellous parties in barracks and at least tonight I won't have to depart over the wall.'

Mrs Forrester was a woman mixed together from a bloodline reaching back to the time of the Danish kings along with a good shovelful of the Yorkshire soil where the family had always been planted, which mixture had produced a character of pure flint. She froze with a card halfway to the table.

'She's teasing, Fenella,' Aurora said calmly and wagged her

finger at Fleur. 'Straight to bed with no supper unless you stop being naughty.'

'I don't want any supper,' said Fleur. 'Have you seen it? Great slices of ham as though we were ploughmen! I'm going to dance again.' She dropped a kiss on all four of our heads and ran on light tiptoes out of the card room with the floating chiffon panels of her party frock streaming out behind her.

'Doesn't she look adorable?' Pearl said, gazing after her.

'Truly like a little flower,' said Aurora. 'That frock makes her look as though she's dressed in petals.'

'Three spades,' said Mrs Forrester, but they were too busy gazing.

'Mamma-dearest and the Major must have seen her whole pretty life ahead of her the day she was born to have given her that name,' said Pearl.

'And yours, Pearl darling,' said Aurora. 'You are the pearl of us all.'

'And you were the dawn of us all, my angel,' said Pearl. 'What does Fenella mean, Fenella?'

'It means my grandmother's name was Fenella and she had her own fortune to leave as she chose,' said Mrs Forrester, making me laugh even though I am not sure she meant to be funny.

I laughed again now, remembering.

'Dandy?' said Pearl down the line.

'Sorry,' I said. 'Do go on. I was just thinking about Mrs Forrester on Armistice night.'

'I must have forgotten,' said Pearl. 'So, dearest darlingest Dandiest, will you help?'

'I will,' I said, interrupting the endearments firmly. 'Of course I will. But you'll have to tell me a lot more about what's wrong. Love or money? It's usually one of the two.'

'Not this time,' said Pearl. 'It's remorse. Black engulfing guilt. I thought Fleur had put it quite out of her mind but, as I say, from her letters I think it's taken hold of her again.'

'Guilt over what?'

'Nothing!' said Pearl. 'How could little Floramundi have

anything to be guilty of? And besides, she's done everything she can to live a different life, a glorious, selfless, saintly life.'

'You make it sound as though she'd taken the veil,' I said. Pearl said nothing. 'She hasn't, has she?' I was not entirely joking now. 'She's not in a convent? Pearl?'

'Not quite,' said Pearl. 'She's in a school.'

'What do you mean? Studying to *join* a convent?'

'No, I mean, she's teaching in a girls' school. A boarding school. In Portpatrick, in Scotland.' Now, *I* was speechless. Sweet little Fleur, pretty and rich, had become a schoolmistress? 'St Columba's College for Young Ladies,' said Pearl miserably. 'And it's worse than it sounds. It's run according to a nasty German theory of education – the Foible Method, or something – and the girls all go on to universities and oh . . . poor little Fleur.'

'It does sound pretty ghastly,' I agreed. 'And so you want me to winkle her out of there? Persuade her to resign? I'm not sure I could—'

'No!' said Pearl. 'She's been there eight years and for all that time she's been almost happy. I want you to find out what's gone wrong with her *now*. I want you to stop her running away even from St Columba's. If we lose her completely again we'll all die of grief. Mamma-dearest, Sunny and me.'

'There, there,' I said. 'Pearl, please. Of course I will, darling. Only why don't you and Aurora hop on a train and—'

'Banished,' said Pearl. 'Forbidden the house. Kept at the gates. "Miss Lipscott is not at home to callers."'

'Miss Lipscott,' I echoed. Of course I should have realised that a schoolmistress could not be a married woman, but to think of that faerie-child, that glittering chiffoned girl, still Miss Lipscott at thirty gave me a pang. Add the fact of her fortune, I thought to myself, and the news would *kill* Hugh.

2

Of course, Alec Osborne was furious.

'A school?' he said. 'A *girls'* school? I thought we had decided, Dandy.' He spiked his fork into his beefsteak and attacked it with his knife as though he were sawing through a plank. (And since the beef from the Mains is excellent, the butcher at Dunkeld a stickler for hanging and Mrs Tilling, my cook, a fiend with a tenderiser, he got clean through it in a second and the blade made a painful screeching sound against the porcelain below.)

'How could we decide such a thing?' I asked him. 'We agreed that it would be fun for you if a case came in that was a little more . . . rugged, but we didn't entertain the idea of turning business away. I didn't anyway.'

'What next?' Alec cried. 'A lying-in hospital? An harem?'

'Trouble?' asked Hugh. He had retired into his own thoughts while I was speaking, naturally, but Alec's distress had roused him.

'The curse strikes again,' Alec said. 'Gilver and Osborne are engaged to infiltrate a dormitory full of schoolgirls. Or in other words, Dandy is in business and I am to stand and hold her coat.'

'No one mentioned dorms, darling,' I murmured.

'Ah,' said Hugh, but his interest had already waned. As far as my husband is concerned any man who mixes himself up with such nonsense as detecting has only himself to blame if his path leads to boudoirs, servants' halls, dress departments or even boarding schools for young ladies.

'Dear Alec,' I said, 'if I could order you up a murder aboard a merchant sea-vessel with a crew of forty bearded sailors in ganseys, I wouldn't hesitate to do so.' Alec regarded me coldly. 'A stolen medicine ball from a boxing gymnasium?' His lips twitched. 'Death and dismemberment in a troop of morris dancers?' Now he really did smile.

'I'm coming to the town with you,' he said. 'Even if I can only press my face against the railings and pine. Where is it, exactly?'

'Miles away,' I said. 'Practically Ireland, and we don't have any friends anywhere about so it's the village inn for you. And me too unless I can wangle an invitation to the staffroom sofa.' Neither of us looked at Hugh. Alec practically strained his neck not doing so.

My husband's opinion of my new life had been through several shades: blissful ignorance, suspicion of something at once both worse than the truth in its betrayal but miles less troubling by virtue of its being so unexceptional (this when all he knew was that Alec and I were spending more time together than he could properly account for), relief on that score swiftly followed by a bewildered huff about why I should do such an unearthly thing, delight in the money, another bewildered huff lest he was being duped in some twisty double-crossing way by Alec and me, wheels within wheels, treachery inside innocence wrapped in treachery, until we had finally arrived at this uneasy three-legged balancing act. Dinner together discussing a case was fine but one arch comment at a party and Hugh was wont to grow mulish again. I tended just to look the other way and whistle since, while nothing is a greater bore than Hugh in a fully fledged sulk, the thought of losing Gilver and Osborne (especially of losing Osborne, if I am honest) was not to be borne.

'And it's not death and dismemberment, is it?' Alec said. '*What* is it?

'Her sisters—'

'Whose sisters?'

'The schoolmistress. Her sisters fear she's going to bolt but they don't know why and they're not allowed to visit her. She's obviously in some kind of trouble and they want us – well, me – to find out what kind, fix it and resettle her.'

'Sounds thrilling,' said Alec.

'And I want to find out what she's doing there in the first place,' I said. 'This girl, Alec, was an absolute darling – pretty, lively, clever, adored and indulged, free to live any life she chose . . . that's the puzzle I want to solve: how on earth she ended up an old maid teaching in a girls' school.'

'I take it back then,' said Alec. 'Sounds a bit *too* exciting when you put it that way.'

'No, but really,' I said. 'Hugh, you remember Fleur Lipscott, don't you?' I had been looking forward, rather meanly, to regaling him.

Hugh considered the name and then shook his head. 'Never heard of her. Lipscott?'

I suppressed a sigh. 'There were three sisters: Fleur, Pearl and Aurora. They were at our wedding. You danced with Pearl at a ball at the Esslemonts'.' Hugh was shaking his head as slowly and steadily as the pendulum in a long-case clock. 'The two elder married rather late on.' More shaking and at last I relented. 'They're all very rich. Left well off by their father, Maj—'

'Johnny Lipscott's girls?' said Hugh. 'Why didn't you just say that? Yes, of course I remember them. One of the Forrester boys got one and some magnate no one knows nabbed another. I don't know who snapped up number three.'

'No one did,' I told him patiently. 'She never married and she's working as a schoolmistress in Wigtownshire.'

'Really?' said Hugh. 'Now, that *is* interesting. Is she merely employed there or has she invested in the place? These single women are notorious for sinking funds into tea shops and dress shops.'

'Hugh, you can't be serious,' I said. 'She's thirty and she's got some dark and dreadful secret in her past, probably a child or an elopement or something.'

'I'm lost,' Alec said.

'It could be anything,' Hugh retorted.

'A spell in burlesque, gambling debts, opium . . .'

'What are you talking about?' said Alec looking between the two of us.

'Hugh – it's too revolting – thinks she might do for Donald, don't you, darling?' I said, expecting to shrivel him. He was unrepentant.

'He's eighteen,' he said.

'Yes, but we're not living in eighteen hundred and eighteen.'

'Osborne?' said Hugh, fixing Alec with a stare. Even a man as lost to silliness as this one, it was to be understood, would side with him when it came to the hard matter of a dowry.

'I wouldn't have thanked my father for a thirty-year-old bride when I was eighteen,' Alec said. 'But of course, I'm thirty-seven now. If she's really so very rich and so very pretty, maybe I can steal her away to Dunelgar. Her sisters can always come and visit her there.'

Hugh cannot tell when Alec is joking and got a look upon his face reminiscent of mild toothache at the thought that he had shown his hand and alerted another to the prize. He fell silent, we arranged to set off on what passed for a fast train the following morning and Alec left early to supervise his packing (Barrow, his valet, is a man of decided opinion and forceful nature, but Alec always tries to have some say) and pow-wow with his estate manager about the many jobs which May inevitably brings. I spent a rueful moment reflecting on how deeply entrenched Alec had become in his pasture and crops and his timber holdings since he arrived at Dunelgar five years before. He sometimes seemed as happy discussing barley or pheasant chicks with Hugh as discussing suspects and alibis with me, and it often made me wonder which was the real Alec Osborne, if either.

I was sitting on my bed describing the little I knew about the case to Grant, my maid, to allow her to choose my wardrobe for me (I, unlike Alec, gave up all thoughts of influence over my outfits long ago) when a knock came at the door.

Grant and I stared at one another and ran through all possibilities swiftly. My sons were at school; we had no guests staying in the house; none of the other maids would dare risk Grant's wrath by attempting to breach the sanctum and if Alec had forgotten to tell me something he would have rung at the front doorbell and sent a message to me. He makes quite free with the downstairs of Gilverton in the hours of daylight but he would never come a-knocking at my bedroom door at night.

'Come in?' I said and Grant nodded, approving my handling of this unheard-of development in our lives.

The door opened, revealing Hugh.

'Ah, good,' he said. 'You're still up, Dandy. Well, I just wanted to say this: Donald is coming down at the end of this term – in a few short weeks, actually. He has no interest whatsoever in university, thank goodness since he has no aptitude for it either, and unless he comes home and takes over Benachally he's only going to racket about and ruin us. Living at Benachally alone would be rather dull and so why not? I wouldn't have ordered her off a menu with that size of an age difference, but you yourself said you like the girl and so . . . a word to the wise. Don't let Osborne have it all his own way.'

I was speechless, and so said nothing.

'Different if it were Teddy,' Hugh said, 'but Donald has had a ribbon in his pocket since he was ten.'

'They don't carry ribbons in their pockets any more, Hugh,' I said. 'Even you didn't carry rib—'

'Just a figure of speech,' said Hugh. 'Don't quibble. He has had a caravan of village girls following him around since he was old enough to wink at them and if we don't get him married off in short order I can quite imagine that someday it will be a caravan of village fathers, with shotguns. Which would you rather?'

Grant was rolling stockings in a kind of paroxysm of embarrassment of which Hugh was sublimely unaware.

'He is too young,' I said. 'And she is too old. If you're worried about shotguns' – I glanced at Grant but Hugh did not so much as follow my eyes – 'then threaten him with your own. Oh, how I wish he would just join the army and get rid of his high jinks with his brother officers where he can do no harm.'

'He's not joining the army,' said Hugh, rather shortly. 'Not now. Not soon and I fervently hope not ever.'

I frowned at him. 'Why not? One would have thought you'd

more quickly shove him into your old regiment than up the aisle with a fading beauty of questionable past.'

Grant was now, frankly, loitering. My case was packed and the drawer she was tidying out was perfectly tidy already.

'If it comes to conscription then of course he shall go. They shall both go. But I will not encourage them into the vanguard.'

I shook my head at him. Hugh is a doom-monger of the very highest order. He was convinced that a nine-day strike a year or two ago was the coming of the revolutionary hordes and managed to get me thoroughly rattled despite my long experience of his dramatic premonitions (not to mention my long experience of my country not going in for revolutions much these days). His latest conviction, a mere ten years after the Great War ended, was that more of the same was on its way and from the very Hun that we had so thoroughly squashed. I do not pretend to follow the domestic politics of Bavaria with the interest my husband manages to muster, but I knew enough to be sure that this was his hobby-horse and nothing more sinister than that; more akin to campfire tales of ghosts when everyone is safe and cosy than a cool appraisal of the state of the world.

'Goodnight, Hugh,' I said.

'Something to consider,' he answered, making no move to leave my open doorway.

I stood and put my hand to the back of my neck as though to unfasten a button there, which did the trick. With a curt goodnight he left me.

'Master's right, you know,' said Grant. 'Madam.'

'About the gathering clouds of war?' I said, unfastening my dress buttons since I had all but started anyway.

'About Young Master Donald,' she replied. 'I caught him up a tree with Eliza McManus once, gazing at her like the crown jewels.'

'Eliza McManus!' I shuddered. She was the daughter of a blacksmith, as broad as she was tall, with a red face and gaps between all of her front teeth. 'How did Eliza McManus get up a tree?'

'This was years ago, before she got so . . . sturdy.'

'So they were children,' I said. 'Stop scare-mongering.'

'Nanny said to me once that Donald said to her – in his bath – that when he grew up he wanted to be a daddy.'

'How sweet. This correspondence is now closed,' I said. 'What am I wearing tomorrow?'

'Leave off wrenching at those buttons and I'll tell you,' said Grant. 'Madam. Turn around and let me at them before they all end up on the floor.'

It was a bright grey day when we arrived at Portpatrick the following afternoon (in Scotland, one must learn to make these distinctions), with a great deal of massing and thinning cloud scudding across the sky on a stiff breeze and, although the sun did not actually break through at all and there was no hint of blue from hilltop to horizon, every so often one could tell that it was getting towards evening from a patch of diffuse light gleaming far out to sea. The station was at the top of the hill and did not run to a taxi, so we descended to the village proper in a cart driven by the porter, a man of dour mien who kept up a droning monologue all the way, in such an impenetrable Wigtownshire brogue that it might as well have been the rumble of thunder.

At the bottom, the cart swung round onto the main (practically the only) street, a straggle of cottages, shops and one or two grander captains' houses snaking along, all facing the harbour. A fleet of small fishing craft were moored for the night, tied together and jostling as they bobbed in the high water, looking like a flock of chickens settling on their perches, with a little squawking and a little shoving but cosy enough and used to the proximity. A few of the men were still at work on their nets in the lee of the far harbour wall and some of their wives were scrubbing out crates beside them, bent double, shoving their brushes back and forth with a steady rhythm. The sound of the clogs on the cobbled ground as the women rocked back and forth, back and forth, seemed to keep time with the clink of the painters, and the soft knock-knock of the boats themselves, making one great percussion section out of the whole scene.

'Delightful,' I said, standing up in the cart as it drew to a stop and spreading my arms to encompass all of the view. It was not in my nature to be so expansive but the last fifty miles from Dumfries to here had been spent on a tiny ancient train with very dark upholstery and very *very* small windows from which the view was of bleak high moors and glowering valleys, so this sight of the sea was as welcome as a toddy.

I breathed deeply in hopes of ozone, but was met instead with the sharp rich smell of fried fish and vinegar from somewhere nearby.

'Fish on Friday,' said Alec. 'I'm ready for my dinner, Dan; I don't know about you.'

At this the dour porter let fly a stream of bitter invective, no more decipherable than his previous offerings in its detail but crystal clear as to its broad intent. Alec and I hurriedly descended and stood on the pavement while he tugged our suitcases out of the back of the cart and dumped them onto the ground.

'Let's go in and try for a cup of tea at least,' I said, nodding at the hotel – not much more than an inn really – where we had alighted. 'Then I think I'll set off and try to find this school. Eh-hem, I say, Porter? Do you know where St Columba's is?'

This innocent question set him off worse than ever, a torrent delivered at top speed and high volume of which I understood not a word, but since he was no longer holding the pony's reins and had finished unloading, this time the words he spat out were accompanied by wild gestures. He shook his fists and jabbed the air with his fingers and, as our gaze followed the way he was so emphatically pointing, up above the roofs of the cottages, up the face of the cliff, all the way up to the headland, we saw a squat grey building, hunched above the village, glaring down. I could not believe – once it was noticed – that it had gone unnoticed before. Almost it seemed to be looming, although in fact it was set back safely with a terrace and a narrow strip of garden, but

I wondered if I was alone in wanting to retreat lest it topple from its perch and flatten me.

'I take it they don't start with a kindergarten,' Alec said. 'I shouldn't want my precious tot running around up there.'

'Eleven and up,' I said. 'What a supremely unwelcoming facade. Or maybe it's very different when approached from the carriage drive. One can only hope so.'

But when I came at it after tea – leaving Alec to stroll the harbour and the single street or so of the town – it was up the cliff path under its cold grey gaze after all, since it appeared that to make a more conventional entrance would involve me in a tiresome round trip, much longer but somehow just as steep-looking. I was wearing stout shoes, for Grant has got into the spirit of my new venture rather splendidly, even sewing extra pockets in my new tweed coats 'for clues and what have you' as she informed me (although none of our cases has yet produced the traditional cigar butt, scrap of unusual cloth, or hair ribbon snagged on a bush and wound around with one long red waving hair, a perfect match for the crowning glory of our chief suspect and therefore her swift undoing under our scrutiny). Stout shoes notwithstanding, though, it was a scramble and I was panting when I gained the terrace. I stopped, meaning to catch my breath, and was still looking down at the rooftops and watching Alec, ant-like, making his way round the harbour, when a voice behind me made me jump.

'This is private property.'

'Oh!' I wheeled round.

'Unless you're Miss . . . ?'

'Gilver,' I said. 'Miss—' I was going to say 'missus' but the woman I found myself addressing was such a very miss-ish miss that it died on my lips and she took it to be my matching curt demand for her name, since I had given mine.

'Shanks,' she supplied. 'Can I help you?'

'Um,' I said, only now seeing the foolishness of (practically) climbing in over the back fence if I wanted to make sure of a ready welcome. Miss Shanks waited, regarding me stolidly. She was a high-coloured woman, hair so yellow there was almost an orange tint to it and face ruddy enough to clash with the hair. I thought again of Eliza McManus. Miss Shanks was similarly robust in her construction, with short thick arms, short thick legs and a middle like Humpty Dumpty. And she did not dress her frame well. She was wearing a capacious pleated frock, which made her look like a lamp.

'I'm the headmistress,' she said, but thankfully it sounded more like an assurance than a threat. Whatever my business was it was also hers, she seemed to say.

'I'm here . . . um . . . I know Miss Lipscott . . .' I said, thinking this was good and neutral.

'Ah-ha!' said Miss Shanks. 'For Mademoiselle Beauclerc?'

'Ah . . .' I said.

'From the agency?'

'Yes,' I said, although surprised at its mention. 'Yes indeed. Gilver and Osborne.'

'*Bon*,' said Miss Shanks. '*Très bon*. We've been expecting you. Well, come in, Miss Gilver, come in. We're just about to start din-dins.' She turned and stumped off towards a half-open door leading from the terrace into the school.

For some reason, probably since Pearl and Aurora were not welcome here, I had taken it quite for granted that Fleur's difficulties – whatever they might prove to be – were secret and I was more than a little nonplussed to be welcomed into the very bosom of the school this way. With one look behind me, I followed her.

Inside the door, which was half-glass, one of many half-glass doors set in pairs along the terrace, I found myself in a long plain dining room, with whitewashed walls and an oak floor washed with soap and left unwaxed so that it was pale and dry-looking. Stretching the length of the room were two narrow tables, set for dinner but with yellow cotton cloths instead of white, jugs of water and cups instead of wine glasses and bottles.

'Sit here,' said Miss Shanks, leading me to a seat halfway up one of the tables, facing the glass doors. 'You can have a nice view of the sea tonight since you're new. *Sehr gut.* If only it were German . . . but there isn't the appetite for German these days and it's not as though I haven't tried.'

I said nothing.

'Sit! Sit!' said Miss Shanks, summoning a maid to squeeze in an extra place for me.

Once the maid had returned I sat, noticing that she had brought bone-handled silver where all around was Sheffield plate, and a crystal water glass in place of a cup.

'Where are your things?' said Miss Shanks. 'At the front door? Still at the station?'

'My things are down in the village at the pub,' I said. 'I was planning to sleep there tonight.'

'In the pub?' said Miss Shanks, rearing backwards a little. 'Dearie me no, Miss Gilver, that won't do. We're quite ready for you. More than ready. After din-dins I'll let one of the big-uns off prayers and she can show you to your cell.' Here she let out a peal of laughter and poked my shoulder. 'I'm joking,' she said. 'I meant your room. Here they come.'

Indeed there was a faint babbling like water just released from a far-off dam. It grew louder and louder and was joined by the tramp of feet, and then two sets of doors burst open at the back of the room and a rabble – there is no other word – of girls, big and small, all dressed in yellow shirts and grey gymslips, spread like a flood through the room and threw themselves into seats at the tables.

'Up, up, upsie-daisies!' shouted Miss Shanks, powerfully enough to be heard above the din. 'If you had a sea view at muncheon you have a wall view tonight. Sort yourselves out, girlsies. Chop-chop. Hurry now.' None of the girls moved but they did stop talking and many of them sat up straight and clasped their hands together. The crowd around me, amongst the tallest, possibly seventeen or so, went as far as to bow their heads, letting the points of their bobs droop almost to the tablecloth.

'Grace!' shouted Miss Shanks. 'Here we go. With a one and a two and a—'

'Dear Lord Above!' Their timing was immaculate but the sound of a hundred girls all droning the words together was not devotional. 'Some hae meat and canna eat and some wad eat that want it. We hae meat and we can eat, sae let the Lord be thankit. Amen.' And the babble began again as maids began to hand round plates of thick soup and baskets of rolls.

The girl who served me spoke very slowly and rather loud, welcoming me to St Columba's, and she called me, to my astonishment, 'mademoiselle'. I blinked and stared after her, feeling realisation begin to creep up on me from far away.

Of course, the misunderstanding had the usual cause. When I did not understand what Miss Shanks meant – spouting French and lamenting German that way – I assumed she meant nothing, and she took the same view of my mentioning Gilver and Osborne. And then what with us both latching on to the shared notion of Miss Lipscott, and our determination not to challenge one another lest we appear to be fusspots, the whole conversation was a failure from start to end. Or rather, it was a failure as far as communication went; from my point of view it was a rousing success for here I was, in the school, sitting drinking soup with half of the sixth form, and if I had the nerve and could remember enough verb conjugations it appeared I was free to stay.

Of course, I did not have the nerve. Not that 'going undercover' was unknown to me, but here at St Columba's there would be a race between the real new mistress turning up, Miss Shanks deciding she had better ask who Gilver and Osborne were when they were at home, and (most likely of all) the paucity of my French vocabulary and the haphazard mess of my grammar undoing my ruse before the first lesson was hardly begun.

I was going to spin it out through this evening, though, since here was a lucky chance to do some detecting, just when I needed all the luck I could find. I was too late, clearly: Fleur had bolted and gone, long enough ago for Miss Shanks to have rung the agency for her successor, but I surmised that the girls must know something and was pondering how much I could ask them. I wondered too if the mistresses – who were dispersed up and down the tables with a view to discipline – would retire to a common room afterwards for coffee and bluestocking chatter; there were certainly no coffee cups to be seen in the dining room anywhere.

For the present, I decided to plunge in with the girls, who had been shooting me little glances and would be more suspicious, surely, if I did not start talking soon, about something, instead of just sitting here.

'Hello,' I said. 'My name is Miss Gilver. I'm the new French mistress. Thank you for not falling on me, but do let's chat now.'

'Welcome to St Cucumber's,' said one of the nearest girls.

'Spring!' said another. I took this to be a Christian name.

'It's affectionately meant,' said Spring. She was an attractive girl of honey-coloured skin and thick honey-coloured hair, with a broad grin revealing a zigzag of pure-white bottom teeth. 'On account of how the late and otherwise lamented Fräulein Fielding was such a one for salad. I'm surprised we don't all have twitching noses.'

'German mistress?' I hazarded.

'Head,' said Spring. 'Well, joint head. And Latin.'

'She wasn't really a Fräulein at all,' said the other girl, a dashing beauty of statuesque proportions with ruddy cheeks and striking pale blue eyes. 'I'm Eileen, by the way. It's just that her name was Fielding and what with the Froebel method and all that . . .'

'One must give one's mistresses nicknames,' I said, 'I quite understand.'

'Miss Gilver . . . ?' said a third. 'What did your last girls call you?'

'Katie!' said Eileen. Katie flashed a devilish smile with a dip in the middle and gave a throaty laugh. If I really were the French mistress I should have to watch out for this one.

'They called me Goody Gilver,' I said, 'because I hardly ever give out prep and I very often give out chocolates.'

'Really?' said a fourth girl, with a sweet heart-shaped face and a dark red bob.

'No, of course not, Sally,' said Katie. 'She's teasing us.' And the look she gave me showed that she was thinking exactly what I had been thinking: need to watch this one.

'What a pity,' said a rather sophisticated-looking girl at the end of our little group. She had the poise of an artist's model and a profile any artist would kill to sketch. 'Stella,' she said, indicating herself with a curl of her hand. 'If you could have substituted cigarettes for the chocolates we might have been *great* friends.' Her cut-glass voice swooped dramatically down on the word 'great' in a way that snagged on my memory and something too about the way she looked was familiar.

'Stella . . . ?' I said.

'Rowe-Issing,' she drawled.

'Oh, right,' said Eileen. 'Rendall.'

'Warren,' said Spring.

'Madden,' said Sally. 'Sally Madden. And Katie Howard.'

I was barely listening as the introductions went on, so surprised was I. The Rowe-Issings were friends of ours, or acquaintances anyway – some of our very grandest connections, in fact, always invited to everything and seldom accepting – and it was the echo of her mother Candide's face in her own which had made young Stella so familiar to me. I looked around the dining hall again. If Basil and Candide were sending their girls here it must be quite an outfit – the odd little headmistress notwithstanding.

'How long has your old French mistress been gone?' I asked Eileen. She seemed, of all of them, the best combination of common sense and eagerness to please.

'Just four days,' Eileen said. 'We've been reading a play with Hammy – Miss Shanks, I mean – but we're thrilled you're here now. In time to help us with our exam prep.'

I hoped my smile was not too sickly. Pearl Lipscott had told me on the telephone the day before that St Columba's went in for university places for its girls but I had not followed the thought through to its conclusion: that to get into a university one had to pass examinations (even though the fast-approaching end of Donald's brush with education had been hastened by his tendency to treat three-hour exams like bear attacks through which one

30

had only to sit perfectly still and keep breathing). The tin lid was firmly pressed on any plan to keep this subterfuge going.

As to the hard fact that Eileen's answer had provided along with the little fright, four days was welcome news in a way, since it meant that I could not have stopped Fleur from bolting if I had set off in a fast car the minute Pearl had engaged me.

'Exams aside, though,' Spring was saying, 'old Pretty-vicar is no loss. She had a mean streak when crossed and it was getting worse.'

'Ill-bred,' said Stella in that same drawling tone. 'Badly brought up anyway.'

I could not help smarting for poor Fleur. She was a little spoiled, it was true, and I had heard her being catty, but I would never have accused her of a mean streak and I could not imagine what she had done to be saddled with 'Pretty-vicar'. Even without knowing what it meant, it sounded beastly enough to have made me cry if someone used it as my nickname. I hoped briefly that Goody Gilver stuck, before reminding myself once again that my schoolmistress life would be over after pudding.

At the moment we were still on meat and potatoes and I shovelled it in as though gardening, but I noticed that the girls – at least the more elegant ones – picked and scowled and grumbled as all schoolgirls ever have always done.

'And where did she go?' I asked, choosing Sally this time to fix with my nearest approximation of a schoolmistress's stare (wishing I had half-spectacles to stare over). 'Rather inconsiderate of her to leave at this stage of the summer term, eh?'

Sally frowned a little and smiled a little, unsure what to make of this woman who did not shush their own gossiping but rather joined in.

'She was called home to care for a relation who'd been taken ill,' she said. 'That's what Ham-miss Shanks said anyway.'

'That's what Ham-miss Shanks always says,' said Katie. 'The relations of our mistresses aren't a very stalwart lot. How many have we mislaid now?'

'Well, science and history,' said Eileen. She leaned back to let a maid take her dinner plate away and then leaned forward sniffing deeply as another replaced it with a pudding bowl. 'Steamed chocolate and coconut, yum. And Latin, of course.'

'And music and PE – although that was just one – and now French,' said Katie, all the devilish sparkle in her face replaced with a frown. 'It sounds quite a crowd when you say them together that way.'

'And no one ever sees them go,' said Spring in sepulchral tones.

'They just vanish,' said Stella, 'leaving no signs of their passing.'

'Except,' said Katie, 'for the deep tracks of their heels where they were dragged across the earth to the—'

'Who's left?' I said, belatedly realising that no schoolmistress in her wits would sit and listen to such impertinent nonsense. 'I certainly can't teach you history and Latin. If Miss Shanks wanted a good all-rounder she ought to have made it clear to the agency. Well, well, we shall just have to see.'

Of course, with this little outburst I was paving the way for a swift retreat back to Alec at the pub but the girls were not listening to me. They were glancing at one another as though the respective totals of mistresses departed and mistresses remaining had only just occurred to them for the first time.

'I shall mention it to my father when I write on Sunday,' said Stella Rowe-Issing. 'It's too bad, really, considering the fees she rakes in. The Fräulein would never have stood for it.'

'She'd have said *Nein* in the strongest terms,' said Spring, making the rest of them giggle again. '*Nein! Ich es* . . . What's refuse to countenance?'

'Something *nicht*,' said Stella. 'Such a dull language and so ugly.'

There was indeed coffee in a staffroom as I had hoped (once the girls got to making up German words and giggling there was no return to sensible conversation and I left them to it). The serving maid collected me after pudding and led me most solicitously through the corridors to a corner room on the ground floor which had probably started life as a business room – terribly masculine and panelled in walnut to within an inch of its life – but was now the haven of the mistresses and their retreat from the grey-and-yellow hordes.

Despite the wave of departures which the girls had related to me, there was still a good handful of mistresses in there, sitting around in what were quite clearly their personal little upholstered empires, each with a table drawn up close at the side and each of these tables bearing evidence of its owner's habits and concerns. Miss Shanks's winged velvet had a lumpy patchwork rug thrown over it and more patches and batting escaping from a cloth bag on the papier-mâché table top. She did not, however, sit down and start stitching, but stumped off to a decanter of port warming by the fire, after pointing me into a low bergère tub chair (which creaked a little but was more comfortable than many bergère chairs I have encountered in my time) and introducing me to a Miss Christopher, a little woodland creature of a maths mistress, and a Miss Barclay, an out-and-out geography mistress of a geography mistress, with tight curls scraped into a crinkled bun, wire-rimmed spectacles and a collar and tie, who were perched at either end of a hard-looking empire sofa in yellow pleated silk with a buffer of exercise books delineating the border halfway along its length.

'Call me Barbara,' Miss Christopher said, once Miss Shanks had gone. 'If you're staying. If you've decided to.'

'Ssssh,' said Miss Barclay softly. 'Help yourself to a chocolate truffle, Miss Gilver. They're very good.' She nodded at a petits-fours plate on the low table between us, as she poured a cup of coffee for me.

'Or are you trying us on appro?' Miss Christopher went on. 'Any other jobs in the offing? You are from Lambourne, aren't you?'

'Barbara!' said Miss Barclay. 'Don't pay any attention, Miss Gilver.' She gave me a smile. I returned it, but I did not miss the tight grip she had on the bon-bon dish as she proffered it to me, nor the sharp look she gave her colleague as she turned back to her. 'Don't quiz the poor woman after her long day,' she said. 'I'm sure Miss Shanks has seen to everything.'

'Excuse me, I'm sure,' said Miss Christopher. 'Naturally nosy. And I can plead overwork too, fraying my manners.'

'You must indeed be run ragged,' I said, taking a sweet. 'Double duties and all that.'

Neither woman answered; Miss Barclay stood, straightened her rather severe coat and skirt (St Columba's, it appeared, did not dress for dinner) and set off to offer the chocolates around the other armchairs in the room. Barbara Christopher busied herself with sugar and cream. My eyes followed the departing sweets and I looked at the three mistresses to whom Miss Barclay was taking them. Right by the fire was a stout woman wedged into a clubbish armchair and knitting very fast; beside her, half-reclining on a red shot-silk chaise, was a black-haired, beak-nosed creature with handkerchief-points to her frock who had to be the art mistress and beside *her* (hence almost escaping notice) was a poor beige slip of a thing who did not benefit from her proximity to such glamour and who blinked and shrank away as Miss Barclay approached her. Or so I thought until I looked again, whereupon I became convinced it was me the poor dear was blinking at, I who had driven her backwards into her cushions with my very presence.

'Who are those three?' I asked Miss Christopher. She wiped her hands – very stubby, very brown little hands, which made me think of a mole's paddles with dirt ground into them – down her frock and made a great display out of swallowing a mouthful of truffle.

'Housekeeper – she always sits in here with us on account of . . . Well, she always does. Miss Lovage, the art mistress.' I was right then. 'And,' she went on, 'the English mistress, Miss Lipscott.'

I made a disgusting noise caused by gasping mid-sip which put Miss Christopher's rough manners into deep shade and had to be banged on the back with one of those little mole hands until I finally managed to stop coughing.

'Miss Lipscott?' I said, staring over at the woman, 'I thought she was missing.'

'No,' said Miss Christopher. 'Why on earth would you think that?'

'And so Miss Shanks sent for a replacement,' I said.

'No,' said Miss Christopher again. 'We need a new *French* mistress. It's Mademoiselle Beauclerc who's disappeared.' She jumped and looked over her shoulder. When she spoke again it was in a low voice. 'I don't mean disappeared, of course. I mean gone.'

'Beauclerc,' I said, light dawning. 'Miss Pretty-vicar.'

'Those terrible girls,' said Miss Christopher, looking rather rattled. Across the room, Miss Lipscott was standing up and brushing down her frock, although as far as I could tell she had not eaten a morsel, 'It's Stella R-I,' Miss Christopher was saying. 'She's the ringleader, but such a feather in our cap to have her here.'

I cleared my throat with one final splutter.

'Are you all right, Miss Gilver?' said Miss Barclay, passing with the plate of petits fours. 'Coffee down the wrong way? Miss Fielding had a marvellous remedy for a frog in the throat. Something to do with opening the oesophagus. Quite yogic.'

From the corner of my eye I could see Fleur – except that how could that faded woman be pretty little Fleur? – lean in close to the headmistress and whisper something. Miss Shanks whispered something back. Fleur looked over at me, whispered again and then slipped out of the room, whereupon Miss Shanks spun to face me like a top which had just been given a good flick with a whip. Her round little pudding of a face was as long as it ever could be, with mouth dropped open and eyebrows arched high. Then, with a jolt, she came back to life and bustled over.

'*Mrs* Gilver?' she said in tones of numb dismay.

'Yes?' I said, trying for an innocent air, even though Fleur had evidently shot my cover to smithereens.

'You're a widow?' said Miss Shanks.

'No, no, not so far,' I said, smiling. 'My husband is alive and well and . . . very modern.'

35

'But I couldn't possibly allow a married woman to teach in one of my classrooms,' Miss Shanks said. It flashed across my mind to ask her why. Presumably all of the girls had mothers who were married women and, universities notwithstanding, were mostly bound to end up married women themselves one day. Perhaps seeing one in the wild at a tender age could be part of the education St Columba's offered them. But Miss Christopher was gawping at me enough already. 'The agency certainly didn't mention anything about it,' said Miss Shanks. I gave it up as a bad job then and turned to extrication.

'Gilver and Osborne?' I said. 'Why would they?'

'Who are they?' said Miss Shanks. 'It was Lambourne Scholastic and Domestic we approached.'

'Who?' I said, eyes wide.

'There seems to have been some considerable misunderstanding,' said Miss Christopher. She had drawn her set of chins right down into her neck with disapproval.

'I agree there must have been,' I said. 'I'm with Gilver and Osborne.' Here I fished out one of our cards from my coat pocket, where I always keep a supply, and blessed their vague wording. Miss Shanks read it with her lips moving. 'We were very much hoping to be engaged to help you with this rather pressing staff shortage you've come in for.' I swept along, feeling the wind of good fortune under me. 'Five, isn't it? Four in the academic subjects – French, Latin, science and history – and also music and PE. What rotten luck.'

'How did you . . . ?' said Miss Shanks. 'I asked Lambourne for a French mistress only. Who told you . . . ?' Miss Barclay had rejoined us, bringing the dashing art mistress with her. I noticed that what I had taken to be a glint of sheen on her dark head was actually a white streak, which only added to her allure.

'I should have to ask one of the secretarial staff,' I said, thinking of how Pallister, my butler, would not even go as far as to set my business letters out separately from my social correspondence on the breakfast table, 'but I rather think it was a parent.'

'But we're fine, we're fine,' said Miss Shanks. 'We feel the loss of poor dear Fielding not least as a Latin mistress, never mind how we all treasured her, but the vicar at St Ninian's is helping and the girls all ado— I mean they're very satisfied with his— and I'm taking PE myself. Dorothy and Barbara have shouldered some extra load, Mrs Tully in the village is an excellent piano and violin teacher. All we need is the right French mistress and we shall be fine. Absolutely fine.' But she did not sound absolutely fine, or even one good French mistress short of it. She sounded, as her voice rose and her cheeks grew hot, as if she were about to let off steam like a tea-kettle. Miss Lovage took a step away from her side to avoid being scalded, but Miss Barclay put out a hand and said a faint there-there.

'Very well,' I said. 'I shall take my leave, if you're sure Gilver and Osborne can be of no assistance to you. Now, just before I go I wonder if you could tell me the way to Miss Lipscott's private room.' The Misses Christopher and Barclay turned wary eyes on Miss Shanks, who spoke up stoutly.

'Miss Lipscott's 'private room' is just that, Mrs Gilver. I'm afraid—'

'But we're old friends,' I insisted. 'I used to know her family.'

Miss Shanks redoubled her efforts.

'Miss Lipscott seems to have made it perfectly clear—' she began.

I put on a guileless look and interrupted her. 'She's all right, isn't she? She was always a shy one, but I can't imagine why she wouldn't want to see an old friend of her family. If she's one of the Somerset Lipscotts, that is. Is she?'

A few of them nodded, but I had not fooled Barbara Christopher, not nearly. No one inhales their coffee because they have suddenly seen an old family friend. Luckily, however, the mood in the room was one of desperation to be rid of me before I asked any more awkward questions about their growing misfor-tunes and my demand for directions, at last, carried the day.

It was a large house, and after climbing to the second storey I walked for quite five minutes through long corridors where the sound of gossiping, giggling, Latin-memorising, violin-practising girlhood squealed and droned away before I found her room, well into the other wing, on the landward side.

She answered before I even knocked, quietly drawing the door just wide enough open to show her face.

'Dandy,' she said. 'It is you, isn't it?'

'It is,' I said. I was searching her for the girl I had known, the gleaming flaxen hair, the flashing blue eyes, the quick dimpling grin of mischief, but I found none of them. The bones were still there, as how could they not be, but she was more changed in ten years than some fortunate women change in fifty, as though the girl had been rendered by Rubens or Botticelli but the woman was a work by Augustus John, a pale oval lozenge of a face with loops of hair drawn back to the nape and a figure which hardly made so bold as to show against the draping of her clothes.

'What do you want?' she said. 'What are you doing here?'

'May I come in?' I glanced up and down the corridor. It was silent and absolutely empty, but who could say whether interested ears were at the many closed doors I saw? Fleur hesitated and then stepped back.

I entered her room thinking only of privacy and a chance to talk, but stopped amazed at the sight that greeted me.

That summer at Pereford we were never out of one another's rooms. It was part of the wonderful air of Liberty Hall (compared with most other houses where the children were not allowed in their own bedrooms during the day and were certainly forbidden to enter any but their own). We lazed on the beds flattening out the feather quilts, borrowed hairbrushes, tried on clothes and dried our hands with any old towel that was nearby, in a way that would have given Nanny Palmer fits if she had seen me. The nanny and nurse at Pereford sat in the shade of the upstairs verandah and did the mending – or rather flipped through the pages of film-star magazines with the mending undone on their knees – and could not care a fig what any of their charges were up to.

So I was quite familiar with them all: the blowsy, rosy confusion of Mamma-dearest's boudoir; the satins and scents of

Aurora's lair which was going through a dramatic season just then; the bookish, boyish campground that was Pearl's particular sanctum, with brown bags of apples for midnight snacking and an army cot under the window for reading in. And little Fleur's room was of all the most exuberant and endearing. She had inherited all the grown-out-of toys of her sisters, leaving her shelves and cupboard-tops stacked three deep with elderly dolls and decrepit bears and then she could never be persuaded to leave the treasures of the day outside in the garden at bedtime, so that her room was full of wildflower posies in jam jars and the floor was covered in watercolour sketches, spread out to dry half-finished and never to *be* finished since the next new day brought its fresh demands and adventures. There were bowls and teacups – doll-sized – she had made from river mud and transported home and in the corner on a piece of board there was a sandcastle made at Watchet which Fleur could not leave behind when the rugs were rolled and the flasks tipped out at the end of a picnic. She had brought it home and tried to keep it damp with an orchid pump full of water before more treasures claimed her. So there it sat, a heap of yellow sand with shells and feathers still adorning it and all her sisters ever said if they strayed too close and felt the crunch under their bedroom slippers was:

'Isn't she a poppet? Isn't she a love? Shall we take it back to the beach, Florissima, and let these grains see all the other grains in their family?'

'I shall rebuild it one day,' Fleur said, very grandly. 'I have that snap of it, remember. And I did sketches too.' Then she turned back to her dolls' house and continued with the endless renovations she was undertaking there.

The study-cum-bedroom of the English mistress at St Columba's shared only the features of having four walls, a window and door. The narrow bed was covered with a plain woollen blanket and the bedside table held only a glass and a Bible. The desk was bare, the dresser top bore not so much as a hairbrush. I thought again of the convent I had imagined, but here was not even a cross on the wall as there might have been there.

Fleur – and I still had to work to convince myself that it really *was* Fleur – drew out the hard chair from under the desk and bade me sit down. She leaned against the windowsill and I thought of her as she had been, sprawled on her bed in her outdoor shoes, eating bread and jam and sharing it with her angora rabbit, who often slept there.

'Did *they* send you?' she said. Her voice was without inflection, no way of knowing whether she feared or welcomed or even cared what had brought me there.

'Pearl asked me to come, yes.'

'And how did you get past— I mean, how did you end up having dinner with the girls?'

'Miss Shanks got the idea into her head that I was a French mistress and somehow I was swept up in things.'

'You're not, are you?' said Fleur, her eyes wide, looking very stark suddenly in her pale face.

'Of course not.'

'Of course – silly. Only all sorts of people are doing all sorts of things these days.'

She was right; but I chose, for the moment, not to tell her. She was studying me very speculatively.

'Miss Shanks doesn't know you're not, though, does she?' she said. 'And she doesn't know you came to see me? That's good. That's something anyway. And so, please, Dandy, just go. Before she finds out.'

'But Fleur – why shouldn't you have a guest? Pearl told me she couldn't gain admittance – or Aurora – but she didn't tell me why and I don't understand.'

'It doesn't matter,' said Fleur. She was speaking in an urgent whisper. 'Please just go.'

'I'm afraid I can't,' I said. 'I promised your sisters I would come and see that you were all right.'

'And I am. It's my choice not to see them. I send letters. I'm fine.'

'Yes, well, clearly that's nonsense,' I answered. 'Clearly you're not. Fleur? Darling, what's wrong?'

'Nothing!' Fleur said, bending over towards me at the waist to make her whisper do instead of shouting. 'I'm quite quite content and perfectly well and I kept telling them that but they wouldn't stop ringing up and bothering me and that's precisely why I don't want to talk to them any more.' She swallowed hard at the end of all this and then straightened up, breathing in a long gathering breath and blowing it out slowly again like someone trying not to panic. I shook my head at her.

'That's not at all what Pearl told me,' I said. 'She told me you were indeed fine for a long time and she and the others knew it, but that something else has gone wrong now and they're worried again. As they were before. They're worried you're going to bolt.'

'What?' said Fleur. It was the loudest she had spoken and I thought I heard the creak of a chair as someone in the next room overheard and turned to listen. Just in that creak and its timing I felt I could see the head raised from study and the shoulders twisted round, the enquiring glance at the wall shared with Miss Lipscott. Fleur had heard it too and when she spoke again she was whispering as she had before, harsh and sibilant.

'Leave me alone,' she said. 'You don't understand and neither do Pearl, Aurora or Mother.' I almost gasped. For one of the Lipscott girls to call Mamma-dearest 'Mother' was like one of *my* children calling me 'you there'.

'Well, I don't understand *yet*,' I said, 'because I haven't heard the story, but I'm very understanding as a rule.' Fleur closed her eyes and murmured through lips barely moving.

'Stay away from me,' she said. 'For your own good. I told them too. Stay away. For their own good.'

'Why?' I said. 'What on earth do you mean?' Fleur swallowed hard. I could hear her dry throat clicking.

'I have killed four people,' she said.

Outside, a barn owl gave its unearthly shriek. I jumped, heart hammering, and was sure that the listening neighbour through the wall jumped too. I had heard the knocking sound of someone startled letting her knee or foot bang against a table leg. I even thought I heard a soft groaning. Fleur did not so much as flinch.

'I have killed four people,' she repeated. 'And no matter how hard I try I have no way of knowing when it will happen again.'

3

'Four?' said Alec. He did not notice as the sandwich he was holding flopped open and a slice of tongue dropped out onto the carpet.

'Four,' I said.

We were sitting in his room at the Crown (his rather than mine because it had a sweet little corner bow with armchairs which looked out over the harbour and seemed made for chatting) to where he had ordered up coffee and sandwiches, thinking my pallor when I banged on his door owed itself to hunger and exhaustion. In fact the exhaustion was not too far from the mark: it had been a long day on the trains, and dinner with a hundred clamouring schoolgirls had taken its toll. Of course, the cold-water shock of Fleur's announcement, swiftly followed by my stumbling, skidding descent of the cliff path in the bad light, had not helped matters any.

'I've eaten,' I had managed to say after he had replaced the house telephone.

'It doesn't seem to have agreed with you,' Alec had said in reply.

Then I told the entire tale, beginning with Miss Shanks, taking in the missing mistresses and the startling change in Fleur – here we were interrupted by the sandwiches' arrival, the girl's eyes out on organ stops at the sight of me in Alec's room, still in my hat and coat – and finishing up with Fleur's whispered pleas for me to leave, her shouting out that odd way at the mention of bolting and finally her bombshell, the words which were still ringing in my ears even now.

'She just said it, right out? "I've killed four people"?' I nodded. 'Then what?'

'Not another word. Well, actually then she said she couldn't say when it might happen again.'

'My, my,' said Alec. 'And then?'

'Nothing further.'

'No, I mean what did *you* say?'

'Nothing. Or maybe a few incoherent mumbles. I left. I fled.'

'Hmph,' said Alec, and it did seem pretty feeble sitting there in his room with a hot cup of coffee warming my fingers and the faint sounds of the public bar wafting up through the floor and in at the open windows.

'Fair point,' I said, although he had not precisely made one. 'There were scores of girls who would have overheard a scuffle even if the mistresses were all still in the common room miles away. And I suppose there must be matrons and maids and what have you. Yes, all right then, I should have stayed put and grilled her. Perhaps next time.'

'Mistresses,' said Alec. 'How many have gone again?' I gave him a grateful smile: he had already forgiven me and moved on.

'Five,' I said. 'That occurred to me too. But five mistresses have disappeared and Fleur definitely said her total – my God, how horrid – was four.'

'So no reason to make the connection.' Alec shivered too. 'I suppose you believed her?'

I thought hard for a moment before answering and then nodded.

'I believe she wasn't lying,' I said. 'She might be mistaken – out of her wits – but it wasn't mischief when she told me. It was more like a warning.'

'Although,' Alec said, 'there is the point of her sister's mysterious message. "Trouble in the past" that they thought Fleur had got over by now and a great dread that it would flare up again. I always wondered why they didn't tell you straight what kind of trouble it was, but if it was four murders then it's less of a puzzle.'

I gave a grunt that was as close as I could get to laughter. 'Yes, I shall be having a sharp word with Pearl if I find out she sent me off to see if a murderer was about to murder again.' Then I shook my head to rattle the idea out of it. 'She can't be, Alec. She simply can't be. She used to decorate her dolls' house for Christmas. How could she kill anyone? And how could she possibly get a job in a good school if she had been in prison for murder? And if she had done it four times why wasn't she hanged? And why haven't we heard about her? She'd be more famous than Dr Crippen.'

'Only if she were caught,' Alec said. 'And *is* it a good school?'

I opened my mouth to answer and then stopped.

'It has some awfully grand pupils for a bad one,' I said. 'And yet . . . five mistresses gone and the head is a funny little creature more like a . . . who she actually reminds me of is Batty Aunt Lilah. Almost one of the girls herself, and not at all suited to being *in loco parentis*.'

'The way she bundled you in and let you loose on them in the dining room certainly doesn't inspire much confidence in her judgement. No reflection on you, you understand, but you know what I mean.'

'I do,' I said. 'Well, perhaps she was the matronly one and Fräulein Whatshername was the brains of the outfit.'

'Who?'

'The other headmistress,' I said. 'There used to be two until she died.'

'Lifting our total to six?' said Alec. 'Six mistresses a-vanishing?'

'No, she's one of the five. She was the Latin mistress as well.'

'So what are you going to do?' Alec said. 'What next? What first?'

Before I could answer there came a timid knock at the door and the same maid who had brought our supper entered.

'Just – eh – wondered if you needed anything else, sir,' she said. 'And madam.' Her eyes were rounder than ever.

'No thank you,' Alec said. 'Here, take the tray, but I'll keep the plate in case I'm peckish later.'

'And can I turn down your bed while I'm about it?' she said, blushing a little and somehow giving off the strong impression that she had been put up to this by a third party.

'No thanks,' said Alec again.

'You could turn mine down,' I said, losing patience with it all. 'Two doors along. And I'd like some hot water too if it's not too late in the evening.' The maid bobbed and disappeared.

'You asked me what *I* was going to do,' I said once she had gone. 'Am I to take it then that your desire to be part of the case has waned as the casualty list has swollen?'

'Not at all,' Alec said. 'Not a bit of it. Only I can see now that you're right. You're much better able to infiltrate a girls' boarding school than I.'

'The pisky vicar has been roped in as Latin master,' I said. 'Could you turn your hand to . . . what was it . . . science or history, I think?' Alec snorted. 'French is taken. Music and PE. Well, I can see the problem with your teaching the girls PE. I don't think the Rowe-Issings would stand for Stella learning rugger. Music?'

'Triangle,' said Alec. 'And I sometimes got that wrong. And anyway, the fact is . . . while you were out I snagged a case of my own.'

'Really?' I said. 'Do tell.'

Alec rubbed his nose and did not quite meet my eye.

'It doesn't have the thrill of yours, but then I didn't know how thrilling yours would be when I agreed to take on mine. A school-mistress in low spirits didn't sound like too much fun, frankly. My case is much more tempestuous than that. Not than five missing persons and four murders, obviously. How untidy to have them not match up.'

'Tempestuous?' I said, cutting through the babble.

'There is a seething tangle of dark passion here in Portpatrick,' Alec said.

'Hang on,' I said, stretching out a toe and poking him. 'A tangle of passion sounds exactly like the kind of case we said Gilver and Osborne would never stoop to.'

'Needs must,' Alec said. 'Since I'm here. One of the good burghers of this fair town wants very much to know which other good burgher has stolen his wife's heart from him.'

'But we agreed!'

'We might have said it would be nice if every case was a juicy one,' Alec said. 'But we never agreed to turn away business. I didn't anyway.' His look of triumph was not to be borne and I took myself off to bed in disgust, not missing the sudden scuffle that told me someone was waiting in the passage to see me go.

He started again over breakfast the next morning.

'It's not at all what we always said we would never do, anyway.'

Our breakfast table was very small and very close to the breakfast tables of everyone else currently staying at the Crown, to wit: three commercial gentlemen who greeted one another and then retired behind their newspapers, three amateur fishermen who sat together and talked of lines and tides and notable catches of old, and a convalescent widow with a companion, who nibbled daintily at soft-boiled eggs and spoke in murmurs. Alec and I attracted no attention at all from the six men but set the two women quivering with interest. The convalescent widow was in danger of letting her egg grow cold, all forgotten, so much effort was she putting in to catching my eye. Alec, leaning in close across the minuscule table, ignored them all.

'He's not asking us to check boarding-house registers to help him with a divorce,' Alec insisted. 'He just wants her back again. And a name. For his own satisfaction.'

'And if he then decides it would be even more satisfying to go after the fellow with a meat cleaver? That wouldn't trouble you?'

'Filleting knife, actually,' Alec said, but absently. He was looking over my shoulder.

'He's a fisherman?' I asked, craning to look over it too. There was a mild commotion taking place in the doorway of the dining room. The little maid who had brought our supper last night, decked out to serve breakfast in a sprigged frock and cotton apron, was remonstrating with another figure who seemed determined to enter the room. A round little figure in a voluminous tartan cloak and a green velvet hat shaped like a hot cross bun:

it was Miss Shanks and, despite the maid's best efforts to protect her guests from the intrusion, she was even now striding towards Alec and me, throwing one wing of her cloak back over her shoulder.

'Mrs Gilver,' she said, arriving at our little table and standing there – still rather swash-bucklingly – with her feet planted far apart and her hands on her hips. 'And Mr Osborne, I believe.'

The commercial gentlemen carried on chewing their toast and reading their headlines; the anglers carried on with their reminiscence of some distant whopper; but the convalescent widow and her companion practically fell off their seats with curiosity and I could feel their two pairs of eyes fastened upon me like magnifying glasses in the desert sun, smouldering dry twigs into fire.

'Miss Shanks,' I said. 'Alec, dear,' – a crackle from the twigs as the magnifying glasses flashed in horror – 'this is Miss Shanks from St Columba's of whom I told you last evening.'

Alec half rose and half bowed then sank into his seat again.

'And how can we help you today, Miss Shanks?' he said.

She regarded him very thoughtfully for a moment before she answered.

'Lambourne, Mrs Gilver, have let me down,' she said, flicking a glance to me and then fastening her eyes back on Alec again. 'And I knew you'd still be here, don't ye know?' Miss Shanks's Scotch brogue was intermittent and utterly bogus, but I was beginning to get a handle on its comings and goings: it carried her over chasms where good taste and fine feeling might send her tumbling. 'I thought, despite our wee misunderstanding yesterday, that I might persuade you to stay, since you've trundled all the way up to us here by the sparkling sea, eh?'

'Down, actually,' I said. 'Not that it ma—'

'And since you're so settled.' She twinkled at me. 'Cooried in, ye might say.'

Alec and I were completely bamboozled.

'But as you yourself pointed out, Miss Shanks,' I said, 'my married state is not at all suitable for employment at your establishment.' I was beginning to sound like the woman, damn her.

'Well, I thought about that, Mrs Gilver,' said Miss Shanks, attempting a girlish air – mostly made up of swinging her skirts from side to side and looking at me out of the corner of her eye – 'and talked it over with one of my colleagues, and I decided that if you would submit to being known as Miss Gilver while you're with us, the girls don't need to know.'

'Your colleague Miss Lipscott?' I could not imagine Fleur clamouring for my return but I could not imagine any of the Misses Lovage, Barclay or Christopher caring one way or the other.

'Mrs Brown,' said Miss Shanks. She stuck her chin in the air and carried on very loftily. 'She's on the housekeeping staff.'

Alec now went so far as to cross his eyes and stick his tongue out to signal his bewilderment to me. Miss Shanks, facing the way she did, missed it but the widow's companion caught it and turned back to her boiled egg with a look of distaste at such vulgarity.

'I see,' I lied. Miss Shanks giggled, although at least the skirt-swinging had stopped, I was glad to see.

'I'm sure your husband won't mind. Since, as you said yourself and as we all can see,' she jerked her head towards Alec like a farmer at a cattle auction, 'he is so very understanding.' She beamed at me. 'Now you finish up your brekkie and then toddle up to see me, eh? I'll arrange for Anderson to collect your things.' She folded herself back into her cloak and beamed again.

'Cheerie-bye,' she said. '*À bientôt. Auf Wiedersehen.* Toodle-oo.'

And with that she was gone, leaving the silence ringing behind her.

We stared at one another and then turned as the little maid arrived beside us and bobbed.

'Beg pardon, madam and sir,' she said. 'I tried to stop her. I – em – well, my auntie, you see. With the eggs. Always on a Saturday. Monday, Wednesday and Saturday. But I never— and she wasn't there anyway,' after which unhelpful communication she bobbed again and scurried away to her kitchens.

'Well,' I said. I leaned in close across the marmalade pot and milk jug as Alec had, but the dining room at the Crown was hardly twelve feet square and the six breakfast tables were huddled together in the middle of it, leaving room for monstrous side-boards all around, and Miss Shanks's performance had gathered the crowd's attention at last, the maid's little coda doing nothing to disperse it either. Eight pairs of eyes were watching us now, while eight pairs of ears, I imagined, were twitching with fascination.

Alec shovelled in the last two forkfuls of scrambled egg and tomato, drained his coffee cup and sat back.

'Care to join me for a stroll around the harbour wall?' he said. 'And a chat?'

I dabbed my lips and stood.

'Excellent suggestion,' I said and we made a poor show of a casual exit, gathering speed until we were fairly trotting through the narrow passageway, making for the front door.

'What in the blazes?' I said as we reeled out into a perfect late spring morning, the sea sparkling, a light breeze just ruffling the air and a few white clouds scudding across the sky. It was nine thirty and the harbour was quiet, the fleet gone for the day, only a handful of old men, their seagoing days long past now, standing around, sucking on their pipes and watching the horizon through narrowed eyes. It would be hours on end before any boats returned, but I supposed they might be watching for passing ships; at least, for the sake of their day's entertainment, I hoped so.

'She leapt away in horror last night when she heard you were married,' Alec said. He had his pipe lit, having come downstairs with it filled in readiness, as usual. 'But this morning, after finding out somehow – but how? – that you're here with me, she decides you'll do?'

'She and Mrs Brown, the housekeeper,' I reminded him. 'And what was the parlour maid on about, for heaven's sake?' I took out my cigarette case and turned away from the breeze to light one. The convalescent widow was just descending the steps and she gave an ostentatious and surely ceremonial cough, waving her hand in front of her face as though my little puff of smoke were asphyxiating her.

'Hardly a surprise,' she said. 'To find you smoking on the street like a flapper!' Alec bristled but it did not trouble me. Grant, who despairs of my tweeds at times and wishes fervently that I would take up life in London where they are unknown, would be delighted to learn that such a word had been used of me.

'I've been coming to the Crown every May for twelve years,' the widow went on, 'but I should hesitate to return now.'

'Righty-ho,' I said. The morning was beginning to take on a tinge of unreality for me.

'I've never seen such a display,' she went on.

'Such a display as two people breakfasting together in a public dining room?' said Alec. 'Well, I'm glad we could add to your life's excitements.'

'A hotbed of gossip and intrigue,' said the widow. Her companion had come out after her with a shawl, and was timidly holding it out towards her employer, almost jabbing her with it, as though she hoped the fleecy wool would simply adhere to the woman's coat shoulders without the one of them taking the trouble of donning the thing or the other finding the nerve to apply it to her person in the usual way.

'I require new-laid duck eggs,' she went on.

'For a digestive condition,' the companion put in.

'Aren't duck eggs richer than ordinar—?' said Alec.

The widow swept on. 'And the cook at the school—'

'Mrs Brown?' I fell on this very slight particle of sense.

'Mrs Brown indeed supplies them to her niece who—'

'Ahhhhh!' said both Alec and I. Then we frowned, in unison, as though we had been practising.

'—repays the favour, it appears, with gossip about her patrons, carried right back up the hill and spread around. Stop dabbing me with that shawl, Enid, do! Give it here, can't you?'

The companion buckled and whimpered as the widow snatched the garment out of her hands and wrapped herself very firmly up in it.

'I am most grievously disappointed,' she announced. 'And now

I'm going for my walk, which I certainly need more than ever today.'

'What an extraordinary person,' said Alec, looking after her as she sailed away, with the benighted Enid sliding along at her side as invisibly as a rather large young woman in bright rust-red tweeds can ever slide.

'Another one,' I agreed. 'So Miss Shanks finds out from Mrs Brown the housekeeper who found out from her niece at the Crown that Mrs Gilver the assumed French mistress is not just unsuitable but actually scandalous and wicked and . . .'

'. . . she hotfoots it down to engage you,' said Alec. 'The plot doesn't exactly thicken but it far from dilutes, wouldn't you say?'

'It curdles,' I said. 'But I tell you one thing, I'm going to do my very best to remember my *avoir* and *être* and see if I can't get myself ensconced up there. I don't know if it's anything to do with whatever's up with Fleur—'

'Or the four people she has apparently killed . . .'

'But there's something very odd about St Columba's.' I turned and gazed up at the long grey facade of the place again. It was not looming this morning, for some reason. If common sense and sanity had not prevented me I would have said it had taken a good step back from the edge of the cliff overnight and was now safely set behind its gardens in an unremarkable way. I saw Alec frowning at it too.

'Very changeable light round here,' he said. 'Must be what draws the painters.' He shivered faintly.

'And I take back what I said about your cuckolded fisherman,' I said. 'Right now, if I thought you could pass as *Miss* Osborne, I'd swap cases with you.'

'Well, come and meet my client to be going along with,' Alec said. 'He's an interesting chap, and not a fisherman, by the way.'

He pointed me on the right course, along under the St Columba's cliff and out around the natural arm of the harbour until we were opposite the main street and could look back over at the Crown, at the housemaids shaking eiderdowns out of the upstairs windows and the grocer's shop two doors down. The grocer was unwinding his awning against the sun for the day and the delivery boy was packing his basket with brown parcels, whistling the same snatch of song over and over again, quite tunelessly. Behind the main street, where a few cottage rows clung to the hillside, washing was being pegged out – heavy overalls and school pinafores on this Saturday morning when the working week was done – and in one front garden a stout housewife was scattering scraps to a small flock of chickens. At one of the villas perched on the high road, a matron in a blue coat and a matching hat (with a feather we could see all the way from the far harbour wall) let herself out at her garden gate and turned to walk briskly towards the station, stepping up her pace even more as the whistle sounded to tell of an approaching train.

'Here we are then,' Alec said and I turned back to face him, then raised my eyebrows.

'I wondered what that was,' I said. 'I smelled it last night.'

'I tasted it last night,' Alec said. 'And very delicious it was too.'

We were standing in front of a rather commodious brick shack of the kind often found at harboursides; an erstwhile boathouse perhaps, or a lifeboat station abandoned when a grateful village or a wealthy patron stumped up for a grander one. They often see out their lives as storehouses for nets in winter or lowly shelters for lobster pots in the off-season. This particular shack, however, had gone on from its beginnings to bigger and better things. Its walls had been whitewashed and its window frames painted a cheerful shade of green. A pillar-box-red door stood open, allowing us a glimpse of shining cream-coloured linoleum, a high counter made out of glass and more of the green-painted wood. A sign above the door said *Aldo's Fish Bar* in red writing, with little flags decorating the corners.

'You dined off fried fish last night?' I asked Alec.

'And fried chips,' he said.

'And then two tongue sandwiches and milky coffee at supper time,' I said. 'You should have the figure of Henry VIII by rights.'

'Come in and meet Joe,' Alec said, and disappeared into the darkened doorway.

I followed, leaving behind the scent of seaweed and yesterday's catch and stepping into a rich, grease-laden, savoury fog so thick one could feel it settle on one's skin. It must, I thought to myself looking around, be impregnated into the very walls, for there was no food in evidence, nor was there any sign of its being on its way or traces of it left over from the night before. The glass counter shone like the windows of an excellent housekeeper, as though vinegar and brown paper had only just been applied, and the metal grilles beneath the counter, where one assumed the hot food waited to be sold, glittered like the radiator of a beloved and expensive motorcar.

Alec had disappeared behind the counter, passing the empty frying vessels and disappearing through a door into the back premises.

'*Buongiorno*, my friend! Good morning. Good to see you. *Avanti*! *Benvenuto*! Come in!'

The voice was as rich and warm as the thick scents that filled the room and must surely have been by far the most exotic sound ever to have boomed out around Portpatrick harbour. Feeling suddenly shy, I peeped around the doorway. On a stool in the middle of a tiny scullery, peeling potatoes into a tub the size of a dustbin clamped between his knees, was a black-haired, cherry-cheeked man, broad-shouldered and thickened with middle age, dressed in a collarless shirt, cambric trousers like a fisherman and a butcher's striped apron.

'You sound pretty chipper,' I heard Alec say to him. 'Is she back then?'

'Cheep-ah?' said Joe. He wiped his face with a forearm as though he had been sweating, even this early on such a fresh spring day; and then, holding his knife like a fairground thrower, he flicked it into the barrel of peeled potatoes. It entered one of them with a whistling sound and a small splash of water.

'Happy,' said Alec. 'You sound happy. Has your wife come home?'

'No, no, no, no, no,' said Joe. 'Not a sight, not a sound. *Niente*. I am happy because you are here to help me. Now I have a friend.' He beamed at Alec, and since the beaming entailed an expansive sweeping glance around the room, at last he spotted me and shot to his feet, wiping his face again and tearing off the blue cotton cook's cap he had been wearing.

'*Scusi, signorina,*' he said. 'How I can help you? The cafe she is closed, but how I can help you? Only say. Giuseppe Aldo is your servant.'

'How do you do?' I said and then immediately blushed to hear such primness responding to his torrent of chivalry.

'Mrs Gilver is a friend of mine,' said Alec. 'My business partner, actually. Also a detective, don't you know.'

'A lady detective . . .' said Joe, or Giuseppe as he seemed to be. He sat back down again at his stool, motioning me into one of the three wooden chairs set around the little table in the scullery. Once there he gazed at me, letting out a long low whistle. 'Okay-dokey, so you breakfass? You hungry? Hah?'

'I could manage a little something,' said Alec, ignoring my look. He had eaten a heartier breakfast than someone who had had two dinners might have been expected to, and not a half-hour before.

'I make you *caffé* and *zeppole*,' said Joe. 'Mos' delectable food you ever have in your life before. Coming up!' He stood and took the two paces needed over to a cooking stove set under the window. There he pulled a heavy, high-sided pot onto the ring and lit the gas with a match. I suspected from the look of the pot's outside what it contained, and very soon my nostrils told me my guess was accurate. It was a pan of beef dripping slowly warming up for things to fry in.

As to what might be fried, once Joe had changed his striped blue apron for a white one, long enough to reach the top of his boots and wide enough to meet at the back of his considerable girth, he fetched an enormous bowl from the cold larder, washed his fingers in water from a kettle – hot enough to make Alec and me both wince, although Joe just chuckled and shook his reddened hand dry – and started breaking off little pieces from a mound of dough which was mushrooming inside the mixing bowl like a puffball.

All the time he worked he was talking, and soon the strange sing-song of his voice, as odd as it had sounded when first I had heard it, came to seem quite natural so that I would not have said he had any accent at all.

'She is gone like the setting sun,' he said. 'Like the sun she will return, but I cannot deny she is gone. Gone from my arms but not from my heart. I work too hard. I leave her too long and she is lonely. I do not blame the poor child. She is a child to me. Fifteen years since I marry my sweetheart and she is still that sweet girl to me. So, my friend, you will find her and bring her home and I will rejoice and I will never again work so hard and let my sweet love be lonely. Eat, eat, eat, eat!'

For the fat had got hot and into it he had dropped little spoonfuls of his mixture, watching them (as tenderly as any mother watching her children at play) before fishing them out again and laying them down gently on a plate of sugar. He rolled the plate around until the sugar was crusted all over the little puffs of pastry, and then he tipped the first one onto a clean plate for me.

'Wait, wait, wait, wait,' he said. He poured me a tiny cup of evil-looking black coffee from a fat little pot which had been spluttering on another gas ring, then he swept his arm down like a starter at a race meet and said it again. 'Eat, eat, eat, eat. *Buon appetito.* Enjoy!'

And despite the fact that I knew it was fried in dripping, and the fact that I had eaten my breakfast along with Alec and that the coffee was strong enough to give me goose pimples, I *did* eat – and it was the tastiest little pastry I had ever had in my life. Light, warm, sweet, almost salty – just far enough from being salty to make one yearn for another bite to see if the salt was *there*. I finished it, licked my sugary fingers as delicately as I could, and craned forward to peer at the pan of hot oil.

Joe Aldo burst into a cascade of delighted laughter.

'That is it!' he said. 'That is the secret. The genius in the lamp, and only a true cook can rub it! I make them one little bite too small. Just one tiny little bite too small and no one, no one, no one, no one ever refuses another. Hah!'

Alec wagged his finger at me and laughed along and I managed to muster a sheepish smile too. I sipped another incendiary mouthful of the black tar Joe Aldo called coffee and asked for a second pastry like a good girl, not wanting to spoil his fun.

When there was a pyramid of them on a plate between us and the fat little coffee pot was sitting on the table too, at last Joe moved the shimmering pan of fat back from the gas ring (setting it on the windowsill, I noticed, where it was sure to taint the wash hung on a rope in the tiny back yard). He removed his white apron, put on the striped one again and went back to his potato peeling, flicking the potato off the knife with an expert twist and plunging his hand into the bucket up to his elbow, wetting his rolled shirtsleeve and not noticing.

'So,' he said. 'I am a bad husband, working and working and never a rose, never a song, never a dance in the moonlight for my lovely wife. Not since her birthday, February, have we danced together in an empty room.' I took in my stride this hint about the home life of the Aldos and its distance and different nature from my own. 'And someone saw her, her beautiful black hair and her eyes like rubies. Ah! No – sapphires. And her cheeks like peaches in the evening. I can't tell you in English how beautiful is my wife. If you spoke my language . . .' He decided, apparently, to try it anyway and spent the next minute regaling us about the many wondrous charms of his wife in swooping, elated Italian of which we understood nothing except – in my case – the oft-repeated '-*issima*'s, which gave one the distinct impression that he really meant it.

'And you're sure it's someone in the town?' said Alec when Joe finally stopped talking.

'She never get letters I don't see. She never leave the village. It must be someone she met here.'

'But you don't know who?' said Alec. 'You weren't able to think of anyone?'

'Most of the time she see only ladies. Washing, see?' He pointed out of the window at the waggling rope of laundry. 'Rosa can wash the lace as fine as web of a spider. She can wash wool as soft as the day the lamb is born.' I looked askance at the washing outside, just beyond the reach (I hoped) of the oily smoke from Joe's cooking pan. It looked to be plain yellow cotton shirts and white calico underclothes to me, and I wondered if Rosa's beauty and prowess in laundry were to be believed. But then, the pastries had been as delicious as their advance press, so perhaps I was being unfair to him.

'She must see *some* men,' said Alec.

'She see postman, milkman, grocer boy, farmer on top of the hill. He kill a lamb for us and butcher it just how we like it, Rosa and me. I fry fish for my living, *bella signora*, but my wife Rosa she is the cook. She make a two-day pot of lamb and tomato would raise the dead from their graves. A *pollo con funghi* could cure a plague.' He turned back to Alec again. 'But it could be anyone. Bank manager, fisherman, pub landlord, anyone who ever see her face or hear her voice. I not angry. How he help it, this man, whoever he is? But she has to come home. She will come home. And before Sabbatina even knows she is gone.'

'Sabbatina?' I said.

'It would break her heart. And so also mine. Sabbatina is our daughter. A beautiful child and a genius, *una prodigia*, a student of the arts and the sciences. Rosa and me so very proud of our girl.'

'Ah,' I said, nodding out of the window. I had thought there was a preponderance of yellow amongst the family wash and it was a shade of yellow, very buttery, that had seemed familiar to me. Now I understood: Sabbatina Aldo went to school at the top of the hill.

'Yes, *signora*,' said Joe. 'Sabbatina is a student at St Columba's College for the Young Ladies! Can you believe? Hah? Hah? Can you?'

Frankly, I could not. And I was sure that Basil and Candide Rowe-Issing could not possibly know that young Stella was at school with the child of a fish fryer and a washerwoman.

'A scholarship, I presume?' I murmured.

'A scholar of such promise and so very young,' said her father, perhaps misunderstanding or perhaps unable to resist another chance, however tiny, to brag. I would not know. Poor dear Donald has never given Hugh or me anything to brag about, being dim-witted, gawky, and shy amongst strangers. It is too soon to tell with Teddy, or at least I dearly hope so.

'But how can you hope to hide the fact that her mother is missing?' said Alec.

'She is full scholar, see?' said Joe. 'Sleep up there, eat with the girls, that terrible food. Study in her evenings in the common room of the girls. She will visit tomorrow for dinner with her family – *cena in famiglia* – unless I stop her. Today I will send note to say Rosa is ill, very catching cold, and Sabbatina must stay away.'

'Giving me a week to find her and persuade her home,' Alec said.

'And if you like,' I offered, 'I'll take the note. Sabbatina might know something.' Joe rumbled a little and I fell over myself to reassure him. 'I'll be very subtle, Mr Aldo. I won't arouse any suspicions.'

'She love her mother so very very much and I love both of them so very very very—'

'I'll be careful,' I said. I had not heard such sustained protestations of love and affection since my Pereford summer and it was beginning to grate upon my nerves.

Back up at St Columba's twenty minutes later, I marched right in at the front door like the welcome guest I evidently was (though the reason for my welcome was a continuing mystery to me) and collared a passing twelve-year-old.

'Where would I find Sabbatina Aldo at this moment, child?' I said. The little girl encouraged her spectacles back up her nose by means of a most unattractive screwing up of her face and pouting out of her lips before she answered.

'Who?'

'Sabbatina,' I said, slower. Surely there could not be more than one.

'What form's she in?' said the girl. She was sidling away as she spoke, clearly bent on getting to wherever she had been headed when I stopped her.

'Stand still when I'm addressing you, please,' I said. 'I'm Miss Gilver, the new French mistress. Now, take your hands out of your tunic pockets and show me the way to Miss Shanks's study.'

'Oh, Miss!' said the child, instantly woebegone. 'I've got thirty-five minutes of tennis before I have to start horrid Latin with old Plumface and the big girls said last night you were nice. Please?'

'Don't say Plumface,' I said, even though my lips were twitching.

'Goody Gilver, Eileen Rendall said.' The little minx was practically batting her eyelids at me now and I am afraid to say that I succumbed to it.

'Oh, go on then. Point me in the right direction and then run along.'

I had to raise my voice towards the end of it, because at the first hint of relenting she was running already.

'West stairs,' she called over her shoulder. 'First floor. The one with all the chairs!' And she was gone.

A child after Hugh's heart, I thought bitterly, turning around on the spot and trying to deduce which way west might lie. I closed my eyes. The sun set over the sea, beyond the far harbour wall, and the school faced the harbour mouth and since it was May and the sun was setting to the north-west, that meant that the west stair was probably . . . I set off rather uncertainly towards the farthest corner of the building from the carriage entrance and climbed a set of broad oak stairs I found there.

The first floor – the drawing-room floor in the heyday of the house, one supposed – was quite a good bit grander than the labyrinth of corridors upstairs where Fleur had her little bolthole and had suffered less in the metamorphosis from manor house to boarding school than had the ground floor with its noticeboards and clattering canteen of a dining room. Here was a wide corridor with Palladian over-lintels to its doors – or perhaps Palladian-style would be more accurate, Palladian-esque, even Palladian-ish (for it seemed that the architect had been more entranced by ornament than he had been constrained by authenticity), plasterwork niches so highly decorated they were almost grottoes punctuating its walls, and pelmets above its windows encrusted with bosses and curlicues like a barnacled wreck on the bed of the sea.

With that weight of unavoidable decoration, the thin school carpet and drab school curtains did little to reduce the overall splendour and also there was no need for occasional furniture to break up the yawning blankness as one sometimes sees in plainer houses, where the corridors become a slalom of tables, long-case clocks and even suits of armour. Here it was easy to tell that I had arrived at Miss Shanks's room, from – as the tennis-bound child had shouted to me – all the chairs. A row of mismatched dining chairs stood along the wall on either side of her door, awaiting, one would surmise, the bottoms of miscreants sent to be dealt with and left simmering so that the prospect of punishment delayed might be half the punishment all on its own.

I knocked. Miss Shanks's welcome came as a burst of song.

'Come in, come in, it's nice to see ye!'

I opened the door and entered, trying hard not to let my eyebrows rise.

'How's yersel', ye're looking grand!' she carolled on.

'Hello again,' I said.

'Harry Lauder,' said Miss Shanks. 'A wonderful entertainer. I have some gramophone records and I play them for the girls for a treat sometimes.'

'How delightful,' I said with a tight smile, thinking how odd her mood was for the current state of her school. One would not have been surprised to find her wringing her hands and tearing at her hair. Skittish hilarity seemed to me to have no place here.

'And how delightful to have you safely with us after our wee misunderstanding,' Miss Shanks said. She pointed me into a chair – a miscreant's chair, clearly, being rather low and set alone before her desk, facing the window. It was a busy, rather messy room: more of the interminable patchwork abandoned on top of a cocktail cabinet and books lying open and face-down on the arms of chairs. There was even a fox's head, stuffed and mounted, which was serving as a coat hook, scarves and satchels slung over it with abandon. I brought my gaze back to Miss Shanks who was watching me with a small smile curling at her lips.

'I have no formal qualifications,' I began.

'Pouf!' said Miss Shanks. 'You speak French, don't you?' I nodded. 'And read it and write it and are familiar with the classics?' I stopped nodding halfway through this but she did not notice. She sailed on. 'Then I'm sure you'll do very nicely. My dear departed Miss Fielding was a great one for certificates and methods and all that, don't ye know . . .'

'Ah, yes, the Froebel method,' I said. 'The girls mentioned it to me.'

'But I have faith in my mistresses no matter what their path to St Columba's. Once they are here, now that you are here, my dear Miss Gilver, all is sure to be well.'

I nodded even less certainly. Faith in her mistresses? Four of them had deserted her and one had died; her school was surely teetering on the very brink of disaster. And she knew not the first thing about me.

'Our sixth formers are four weeks from their Higher Cert exams,' she was saying. I redoubled my efforts at concentration. 'They must be your particular concern, naturally.'

'That kind of certificate does interest you then?' I said. Miss Shanks opened her eyes very wide.

'Och, but of course,' she said. 'Of course, of course. Five of our sixth form are bound for university, Miss Gilver. Five! Out of only twenty. And three of the others could have gone if they'd a mind to. Two off to Edinburgh, one straight to St Andrews, one to St Andrews after a year in Switzerland and one, can you guess?'

'Oxford?' I said.

'Somerville College, Oxford,' said Miss Shanks in tones of wonder. 'If my dear Fielding is looking down on us she will be tickled pink.'

'And are any of them going up to read French?' I said, resisting with some effort the impulse to cross my fingers for luck.

'One,' said Miss Shanks. 'I forget which one, but one certainly. French, two for history, one for chemistry if you can believe it and one . . . oh, geography I think. Not that it matters.'

'I see,' I said. I was furiously trying to remember what I had ever known of Donald and Teddy's French at Eton, furiously trying to convince myself either that I could coach one clever girl through the last few weeks – she was surely more or less running under her own steam now? – or that I could fulfil my obligations to Pearl and Aurora in a hundred other ways besides passing myself off as a mistress in this school.

'Well, I suppose I've got until Monday morning to prepare, have I?' I said.

'Yes, I'll show you to Mademoiselle Beauclerc's room and you can acquaint yourself with her lessons. It makes sense for you just to take over her room, I suppose, although it's one of the nicest ones and with you being new, strictly speaking, it should be "all roll over and one fall out", don't ye know.'

'I'm sorry?'

'One fell out and so we all roll over and the new girl comes in at the far end. Just my bit of fun, Miss Gilver. I daresay no one will make a fuss for the last few weeks of term and then we can all bags new rooms in September.'

I managed a smile, but my head was reeling. I had fraternised in the course of my detecting career with circus performers and music-hall turns, cottagers and publicans, opium fiends and charlatans and once – frankly – witches, but I had never met anyone whose conversation left me feeling as rudderless as little Miss Shanks. No one even came close to her.

'Right then,' I said, and stood.

'We'll soon have her things cleared out of your way and everything shipshape.'

'She . . .' I swallowed. 'She didn't take her things?'

'Not all of them,' Miss Shanks said. 'Not many, actually. She left in a bit of a rush. But one of the maids will soon get her study and bedroom ready for you. Or one of the girls maybe.'

'Oh!' I said, sitting again. 'I was forgetting. I have a message for one of the girls. Sabbatina Aldo?' Miss Shanks's face turned blank and she shook her head.

'Who?' she said.

'Sabbatina? From the village. Her father asked me to say that her mother is unwell – a contagious cold – she is not to visit tomorrow as is usual.'

'Ah!' said Miss Shanks. 'Betty. We call her Betty Alder, Miss Gilver. Much more suitable. I'll make sure she gets the message.'

'I look forward to meeting her,' I said. 'I take it she studies French, doesn't she?'

'I couldn't say,' said Miss Shanks. 'I don't know the child.'

'Oh?' This was odd for two reasons: in a school of one hundred girls one would expect the headmistress to know all of them and, besides, Sabbatina Aldo was hardly run of the mill. 'Isn't she a scholarship girl?' I said.

'No,' said Miss Shanks. Her voice was cold and the brogue was quite gone.

'Oh,' I said again. 'I got the impression that she was a tremendously bright pupil. Perhaps I imagined the scholarship angle all on my own.' I was sure I had not, but there seemed nothing else to say.

'She is,' said Miss Shanks, 'extremely clever and bookish. And here thanks to a wealthy patron. She is of absolutely no interest to me.'

Which, coming out of the mouth of the headmistress of a school which went in for sending its girls to college, was a mystifying remark even set against Miss Shanks's inexhaustible supply of them. I stared at the woman; quite honestly I gawped at her but, before I could think of a reply, a knock came at the door.

'Come in, come in, it's nice to—' Miss Shanks did not get to the end of her little ditty. The door opened and Fleur Lipscott blundered into the room.

'Miss Shanks,' she said. She put both of her hands on the back of my chair and leaned her weight on it. I would not have risked a wager that she even noticed I was sitting there. 'There are policemen downstairs.'

Miss Shanks said nothing but she sat up very straight and drew in a sharp breath.

'They were asking Tessie to take them to you but I happened to be passing the door. They've found a body. Washed up out of the sea. At Dunskey. A female body.'

Miss Shanks and I had both scrambled to our feet and Fleur noticed me for the first time.

'What brought them here?' said Miss Shanks. Her voice was high and tremulous. 'Oh my good Lord, it's not one of the girls, is it? Was anyone missing at breakfast time?'

'It's a woman,' Fleur said. 'Not a girl. They came here because they thought it might be one of us. One of the mistresses. From the way she was dressed, I suppose.'

'How long—' Miss Shanks had to clear her throat and start again. 'How long has it been in the water, did they say? Which one did they think it might be?'

The room swirled just a little around me then and I put my hand out to steady myself, finding Fleur's icy fingers under my own. She flinched and then grabbed my wrist.

'Dandy,' she said. 'They – the policemen – want someone to go and look at it – her. I'll go but only if you come with me.'

Miss Shanks pattered around the side of her desk and came to stand, shifting from foot to foot, between us.

'It should be me,' she said, but plaintively with not a shred of determination. 'As headmistress it falls to me. Oh, how I wish Miss Fielding were here! Perhaps Mrs Brown would . . . I can't!' she said. 'I can't do it. The sight and the smell of it. I'll faint or be sick. I feel ill just thinking about it. How long did they say?'

'I'll do it,' said Fleur. 'Mrs Gilver will come with me.'

It seemed that I was not to have a say and I was feeling rather green myself at the prospect, especially since Miss Shanks had brought the rude facts of the matter right out into the open that way.

'I shan't forget this, Miss Lipscott,' said the headmistress. 'I shall never forget that you did this for me.'

Fleur gave her a long cool look which I could not decipher before she turned back to me.

'Dandy? No time like the present. The policemen have a motorcar with them. They can take us there right away.'

There turned out to be a small cove a mile or two north of Portpatrick. Four of us – Fleur, me, a sergeant and a constable – trundled up out of the village on the road I had taken from the station the evening before and onto a little farm lane before turning to the sea again and following an even smaller lane down through the woods to a headland. The constable pulled off onto a patch of ash beside a cottage and stopped the engine.

'This is as far as the road goes,' he said. 'There's a wee path'll take us down from here.'

'Where is she?' I asked, horrified to think, no matter how long the body had been in the water, that they had simply hauled her up the beach, covered her with a tarpaulin and left her there.

'Dinnae worry, miss,' he replied. 'She's inside, decent as decent can be.'

The cottage wife looked with wary interest out of her kitchen window at us all alighting from the motorcar, and a clutch of her children peeped around the side of the house wall, going so far as to follow behind us as we set off two by two towards the track we were to take to the shoreline.

'Scat!' said the constable, turning round and stamping his foot at them. 'Gah!' The children scattered, giggling. 'They'd no' be laughin' if we let them come with us and they saw her,' he said. 'Or smell—'

'Tsst!' said the sergeant and his man fell silent, but not soon enough for me. The succession of sugary little pastries and the two cups of coffee-flavoured tar were lurching around inside me. I stole a look over at Fleur but nothing could be gleaned from her pale, set face and her timid posture. She had looked terrified since the first moment I had laid eyes upon her, last night in the staffroom.

66

The path was not long and within minutes we had come out onto a pebbly cove between rocks, where there was a curious little wooden building like two hexagonal beach huts stuck together, their pointed roofs and arched windows looking straight out of a fairy tale.

'What is that?' I said, thinking that if it were my little summerhouse I would not have been best pleased to have had the police commandeer it to lay out a body, new-plucked from its fishy grave.

'Cable station,' said the constable. 'It was built to house the machinery for the telegraph cable. Quite interest—'

'Tsst,' said the sergeant again. He had taken off his cap and nodded at the constable to do the same. Then he drew a deep breath and turned to Fleur and me.

'If you've a handkerchief, ladies,' he said, 'you might want to . . .' He demonstrated with his own large cotton square, clamping it hard over his nose and mouth. I fished my little bit of lace out from my pocket and did the same. Fleur shook her head slightly. The sergeant opened the door and we stepped inside.

On a table against the far side of the room – only seven or eight feet away at that – a humped shape under a sheet lay as still as a stone. I concentrated hard on breathing through my mouth, after hearing a soft groan from Fleur.

I had seen corpses before now. I had watched men *become* corpses once or twice in the convalescent home during the war, where convalescing was predominant but not guaranteed. And in latter years I had been forced to look at and sometimes touch no fewer than seven dead people, some of them dead by the most violent means that wickedness could bring. But all of these corpses had been newly departed this life, a few hours gone at most since they had been breathing. What awaited me under the sheeting in the cable station that bright May morning was something else again.

The sergeant took another of his enormous breaths and swept back the cover from the remains it had been shrouding.

Fleur let out a shuddering kind of moan and put her hand up to her mouth at last. I stared straight ahead out of the window, attempting to bring my panicky breaths back to something near normal before I tried to look at the thing.

'Well?' said the sergeant. I glanced at him. He was talking to Fleur, but as he looked from her face down at the table my eyes, without my bidding, followed his gaze.

'Oh God,' I said and then the most surprising thing happened. I was not sickened nor frightened by what was lying there. Instead, I felt a tear bulge up in each of my staring eyes and drop down my cheeks.

Her hair was matted and stiff with salt, straggling over one shoulder and lying in a clump on her breast. Her clothes were dark with the water and twisted around her body from where she had been roughly humped onto the table. Her shoes were gone, her stockings tattered and her feet, puffed up like monstrous toadstools, were mottled with wounds and sores. Her hands were half-hidden in her clothes, but I could see that they looked just like her feet, swollen and nibbled. Terrible to think they had put on those clothes and brushed that sodden hair.

I wiped the tears away from my eyes and looked at her face, or at the dreadful, pitiable sight where her face should be. And finally I felt the floor begin to tilt.

'Steady there,' said the constable and put his good strong arm across my back. The sergeant was already holding Fleur by her elbows and I could tell from the grim look upon his face that she was buckling.

'Is that one of your colleagues, miss?' he asked her. She shook her head and the movement seemed to strengthen her. The sergeant took his hands away.

'Do you know who it is?' said the constable gently. Fleur took a step forward and bent over the body, looking at the buttons on the high-necked dress, staring at the lace around the collar. I could not have put my face so close to that grey skin with the ragged edge where her face should have begun if all our lives had depended upon me.

'Miss?' said the constable.

'It's not Jeanne Beauclerc,' said Fleur.

The constable swallowed audibly.

'Who is it?' he asked.

'I – I don't know her,' said Fleur.

'Madam?' said the sergeant, looking back at me.

'Nor I.' My voice sounded thin and high, like a child's.

'Right,' he said. 'That's that then.' He must have been struggling, poor man, because he turned very sharply and almost ran out of the little room back to the open air.

'You can go now,' said the constable. He was staring at Fleur, with his face twisted up, staring at the way she was crouched over the body, six inches away from the soaking cloth and the flesh. He was horrified and I was not far behind him.

'Fleur,' I said. 'Darling, let's go.'

She spoke, just one muttered word, and then straightened and turned away.

'What was that, miss?' the constable said. 'What did you say?'

'Nothing,' said Fleur, and walked out onto the beach. But she had not said nothing. I did not repeat it, but I had heard it.

She had said, 'Five.'

4

The word seemed to echo throughout the dank dimness of the cable station, until it and the walls around me and the low ceiling above my head were all pressing closer than I could bear and I stumbled out into the sunshine.

Fleur had walked down to the water's edge – even though the tide was low and the going must have been unpleasant with such a great deal of seaweed lying in bands across the beach – whither the constable looked on the point of following her. At least he was standing shifting from enormous foot to enormous foot, working himself into a little hollow in the shingle, and was twisting his cap in his hands with a rhythmic efficiency which promised to ruin it for ever.

'Where's Sergeant . . . ?' I said, looking around.

'Turner,' said the constable. 'Away to get a wee drink from the burn. His wame's no' fit for thon.' He jerked his head back towards the cable station.

'It didn't do *my* tummy much good either,' I said, swallowing hard. (I am a past master at Scotch after all my years immersed in it.) 'She, I mean. Not it. She.'

'Aye, well,' said the constable, and he gave me a kindly look. '*She's* long gone and past carin', missus.'

'I suppose so,' I said. 'How long would you say, Constable . . . ?'

'Reid,' he replied. 'A wee while, anyway.'

I sighed. Even a past master cannot distinguish the Scotch whiles – a wee while, a fair while and a good while – without some reference point at which to start.

'Not today then?' I said, employing imbecility to shake him into further detail.

'The day?' he said, with ready scorn. 'Naw, never. Three, four days easy. No' a week. I'm sayin' three days, missus.'

'You can really be that precise?' I said, wondering at how much practice a village constable could have had in this grisly specialism. Reid swept his arm across the view before us.

'Fishin',' he said and did not need to say more.

'Right,' I replied, and then we both stood and watched Fleur in silence.

'I tell you what else, missus,' Reid said at last, when the three of us had held our tableau long enough for seagulls to alight on the bands of seaweed and start their scavenging, 'I bet I can tell you where she went in too. If she went in off the cliffs and no' out a boat, anyway.'

'That would be handy,' I said.

'Likes of if she left anythin' behind with her name on,' said Reid. 'Find out who she was.'

'Hm,' I said. I was thinking how best to suggest that they should ask someone else from the school to confirm it was not Miss Beauclerc lying there (without absolutely dropping Fleur in it) since clearly if Fleur had added this latest body to her growing collection she would not be above lying. I stole a glance at Reid wondering how to broach it.

As a rule I am beyond scrupulous. I break no laws and I do not collude to help others break them, and if I had known there was a body in the offing I would have made sure and said all that to Pearl on the telephone. As matters stood, however, I was hogtied. I had promised Pearl to help her sister; telling a police constable she was a self-confessed murderer did not fall comfortably within the bounds of helpfulness as Pearl would understand it, I was sure. On the other hand, how could I get a second opinion organised without explaining my doubts about the first?

All in all then, Reid's hope for a tidy parcel of belongings left on a cliff top was mine too.

'So where would that be?' I said.

'Down Dunskey Castle way,' said Reid.

'Isn't this Dunskey Castle?' I asked him. He gave me a pitying look.

'This is Dunskey House,' he said. 'The castle's away the other side o' the town. And I'm thinking maybe if we go and have a wee scout round down there, we'll find a clue. Otherwise . . .'

'Quite,' I said. 'I suppose there aren't name tags sewn into her clothes, are there? Her underclothes?'

'No' checked yet,' said Reid, and who could blame him? 'The police surgeon's the man for that.' He paused. 'Or a mutch-wife.' He sighed. 'Or maybe somebody'll report a woman missin', and we can leave the poor soul be.'

How to explain that it took so long for the notion to strike me? Rosa Aldo had disappeared and here was a body, yet I had made no connection between the two. I put a hand to my mouth, picturing Giuseppe's grief if that was his adored and beloved wife lying in there.

'Missus?' said Reid.

But why would Fleur Lipscott kill a washerwoman?

'You all right?'

But might not the killer of five people be indiscriminate in exactly that way?

'You feelin' sick?'

I took my hand away from my mouth again.

'I think I know who it is,' I said.

'Good grief!' said the harsh voice of the sergeant behind me. 'You might have spoken up before now, madam.' I turned to see him glaring at me out of a pale face. 'This is a serious business, you know.'

'I didn't *recognise* the woman,' I said, drawing myself up and glaring back, out of a face as pale as his I am sure. 'I just remembered something. Mrs Aldo from the village is missing.'

'Who?' said Reid.

'Mrs Giuseppe Aldo. I don't know her address.'

'The Eye-tie's wife?' said Sergeant Turner. He wheeled around and stared at the cable station door. 'Aye, it could be, it could be.

All dressed in black that way. And more like a foreigner to go flinging herself in the water than one of our own.'

Reid's eyes narrowed and his head shook a little, too small a movement for his boss to see. I noticed it, though, and I knew we were in accord. The man was a fool.

'So, shall we fetch Mr Aldo?' I said.

'We?' said the sergeant, staring coldly.

'I beg your pardon,' I said. 'He's a . . . friend of a friend of mine. In fact, this friend of mine – a Mr Osborne – will probably want to come with him, as I came with Miss Lipscott, don't you know.' Which was stating it rather strongly; the truth was *I* wanted Alec to come along with Joe Aldo. If there was a body in his case he should see it.

'Are we talking about the same folk?' said the sergeant. 'Black-haired Eye-tie that fries fish at the end of the harbour?'

'Giuseppe Aldo,' I said. 'That's the chap.'

'Funny friend for you, madam,' he replied.

'My acquaintance is wide and varied, Sergeant,' I assured him. 'And speaking of friends . . .' I jerked my head towards the shoreline. 'I'd better get Miss Lipscott home, hadn't I?'

'Where is she?' the sergeant said.

I wheeled round to look at where Fleur had been. There was no sign of her.

'Where's she gone?' I said, stupidly, and exchanged a glance with Reid.

'She'll have walked round the head to the other wee beach there,' he said, pointing. I set off after her, trying to hurry in the deep shingle which only produced the mired feeling of a nightmare, when one surges and struggles and gets precisely nowhere. At last, however, I gained the hard, wet grit below the tide line and could break into a trot as I rounded the promontory dividing the cable station cove from the next one down. This was a sandy, sheltered spot with a deep swathe of meadow grass at its back stretching up to the lane. There were no rocks; nowhere to hide. And there was no Fleur.

Constable Reid came puffing up behind me.

'Did she have time to come round here and go up the path?' I asked him.

'Must've had,' he replied.

'But weren't we more or less watching her the whole time?'

'Cannae have been,' said Reid. 'Else where is she?'

I could not fault his reasoning and so I set off up the path, which meandered back past the cottage with its party of peeping children and on to where the motorcar awaited our return. The sergeant was there, sitting stiffly in the passenger seat, displeased to have been abandoned by his underling, but of Fleur there was not a sign.

'I'll ask at the cottage,' I said, turning back, but the sergeant stopped me with a throat-clearing sound that was almost a growl.

'You'll both have to walk home if you don't come now, madam,' he said. 'We're not a taxi.'

'Likely we'll pass her on the road,' said Reid, stooping to the starter. 'Maybe she just set off on her own for a wee breath of fresh air after yon.'

I nodded and climbed into the back seat, still craning around, expecting Fleur to appear from amongst the trees. It was not until later that I realised the absurdity of what he had said; one does not leave a seashore in search of fresh air. As it was, the motorcar bore me away while I sat on the edge of my seat, peering into the hedgerows and scanning the road ahead for a figure and ignoring the sick cold feeling inside me.

And since a sick feeling inside is not something one can tell of to a rather stupid police sergeant – or even a tolerably bright constable – I kept my worries to myself as the little motorcar descended to Portpatrick's harbour and trundled around towards Joe Aldo's shack there. Also, like a child at the approach of its bedtime, I was hoping that if I kept quiet the men would forget I was there. I wanted to soften the blow of what was sure to be a bald announcement from the horrid sergeant that a body had appeared and would Joe come and see it, please.

The little shack on the harbour was a very different place this Saturday luncheon time, thronged with people: a long queue of men and women snaking out of the door and coiling around the side, and on the bollards and lobster pots and the harbour wall itself there were gangs of little boys and girls, rabblesome families and courting couples all intent on the fragrant contents of the newspaper nests they held open in their laps. As we stepped down from the motorcar a gaggle of well-dressed but rather grubby little boys came tumbling out of the open doorway, holding folded newspaper cones of fried potato and stone bottles of ginger beer, and in spite of the recent sights in the cable station my stomach gave a slow, luxurious rumble.

'That's Mr Tweedie's son!' said the sergeant in tones of high astonishment. 'The bank manager,' he explained to me. 'I don't know what this place is coming to.'

'Sodom and Gomorrah, Italian-style,' I murmured. He did not hear me but Constable Reid gave an explosive snort which he turned into a cough with the skill of long practice.

'You're not a patron of Aldo's then, Sergeant Turner?' I said.

'I most certainly am not,' he said. 'Mrs Turner won't hear of it.'

The families and couples who had boggled to see the arrival of a police motorcar were now openly listening, all conversation stilled, only the rustle of newspaper and the crunch of batter disturbing the quiet around us (that and the hopeful screeching of a perfect battalion of seagulls with designs on the crumbs).

'Take him through the back, Reid,' said the sergeant, returning to his seat in the motorcar, 'and I'll come round and speak to him there, away from the frying pans.' But I do not believe it was the cooking smells which troubled him. The sergeant simply did not care to jostle into the shack with the hoi-polloi, which gave no quarter to the comings and goings of anyone not in the queue for luncheon. Even as we watched, an emerging figure had to turn sideways to squeeze through in the small space left by a stout man in brown overalls with his eyes fixed on the counter.

This figure, once outside, revealed itself to be Alec. He was wiping his lips with his handkerchief and breathing hard, but when he saw me he broke into a jog.

'Marvellous news, Dandy!' he said. 'Guess what?'

'Alec, have you really just eaten fried haddock and chips?' I said.

'Certainly not,' said Alec. 'It was cod. The man is an artist.'

'I've got news too, I'm afraid,' I said. 'This is Constable Reid, Alec. Reid, this is my associate, Mr Osborne.'

'Associate?' said Reid.

'Glad to make your acquaintance,' Alec said, holding out a greasy hand. He says he can always tell by my introductions of policemen and the like whether I have filed the man under 'idiot' or have turned down the corner of his card as a possible ally. I am not sure I believe him; more like lucky guesses on his part, I should imagine (for one would rather not be so transparent when one is bent on detecting). 'But my news first,' Alec went on. 'She was seen.'

'Fleur?' I said.

He gave me an odd look. 'Mrs Aldo.'

'Thank God,' I said. 'When and where?

'Tuesday night,' said Alec. 'On the cliff path, heading for Dunskey Castle.'

'Ah,' I said. Reid and I exchanged a glance.

'And . . .' Alec began.

'Could still be her, missus,' said Reid. 'Looks more like it now, if aught.'

'What's this?' Alec said.

'I've just come from viewing a body,' I told him. 'A woman's body. Three days in the sea, washed up this morning.'

'Just where it *would* wash up if it went in at the castle too,' said Reid.

'We came to ask Joe to take a look at it,' I said, and we all three turned and looked in at the door. Over the heads of the waiting crowd we could just see Joe Aldo in his white hat and capacious white apron, tipping a sizzling basket of fried potatoes into a trough behind his glass counter.

'Did your witness say anything about Mrs Aldo's demeanour?' I asked. 'If she was walking alone at night on a cliff top it begins to look like suicide.'

'She wasn't,' Alec said. 'Walking alone, that is. She was with a man. And Dunskey Castle is a well-known local trysting place, I believe.' He raised his eyebrows at Reid, who nodded and blushed a little, as though his knowledge of the spot might have been gained in his off-duty hours.

'What man?' I asked Alec.

'My witness didn't know him but she did go as far as to say she'd recognise the chap if she saw him a second time. She did go that far.' He heaved a heavy sigh. 'This is going to kill Joe,' he said. 'Absolutely kill him. He's already beside himself even just hearing that she was seen with her lover.'

'But he knew she had one,' I said.

Alec nodded. 'It's one thing to suspect one's wife of a dalliance, but it's quite another actually to hear proof.' He shook his head. 'It hit him like a brick.'

'He'll need a good hard nut on him now, then,' said Reid, not quite unkindly. 'Cos here's what I'm thinking. *Maybe* she fell and her fancy man didnae tell a soul so's nobody would know his wee secret. And *maybe* she flang herself down and he kept *that* quiet. But most likely of all, if ye're askin' me, if he was up there with her . . .'

'Quite,' I said.

'I agree,' said Alec.

'Aye,' said Reid, 'he pushed her.'

'But the witness was sure she'd know the chap again?' I said.

'Seemed to be,' Alec said. 'Although to be perfectly honest she scooted off again before I could grill her.'

'Who was she?' said Reid.

'A little servant girl from one of those villas up there,' said Alec, pointing. 'I rather suspect she was out walking with her true love too and didn't want it known that she had been.'

'A wee servant girl?' said Reid.

'You'll have to have another crack at her,' I said.

'Out walkin' with her felly?' He was frowning.

At that moment the motorcar door opened and the sergeant leaned out and barked (the only word for it) at the constable.

'Reid!'

'Aye, Sarge,' said Reid. 'We're just away in the noo.' He dropped his voice before he spoke again. 'I tell you what, though. I'm no' taking the poor man through and letting the sarge tell him. I'll tell him myself and get Sergeant Turner after. He's no' got a good touch with folk tae my mind.'

But his concern was wasted, for when we entered the cafe it was to find Joe Aldo already in a state of shock so all-consuming that one wondered whether any fresh horrors could touch him. Even so, we shooed the hungry crowd out of the door (to gales of protest) and I scribbled a sign – *10 mins* – and propped it up in the window. Then all four of us crushed into the back kitchen, Alec urged Joe into a chair and Constable Reid told him very gently that 'a lady had passed away' and would he 'just glance at her to say it wasn't his wife, please' before leaving to fetch his sergeant for the rest of the interview.

'Where?' was the first word Joe uttered, when the two policemen had returned.

'Up in the wee cove at Dunskey,' said Reid. Joe's face paled to an ugly cream colour and he rubbed his hand over it roughly.

'From – from the water?' he said.

Reid nodded.

'Is Rosa?' asked Joe.

'I couldnae say,' said Reid. 'I've never met your wife, sir. Sarge?'

'*I* didn't know her,' said the sergeant, his past tense making me wince.

Joe threaded a hand in under his apron and drew a wallet out of his waistcoat pocket. He flapped it open and held it out to us all, showing us a small photograph, rather dark, of a young woman in old-fashioned dress staring solemnly ahead. She might have been a great beauty; it was hard to say.

'My Rosa,' he said. 'Is Rosa? In the cove?'

'Can't say,' said the sergeant. Luckily, Joe Aldo was mystified by this response, blinking slowly and looking around us all. If he had realised why we could not say he might well have fainted.

'So . . .' said Reid.

Joe nodded, rummaged under his apron front again and pulled out a watch.

'After the dinner time,' he said. 'One hour is the very most. Once my customers all are gone.'

'Now hang on, pal,' said the sergeant, causing a stir of protest from both Alec and me – he really was one of the most abrasive characters I have ever encountered and police sergeants are not known for being soothing. Constables and inspectors, in my experience, reflect the sweep of humanity but a sergeant always has something of the fox terrier about him. 'We're needing to crack on. We can't hang about for you.'

'Quite right, Sergeant,' I said. 'We'll bring Mr Aldo to the cable station and you can, as you say, crack on. You've a case to solve and an obvious place to start from.' I raised my eyebrows at Alec. He stared blankly back at me. I glanced at Reid. Both he and Alec continued to gaze back as though unable to guess at my allusion.

'Taking statements from witnesses, for instance,' I supplied, with another eyebrow wiggle at Alec and Constable Reid. They were two statues. It seemed 'the sarge' was not to be told of the servant girl and her observations.

'I'm the best judge of my business, madam,' said the sergeant, rather primly. He stood, straightened his suit coat and walked away. Joe shook himself, gave one last miserable look at Rosa's photograph and went to reopen the shop. The three of us remaining – Reid, Alec and me – kept our seats in the back kitchen and as soon as the crowd had re-entered and their clamour would cover our voices I charged them with it directly.

'Why on earth not tell Turner about the witness on Tuesday night?' I said.

'I found her,' Alec said. 'I'm not going to hand her over to him.'

'Quite right, sir,' said Reid. 'I agree.'

I turned on him.

'Why?' I said.

'She's as timid as a little rabbit,' Alec said. 'Sergeant Turner would terrify her.'

'Sergeant Turner *does* terrify her,' said Reid. 'The both o' them do.' To our puzzled looks he offered an explanation. 'It's the Turners she works tae, see?'

'She's Sergeant Turner's very own servant?' I said. 'How do you know?'

'Well, Mrs Turner's really,' Alec said.

'Well, then of *course* you should have—' I began, but Reid cut me off.

'Can I just ask, sir? How did you track her down?'

'Well, I didn't so much track her down as run into her,' Alec said. 'She came down here to the shack at the same time as me this morning.'

'To buy an early luncheon?' I asked.

'Never,' said Reid. 'Cissie Gilhooley hates thon greasy muck.'

'How on earth do you know that?' I asked.

'It's not the least bit greas—' Alec began, but then shook himself. 'Cissie came down because Mrs Aldo was supposed to go and collect the washing yesterday and she didn't show up. So the lady of the house sent the girl to see what was wrong.'

'And you pounced on her?' I asked.

Reid shifted in his seat.

'I asked when she'd last seen the woman,' Alec said, 'and she blurted out "Tuesday night" and blushed to the roots of her hair. It was *then* that I pounced on her. And she's obviously going to get into considerable trouble if her mistress gets wind of her wanderings, so I'll have to get even firmer with her if I'm to learn any more.'

'Naw, no' really,' said Reid. 'It's right enough the wee lassie would get her papers if she got found out and we'll can get it out of her without any o' that anyway.'

'You're sure?' I said.

'Fine an' sure,' said Reid, shifting in his seat again. 'It was me she was comin' to meet.' He turned as red as the big glass bottle of tomato ketchup on the table between us.

'Ah,' I said. 'I see. You'd get into more trouble with your sergeant than she would with her mistress? Not that a little chivalry isn't a welcome sight in these discourteous days. At least . . .' I lowered my head and looked at him from under my brows. I have rather suitable eyebrows for the gesture, black and straight and formed for knitting. '. . . I *hope* it's chivalry. I'm assuming your intentions are—'

'She's got a diamond ring on a chain round her neck, till we've a bit more saved and she can put it on her finger.'

'Jolly good,' I said. 'And I suppose you didn't see the mysterious stranger?' He was shaking his head before the words were out of my mouth.

'I did not. Cissie said she wanted to go a walk instead of sittin" – the blush deepened until he was almost purple from collar to hairline – "cos of there bein' other folk about and, to be straight wi' youse, I didn't really believe her.' I pulled my eyebrows down again, not liking the sound of this at all. 'Sitting', as Reid called it, had to be at the lady's discretion, surely. I could not think how to put this into words, however, without killing him off from embarrassment and quite possibly sending Alec with him. Besides, my eyebrows seemed to be doing the job on their own. He hung his head and scraped his boots against the floor and we left it there.

Outside in the cafe the luncheon trade had picked up again to full strength after the break in service. Orders were being shouted, the bell on the till was dinging, the rush and sizzle of hot fat as cold chips poured into it broke out over and over again. All that was missing was Joe's voice, describing his wonders and urging the crowd to 'eat, eat, eat, eat' as he had with Alec and me at breakfast time.

'Quiet the day, Gee-seppy,' one wag called over the counter.

'Don't tell me you've dropped yer tongue in the batter there,' said another and a chorus of laughter rang out all around. Not quite friendly laughter. Perhaps these villagers, more than happy to eat his food and give him their money, had not yet welcomed him in as one of their own. Joe nodded, unsmiling, and carried on plunging, shaking, wrapping, telling the price and counting out the change until at last the crowd thinned to a stream, broke into dribs and drabs and finally stuttered out, just one or two stragglers looking for bargains. Then, at last, silence and emptiness and Joe turned the sign on the door.

'Right then,' said Alec. 'To Dunskey Cove with us all.' Joe was out in the privy in the yard washing the luncheon-time lard from his hands and face.

'Not me,' I said. 'Not twice in one day.' Alec nodded as though only just remembering.

'In all the commotion I never asked you, Dan,' he said. 'Why *were* you there? How did that come to be?'

'The police thought it might be a mistress from the school,' I said, turning to Reid. 'You heard that Mademoiselle Beauclerc was missing?'

'Who?' said Reid. 'No.'

'Well, not to say missing, but gone anyway,' I said. 'Like so many before her.'

'But how could you help?' Alec said. 'You never met the woman.'

'Fleur volunteered and I tagged along,' I said. I turned to Reid again. 'You must have heard about all the departures.' Reid pushed out his lips and shook his head.

'Don't have much to do wi' them up there,' he said. 'Gey queer set-up havin' a bunch of women all doing science and geography and out on the cliff in their semmets at dawn.'

'Really?' said Alec.

'Gymnastics,' said Reid.

'Ah,' Alec said. Then to me: 'Fleur volunteered?' I nodded.

'And if you don't mind me askin', missus,' said Reid, 'what did she mean by what she said when she was in there?' I stared at him.

'I thought you hadn't heard,' I said. 'You asked her to repeat it.'

'I thought maybe I hadn't heard *right*,' said Reid. 'I asked to make sure.' He turned to Alec. 'Five, she said, sir. She looked at the corpse and said the word "five".'

'No!' said Alec.

'So what I was wondering,' said Reid, 'was five what?'

'Bodies,' said Alec.

'Alec!' I said, putting up my hand in front of his face and startling him.

'Murders,' said Alec.

'Stop it,' I said, almost loud enough to call it shouting. 'That's not fair.'

'What's goin' on?' said Reid.

'You refused to tell the sergeant about your witness just because you wanted to keep her to yourself!' I said. I was glaring at him and I knew my cheeks were reddening with anger. 'And then you blurt that out before I've even had a chance to talk to Fleur!'

'What do you mean?' Alec said. 'Why didn't you talk to her right away?'

'What five murders?' said Reid.

'She was upset,' I said. 'I was upset. Wait till you've been and looked at it and then carp at me.'

'What five murders?' said Reid even louder. I rounded on him.

'Constable,' I said, 'unless you want me to march right up the hill and tell Mrs Turner that you and her maid are in the habit of "sitting" on the cliff at Dunskey Castle on your free evenings, you'll forget all about Mr Osborne's indelicate outburst until I'm ready to discuss it with you. After I've discussed it with Miss Lipscott.' I ignored the whispering little voice inside me.

'Five mistresses have gone missing from St Columba's,' said Alec.

'Aye?' said Reid, his interest in the 'bunch of women' piqued at last.

'And Miss Lipscott . . .' said Alec.

'Miss Lipscott said an unguarded word in a moment of great strain,' I finished for him. 'She is clearly . . . troubled. Perhaps ill. But her story is too preposterous to be true.'

'Why not tell me what her story is and if ye're right I'll no' believe it,' said Reid. 'Five mistresses missing and Miss Lipscott . . . ?'

I glared a little more at Alec and then let my breath go and sat back in my chair.

'All right, I give up,' I said. 'Miss Lipscott said last evening that she had killed four times.'

'And then today . . .' said Reid. 'She saw that poor corpse and said, "That makes it five"?'

'She said "Five", as you well know,' I reminded him. 'Why, it might not even have been connected to the four from yesterday.'

'Oh, come off it, Dandy,' said Alec.

'You should have told me there and then,' Reid said.

'I ready as ever I be.' Joe Aldo was standing in the kitchen door. His hair was slicked flat and his face was scrubbed red and raw. His shirt cuffs were rolled down and his cuff-links fastened. He took a coat from the back of a kitchen chair and shrugged into it.

'Right you are, Mr Aldo,' said Reid. He stood and gave rather a withering look to be coming from a boy in his twenties to a great grand lady like me. 'I suppose,' he said, 'since you're all ready to go an' that. It would be a shame to keep you hangin' around while I just run and arrest somebody.' Joe Aldo was blinking in some confusion.

'I'll fetch the sergeant if you like and tell him everything,' I said. 'Everything.' Reid blushed again.

'But look on the bright side,' he said to Aldo. 'From what I've just heard, chances are, it's no' your wife at all. Chances are, your wife'll be back here wonderin' where you've got to before we're halfway home.'

Alec nodded but I could not bring myself to agree. Rosa Aldo had been on the cliff top on Tuesday evening and now was gone. A woman's body had washed up at the cliff foot on Saturday after three days or so in the sea. I did not see why Fleur Lipscott would have killed her and I agreed that the five mistresses gone and five murders claimed was a neat little balance, but I would not have raised Joe's hopes that way.

I waved them off in the motorcar – the sergeant was nowhere to be seen and one could only conclude that he had walked back to the station or perhaps climbed the hill to his wife and home. Reid drove and Alec and Joe sat in the back. I watched after

84

them until the little car had disappeared from view at the top of the hill and even then I followed them in my imaginings, along the road and onto the lane, down the track and onto the path, across the shingle and into the building there. I remembered all I could of the woman I had seen. Were her clothes and her stockings French like Mademoiselle Beauclerc's would be? Were they Italian? Would Rosa Aldo have Italian clothes or would she be dressed like every other washerwoman in Portpatrick, in clothes made up to Woolworth's patterns in cloth from the local Co-operative store? I tried to think of the look of her dress and the scrap of lace at her neck. But it had been soaked and clumped with water and the frill at her neck was rusty with blood and brine mixed. For just a moment I wished I had returned in the motorcar. I could have looked at her clothes and tried not to see the rest of her. I could have surely found something to tell me *something*. I leaned over the harbour wall and looked down into the water, just beginning to slosh against the stones. If I fell in there when it was deep and was fished out after three days, what could they tell about me? Good underclothes made of decent silk and fine wool, skilfully mended here and there. A rather flashy shirt that Grant had got from London on postal order and Jenner's Ladies' best tweeds in greenish grey. I would look – on a slab in the cable station – like a Scotch matron of exactly my type and exactly my years, and I determined there and then to let Grant buy me some flashy skirts and coats to go with the shirt next time she was ordering.

Then I remembered Miss Lovage from the evening before – and Miss Shanks with her cloaks – and I shuddered. I had been inoculated against theatricality in dress by my mother's trailing sleeves and by her penchant for the sort of embroidery that belonged on the back of a kimono, if anywhere. Perhaps Fleur in her beige had it right after all, dressing like the schoolmistress she had become, with not a scrap left about her of the child I remembered so well.

I smiled. Even then, when every girl and boy was beribboned and befrilled to the point of immobility and forced to be good (given the effort required to be naughty when one had so many elaborate garments to haul around with one), Fleur Lipscott had been renowned in the family, the village and beyond for the costumes she concocted day by day. There was a foundation layer – what archaeologists, or quite possibly geologists, call a substratum – of woollen underclothes, linen and lace petticoats, muslin and lawn frocks: the stuff of Edwardian childhood, but to it Fleur added trimmings of her own devising, unearthed and scavenged from all around her domain. She wore camphorous stoles and tippets found in the attic trunks, voluminous plaids spun by the crofter women around the Highland hunting lodge, a cage of crinoline hoops embellished with rag ribbons so that she looked like an enormous birdcage full of fluttering budgerigars. She found amongst the Major's uniforms more items of interest than might have seemed likely: epaulettes and medal ribbons, sashes and spurs, hat-bands and waistcoats, and a greatcoat of such length and girth and unyielding thickness that she rather inhabited it as a dwelling than wore it like clothes. When she walked in this last item it made one think of how the pyramid stones were moved, impossibly slowly, on rolling logs. She always emerged with hot cheeks and damp hair and to our laughter and quizzical looks she would say that it was indeed rather warm but good for thinking. Then she would resettle her Indian headdress or pirate's tricorne and sweep grandly off to another adventure.

'Darling little goose,' I remember Pearl saying once, gazing after her.

'And she slogs like a slave at it,' Aurora had agreed. 'That hat was miles too big until she put the rats in it.'

Batty Aunt Lilah let out a small shriek and shot to her feet, calling Fleur back and demanding explanations.

'Not *rats*, Batty Aunt,' said Fleur, bowing so that her hat fell off into her hand. 'Not *Rattus rattus*, although I don't hate them like you do.' She rummaged inside the tricorne and extracted an object which looked distressingly like a member of the *Rattus rattus* family to me. Batty Aunt Lilah shrieked again and recoiled from it.

'It's my hair!' said Fleur, holding the thing in the palm of her hand to show it clearly. 'Stitched up in a net. You know I found that old ratter of Granny's and couldn't resist it? Still in its box, with instructions and everything. I made three of my own and now I'm doing Aurora and Pearl. Separately, for hygiene, but I must say, Pearl, either you're not brushing properly or Rora's going bald, because she's surging ahead of you. Come to my room and I'll show you.'

'You horrid child!' said Pearl, pretending to shiver although really she was laughing. 'I knew you'd been skulking in the bathroom. I never dreamed why!'

'You'll thank me when fashions change back again and you're all ready for them,' said Fleur, carefully inserting the rat back into the crown of the tricorne. 'It's not everyone who can be out of fashion and look remarkable instead of just peculiar.' Then – dressed, under the greatcoat, in pale grey patent skating boots with the blades removed and an old sari – she had gone about her day.

How I wished that little ribbon-ringleted Fleur was here today, prattling on without a care for who heard and what they made of it. Even the second Fleur, the painted and sequinned girl I had met only once and who had left such a searing impression upon me, would have been welcome; for although she was far from that innocent child who spoke without thinking, at least she *spoke*. She twittered and giggled and made spiked little jibes and, like any flirt, at times she gave away more than she meant to, reaching for a joke, playing out her line to its end to hook the laugh she had spotted there.

Still, I should go up and find her, even the silent self-possessed woman she was now. I turned and leaned my back against the harbour wall, staring up at the school. She must surely be back by now, no matter how rambling a path she had taken home from the cove. With the thought, that sick feeling returned to somewhere deep inside me, but once again I swallowed and let it pass, not giving it form in my mind, not even examining it to see what form it would take. Instead I pushed myself up off the wall and strolled around the arm of the harbour, just like the fisherwives, all of us waiting for our men to return.

Fisherwives, I soon concluded, were better at waiting than I. In less time than it would have taken one of them to retie her shawl, fill her pipe and enquire in that rolling Gallovidian drawl after the health of the next fisherwife along the wall, I had grown bored and was marching back into the heart of the town. I was bound for the kiosk to ring home and tell them all where I was if needed, thence to St Columba's, but I had hardly begun the long haul up the Main Street when I saw the police motorcar trundling down. Alec's arm appeared, waving madly, in the side window as he saw me too and he jumped out while Constable Reid was still in the early stages of braking.

'It's not her,' he said, lolloping towards me in enormous strides. 'It's not Rosa. Joe was quite certain.'

The motorcar crossed the street and drew up beside us. Constable Reid was in the shadows, but I thought I could still discern a frosty look on his face as he nodded a greeting. I ignored him and leaned in at the back where Joe Aldo was sitting bolt upright with a fist clenched on each knee, staring straight ahead.

'You're sure, Mr Aldo?' I said. He turned his head immeasurably slowly and showed me stricken eyes with black circles under them.

'My head,' he said, in a whisper. 'My head is to break in pieces.'

'Tension,' I said. 'You must go home and rest. It must have been horrid for you until you knew.'

Perhaps his headache was too severe to let him nod, but he squeezed his eyes shut and tilted his head just a fraction.

'Is not Rosa,' he said. 'Dress, hair. I roll her sleeves and is not Rosa's skin. Rosa has . . .' He poked his finger here and there over his other forearm as if to dot it.

'Freckles?' I said.

'From the soap.'

'Ah,' I said. 'But might not the sea water have . . . ?'

'*Sottoveste*,' said Joe, gesturing. 'Under. Underneath.'

'Petticoats?' I said. He nodded. 'But—'

'Dandy,' said Alec. 'It's not her. They were married for fifteen years.'

'And the lady, poor lady, is too . . . Rosa is a little apple. My little peach, my little plum.'

But it was what Alec had said that convinced me. I can never understand it when one reads in the Sunday papers that a headless torso has been found *sans* legs, *sans* arms, in a suitcase, and no one can guess who it might be. If the torso were part of a husband then I should think the wife would know. I could tell any part of Hugh big enough to fill a suitcase, certainly.

Besides, this tussle between Alec and me was becoming ridiculous. He could carry on alone desiring my client's sister to be a murderess; I was no longer going to desire his client's wife to be drowned.

'If you're gettin' out here, Mr Aldo,' said Constable Reid, 'I'll swing round and get up by.' He jerked his head in the direction of St Columba's. 'Are you comin'?' he asked me. I was not, I noted, worthy of even a 'missus' now, never mind a 'madam'. I hesitated; I did not want to consign Fleur to being arrested without an ally, but I could not promise to be a staunch one. I would not lie.

Before I had decided, we were interrupted by the sound of a bell being rung with great energy a little way up the street. I squinted, shading my eyes from the sun, and could see a large woman dressed in a shopkeeper's overall pulling on a bell chain as though her life depended upon it. The bell itself was attached to a cottage wall, accompanied by no blue light or red plaque and quite a way from the harbour.

'Is that the lifeboat bell?' I said, nevertheless.

All around, street doors were opening but it was not burly lifeboat men who emerged. Instead, housewives in their aprons and old men in carpet slippers, holding their newspapers open at the racing news, stepped out and looked up the street.

'Post office telephone,' said Reid from inside the motorcar.

'It's for that Mr Al-do,' cried out the bell-ringing woman. 'Him fae the chip shop.'

A cluster of children had gathered around her, Pied-Piper-style, and were clamouring.

'Me, me, Miss Broon.'

'I'll gan, Miss Broon.'

'I've no' been chose for donkey's.'

The doors were closing on withdrawing villagers and, as the street cleared, Miss Brown (could it be another tentacle of that same family, I wondered) noticed us standing further down; noticed Joe Aldo, anyway.

'Mr Al-do?' she called, again managing to make two blameless little syllables sound as though they had taken a huge effort of concentration to pronounce. 'There's somebody asking for you on the telephone.' She looked back at the post office door and deigned to walk a little way down the street towards us.

'I'll get 'im, Miss Broon,' said the most tenacious of the children, the others having given up and begun a game of marbles in the gutter. 'You cannae leave the desk and all the stamps and money. I'll tell him. Save you shouting.' But Joe was walking up towards her now. Alec and I trailed after him, and Constable Reid threw the police motorcar into its reversing gear and backed slowly up the hill too.

'Me?' said Joe as he drew near Miss Brown. 'Inside?'.

'It was pure luck you were so close,' she said, with a strong note of disapproval which I could not easily fathom. 'By rights you should be tipping a message boy a penny.'

'Aye!' said the tenacious child.

'Somebody on the telephone for me?' said Joe again.

'And she'll no' be best pleased if you keep her hangin',' Miss Brown told him. 'Never mind me needin' to get back to the counter. Are you comin' or no'?'

'She?' said Alec. Joe had returned to his blank, dead state again. 'It might be her,' Alec prompted him. 'It might be Rosa.' Joe blinked and then started as if a shock had passed through him. He barrelled inside the post office, fairly shoving Miss Brown out of the way. Alec and I started after him but she stepped in front of the doorway.

'Do youse two have Post Office business?' she said. 'For there's no loitering.' Then she turned on her heel and swept in, muttering about 'you people', whoever that might be. Of course, all that happened was that we loitered outside instead, and with us Constable Reid, his engine running. In under a minute, Joe was back, the circles under his eyes darker than ever and his face paler. His hand shook as he opened the door and his voice shook as he spoke.

'Is Rosa,' he said. 'Rosa to say she is leave me. No say where she is.'

'Excuse me, Mr Al-do?' said Miss Brown, coming fussing out after him. 'Do you know you've left my good telephone hanging down where it'll scratch all my varnish?'

'Talk to her!' said Joe, taking hold of Alec's lapels and clutching him until they were nose to nose.

'If you've damaged Post Office property . . .' said Miss Brown.

Joe swayed and his face turned a ghastly shade of grey. Alec reached out and put both arms around him. He threw me a desperate look. Quickly, I slipped into the post office to the kiosk in the back corner and caught the earpiece, which was indeed swinging at the end of its cord.

'Mrs Aldo?' I said. There was a sharp buzzing as she sobbed, or possibly gasped, at the other end of the line. 'Mrs Aldo?'

'*Si*,' came a faint whisper. 'Is me.'

'Mrs Aldo, I know I'm a stranger but if you could see the state of your husband at this minute, you couldn't, no matter what the temptations . . .'

Now she was sobbing for sure.

'And think of your daughter,' I said.

The sobs grew to wails. Behind me I was aware that Miss Brown had come back in from the street and was watching me, arms folded, eyebrows lost in her hair. I drew the door closed so that at least she could not hear me. In the new muffled air of the kiosk, Rosa Aldo's sobs were louder than ever in my ear.

'Come home,' I said. 'Just come home. This man, whoever he is, who has lured you away, he can't possibly have honourable intentions. Or a good heart, I have to say. Your husband loves you. Not one woman in a hundred has a husband who loves her so.' But the more I spoke the harder she cried, until it felt cruel to go on.

'I go,' she whispered. 'Tell Giuseppe, *mi dispiace tanto*.' And with that the line stopped all its buzzing and the soft, close quiet of the kiosk filled both my ears.

'She hung up,' I said, rejoining Alec and Joe on the pavement.

'She say nothing?' asked Joe, stricken all anew by this, it seemed. 'Not one word?'

'She said, um, "Me dispassy tanto",' I repeated, feeling foolish. Joe Aldo let all his breath go at once. 'What does it mean?'

'It mean – so very sorry,' said Joe. 'She is leave me, for true.' At this he buried his head in Alec's shoulder and began to weep, louder and more noisily than his wife even. Alec patted him awkwardly.

'We'll find her,' he said. 'I'll get onto the exchange and ask them about the call and we'll find her.'

I thanked all my stars I was English, turned to Constable Reid in the motorcar and nodded.

'Let's go,' I said. Alec's case had had its moment of excitement, but now the faceless corpse – Mademoiselle Beauclerc, in all likelihood – was mine again, her identification my problem and her possible murderess my particular responsibility.

Reid nodded back, but did not make any move to step down and open a door for me. Alec had his hands full supporting Joe and so I opened it myself and climbed in.

'I can explain, Reid,' I said as we drew away.

'No need to explain it to me,' said Reid, swinging the motorcar around and beginning to ascend the hill.

'She's an old friend. I've known her since she was a child. You understand a protective instinct. I know you do.'

'Right,' said Reid. My patience was exhausted.

'Poor Cissie,' I said. 'No man is perfect but a man who pouts and sulks is a fearful drag. I shall tell her so in a spirit of warning when I meet her.'

'Aye well,' said Reid. 'Fine enough. I'm just sayin'.' Scotch has an inexhaustible supply of quite meaningless little bons mots with which to convey one's determination to hang onto a huff; Reid seemed to know all of them.

Up at St Columba's, Saturday afternoon was unfolding in leisurely fashion. The tennis courts were thronged, but for each foursome engaged in patting the ball back and forward, forward and back, sending it sailing over the net into the reach of the waiting racquet, there were at least a dozen lolling on mackintosh squares behind the service lines, chatting desultorily and sipping lemonade. In the rose garden, the girls were soaking up what watery sunshine there was by stretching out on their backs on the wide stone benches and even the narrower terrace balustrades. Their hair fanned out – St Columba's seemed not to be the firm supporter of pigtails one might look for in a girls' school – and their arms flopped down, letting their hands graze the ground at their sides. Just for a second that morning's image swam before my eyes and I shuddered.

'Aye,' said Constable Reid. 'We'll no' forget that yet awhile, eh no?' And, sharing a look, we took the first steps towards cordiality again. 'Here, youse!' he said, clapping his hands. 'Mind out and no' fall off they banisters.' It was hardly police business, but his hectoring did the trick, rousing all the girls until they were sitting or at least propped up on their elbows, blinking and scowling and no longer looking like corpses, which was fine by me.

'And . . . put your hats on,' I chipped in. 'Or move into the shade before you all end up as brown as ploughmen.' Reid nodded and we left the garden, to whispers of 'Gilver' and 'French, I think' and stifled laughter at how old-fashioned I had shown myself to be.

'So where is she?' said Reid, when we had slipped in through the open french windows to the empty dining room. He stood sniffing the air, which was still thick from the luncheon-time cabbage and gravy – the poor girls; small wonder they were drowsing like bumblebees – and looked so very efficient and eager that once again I felt an urge to shield Fleur and none at all to deliver her unto him.

'I'll take you to her rooms,' I said, hardly knowing why I gave the little cell this lordly title – more shielding, probably.

The same cold feeling which had descended upon me at the cove was back again, stronger than ever. I wondered if Reid felt anything of the like and I stole glances at him as we crossed the hall and climbed the stairs. He seemed calm enough, grimly confident if anything, but he was a bright lad and surely he must be wondering if we would find her there. I was long past wondering myself; I was sure. We wended through the corridors, past rooms absolutely silent this sunny afternoon, and stopped at Fleur's door. Constable Reid rapped on the wood with a firm authority that no one inside could have ignored, not for a pension. There was no answer. He tried the handle, found the door unlocked, glanced at me and just as firmly as he had knocked he swung it open.

The room, needless to say, was empty. Reid let his breath go – the first sign that he had been suffering even the smallest measure of tension.

'Righty-ho,' he said. 'So where will she be if she's no' in here, then? Classroom? On a Saturday afternoon?'

I shook my head and gazed at the room that lay before me. It had been so bare before that it was hard to account for what made it barer now. Perhaps there had been a book on the beside table; certainly there was none today. And the water glass had been rinsed out and was resting upside down on a folded flannel facecloth by the washbasin. But perhaps Fleur rinsed her glass and moved her Bible every morning. What was it? Then my eye was caught by the dark lines along the front of the little chest and I bit down on my bottom lip. The drawers were not fully closed – the top one open half an inch, the next an inch and the third an inch and a half, so precise and so familiar. It was what Matron in the convalescent home in the war required us to do when one poor soldier had limped off home and the next had not arrived. The drawers were being aired. The drawers were empty.

And what had happened was my fault, entirely mine. I knew it had happened the moment I turned and saw the empty beach behind me, but I had done nothing. Later I would argue that I had tried and the stupid sergeant had stopped me. Later still, I would tell myself that if I knew the sergeant was stupid then it was up to me to ignore him. She could not have gone far; she had only had a five-minute start at most. I should have searched and listened and called her name and – surely – I would have found her. It was too late now.

Fleur was gone.

5

'Yep,' said Constable Reid, slamming shut the wardrobe door which gave an echoing boom. 'She's away.'

'I can furnish you with the address of her family home and those of her sisters and . . .' I said.

'Right,' said Reid, but his tone was not one of huffy offence any more. He stood looking out of the window, tapping a tune with one finger on the hollow of his cheek. 'Only . . . how come she got packed up and off so quickly?'

'Maybe,' I said, slowly, thinking of the bareness of her room the night before and the way she had yelped when I mentioned the possibility, 'maybe she was planning to go anyway.'

'Seein' as how she'd killed somebody?' he asked. Then he frowned. I frowned.

'Why would she wait until the body had washed up?' I said. 'To see it?'

'She had a good enough look at it, right enough,' Reid said. 'And there's something no' right about what she said. It's like . . .'

'I know what you mean,' I said. 'It was too . . .'

'Aye,' said Reid, staring at me like a cow looking over a fence at another cow staring back. Where, I asked myself, was Alec, when one needed him?

'Also,' I went on, 'why would she pretend it wasn't Mademoiselle Beauclerc? She'd be so easily caught out.'

'If it *is* that French one,' said Reid. 'We'll need to get another one of them up there and see, eh?'

We had left the door open behind us when we entered and now heard footsteps approaching along the passageway; a very steady tread which already I recognised as belonging to the sturdy little booted feet of Miss Shanks. I braced myself for the encounter as she hove into the doorway and stopped there.

'Aha!' she said. 'Miss Gilver and . . . escort. Thank you, young man, for bringing my bonnie back home. Most thoughtful. And I take it the poor unfortunate was no one we know? Since I haven't heard otherwise? Splendid, splendid, jolly good.' Reid tried to break into the stream but was unsuccessful and retired into silence.

'So, my dear Miss Gilver,' Miss Shanks went on. 'I thought I'd find you in Miss Lipscott's rooms. Where is she, by the way? Sad news, I'm afraid. Look who's here!' She drew to her side a middle-aged woman dressed in a gunmetal-grey travelling costume whom I had never set eyes upon before in my life.

'Such a shame,' she said, 'I had very high hopes of you, my dear. But Miss Glennie comes with the Lambourne Agency's highest recommendation and, besides, she has been a governess to— Well, let's not tell tales in school, eh?' She broke off to utter a series of whinnying high-pitched giggles with her hand in front of her mouth.

'How do you do, Miss Glennie,' I said. 'Welcome to St Columba's.' She nodded slightly. 'Might I though, Miss Shanks, before I go, have a quiet word?' I shrank from speaking freely in front of the new mistress of the faceless, handless corpse who might well be the old one.

'Why certainly, for sure, for sure,' sang out Miss Shanks. I did not recognise her words as a quotation, but her habit of speech was beginning to make everything she said sound like a snatch of some music-hall ditty, or like the last line of prose in a light operetta just before the band strikes up and the cast bursts into out-and-out song. 'You'll find your way back to my sitting room all right, won't you, Miss Glennie?' she said, to the new mistress's astonishment. Miss Glennie blinked and gave half a look over her shoulder at the turn in the passageway.

'Perhaps one of the girls . . . ?' I said, gesturing to the doors on either side. Miss Shanks gave them a swift glance and then shook her head.

'Just keep turning left, Miss Glennie,' she said, 'and you'll come soon enough to the top of the stairs. It works for mazes too if you're ever lost in one. I'll not be a tick.' She went so far as to give the woman a little shove in the small of her back as she set off, and then she came inside and held the door open like a commissionaire, twinkling at Constable Reid.

'Thank you again, laddie,' she said, 'and give my kind regards to the inspector when you see him.' She turned to me. 'Inspector Douglass's girl comes here, you know. A very promising scholar.'

'I'm stayin',' said Reid, and something in his tone caused Miss Shanks to turn abruptly and shut the door.

'Don't tell me!' she said. 'It was never? Was it? Wee Mademoiselle?'

'We don't know,' I answered. 'Miss Lipscott said not.'

'Well then!' said Miss Shanks.

'She was very upset, though, and might have been mistaken.'

'She's a steady sort as a rule,' said the headmistress.

'Steady!' said Reid. 'She's hooked it.'

'She's what?'

'She's gone, Miss Shanks,' I said. 'And one has to wonder – that is, the police have to consider – I mean to say. A body turns up, dead by some misadventure, and someone runs away. One has to ask oneself whether one is connected to the other. It would be best to have a second witness try to identify the body, don't you see?'

'You mean . . .' said Miss Shanks, 'that Miss Lipscott feared . . . she might be next?' This sudden suggestion startled both Reid and me and we opened our mouths to protest. 'Or even worse! Oh, surely not! You don't mean you thought Miss Lipscott . . . ? You do! I can tell from your faces!'

'Were they enemies?' said Reid. 'Had they fell out?'

'Certainly not!' cried Miss Shanks. 'They were great friends. If Miss Lipscott said the corpse was a stranger then why not leave it at that? If Miss Lipscott chose to go – most inconvenient but there's no need to make a penny dreadful out of . . . I say!

Every cloud, Miss Gilver! How d'ye fancy English instead of French and you don't have to leave us after all?'

'Miss Shanks,' said Constable Reid, barely containing himself. 'I'm no' just so sure you appreciate what we're sayin'. Miss Lipscott has run away. Look.' He opened the door of the wardrobe upon the pitiful sight of a half a dozen empty coat hangers, padded and covered with cloth, a lavender bag drooping sadly from each.

'I worked those covers, you know,' said Miss Shanks. 'They're just a nice wee size of job for teatime in the staffroom.'

'And I'm going to have to ask another of youse to come and say aye or no once and for all about this poor soul we've got lying up there.'

'Miss Barclay,' said Miss Shanks at once. 'She has the constitution of an ox. She'd have had a better time of it than poor Miss Christopher with all those nasty dissections. After the science mistress left us, you know.'

'I wonder you didn't think of her this morning, then,' I said. 'And save poor Miss Lipscott a sight that might well have caused to her to pack her bags and flee.'

'Oh no,' said Miss Shanks, turning round and causing us almost to collide with her – we had begun our journey to Miss Barclay's rooms already. 'It wasn't the shock of the corpse, Miss Gilver. And it wasn't fear for her own skin. Nor that other thing either – what an idea! No, this has been on the cards for a whiley. Quite a wee whiley, aye.' She beamed at us, turned to face front again and tramped off. Reid lifted one finger and twirled it around by his temple. I nodded. Either that or drink, I was thinking, though her progress up the passageway was as straight as a plumb line.

Miss Barclay gave us a look of pure terror as we entered her room. At least, for a moment I thought so. She was hunched over her desk, a towering pile of test-papers at one elbow and a sliding heap of open textbooks at the other, and she looked up like a rabbit who has seen the shadow of an eagle passing over. She dropped her pen into the inkwell with a little splash and took the red pencil out from behind her ear.

'Headmistress?' she said.

'So sorry, Barclay,' said Miss Shanks. 'But don't look like that, my dearie! I'm not going to bite. You'll be giving Miss Gilver here the wrong impression of our happy band, so you will. Now, I'll make the cocoa myself for your return – or chicken broth, if you've a mind that way – but I need to ask you to go with this laddie here and look at that body they've fished up out of the sea.'

'You said at lunch Miss Lipscott had done it,' said Miss Barclay. She stood up and walked away from her desk.

'She did,' said Miss Shanks. 'Then she packed up her troubles in her old kit bag! Leaving our boys in blue not very happy to take her say-so on who the corpse might be.'

'Gone?' said Miss Barclay. Her expression, back to the light coming in the window behind her, was unreadable and I started edging round the wall hoping for a better view.

'But Lambourne have sent us Miss Glennie, like manna from heaven. Miss Thomasina Glennie who used to be an under-governess at Balmoral when—' Miss Shanks then clamped her hand to her mouth and gave that high-pitched giggle again. 'I wasn't supposed to say,' she said. 'And so she's the new French mistress.'

'Balmoral, eh?' said Miss Barclay, with shrewdly narrowed eyes. Mine, I suspected, were as round as plates. How could anyone swallow a story like that? Even someone as odd as Miss Shanks had to see it for the trumped-up nonsense it must be.

'And so Miss Gilver here is the new English mistress.'

'Um,' said the new English mistress.

'*Miss* Gilver?' said Miss Barclay.

'Grammar?' I said. 'Or novels and what have you?' But truth be told, I would gladly have parsed all one hundred stanzas of *Sir Gawain and the Green Knight* if it meant I could stay put and take a crack at this oddest of cases. (I had been exposed to the thing by a tutor of my brother's, introduced into the household by my father but shortly expelled from it again when Nanny Palmer saw what he had us reading.)

'All roll over and one fall out!' said Miss Shanks, as she had before.

'You know best, Headmistress,' said Miss Barclay. She fished her pen back out of the inkwell, wiped it and capped it. Then she stood and followed Constable Reid out of the room.

'A bit of spelling, a spot of composition,' said Miss Shanks, once we were alone. She had gone to the window and was gazing down into the grounds. 'As long as they've read some Scott and some Shakespeare their mummies and daddies are happy. Clear lungs and rosy cheeks, that's the main thing. Just look at them, would you?'

I joined her at the window, which was on the west front and gave a view I had not seen before now: a view of grassy headland with the blue-green sea sparkling in the middle distance and, sparkling in the immediate foreground, a bathing pool of impressive proportions in that shade of turquoise unknown to any sailor of the world's oceans but apparently very dear to every maker of ceramic tiles. Around the pool were more of the draped and drowsing girls, none of them actually swimming. Those in the water seemed to be floating on rafts, while at the edges girls were stretched out in deckchairs, not quite naked, but close enough so that I felt stupid remembering what I had said to the others regarding hats.

'Won't they get cold?' I said. It was sunny, but it was Scotland.

'The water's heated,' said Miss Shanks. 'Such a treat to dip into warm water for a wee splash about.' I nodded, secretly scandalised by the idea of such luxury. Besides, there was no splashing down there, barely a ripple as the little rafts eddied around. 'Still,' Miss Shanks said, 'it's early in the season and we don't want them sniffling for Parents' Day. Just you slip down, Miss Gilver, and tell them to get in to the kitchen for cocoa and I'll just slip down and ask our good Mrs Brown to put the milk on.'

Now this was going far beyond the heating of a little bathing water. Every nanny and every girl and boy who had been brought up by one knew that there was only one thing to do when one was cold from languid bathing: one ran up and down until one was warm again. Then one went back to the water until one was blue and shivering, then more running, and so on and so on until teatime. In fact, it was my considered opinion that the wonderful night's sleep which followed a day at the seaside was nothing to do with fresh air at all but owed itself to athletics alone.

'And shall we try to find out where Miss Lipscott has gone?' I said.

'Oh, I think Miss Lipscott has made it clear she's done with us, don't you?' said Miss Shanks. 'I had high hopes of her once but she never did shape to the job and this bolt has been a long time coming.'

'But still—' I said.

'If the police want to find her then they can do the searching,' Miss Shanks said. 'Finders keepers, losers weepers.'

'Well, shall we at least ring her sisters and let them know? Shall I? Since I'm acquainted with them?'

'Yes, yes,' said Miss Shanks. 'Now, go and tell those girls to put on their wraps and come inside.'

I took this to give me carte blanche to do what I chose in the matter of Fleur. And what I chose to do was find her. (Of course, I should also have to spend some little time on the question of why Miss Shanks left it to me, of why she had been so frantic about the mademoiselle and cared not a fig for Miss Lipscott. It was Betty Alder all over again.)

So it was with a great many questions bumping around inside my mind that I let myself out of the front door of the house and made my way around to the bathing pool. It really was getting rather chilly, even though the northern sun was still high in the sky, and my task was being taken out of my hands as the girls themselves variously sat up, stood and tried to rub the goose pimples from their bare arms. In the pool the bathers were slipping off the rafts, out of the cool air and into the warm water.

'Jolly good,' I called to them. 'Hurry up and get dry and there's cocoa in the kitchens for you.'

Then there came again the rustle of whispers – 'Who's that?', 'Miss Gilver', 'French mistress' – as they folded their deckchairs and leaned them together like playing cards (in Scotland, even on an afternoon where the sky is clear to the far horizon, one is always preparing for rain).

It was a very pleasant scene, the mild sunshine and the girls in their colourful bathing suits; even the pool itself was not so monstrous viewed from down here. The steps and rails were of painted wood and not the nasty chromium of a common lido and the turquoise-blue tiles stopped at the water's edge; the lounging terrace around it was good grey granite and weathering nicely. I stepped over to read the inscription carved into an especially large granite slab. *The Rowe-Issing Bathing Pool*, it read. *By the kindness of Cmdr and Mrs B. T. H. Rowe-Issing. Opened 21st June 1925.*

I stared until my watering eyes reminded me to blink. It was unthinkable that Basil and Candide Rowe-Issing had given Miss Shanks's funny little school a bathing pool. For one thing, they had no money these days. For another, what bent pennies they ever did find down the backs of sofas were spent on their son, as could only be expected. And finally, even had they no son and had they pots of money as before, a garish blue bathing pool with their names etched in black on a granite slab by the deep end . . . nothing would have possessed them. I could picture Candide's little shudder and the pursed little moue of her mouth at anything half so vulgar.

It was hardly less unthinkable, though, that there could be two Commander B.T.H. Rowe-Issings and that one would donate a pool to the school where the other's daughter happened to be boarding.

Such a puzzle, and such a delicious morsel too. Not that I was a gossip; at least, I had not been until I took up detective work, but of late I had begun to wonder. Perhaps the very habit of sleuthing was working on some neglected part of me, like eurhythmics for posture, causing it to grow brawny from frequent use. Perhaps, on the other hand, the question of the Rowe-Issing bathing pool would have piqued the interest of a swami sitting cross-legged in a tree. In either case, for the first time that day

I did not wish that Alec was there to listen and enlighten. For the first time in my professional life, I think, I simply longed for Hugh.

The longing passed and when Alec arrived at my side I was as happy as ever to see him, bursting with news and questions after a frankly rather lonely early evening. Saturday supper at St Columba's was a kind of picnic cum buffet, it appeared; the kitchen staff loading up the long refectory tables with boiled eggs, cold ham and salad and the girls drifting in to fill their plates, pour themselves lemonade from the tall jugs set on the sideboards and drift out again. One could hear them giggling and yelling inside all the dorms and studies as one passed. Indeed, going by one particularly raucous gathering I felt the spirit of Nanny Palmer move within me and I opened the door after one sharp rap.

Five small girls in pyjamas, their mouths full and their eyes wide, turned to stare at me.

'Simmer down a little, please,' I said in my best attempt at clipped exasperation.

'What . . . ?'

'Who . . . ?'

'It's Saturday night!' This was from a child eating her supper sprawled on her bed like a Roman at a Bacchanalia, except that such a Roman would not be absorbing a wedge of bacon and egg pie.

'You'll get a sore tummy if you eat lying down like that,' I said to her. 'Not to mention the crumbs.'

'But it's Saturday night!' she said again.

'Well, be sure to put on your dressing gowns and slippers before you take your plates back down,' I said. 'It's getting chilly in the passageways.' For the sight of their bare feet, little toes either red or white with cold, was bothering me and they were at the age where frequent spurts of growth ensured that there were stretches of bare leg at the bottoms of their pyjamas and draughty little gaps between jackets and trousers too.

'Oh, we don't take them down, Miss Gilver,' said another. She was sitting on a dressing-table top with her plate of ham and salad resting in amongst the hairbrushes in a most unsavoury way. 'We just stick them outside for the maids in the morning.'

'You . . . ?' I was rendered quite speechless with disapproval, and did not know whence the worst of the shock hit me. Such indolence in the young, such sloppy housekeeping and such inconsideration towards one's maids were neck, neck and neck. I left them to it and ignored the surge of giggles which followed upon my closing the door.

I might even have dipped a careful toe into the subject with my fellow mistresses but when I edged open the staff room door, holding my own supper plate, it was to find the room empty and the fire cold. When I happened to pass Miss Christopher's rooms on my way to Fleur's (which were now to be mine) I saw a light under the door and, listening a little, heard the scrape of a pen and the crunch of an apple being eaten. The maths and science mistress was hard at work. Saturday evening, evidently, was a jamboree for the girls and another night in the salt mines for everyone else; maids and mistresses, anyway.

So when the knock came at my own door a short while later I was glad at the prospect of company.

'Come in,' I said.

It was Mrs Brown, and I was pleased to see her.

'Ah,' I said. 'Good, I was wondering . . . Might I trouble you to have my things sent up from the Crown, Mrs Brown? I know you're in frequent contact with your niece. Perhaps you would ring down to her? And then I wonder too if I might ask for the bed to made up in here? And perhaps an armchair or two? Unless the English mistress has a study elsewhere?'

She was nodding.

'Surely, surely,' she said. 'Of course, but I'm here, Miss Gilver, to bring you a visitor.' And with that she stepped back and let Alec fill the doorway. He paused on the threshold and Mrs Brown, from behind him, spoke again.

'I'll get your bags and get one of my girls to bring your sheets so's you can get your bed made, Miss.' And with that she was gone.

'Good evening, Miss Gilver,' Alec said, still standing neither in nor out of the room.

'I can't believe you asked to be brought to my rooms!' I said.

'I didn't!' Alec replied. 'I asked if you could be fetched and that doughty woman said "Oh, away and come on with you" and delivered me. I must say, Dan, I thought a girls' school would be a bit more circumspect.' He looked around with some interest. 'And a bit frillier too.'

'Oh Lord, I suppose you'd be better inside than standing there,' I said, grabbing him. 'But keep your voice down and don't light that accursed pipe.'

When we were arranged, Alec on the hard chair and I on the end of the bed – sitting much more primly than the little girls at their picnic – we shared the fruits of our afternoons. Alec went first, unusually (he prefers to be the finale).

'Glasgow,' he said. 'That's where Rosa called Joe from. We'll have a hard job finding her in that teeming anthill of a place.'

'Did she call from a kiosk?' I said. 'If it's near where she's staying . . .'

'At the Central Station,' said Alec.

'Ah.'

'Quite. There must be dozens of kiosks there. And hundreds of strangers every day and no chance of anyone remembering one of them. Even a black-haired Italian one.'

'Well, actually, darling, there are quite a lot of black-haired Italians in Glasgow. That's a thought – does she have relations?'

'I asked Joe and he said not.' Alec took his pipe out of his pocket and looked at it sorrowfully.

'Well, missing persons are the usual bread and butter of a detective agency, or so one is led to believe,' I said. 'You could look on it as a belated apprenticeship.'

'Hm,' said Alec.

'Or you could retire gracefully from your case and help me

with mine,' I said. 'Lord knows I could do with it.' He looked up at this. 'Fleur has gone,' I told him. 'Packed her traps and slung her hook. This is her room, as it happens, so you can see she meant it.'

'How many is that?' said Alec. 'Six?'

'The balance shifted a little the other way,' I said. 'A Miss Glennie turned up to teach French. But yes: Fleur was the sixth departure including Miss Fielding's death.'

'And how is Miss Shanks taking it?'

'She doesn't seem all that troubled,' I told him. 'That's the puzzling thing! There's something very odd about this place, Alec.' He spread his arms and gestured around him. 'Well, yes, it's most peculiar that the housekeeper showed a gentleman up to my chamber, but there's more.'

'And what about the police?' Alec asked. 'Are they closing the ports and combing the land till they find her?'

'Miss Barclay has gone to the cable station with PC Reid,' I said. 'In fact, she must be long back by now. If she says the body is Miss Beauclerc, then I suppose they'll have to go after Fleur with bloodhounds.'

'Leaving aside the other four murders,' said Alec.

'I suppose that too,' I said and then I cocked my head. 'Someone's coming.' Indeed someone was, and I knew who, flitting along the corridor at a tremendous rate. There was a squeak of shoe leather right outside my room and the door burst open.

Miss Shanks swept the room with her gaze and then let go a huge held breath.

'Good evening, Miss Gilver,' she said. 'Mr Osborne.'

We waited, both Alec and I, for the expected tirade on the subject of his presence in my bedroom, but nothing came.

'Miss Shanks,' I said at last, 'has Miss Barclay returned?'

'Oh, she has, she has, she certainly has,' said Miss Shanks, still standing there, with her hand on the doorknob and breathing heavily after her sprint along the corridor.

'And?' I said.

'It wasn't our mam'zelle,' said Miss Shanks. 'A complete

stranger. Nothing to do with St Columba's at all, whoever she was, the poor soul.'

'Well then,' said Alec. 'Not that one would wish drowning on a stranger, but good to know it wasn't a mistress. Or a parent.'

'A parent?' said Miss Shanks, her voice rising to a shriek.

'There was a suspicion it might be Sabbatina's mother,' I said. 'Betty Alder?'

'Quite,' I continued. 'But it's not.'

'Why on earth would Betty *Alder's* mother want to kill herself?' said Miss Shanks, in that same dismissive way which had puzzled me earlier in the day. 'Right then,' she went on. 'I'll leave you two to it. Goodnight, Mr Osborne. Chapel at nine, Miss Gilver. Breakfast at eight. Long lie on a Sunday.' She gave the room another searching look and then was gone.

'She is the oddest creature I have ever encountered,' I said, when her footsteps had pattered away and there was silence again.

'What was she looking for? She quite obviously didn't come to tell you the news of the body.'

'Ah yes,' I said. 'The body. The mysterious body.'

'You're right, Dandy,' said Alec. 'You need my help. So where do we begin?'

In response, I stood and wrestled open the sash window.

'I can't even begin to begin without a cigarette,' I said. 'And you may as well light that filthy thing, Alec, since the powers that be know you're here anyway.'

'Gladly,' Alec said and busied himself with the considerable paraphernalia.

'So,' I said, once calmed by a good few lungfuls of delicious Turkish smoke. 'As I see it, we have three separate problems. We need to find these mistresses – and actually, since I'm employed by the Lipscotts, finding Fleur is the only bit of the whole case that's really my business.'

'When did that ever matter to you?' Alec said. 'Agreed, though. Number one. Find mistresses.'

'Number two – possibly related and possibly not – solve five murders. Or at least find out if they really happened.'

'The fifth corpse is real enough.'

'And three – again possibly related and possibly not – identify the all-too-real corpse.'

'I can't see us chasing off to Glasgow after a missing wife, then,' said Alec.

'There might *be* some chasing off, though,' I answered. 'I can root around at this end as to where the mistresses might have gone – good God, I don't even know the names of the first three! – and if the search for any of them should take you to Glasgow . . .'

'As for the corpse,' Alec said, 'I'd be best to ask around about here, don't you think? If anyone saw anything? If anyone's missing? And actually, if I were to pretend to be asking after the departed Mrs Aldo and her paramour, I'd have a handy way in.'

'I suppose so,' I said. 'And I shall try to find out if Fleur was close to any of the remaining mistresses or perhaps some of the girls and see if she ever spoke of her . . . exploits . . . to any of them.'

'And so you might take a moment to chat to Sabbatina, in case she knows or can guess where her mother might have gone.'

'I'll try,' I said, 'but I can't promise, Alec dear. There are rather a lot of other matters more pressing.'

'Let's start with the easy bit then,' said Alec. I waited. 'How do we determine whether Fleur Lipscott killed this unknown woman on Tuesday or Wednesday of this last week?'

'Alibi.'

'Exactly. Where was Miss Lipscott on those two days? Could she have gone out on the cliff and shoved someone off it?'

'We don't know that that's how our corpse got in the water, though, do we?' I said.

'True,' Alec agreed. 'So . . . more generally, did Miss Lipscott have any periods of solitary time long enough to go boating? Or any time at the high tide to go swimming? If not . . .'

'You're beginning to doubt it?' I asked. 'You seemed sure enough when you were gaily telling all to Constable Reid.'

'I *am* doubting,' Alec said. 'It's what we're taking to be the confession.'

'You too? That's been niggling at Constable Reid and me.'

'Bright boy,' Alec said.

'But what else could she mean by saying "five"?' I countered.

'No, it's not what she said, it's when she said it.' I sat up and snapped my fingers at him. 'She looked at the corpse three days later and said it then.'

'Of course,' I said sinking back again. 'She should have said it when the woman was plummeting down the cliff face, or just after she'd tipped her out of the boat, or held her under.'

'Exactly. It was too late by miles by the time it came to the cable station. On the other hand, if it was said for your benefit, then the whole thing is so stagey I don't believe it can actually be true. Why would a murderer say such a thing at such a moment? Was she the theatrical sort, when you knew her before?'

I smiled in spite of the dreadful conversation. Was little Fleur Lipscott theatrical? Not in the way Alec meant it. There was nothing insincere or calculated in the extravagance with which she lived. One always got the impression, on the contrary, that she would go on in just the same way in an empty room in an empty house, or indeed if washed up all alone on a desert island. I watched her once that summer, from under the walnut tree where we had tea almost every afternoon. She had been painting, dressed in a calico smock and a black beret (stuffed with the rats to stop it slipping over her ears), and she was about to leave her easel and palette on the lawn while she went in to change. I watched her dab two unused brushes into the paint and then thread them through the thumbhole of her palette along with the one she had really been using. I watched her reposition the palette on the grass, walking around to view the composition and replace it twice before she was happy. She even dragged the easel round a bit – away from the view – until it was framed against a yellow rose which scrambled over a pergola. Then she quickly added some blobs of yellow to her picture, walked round the whole thing again, nodded firmly and pelted off to the garden door and the nursery stairs, turning twice on the way to look at the pretty arrangement she had left behind her.

'No,' I said to Alec. 'Not the least bit attention-seeking. Quite the most self-possessed little girl you could imagine.'

'And once she was a big girl?'

'Well, she was very silly and shocking,' I said. 'And I suppose she did play to the gallery. But in a very sort of full-blown way. For one thing she was still as lavishly fond of her family as ever. Not at all like those hard-faced little flappers who always made such a great point of being cold. Catch them coming to kiss their married sisters at a party! No, Fleur Lipscott, even at her silliest, was never furtive or calculated. If she seemed to be speaking to herself then she was, and if she whispered "Five" to herself then she meant it.'

'Which makes no sense at all,' Alec said.

'Not much,' I agreed. 'But I like things not to make sense, Alec dear, as you know. For then there is something to catch hold of and straighten out about them.' We smoked in silence for a while, each hoping to catch hold of a loose end immediately, each failing to do so.

'Right,' I said, at length. 'First things first, I have to ring Pearl or Aurora and tell them the unwelcome news that Fleur is gone.'

'Perhaps she'll have been in touch already,' said Alec. 'Perhaps she's on her way home to them.'

'We can hope. Now come with me and help me find a telephone. I only pray that there's not just one on a table in the entrance hall. This conversation is going to be ticklish enough without eavesdroppers.'

We were in luck: finding an instrument I had not noticed in the staffroom, I sat down beside it and dialled for the exchange. While we were waiting, though, I changed my mind and held the earpiece out to Alec.

'You talk to Pearl,' I said. 'She knows about you and I'd like to get your impression of her. Also, she won't be so airy-fairy with you. We might actually learn something.'

But about that I was wrong, quite wrong. Alec started off the call in businesslike fashion, introducing himself and asking Pearl if she was alone, since he had some upsetting news and she should prepare herself to receive it. A wail came out of the ear trumpet and Alec flinched before trying again.

'Not so bad as all that, Mrs Tennant,' he said hurriedly, 'but I'm afraid I have to tell you that Miss Lipscott has gone away. She has left St Columba's, clearly not meaning to return. Now, I take it you have had no word from her?' There was a pause. 'And would you know if Mrs Forrester had heard from your sister?' Another pause. 'In that case, Mrs Tennant, I hope you'll oblige me by answering a few quest—' Here Pearl obviously cut him off again and during this pause, he blushed. 'Osborne, yes,' he said. 'Dorset. No, in Perthshire these days.' Then he blushed even harder, turning quite purple and making his freckles appear yellow. 'She is indeed. Yes, we do. I most certainly am— Mrs Tennant, if I can just— A splendid chap. Most helpful to me in the matter of the farm. Mrs Tennant' – his voice rose – 'can I start by asking you this: as far as you know, has your sister ever committed any cri—' I could hear Pearl squawking into the telephone from where I sat across the room (I had chosen a fireside chair as one does even when the grate is empty). 'No I don't mean the high-spirits of youth, my dear Mrs Te— Yes, indeed, I've snatched many a police helmet on treasure hunt nights myself, but that's not what—' Alec shook his head at me in dumb disbelief. It was his first exposure to a Lipscott outpouring and I took it that Dismay was just as profuse as Delight. 'She hinted – no, she more than hinted – that she might have killed some—' This time Alec tucked the earpiece into the crook of his neck and refilled his pipe while Pearl's voice squeaked on and on. 'Well, yes, we did wonder. Hm? Dandy and me. Yes, she is. Yes, I'm sure she would.' I was signalling madly but he ignored me.

'Hello, Pearl darling,' I said, taking over and watching Alec go to flop in a chair.

'Dandy, honestly!' said Pearl down the line. She sounded tearful. 'I asked you to take care of her and I told you to be gentle with her and it sounds absolutely as though you've trampled in in hobnailed boots like some beastly policeman.'

'No need, dear,' I said. 'There is a real beastly policeman with perfectly good hobnailed boots of his own. And I should think he'll be in touch very soon to ask you just what we're asking you. There's been a murder.'

'Oh, nonsense!' said Pearl, rather surprisingly.

'Or a death anyway,' I said.

'See? Don't make such a melodrama, Dandy, you're hardly helping.'

'I had to go and look at the corpse, Pearl. It was melodramatic enough without anyone making it so. And Fleur as good as confessed that she—' Pearl interrupted again.

'Nonsense,' she said. 'Dandy, if I had thought for a moment you'd take this line . . . You *know* Fleur. She's a darling, an angel, a cherub on a white clou—'

'She *was*,' I said, interrupting back. 'She's changed. I would like to know what changed her.'

'I can't listen to this,' said Pearl. 'From you of all people.' I heard an ominous fumbling sound.

'Don't you dare hang up!' I said and before I knew it Alec had taken the instrument back out of my hand.

'Mrs Tennant,' he said. 'I'm well aware that Mrs Gilver is an old friend of your family but she is also a professional detective of the utmost integrity and moral scrupulousness. She cannot – we neither of us can – condone any—' His voice was getting louder and lower and Pearl's voice was getting higher and faster and they went on in this fashion for another good minute and then very abruptly Alec hung up the telephone.

'What happened?' I said.

'The pips went,' he said. 'But she got a good one in just before. We've been sacked, Dandy darling.'

'Oh God,' I said. 'Not again.'

After which it seemed immediately necessary to take a walk down the cliff steps to the lounge bar of the Crown and a restorative glass of brandy. It was rather shudder-making, as even the best brandy in a small village inn is wont to be, but all the more invigorating for that.

'Ugh, a little more soda, please,' I said, after the first sip.

'You should really develop your palate for whisky,' Alec said, which suggestion made me shudder even more. 'It's a safer bet in these parts. This' – he swirled his glass – 'is delightful.'

'So she didn't take too kindly to the suggestion that Fleur is a killer, it's safe to say.' I was resuming the conversation which had begun as we picked our way down by the path.

'Ah yes, but it wasn't the outrage you'd feel were I to accuse Donald, Teddy or Hugh. It was a much more well-honed rejection.'

'She'd heard it oft before?'

'And she wasn't having any of it.' Alec nodded. 'She didn't actually put up any counter-arguments, you understand. Just poor little Fleurikins and how dare I. Poor sweet pixie and poppet and dear little elf, their poor darling mamma and sorry old pa and it was all extremely sickening, I must say.'

'It seemed adorable when we were girls,' I said, not liking to hear the familiar pet names repeated in quite that sneering way, no matter how nauseating I might find them myself on occasion.

'But she was genuinely rattled,' Alec went on, with a relish which was worse than the sneering. 'Doing her best to pooh-pooh any notion of a murder but stammering with the strain. Poor little elf-f-f-f-f.'

I set my brandy glass down hard and stared at him.

'That wasn't stammering,' I said. 'Elf-f-f-f? Apart from anything else, no one stammers at the *ends* of words, do they?'

Alec, like most men, does not welcome criticism. Unlike most men, however, he sets that aside without a care when more important matters are in hand. At that moment, he barely noticed the criticism at all, but only sat forward in his chair as eager as a puppy and stared back at me.

'You've got that look, Dan,' he said. 'What is it?'

'Elf-f-f-f,' I said, 'and I can't believe you don't know this but I suppose you're rather young and from darkest Dorset, but Elf-f-f-f is the rather silly nickname of Edward Lionel Frederick Forrester-Franklin. Some sort of cousin of Aurora's husband's family.'

'And?' said Alec.

'He died,' I said. 'In '19 or possibly '20.'

'Eight years ago,' Alec said. 'And didn't Pearl tell you . . .'

'She did. That Fleur had got over the old bad time and been fine for eight years.'

'Dear God, Dandy. What did he die of? Not old age, I take it.'

'He was twenty-five,' I said. 'Suicide was the whisper, accident was what they put in *The Times*, but here's the thing, darling. He died at Pereford. He died at Fleur's family home.'

6

I slept more soundly that night than I had any right to expect I would after the horrors of the day and I dreamed, blamelessly, of Hugh and the boys and some task unknown and undone, very glad upon waking that the poor ravaged corpse and the ghost of Edward Franklin had not visited me. I stretched out in my narrow bed feeling the sheets, which were adrift under my body, twist and wrinkle with my movements. (I had never perfected the art of bed-making even after some very fierce lessons from Matron at the convalescent home and had never imagined that I might feel the want of it, but those same maids who carted dirty supper plates around for the girls of St Columba's really did leave tender new mistresses to struggle with their own linens.) My pillow was bursting out of the end of its case too, giving it an uncomfortable sort of waist and ruining any chance of a snooze.

With a sigh, I swung my legs down and felt for my slippers on the cold linoleum floor. If moved to thank heaven for small mercies, I could always be glad that the Crown's brandy was too unpleasant to tempt me to a second and my head was clear this morning. I wondered how Alec, so delighted by the quality of the whisky, was faring; and I hoped that, at least, he remembered the rather detailed plan of attack we had formed the evening before.

I set the first part of the plan in motion over breakfast with the girls, choosing again the gaggle of sixth formers I had met at supper on Friday.

'With a one and a two and one two three and!' Miss Shanks shouted from the end of the room, the girls rose to their feet and the slow chorus began.

'Dear Lord, thank you for this new day and this good food and all our friends. Amen.'

I mumbled along, unfamiliar with the wording, and then sat and spread my napkin as the girls flopped down all around me.

'Dear Lord,' said Katie as she did so, 'thank you for the fact that Hammy doesn't make us do that music-hall routine at breakfast at least.'

'I thought the dinner grace was rather sweet!' I said.

'So did we for the first year or so,' said Stella, breaking into a roll and craning her neck for the maid. 'Ah, good,' she said, when the child arrived at her elbow. I was astonished to see and smell a stream of dark steaming coffee pouring into Stella's breakfast cup.

'Miss?' said the maid.

'Th-thank you,' I managed, holding my cup up across the table to her.

'Ugh!' said Eileen. 'I dread being grown-up and married and having to drink nasty coffee in the morning instead of delicious chocolate.'

'Oh, that won't be the worst of it,' Stella said, drooping one lazy eyelid and making Spring and Katie giggle.

'Now, now, girls,' I said mildly, although privately just as startled by the talk as I was by the coffee. 'Now, let me see . . . what did I mean to ask you . . . ? Oh yes, what are you reading in English just now? I have a great deal of prep to do today.'

'You mean French, Miss Gilver,' said Sally, smiling rather shyly at her own temerity in correcting me.

'Ah no, English,' I said. 'I thought perhaps you would have heard, but I suppose Miss Shanks will announce it at chapel. Miss Lipscott has been . . . called away and, since Miss Glennie came to help out with the French lessons, I'm taking over English.'

'Juliet's gone?' said Spring. 'Miss Lipscott, I mean? Not another one!'

'She has been forced to take a leave of absence owing to a family emerg—' I began before remembering that 'family emergency' was precisely the tale Miss Shanks had been spouting about them all.

'Thank God,' said Stella. 'Escape! Relief! We can read anything you like, Miss Gilver, and we'll be your devoted slaves if it's not what we've been reading, I can tell you.'

'Stella!' This was in chorus from Eileen and Sally. 'We can't change books now. We've been studying all year for our Higher Cert.'

'Speak for yourselves,' said Spring. 'I've been *not* studying all year and just hoping to be overtaken by a natural disaster before the exam!'

'And the papers might be written already,' said Katie.

'Surely not,' I said. 'Examination papers can't be written and lying around.'

'Not lying around,' said Spring. 'Locked up in the safe until they go to the printers and then locked up again when they return. Miss Shanks is nuts on cheating.'

'Well, I'm not about to change books this late in the term anyway,' I said stoutly.

'You know best, Miss Gilver,' said Stella. She had a special way of being horribly insolent without saying anything on which one could lay one's finger.

'So what *are* you reading?' I asked them.

'*Paradise Lost*,' said Eileen. 'Miss Lipscott loves it.'

'Juliet hates it as much as the rest of us!' said Katie. 'She just thinks that reading hateful boring tripe is good for the soul.'

There was so much about this remark I should have pounced upon, from the casual use of the nickname, past the intemperate language, to the disparaging of the great John Milton, but so panicked was I by the thought of having to teach a single sensible thing about such a poem that I said nothing, instead shooting off to the sideboard, ostensibly to fetch some eggs and bacon, but really because Miss Shanks was standing there and I felt an urgent need to reassure myself. A bit of Scott and Shakespeare, she had said. *Paradise Lost* was far beyond both my brief and the pale.

'Exams, Miss Shanks,' I said. 'The papers. The girls said they were written and that the upper sixth is studying Milton. I'm sure they're just teasing the new girl?' My voice went up at the end and sounded as unsure as could be.

'Milton, eh?' said Miss Shanks. She was stirring a pot of scrambled egg with a wooden spirtle and in her black church costume and already wearing a black church hat she looked rather witchy. 'Well, Miss Lipscott was a one for that kind of thing.'

'But the papers?' I said. 'Do I have to write an exam paper? On *Paradise Lost*?'

'No, no, no, it's written, Miss Gilver. The upper sixth and the fifth form are accounted for. School Certs, you know. It's just the first to fourth forms and the lower sixth you need to take care of.'

'Oh!' I said, standing with the chafing dish lid in my hand, letting the uncovered bacon get cold. 'Is that all? And do you happen to know what sort of stuff . . .'

'You've all day after chapel to prepare, Miss Gilver,' said Miss Shanks. She had finally got the scrambled egg stirred up to her satisfaction and now she scraped a great heap of it onto her plate with the spirtle and left me there. As my eyes followed her back to her place I saw that our little interchange had not gone unnoticed. Miss Christopher was watching me. She glanced at Miss Shanks and at Miss Barclay and back to me, saw me looking at her and finally lowered her gaze as though to spread toast with butter took all the concentration with which she had learned to subject a frog to dissection.

'Well,' I said, sitting back down. 'Why ever Miss McLintock and Miss Stanley left, it wasn't because of muddle in the organisation.'

'What?' said Spring.

'Who?' said Sally.

'You were right, girls,' I said. 'The Higher Cert exam papers are written already and safely under lock and key.'

'Who's Miss Stanley?' said Katie. 'Was she before our time?'

'Golly, how long have the mistresses being fleeing St Cucumber's?' said Eileen.

'Maybe,' I said, mentally crossing my fingers, 'I got the names wrong. Weren't they the science and history mistresses?' I looked around their faces. 'No?'

My ploy worked, as I had thought it would, for who can resist the chance to correct another's mistakes, especially when that other is an elder and better? They filled the air with all the information I needed, babbling and chirruping over one another like a family of day-old chicks squabbling in their dust bath and, concentrating hard, I caught it all.

The science mistress had been a Miss Bell (called Tinker, affectionately by the girls) who had departed two years ago. Miss Taylor the history mistress, mystifyingly referred to as The Maid, had gone with her; and a Miss Blair, who had taken the girls for gym and music, had left just before an important hockey match.

'And of course, dear Fräulein Fielding, who died at Christmas time,' said Sally, her eyes misting. 'She was the most marvellous Latin scholar, Miss Gilver. Not like old Plumface who just translates battle after battle and makes us draw tables of verbs.'

'Miss Fielding died just this last Christmas?' I said.

'Golly no, two years since,' said Sally. 'And a half. And no one left when she was here. Misses Taylor and Bell were pals of old.'

I was rather disappointed in the selection of names – I had been hoping for something more prominent upon which to hang the next part of my ruse, but I did my best, walking to chapel alongside Miss Lovage, the art mistress.

'The girls seem very fond of you all,' I said, to start things off. Miss Lovage raised her striking profile to an even more glamorous angle, whether from pride in her girls' fondness or the better to sniff the sea air I could not say. 'They seem terribly to miss Miss Fielding and Miss Blair.' The imposing chin came down a bit at that and Miss Lovage turned to look at me.

'Miss Blair?' she said.

'I wondered if it could possibly be the same Miss Blair I know from my own schooldays,' I said. 'At St Leonards. Over twenty years ago now. A little Irishwoman with flame-red hair?' Of course I had not been to school at St Leonards or anywhere else for that matter and the flame-haired Irishwoman was my own invention, but once again it worked for me.

'Can't be,' said Miss Lovage. 'Emily Blair was Scotch and Amazonian and what hair she let grow on her head was mouse. Did you say the girls loved her? Who have you been talking to?'

'Ohh . . .' I said.

'My girls – the painters and sculptors – hated all that. *Endless* hockey all winter and cricket, if you can believe it, in the summer term. Cricket!'

'That does seem a little odd,' I said. We were nearing the church now and I plunged on before we should arrive and have the conversation cut off by song and prayer. 'Odd too to find a Scotswoman with a yen for cricket. I wonder if she gets the chance where she is now.' I paused but nothing came out of Miss Lovage's ruby-red painted lips. 'Do you know where she moved on to?' I said but, as usual, the direct question shut the conversation down like a slammed door. Miss Lovage merely stared at me down her dramatic nose and then threw her dramatic scarf back around her neck with a gesture (dramatic, of course) presumably meant to brush me and my question away. I was not, however, to be so easily brushed.

'Or perhaps she didn't take up another position?' I said. 'If she left in the rush she seems to have . . .'

'You are remarkably inquisitive about your fellow man,' said Miss Lovage.

'Inquisitiveness is rather to be encouraged, though, wouldn't you say?' I replied. 'As a schoolmistress and a shaper of young minds, one would expect you to be all for it.'

'A mind which enquires into Life and celebrates Beauty,' said Miss Lovage, 'is greatly to be encouraged, of course. But the quotidian minutiae of strangers' lives has never enthralled me.'

She sounded, as Donald and Teddy say, as though she had swallowed a dictionary.

'Miss Blair was hardly a stranger to you,' I insisted, 'and although she and I did not overlap, as a new mistress where she was an old one, I'm naturally interested in what became of her.'

'What do you mean "new mistress"?' said Miss Lovage, quite forgetting to drawl and letting her face fall into its natural lines, without arched eyebrows or stretched neck. 'Miss Shanks said a French mistress of impeccable pedigree had arrived from the agency.'

'Oh, she did,' I said. '*Incredible* pedigree, really. But haven't you heard? Miss Lipscott is gone. I'm taking over English for her.' Miss Lovage reared backwards like an adder about to strike. 'For a while anyway,' I said.

'But how can you switch from French to English?' she said. 'Which are you?'

'Oh, I'm a . . .' I sought desperately for some phrase other than that – jack of all trades – which had sprung to my mind. 'I'm a generalist, Miss Lovage.'

'This is an outrage,' Miss Lovage said, rather rudely to say the least. 'Excuse me, Miss Gilver. I must speak to the headmistress right away.'

With that, she shot forward to where Miss Shanks was stumping along and I dropped back and fell into step with Miss Barclay and Miss Christopher, together again like Tweedledum and Tweedledee.

'I've upset Miss Lovage,' I told them.

'Not difficult,' said Miss Barclay, with a world of scorn in her voice for artists and their flighty ways.

'What's wrong with her?' said Miss Christopher.

'Well, I was asking about Miss Blair to start with,' I said. 'Which she didn't like at all.' The chalky little titter of Miss Barclay and the rattling chuckle of Miss Christopher were loud enough to cause some of the girls to turn and stare.

'Hardly a surprise!' said Miss Barclay. 'Not much kindred spirit there.'

'Because of the cricket?' I asked.

'Oh, you heard about the cricket, did you?' said Miss Christopher. 'Some of the mummies and daddies didn't think it was quite nice. And such a waste of the lovely new tennis courts too. Not to mention her taste in music.'

'Violins?' I asked. I could think of nothing worse than the sound of children learning to play the violin.

'Bagpipes,' said Miss Barclay.

'Dear God!'

'But Miss Shanks took over when Blair left us in the lurch, and the girls are just as well off with callisthenics and country walks. And Mrs Tully in the village is happy to listen to them playing their scales.'

We were at the church gate now, joining the rest of the flock being gathered in under the stern eye of a black-garbed minister who stood on the step, and it was impossible to resist the unspoken command to stop talking and stare at the ground as one passed him. Just as well, I daresay, for how could I relate Miss Lovage's horror at the makeshift way I had dropped French and taken up English to two women who were cribbing science and history by staying one page ahead of the girls in the textbooks?

During the service I had plenty of time for quiet reflection, for the rites of the Church of Scotland – in which there are no kneeling and no responses and what little standing is required is heavily cued by the organ – give one's mind a blissful chance to wander with no one able to tell. Actual snoring is frowned upon, but pew after pew of glazed, slumping parishioners dreaming of their dinners is the sight which greets many a minister of that kirk every week, I am sure.

And so after the service, when I excused myself from the walk along the promenade and dodged into the Crown by the back way, I felt I had plenty to tell.

To my surprise and slight annoyance, Alec was not alone in the parlour but was sharing a glass of beer and a plate of sandwiches with an off-duty Constable Reid, rather resplendent in britches and a golfing jersey and with a pancake of a golfing cap lying beside him on the settle.

'The sarge's no' buying it,' he said. 'Good news for you, missus.'

'Buying what?' I asked.

Constable Reid took a pull at his pint glass before replying.

'Five murders. Or even one murder. I've telt him all about

123

Miss Lipscott – good family, went off the rails, teachin' in a school, livin' like a nun – and he reckons she's likely a wee bit' – he twirled his hand beside his head and whistled – 'and no need to listen to her.'

'But she has to be found!' I said. I had had a complete change of heart in the matter of Fleur's protection, thinking that if the police wanted her for murder, they would work all the more for her safe return.

'We don't know how she got away,' said Reid. 'She didn't get on the train here nor Stranraer nor Glenluce as far as the station masters can recall – and she'd have had a wheen of luggage, mind.'

'Stranraer?' I said.

'I already asked about a ferry-boat,' said Alec. 'No joy. And she didn't hire a car or ring anybody to come and get her.'

'And she's no' holed up in any wee place in town or in Portlogan that takes in guests unless they're lyin' and why would they? So there you have it. She's gone.'

'And Sergeant Turner is simply washing his hands of her?' I said.

'I told him what you told me,' said Reid. 'That they women are always taking off. He'll send her lines out – her description – to the other forces but nobody's reported her missin' and so . . .' He shrugged.

'Can I report her missing?' He was shaking his head already. 'Her headmistress? Or one of her sisters?'

'Aye, a sister for sure,' said Reid. '*Then* we'll have another wee look-see.'

'But in the meantime, Dandy,' said Alec, 'it's you and me.'

'And what about the corpse?' I said.

'It'll be in tomorrow's paper,' said Reid. 'We're asking the ferries and the fishing boats – no' that our fishermen would have a woman aboard, mind – and asking down the coast if anyone's missin' and we'll just need to wait till somebody pipes up.'

'And no clues from the body itself?' I said. 'Did someone search the headland?' Reid was nodding. 'And question passers-by?' Now his eyes flashed. 'Yes, I *do* mean Cissie,' I said. 'If she was there on her own, noticing Mrs Aldo with her mysterious companion, she might have noticed someone else too.'

'But only on Tuesday evening and only at that spot, Dan,' said Alec.

'Better than nothing,' I said. 'I'll talk to the girl and do it gently.'

'Or me,' Alec said.

'I think you'll have other fish to fry,' I said. 'Do you suppose you could impersonate a distressed headmaster, or a doting and wealthy father of at least five?' I sailed on without waiting for a reply. 'Here's what I'm thinking. How many gym-cum-music mistresses can there possibly be in this rather small country – Scotland, that is – who like to get their charges playing cricket and bagpipes?' Neither man answered. 'Now, if Miss Blair left suddenly in the middle of a term – and I think she did – wouldn't she most likely apply with some haste to an agency to find work? And even if she didn't, mightn't an agency know her of old?'

'And I what?' said Alec. 'I ring up pretending to want a woman to teach cricket?'

'Exactly,' I said.

'Wouldn't it be easier for you simply to keep digging for a home address or something?' he said.

'No,' I said. 'On two counts, no. First, if I "dig" they'll get suspicious, and secondly you can do this right now instead of waiting. And if you find one ex-mistress you can ask her about the others.'

'But why start with Blair?' said Alec.

'The other two have even more dispiritingly ordinary names – Taylor and Bell.'

'What's ordinary about Lipscott and Bow-clark?' said Reid, making me flush.

'Very sound point, Constable,' I said. 'Although it's a bit quick to expect Fleur to be back on the books.'

'I'll eat my hat if she turns up on agency books at all,' said Alec. 'She's lying low, mark my words. Mademoiselle Beauclerc though . . . could be.' He thought for a moment, sucking on his unlit pipe in that disgusting way (the very thought of what it must taste like made me grimace). 'Of course,' he went on, 'not getting a whiff of them doesn't mean anything. They might have gone home to their people.'

'I know, I know,' I said. 'But if we *did* find Miss Blair, for instance, happily coaching some pigtailed first eleven somewhere, we could stop worrying that she'd been murdered.'

'No' that again,' said Reid. 'If the body we've got the now isn't the French one, why think there's anything in it that four other teachers went away?'

'Because I still don't believe we can be sure that the corpse *isn't* Miss Beauclerc,' I said, to a chorus of their groans. 'I know Miss Lipscott said not, but she ran away straight afterwards. And I know Miss Barclay said not, but . . .' Both of them sat forward and opened their eyes very wide. 'I don't trust her,' I finished lamely. 'I don't trust anyone in that place.'

'So there's nae use gettin' a third opinion then?' said Reid. 'If they're all as bad as each other.'

'I'd trust one of the girls,' I said, 'but we couldn't possibly ask it of them. No, I think we just have to try to track down Miss Beauclerc and if we fail to . . . then track down her family and . . . no distinguishing marks at all, Constable? Moles, scars, birthmarks?' Reid, brick-red in the face once more, simply shook his head. 'Very well then,' I said. 'When can I speak to Cissie?'

'We're all quits, aren't we?' said Reid, rather wary. 'The police are no' botherin' your friend and so you're no' tryin' to set Cissie against me, eh no? Aye, well come and meet us on the links this afternoon then. After three. It's right behind the school. You can't miss it.'

'She's a golfer too?' I said. This was surprising in a parlour maid, to my mind.

'Naw,' said Reid, blushing a little again. 'She's . . . she just, if I'm playin' a round she . . .'

'You're not trying to say she *caddies* for you?' said Alec.

'She lugs your clubs around on her afternoon free?' I said.

'Naw!' said Reid. 'They're on a wee set o' trolley wheels. She just pulls them along.'

He retired with a great air of wounded dignity, leaving Alec and me to burst into laughter behind him, like a pair of school-girls when a mistress leaves the room.

'My God,' I said. 'This Cissie must be a bit of limp rag.'

'She seemed lively enough to me,' Alec said. 'Perhaps PC Reid has hidden charms. Now, to the part we couldn't discuss in front of him.'

'Elf,' I said. 'Where does one begin?'

'With the newspapers of the day and the report of the inquest, I suppose,' Alec said.

'But those will only tell you what I've told you anyway.'

'Oh quite, quite, but I was thinking more of gathering names of individuals one might talk to. I still think that's a better use of my time than haring after Miss Blair in that unlikely way. Either that, or asking around for anyone who might have seen our corpse when she was alive. Under cover of tracing Mrs Aldo, you know. For today at least, since it's Sunday and I can't start pestering librarians *or* teachers' employment agencies until tomorrow.'

'I suppose so,' I said reluctantly. 'And I could try to think of a way to dig some more without arousing suspicions. If only they hadn't met me already I could present myself as an inveterate nosy-parker and they'd think nothing of my questions.'

'Ask the girls,' said Alec. 'No one so self-centred as the young. They'll think nothing at all.'

'True,' I said. 'And I need to establish Fleur's movements during the time our corpse might have died anyway. I hate having to call her "our corpse". Can't we think of something less grisly?'

'Why don't we call her No. 5?' suggested Alec. I stared at him, disbelieving, for what could possibly be more grisly than that?

'I'll start with Sabbatina Aldo,' I said, pulling on my gloves and preparing myself for departure. 'You never know – she might be able to tell us something about her mother's movements too.'

'Onwards, then,' said Alec, rising as I did.

'And most certainly upwards,' I replied, thinking of the cliff steps to St Columba's, which were not getting any less steep and arduous for the number of times I had climbed them.

It was a pleasant prospect, however, the gusting clouds and the sparkling sea, and I noticed for the first time the golf links on the headland behind the school, where the pancake caps of the men could be seen sprouting on the greens and fairways like mushrooms. I saw, too, a fair few splashes of custard yellow: St Columba's girls in their shirtsleeves, getting in a round before luncheon on this unusually mild day.

The entrance hall was deserted and the corridors silent, only the good rich smell of roasting beef wafting up from the kitchens to say that anyone was at work inside these walls, so instead of trying to find the needle of Sabbatina Aldo in the haystack of girls around the pool and courts and grounds I set off for Fleur's classroom – Miss Shanks had given me sketchy directions the evening before – in slim hopes of some letters or papers she might have left behind and in rather plumper dread of what reins, besides Milton, I might discover I had to take up when the following school day dawned.

Her classroom was on the seaward side, long and sunny, with high glittering windows, white-distempered walls and broad black floorboards, surely as Spartan as even the tenant of Fleur's monastic sleeping cell could desire. There was not a picture, nor a bookshelf, nor the lowliest pot of daisies on the mustard-painted fireplace, just six rows of forms facing a large desk set up on a small dais, with a blackboard behind.

I sat in Fleur's chair and opened the top of the three desk drawers, finding in there such tidiness and order that my hopes, slender as they had been, dwindled to threads and blew away. Pens and ink, a wiper, fresh sheets for the blotter, a red pencil and its little box sharpener, a cloth-covered block for cleaning the board and a packet of white chalk. In short, nothing.

In the second drawer, however, there was something indeed. I drew it all out and spread it on the desktop, letting my horrified eyes rest on each item in turn until I had been round them all.

Milton, to my creeping dismay, was not the half of it. The

lower sixth were engaged, granted, on studying Shakespeare (as Miss Shanks had so airily suggested all her girls might be) but no frothy comedy or worthy history for them! *King Lear* was the order of the day. Fleur's copy had girls' names pasted over the list of dramatis personae, which I took to indicate that it was being read aloud in the classroom, but there were also some beastly comprehension questions scrawled on slips of paper and tucked into the pages here and there.

I turned, faintly, from the long, frantic speech towards the end of Act IV where the volume had fallen open and gave my attention to the books upon which Fleur had decided the budding minds of the middle forms should grow rich and be enlightened. *The Pilgrim's Progress, Piers Plowman* and *The Canterbury Tales* glared balefully up at me from the desktop and my heart sank deep down into me like a pebble lobbed into a well. The poor girls! I had slogged through *The Pilgrim's Progress* myself as a small child, weeping with boredom and hating Christian like poison, but those were the times and that was the excuse for it. These days there could surely be none. As for *The Canterbury Tales* and *Piers Plowman*, I had managed to stagger thus far through my life without knowledge of a single line of either and, leafing through a little of each, was only sorry that my run of luck had ended. John Donne for the lower fourth seemed a bright spot until I cast my eyes over Fleur's notes and saw that, of all his works, she had selected the Holy Sonnets, which was tiresomeness beyond imagining.

The first and second forms, in their tender years, had been spared maddened kings, pious allegories and epic poetry and were allotted instead novels, and nineteenth-century novels at that, but of all the wondrous outpourings of that miraculous age Fleur had plumped – as though to quell any danger of enjoyment – for *The Water Babies* and *Silas Marner*.

'*Silas Marner*?' I muttered, remembering how I had snorted with impatience at the tiresome old fool and his sickening little darling. I closed it and pinched the pages between my forefinger and thumb. 'Well, at least it's short.' *The Water Babies* I had, admittedly, loved when I was too young to know better but when I unearthed it to read to my sons in their nursery, I had very soon re-earthed it again, deep into a trunk in an attic, aghast at its feverish insistence on death and sacrifice and its unwholesome obsession with staying pure and clean (and with fish, one has to say). Mr Kingsley would have given those Austrian doctors a good gallop round the paddock if he had ever submitted to them, I remember thinking.

And so this was what little Fleur Lipscott had picked to share with the poor unfortunate girls. I could hardly believe it. Where was Robinson Crusoe? Where Gulliver? Where Oliver and Pip and Alice and Cathy and all her friends from childhood? For Fleur had spent all day every rainy day – and portions even of fine ones – holed up in a loft with a bag of toffees, and I recalled her emerging with shining eyes and demanding paper and pens and solitude while she began her Great Novel.

'With islands and pirates and pickpockets and a raging fire and orphans and a stolen inheritance and a wedding,' she had announced to us all. 'And a ghost. Don't disturb me until it's done.'

I cast my eyes over the seven volumes before me on the desk, doubting whether there was a single pirate amongst the lot of them, and went on a treasure hunt for what I was sure must exist somewhere.

I was right: in the big cupboard built into the corner of the room, where exercise books and bottles of ink were stored (and also, I noticed, a large trunk full of veils and swords and the like to help with the acting out of the plays), there was a bookcase, and upon that bookcase by the mercy of Providence were still ranged the books which had held sway in the English classroom of St Columba's before the strange Miss Lipscott had swept them away.

A very happy twenty minutes later I had made my selections. The little ones were to have *Kidnapped*, the second form *Rob Roy*, the third form (who deserved the most pity of all after *The Canterbury Tales*) were to be rewarded with *Tam o'Shanter*.

The lower fourth were going to see a side of Donne at which his Holy Sonnets had not hinted, although I would avoid the farthest reaches: they were fifteen, after all, not forty. The fifth had to stick with *Piers Plowman* for their exam but I would intersperse it with *Jane Eyre* as a corrective. The lower sixth, I decided, could leave King Lear out on the moor to take his chances and turn to the rather more thrilling adventures of Macbeth instead and, to soothe the troubled brains of the upper sixth, busy cramming *Paradise Lost*, I would require them to read one each day of Shakespeare's sonnets starting with 'O, never say that I was false of heart', Sonnet 109, which was my favourite. (Already I could tell that the power of being the schoolmistress, with the key to the cupboard where the books were kept, was going to my head and threatening to ruin me.)

At luncheon, where the roast beef fulfilled every bit of its fragrant promise, although one could have played deck quoits with the Yorkshire puddings (for no doubt the cook was a Scotchwoman and it will out somewhere), I slipped the tiniest little border trowel into the palm of my hand and did as minute and discreet a portion of digging as could properly be called digging at all.

'What of your extra-curricular hours, girls?' I said. 'I'm very happy to take over Miss Lipscott's duties there.'

'Cramming,' said Katie.

'Yes, stuffing *Paradise* down our gullets like pelicans with herrings,' said Spring. She had taken the news that it was too late to change the examination paper very badly.

'Ah,' I said. 'Yes, poor dears. I remember it well.' This was a lie, of course; I had never sat an examination in my life unless one could count the beady-eyed way I was watched making introductions at finishing-school sherry parties (and in all honesty one could not). 'But the other forms? Do you happen to know? Did Miss Lipscott have a weekly round?' Five pairs of eyes gazed back at me, with varying expressions of interest and disdain, but none with comprehension. 'Sewing Club on a Monday, Rambling Club on a Tuesday, Country Dancing on a Wednesday, that sort of thing . . . ?' I had put the notion of rambling on a Tuesday into the list with great care.

'Oh no, the mistresses don't concern themselves much with our Societies,' said Sally. 'Too busy marking.'

'I see,' I said. 'And what Societies are there?'

'Well, not sewing, thank goodness,' said Stella. 'And not country dancing – what a thought.'

'We used to have all sorts of dancing but there's none now,' said Sally.

'Miss Lovage does teach *Dance*,' said Eileen. 'But *Dance* isn't dancing, really.' Spring and Katie began to giggle.

'Imagine going to a party and doing Miss Lovage's *Dance*!'

'Imagine at our coming-out balls. If we did *Dance*!'

'We'd be taken to a sanatorium and tied to our beds with stout rope.'

'Now, now,' I said, although my lips were twitching. 'And what about rambling? One would have thought with these lovely cliff walks and the ruined castles and all . . .'

'I think some of the younger girls tramp about a bit,' said Stella. 'Especially the Scotch ones.'

'It's on Sunday afternoons,' said Eileen. 'Quite fun, actually. We – they, I mean – they take nature sheets and try to collect things. Almost like a treasure hunt, you see?'

'Sunday afternoons,' I said. 'Right-ho.' There was no chance that No. 5 had been in the water six days so, no matter how many girls had been tramping about the cliffs with nature sheets at the last ramblers' outing, they could not have seen anything useful to me. I tried another tack. 'I didn't realise that the art mistress might teach dancing too,' I said.

'Not dancing, Miss Gilver,' said Katie. '*Daahhhnce*!' The giggles started to break out once more and I did not have to summon any schoolmistressishness to start tutting.

'You're all very silly for such great big girls,' I said. 'I could excuse it in the little ones. What of Miss Taylor and Miss Bell? Had they other strings to their bow? I'm afraid I shall only be teaching English to you. Although I do have some circus training,

I suppose.' Thus I attempted to ingratiate and glamorise myself with them, and certainly I loosened their tongues.

'Tinker Bell and The Maid were scholars, Miss Gilver,' said Spring.

'The Maid?' I said.

'Of Orleans,' said Katie. 'History mistress, you see?'

'Ah,' I said. 'And so Juliet for Miss Lipscott, because of Shakespeare?'

'Scholars,' went on Spring without answering my interruption, 'dry, dusty and devoted. No time for anything else. They and Miss Fielding were all at Somerville together – pioneers of the day – and we always thought – that is, Mummy always told me – that they had to be whiter than white. No high jinks or they'd be out on their ear.'

'I didn't mean to suggest high jinks!' I said. 'Astronomy, perhaps. Or woodcarving.'

'Or circus tricks, quite,' drawled Stella.

'What kind of circus tricks?' Sally asked. 'I'd love to be able to juggle.'

'Oh, me too,' said Spring. 'Or standing up on a horse in a bathing suit. Just to annoy Daddy. He's still quite keen on side-saddle, Miss Gilver, if you can believe it these days.'

'Dogs,' I said, and it was rather difficult to keep mopping up gravy with the last of my Yorkshire pudding while crossing my fingers. 'I can't juggle myself but I have a Dalmatian at home who can.' I warmed to it and uncrossed my fingers. There was a kernel of truth in this. Bunty had never quite forgotten the wonderful things she had learned in her short sojourn at the circus three years before and even my bumbling instead of the expertise of the circus folk could not dislodge it.

'Golly,' said Eileen. 'I wish you'd brought him. What fun.' I nodded and smiled, knowing that Bunty was safely stuck in Perthshire and my fibs would never come back to haunt me.

The maids appeared then to clear the main course and the girls went through their familiar craning and straining to see what pudding might be, looking quite a bit like liberty horses arching their necks in formation in the ring. I was content with what the luncheon table had given to me and did not need the delights of the pudding. Miss Bell and Miss Taylor had been at Oxford with Miss Fielding. It would be easy, I was sure, to track their movements now, for were not these bluestockings all as thick as thieves and did they not gather together for reunions as regularly as migrating flocks of birds alighting on their oceanic islands?

'What about bird watching?' I said, as the thought struck me. 'I'm rather an ornithologist.' More lies, but I was thinking, rather desperately, of what might be seen through binoculars. 'Or does one of the other mistresses already help out there?'

'Not any more,' said Sally.

'Miss Beauclerc?' I asked, with a leap of hope. For how easy it would be, if one's attention was trained on a distant speck, to take a fateful step too close to the cliff edge and plunge into the sea.

'Miss Lipscott,' said Eileen. 'Owls.'

'I thought it was bats,' said Katie.

'Making her a chiropterologist,' said Eileen, 'and not an ornithologist at all.'

'Well, it was night anyway,' said Spring.

''Twas the nightingale and not the lark,' said Stella.

'Oh Romeo, Romeo, wherefore art thou?' said Katie in a fluttery voice and all five of them, even the haughty Stella, were soon tittering.

I had meant to ask them to point out Sabbatina Aldo for me, although I could not quite see what reason I could give to allay suspicion about my interest in her, but rolling my eyes at their silliness and looking away to other parts of the room, I thought I had spotted her without assistance. Amongst the third form there was a child with luxurious raven tresses who could not possibly be either an English rose nor a Scotch thistle (as Grant always described her countrywomen, on account of their dry fair hair and their cheeks purple from the cold). Besides her colouring, she was sitting slightly alone although at a table of twelve, looking as diffident in her neatness as a scholarship girl (or the beneficiary of a wealthy patron anyway) would look amongst the Stellas and Springs of this world.

First, though, for the obliging Cissie, who might have seen all manner of going-on on the cliff top last Tuesday evening and might yet have more to tell of Mrs Aldo's mysterious lover, if one asked the right questions and if one were a kind lady of forty-one instead of a mortifyingly handsome young man.

She was a short and wiry little person, with a slight cast to her left eye and an upper lip larger than the lower one by just about the proportion that a lower lip should be larger than the upper. She was saved, however, by a finely chiselled nose, apple cheeks and a shining cap of bright hair done in the latest style, of which one could see rather a lot owing to the tiny dimensions of her fashionable hat, chosen for the company rather than the setting. All in all, one could see what a young man might find appealing about her, especially since when I discovered her with Reid at the third tee she was gazing at him with slightly cross-eyed but nonetheless heartfelt devotion and hugging his clubs as an obvious substitute for his manly form.

'Reid,' I said, nodding. 'And Cissie.' She let go of the clubs and bobbed nicely. 'You'll just have to slum it for a while,' I said to the constable. 'Carry your own clubs – it won't kill you. Cissie, my dear, I'd like you to come for a little walk with me.' She looked at Reid for approval and when he gave a short nod – although with not a whisper of good grace about it – she opened her little bag, put on her Sunday gloves and waited expectantly for me to lead her.

'Now then,' I said, when we were under way, before remembering the kind lady and hastily parking the schoolmistress-cum-nanny as whom I had begun. 'That's a very pretty hat, is it new?' Cissie nodded and put a hand up to touch it. I wondered if she was still at the age when she would stop walking and bend over her skirts to look at a new pair of shoes she was wearing. 'So your mistress doesn't have any silly notions of you dressing plainly even on free afternoons then?' Cissie very properly said nothing. 'Only Reid said she was a bit of a tartar.' Again, Cissie said nothing but she did allow herself a small smile. 'I'm glad to hear she's not as unreasonable as all that,' I said, 'but I do want to assure you, my dear, that anything you say to me is in the strictest confidence.'

'I brought it out in ma handbag,' said Cissie. It took me a moment to realise she was talking about the startling hat, but only another moment to realise that she had shown herself to be my ally.

'Dear me, how old-fashioned of her,' I said. 'Now then,' – cosily, this time, with nothing of the nanny anywhere – 'I know because your fiancé told me' – there was a gasp – 'oh, yes he told me that too and as I say – strictest confidence – anyway, I know that last Tuesday evening you saw someone on the cliffs at Dunskey Castle. I would like you tell me all about it in your own words.'

'Rosie the washerwoman, ye mean?' said Cissie.

'In your own words,' I said.

'Aye, I seen her,' said Cissie. 'Walking along the path with a man. So I just ducked in a wee bit behind a bush – gorse it was and right scratchy – so's she didnae see me. That's all, madam.'

In story books, witnesses invited to speak in their own words always obligingly rattle on for hours spilling reams of detailed clues and red herrings, so the disappointment was a heavy one. I started the list of questions I had hoped to avoid.

'You didn't know the man?'

'I didn't.'

'But can you describe him?'

'He was quite big.'

'Fat?'

'Aye, a bit. And tall. Dark too. Well, it was dark, but he didn't look fair.'

'Young? Old?'

'No,' said Cissie slowly. 'I wouldnae have said he was young. And he couldnae have been old because of . . .'

'What?' I said.

'I never said this to that other man,' she whispered and my heart quickened. 'But he couldnae have been old because of how

136

they were . . . I mean, they were definitely . . . I mean, he wasn't her uncle.' My heart slowed again, so suddenly that I felt the slump as a slight dizziness. What an innocent she was, despite the 'sitting'. Of course, we had guessed at once that the partner of a moonlit walk on the cliffs 'wasn't her uncle'.

'And what exactly makes you say so?' I asked. 'What did you see them do?'

'Do?' said Cissie, blushing. 'Nothing. Just the way they were walking along and the way they were talking. Well, the way he was talking to her.'

'You heard what they were saying?' I said.

'I heard them talking,' Cissie said. 'I didnae understand it, though.'

'Hm,' I said, almost blushing myself at that. 'Just as well, I daresay. And they passed along and didn't turn back while you were there? You only saw them once?'

'Aye,' said Cissie. 'And I was watching out for them too – didnae want Rosie to see me.'

'And so you would have seen anyone else who was about?' I said.

'Who?' she said, glancing at me. 'Did somebody see Wullie and me?'

'Not that I know of,' I said. 'I just wanted to find out if anyone was around. If you saw or heard anything. Anyone calling out, or any kind of disturbance?'

'No,' said Cissie. 'It was right quiet for such a nice warm night. Sometimes you can see smoke or wee red dots if it's dark. From folks' cigarettes that are sittin' in the dips. But no last Tuesday.'

'And you heard nothing either?' She shook her head. 'And I don't suppose you were there on Monday and Wednesday.' Cissie took great offence at this, as though one unchaperoned walk a week was blameless but three would ruin her.

'I was not, madam,' she said. 'And I tell you somethin' else too. I wish I hadn't gone the night I did. I've had it up to here wi' all these questions.'

And so since there was really no point in badgering her – she had been at only one of the places on the cliffs where No. 5 might have gone over, and at only one time when it might have happened – I let her go back to the honour of trundling 'Wullie's' golf clubs around all afternoon and turned my own steps to the school.

What I really wanted was to find the mistresses in their staffroom together and in the mood for chatting. How difficult could it be to get them talking about their departed colleagues? How I should love to be able to present Alec, in the morning, with a list of their full names and approximate home addresses. My quick peek around the staffroom door, however, revealed that chamber empty of grate and of armchair again, and my surreptitious pause outside Miss Christopher's door yielded only the scratch of a pen and the rustle of paper. I abandoned the plan, grabbed a passing child and demanded that she find Betty Alder and send her to my classroom to meet me.

If it were not for my hidden but primary purpose – were I in reality only the new English mistress and not a detective as well, I thought – I should be at a pretty loose end by now and rather disappointed by my welcome. This thought brought another on its heels. What of Miss Glennie, who was not (presumably) sleuthing and skulking like me, but really *had* just joined the happy band of mistresses? What must she make of the utter lack of collegiate chumminess I had found here?

'Here, little girl,' I called out to a figure crossing the end of the passageway. To my astonishment, instead of meekly trotting up to see what I wanted, she put on a spurt of speed and disappeared from sight. 'Hey! Young lady!' I shouted after her and marched to the corner to find her dragging herself back as though she had weights attached to her ankles.

'Yes, Miss Gilver?' she said.

'That was very naughty of you,' I scolded. 'I'm half-inclined to hand out . . .' My voice trailed off as I realised I did not know whether St Columba's went in for demerits, detentions or the slipper. 'Anyway, don't do it again.'

'You know what the girls are calling you, don't you?' said the child with blithe impertinence.

'I do,' I replied. 'Goody Gilver, but I'm willing to relinquish the honour.'

'Grabber,' she said. '*Grabber* Gilver. Always collaring us and sending us on errands quite out of our way.'

'Well, I'm only after information this time, you little scamp,' I said, secretly quite pleased to have got a nickname already and one I did not make up for myself, not to mention one which made me sound so efficacious as a moderator of youthful indiscipline. I only hoped I was not noticeably beaming. 'Where is Miss Beauclerc's old room?'

'Oh! All right then. It's up those stairs at the end there and halfway along the land-side passage. Just beyond the horrible picture.'

'Thank you, peculiar child,' I said. 'And run along.'

One could see what she meant, I thought, as I drew even with the painting, in which Ophelia floated rather smugly in what looked like a fishpond; a paean to suicide which surely had no place in a girls' school. (Although if the artist had painted what a young woman *really* looked like once good and drowned, one would no more have hung the results on the wall.)

Passing by it, I stopped at Miss Glennie's door, which still bore the name of Mademoiselle Beauclerc, and knocked. There was a pause, a scuffle and then a reply.

'Yes?'

I opened the door and leaned in with a friendly smile arranged on my face.

'Miss Gilver, Miss Glennie,' I said. 'The other new girl. Just wondering how you're getting on?' Then my smile faltered a little. Miss Glennie was getting on, or so it would seem, a lot better than I. She had a pile of jotters on her table and a large dictionary with gold-edged pages open on the floor at her side, and it occurred to me that there might be all manner of things I should have been busy doing yesterday and today.

'Oh, I'm fine,' said Miss Glennie. She did not look fine. She looked as though she had recently had some dreadful shock and was still reeling.

'Had you far to come?' I asked her. 'Shouldn't you be resting today after your journey?

'Only Edinburgh,' she replied. 'And I'd rather not fall behind.'

'And you're new at this schoolmistressing lark, aren't you?' I said. 'Miss Shanks said something about your having been a governess before?'

Miss Glennie looked less fine than ever on hearing me mention what I was still sure must be her fictitious royal past.

'I told the Lambourne Agency only with great reluctance,' she said, 'and they promised not to divulge my personal affairs to *anyone.*'

Or rather, I thought drily, she had made up a silly story that she heartily wished would go away and stop following her around.

'One would think you'd be proud of such a connection,' I said, smiling, 'hardly ashamed.'

'We're not supposed to talk about it,' she said miserably. 'That was always made very clear.' I nodded but said nothing. Teddy had been a one for tall tales set about by secrets when he was a child (a Foreign Office appointment requiring him to spy on the Germans with a secret radio he was not allowed to show us; this was one notable episode from wartime) but he had been six and Miss Glennie was forty-five if a day. 'And now, Miss Gilver, I really am grateful but I must get on with all of this. Do you know there's a girl going up to Edinburgh to read French? But only if she passes her Higher Cert.' I nodded, but now it occurred to me that I could not remember whether Miss Shanks had said one of the crop of scholars currently incubating in St Columba's bosom was bound for a degree in *English*. Chemistry she had mentioned, and I rather thought geography and history were the others, but I had not been thinking of English then, during my interregnum as the French mistress. I took my leave and hurried away to Fleur's classroom, thinking there would be some note of such a scholar in the papers there. It was only when I opened the door and entered that I remembered having summoned Sabbatina Aldo, who was waiting in a desk in the front row and stood politely on seeing me.

'Miss Gilver?' she said. 'I'm . . . Betty. You wanted me?' Her voice was a curious mixture: the village Scotch of her early youth overlaid by a smattering of the Queen's English, no doubt copied from her new school friends and her mistresses in admiration or to allay the teasing which must have come her way, and somewhere in there too was a trace – just a trace – of her Italian roots, in a kind of emphatic landing on the consonants and a slight reluctance to leave them behind.

'Yes indeed, Betty,' I said. 'You don't mind 'Betty'? Sabbatina is a beautiful name.'

'Sabbatina is a beautiful name for a Sabbatina,' she replied, and her voice was pure Italian as she repeated the melodious word. 'I am a Betty, though. You can have no idea, Miss Gilver, what a trial it is to have a name so at odds with your life.'

'My Christian name is Dandelion,' I said and was gratified to see a spark jump up and dance in her eyes. 'You have my permission to chortle.' Good child that she was, she only gave a very small smile before composing herself again.

'Now, Sabbatina,' I went on. 'You know that Miss Lipscott is gone, don't you? And I am the new English mistress?' She nodded. I hesitated. All of a sudden I could not quite remember why I had thought I should speak to this girl at all. Or rather I had imagined a casual conversation somewhere, not this stark interview in an empty room.

'I met your father,' I said. Sabbatina gazed back at me very blankly. 'I should like to be able to give him a good report of you. Tell him you are well and happy. I know you missed your visit home to see your parents yesterday.' She was still gazing but her eyes were shining with unshed tears.

'To see my father,' she said. 'Not to see my mother. Not yesterday.'

I had thought her father meant to hide the news from her but clearly he had changed his mind and although she was too polite to wail about her private woes to a perfect stranger her misery was palpable.

'Are you all right?' I said.

'Just sad,' said Sabbatina. 'And a little confused. I don't understand what is happening. I don't understand how she could just go away.'

'It's a very odd world, the world of grown-ups,' I said. 'They often do inexplicable things and don't usually stop to wonder how it looks to the innocent around them.' I shut my mouth rather firmly at the end of this speech, having been mildly surprised to hear it coming out of me. Thankfully, she appeared to take it as yet another of the odd things that grown-ups do and not as the rebuke of her mother it most impertinently was. Besides, her loyalty was severely shaken. She looked fiercely angry as she looked at me and spoke again.

'She was supposed always to be there. She said so.'

I nodded, dumb with pity for her, and could not think of a single platitude to serve up, for what woman in a thousand could leave her child? I am not the most maternal woman ever born, and often shut the numerous doors between drawing room and nursery, leaving Nanny to deal with the wailing. Frequently, too, I wilted with boredom listening to their stories and watching them at play (not to mention the fact that I faced the dreary prospect of Donald's uncertain future with all the enthusiasm one usually takes to the dentist) but even I could not imagine just cutting loose and letting them tell their stories to the empty air, letting them listen to silence instead of adoring 'good shows!' when they scored a point or cleared a fence. And whatever hash Donald was going to make of his life without masters and prefects to keep him in line, I was determined to be there as a witness to it and, with luck, a hand on the tiller.

For the first time it occurred to me to wonder if her father's early death – the Major had died without ever seeing his youngest child – could be at all to blame for the odd way that Fleur had turned out compared with the other two. Then I dismissed this as the tosh it had to be, for had not the two elder sisters lost their father to the grouse and the deer long before his death anyway, and had not little girls – and little boys, too – grown up without their soldier fathers throughout the whole of history? Mothers were quite a different thing.

'I knew Miss Lipscott as a child, you know?' I said to Sabbatina. This seemed to pique more interest in her than any of my previous offerings; or perhaps she was merely being polite to this odd newcomer who spoke of personal matters in such a way. 'And it has been strange to me to meet her again as a grown woman, so much changed.' Sabbatina nodded. 'Of course, I only met her – this time around – on Friday, and I can't tell for sure but I think perhaps she was not herself?' Poor Sabbatina looked struck with terror at the thought of having to answer such an outlandish remark from a schoolmistress about another. 'Did you see much of her?'

'Of course,' said Sabbatina. 'What do you mean?'

'Just before she left, specifically?' I added. Sabbatina was staring at me and I had to think very quickly. 'When I told her sisters she had disappeared they wanted very much to know all that they could of her last days here. To hear all about her that could be told.'

'Her last days?' said Sabbatina, drawing back. 'You make it sound as though she's . . . dead.' This was true and had not occurred to me until I ran over the words again in my mind. I changed the subject swiftly.

'So, what can I tell your father if I see him, Sabbatina? Are you keeping busy and doing all your schoolwork? Are you finding time for your hobbies? One can't work all the time.'

'Tell him I am very well,' Sabbatina said. 'Working hard and keeping up with my sewing. I'm stitching a bedspread, Miss Gilver. For my bottom drawer. My mother chose the material and I chose the pattern. I've been stitching it since I was twelve. If I go to university I will have to put it in a chest, in mothballs, but I still work on it a little every day.'

'I think,' I said to Alec later on the telephone – I had to use the one in Miss Shanks's study and was listening strenuously for her dreaded return – 'I *think* she was offended at my insinuation that she wouldn't mind sneaking. Or she was offended that I made the slightest, most heavily veiled hint about her family's current misfortune. Anyway, she put me in my place.'

'Did you insinuate?' Alec said. 'Did you hint? And why are you whispering?'

'Just typical,' I said. 'The mistresses' room has been deserted all day – forcing me to grill little girls for scraps of gossip – I probably did, you know: hint and insinuate – but now when I want to use the telephone they're all in there playing cards and having a whale of a time, so I've had to sneak into the head's study and if she catches me I'll be for it.'

'You seem to be making it all very complicated,' Alec said.

'I don't know who to ask or what to ask them or where to turn,' I moaned down the line to him. 'How did you get on?'

'Oh, it was all very straightforward and out in the open,' said Alec. 'I found out from Joe who all Rosa's customers were and went round them, asking if they had any clue where she might have gone. Did they know of anyone else who was missing, had they seen anyone suspicious hanging around; in short, I've started a bit of a panic that there is a lunatic at large snatching women and making off with them.'

'Marvellous,' I said. 'Good work.'

'And I stopped in at all the farms – well, both the farms – and all the cottages on the way to Dunskey Castle, and asked if anyone had seen or heard anything in the first half of the week.'

'And?'

'And was obliged to eat tea four times, one after the other. Not bad in the first farm – Portree – thin bread and butter and warm scones, but cottagers' teas are meant for men who're herding sheep and building dykes. Solid, don't you know.'

'But did you learn anything?' I asked. 'I could be obliged to ring off any minute, Alec. Stop wittering on.'

'At the first of the two farms and at all of the cottages – nothing,' said Alec. 'Except how little apple and how much pie can make an apple pie for working men.'

'And at the second of the two farms?' I asked, suppressing a sigh. 'I take it all of that was by way of an introduction.'

'At the second of the two farms – Low Merrick – I was set upon by dogs.'

I snorted.

'Serve you right,' I said. 'Barging into a farmyard. Some of these sheep farmers are absolute hermits, you know. You're lucky it was one lot of dogs and four teas, not the other way around.'

'But it wasn't a hermitage,' Alec said. 'There's a painted sign at the gate proclaiming bed and breakfast. Sea views and home-cooking. But when I marched up the drive and hallooed, someone – I saw her arm and hand quite clearly – opened a door and shooed out a pack of dogs to see me off.'

'A pack of dogs,' I repeated.

'Three collies,' Alec admitted, 'but those mean little skinny ones, with teeth like ice picks. I had to vault a gate. No joke after the pie. And moments later a bobby turned up to arrest me.'

'For what?' I cried. 'There's no law of trespass in Scotland.'

'Well, with hindsight, I suppose, a strange man – me – going about the quiet country lanes asking if there's a strange man going about does become a bit of a self-fulfilling prophecy. Whoever she was with the dogs at Low Merrick had rung the police too.'

'Oh my God, Alec,' I said. 'What a pair we make!'

'Thankfully, it was Constable Reid,' Alec said. 'He went back on duty at six. So, I wasn't clapped in irons but I don't feel covered with glory.'

'You poor darling,' I said, laughing.

'This would be Mr Osborne, I take it,' came Miss Shanks's voice from the doorway. I had forgotten to listen and, laughing with Alec, had not heard her come in.

'Headmistress!' I said. 'I apol—'

'Oh, no need, no need,' said Miss Shanks. She sat down in the supplicant's chair in front of her desk as though unconcerned that I was sitting in her place behind it. 'Maybe *ask* another time, but don't be sorry. And what ails Mr Osborne that makes you pity him so?'

'Oh, nothing,' I said. I was still dumbly hanging on to the earpiece and could hear Alec's careful breathing while he listened to this odd exchange. 'Just nonsense, really. We're old friends and nonsense is our habit, I'm afraid to say. I shall be much more solemn in the classroom with the girls.'

'Ocht away,' said Miss Shanks. 'The girls could do with a wee bit cheering up in the English classroom. Young Miss Lipscott was solemn enough for us all.'

7

My joy was unconstrained on learning that, while dining with the girls was a daily duty, breakfasting with them was confined to Sundays. On this Monday morning the other mistresses and I were to be served porridge, eggs and bacon – or in my case coffee and rolls – in a little breakfast room off the staff common room. Even better was the realisation that Miss Shanks was not amongst our number.

'Oh, try dragging Shanks away from her girls in the morning!' said little Miss Christopher, looking more mole-like than ever this morning in a dark-grey coat and skirt of velvety nap.

'Well, I suppose that's when any new sore throats and dicky tummies are most to the fore,' said Miss Lovage, with a delighted nastiness I could neither put my finger on nor ignore. I stared as she raked back her black and white hair with a ringed hand, then I exchanged a look with Miss Glennie, who seemed just as puzzled as I .

'You see, Miss Ivy Shanks wasn't always a headmistress,' Miss Lovage continued.

'But she's a fine headmistress now,' said Miss Barclay, and set to buttering her toast so ferociously she all but tore it into rags. Her voice was clipped, her lips pursed, even her head of tight curls seemed tighter than before.

'And,' said Miss Christopher, 'since it was your own dear Miss Fielding who elevated her I wonder at your sneering.'

'I don't sneer,' said Miss Lovage, looking down her aquiline nose and curling her top lip, and so unfortunately producing a sneer which could have stood as the very definition in a pictorial dictionary.

'What Miss Lovage is hinting at,' said Miss Barclay, now trying to patch her toast back together again with globs of marmalade, 'is the fact that when Miss Fielding and Miss Shanks, as colleagues, first conceived of their own school, Fielding was Latin mistress and Miss Shanks was on the less academic side of things.'

'Miss Shanks was under-matron,' Miss Lovage snapped. 'Less academic indeed!'

'A matron?' I said, and once again caught Miss Glennie's eye. She was no less surprised than I but, unlike me, she was trying not to look so.

'And Mrs Brown was the cook,' said Miss Lovage. 'I'm only surprised she hasn't stepped into Miss Fielding's shoes to fill the vacancy.'

'Dear Miss Fielding,' said Miss Barclay, attempting a honeyed tone but failing rather miserably at it owing to her clenched teeth, 'had a vision. For the girls' education, of course, but not only that. She believed that good food and good healthy habits were just as important as what they learned in the classroom. It was absolutely her conviction that a matron was as important as a Latin mistress.'

'And she believed in seeing the good in everyone,' added Miss Christopher. 'We should all remember that without Miss Fielding none of us would be here.'

'It's . . . um . . . wonderful that the school is thriving without her,' I said. 'If she was— I mean *given* that she was such a visionary. One could easily assume that her loss would change things.'

'Oh, things have changed,' said Miss Lovage. 'Things have certainly changed. I'm not sure I should as readily have sunk my savings into a school run by a cook and a matron.'

I thought then about what Hugh had said, on the subject of single women and what they did with their money. It was interesting that Miss Lovage was more than just the art mistress here.

'But Miss Shanks sees the good in people too.' It was the first time Miss Glennie had spoken, and she did so with a tremor in her voice. 'I mean, I think Miss Fielding sounds wonderful but it's Miss Shanks I have to thank for *my* being here.'

'My investment in St Columba's was considerable,' said Miss Lovage, clearly disliking to hear the absent Miss Shanks given all the gratitude.

'You sound as if you're suddenly regretting it, Anna,' said Miss Barclay. 'We don't normally hear you casting it up to the rest of us.' There was a warning note in her voice that I could not interpret.

'It's just gone a bit far, that's all,' said Miss Lovage. 'Double duties here, an obliging vicar there and . . . well, agency staff.' She gave Miss Glennie and me an unconvincing smile as she thus disparaged us. 'Miss Lipscott was a scholar and a lady, and Mademoiselle Beauclerc was teaching the girls true Parisian French. And they both understood the artistic life. Without them, and without Miss Fielding, what does St Columba's have to offer?'

Several of us took in a sharp breath at that. Miss Barclay expelled hers in a speech, delivered with great control, through white lips.

'Geography and mathematics, to name two things,' she said. 'And art.'

'Good gracious, Dorothy,' said Miss Lovage. 'I didn't mean the girls! Who cares about the wretched girls – they'll all just go off and get married anyway. I meant what does St Columba's have to offer *me*?'

There was a stony silence after this remark, which gathered weight until it threatened to crush us. Miss Barclay, once again, got her wits about her first and broke it.

'Let's change the subject,' she said. She did not, however, offer a subject to take up and the blanket of silence settled back down over us, except for the sound of Miss Christopher doggedly crunching on a rasher of very crisp bacon.

'Well,' I said at last, 'not exactly a cheerful topic, but I'd like to ask you all to tell me what you can about Fleur Lipscott's last few days here.' I was aware of all eyes upon me but I looked unconcernedly out of the opposite window and sailed on. 'It's not nosiness – I know how much that offends at least Miss Lovage – it's just that when I told her sisters she'd bolted they badgered me and badgered me for some explanation or assurance and I promised I would try to find something out for them.'

All of them, Miss Barclay behind her little glasses, Miss Christopher under her bushy brows, Miss Lovage inside her rings of black pencil, and Miss Glennie whose eyes were unadorned and so lashless and browless in that fair Scottish way as to make her face appear naked, all of them simply stared at me.

'Explanation of what on earth was wrong,' I went on, 'or assurance that nothing was, but they can't simply leave it as a mystery, shrug and pass on. She's their beloved baby sister and if they don't get some answers they're likely to land here demanding them. They're very worried about her. Taking off like that.'

'Her sisters?' said Miss Lovage. 'News to me she *had* sisters.'

'And didn't she go home?' said Miss Barclay. 'To take care of some sick relation?'

'I think these "sisters" are pulling your leg, Miss Gilver,' said Miss Christopher.

It was my turn now to stare around at them. Even the girls hadn't swallowed the stories of one sick relation after another; surely the mistresses did not really believe it?

'She was fine,' said Miss Barclay. 'Just the same as ever.'

'But can you be sure?' I asked. 'You all seem to spend such a lot of time alone in your rooms. Would you know?'

'We saw Miss Lipscott at every meal, and she was in her classroom all day every day,' said Miss Barclay. 'She was quite fine.'

'And what about the evenings?' I asked. 'Did you see her then? Did she sit in the staffroom with you?'

'We are very busy women,' said Miss Christopher. 'We sit in the staffroom when we can but we all have work to do. And none of us nursemaids the rest.' She had rolled up a piece of bread into a sort of pad and now proceeded to wipe the egg yolk and bacon fat from her plate with it. She popped the little piece of bread into her mouth and chewed it resolutely. When she had swallowed she washed it down with a swig of tea. She really did have the worst table manners I could remember seeing.

'Have you considered, Miss Gilver,' she went on, 'that Miss Lipscott's sisters are simply stringing you along? They knew what she was and how she lived, but they would rather *not* know, and so they wring their hands and call her their baby sister and ask – wide-eyed – for explanations.'

'What *can* you mean?' I said. She was spot-on about Pearl and Aurora's habit of singing tra-la-la and looking the other way rather than face troubling facts head-on, but I was lost as to specifics.

'Miss Lipscott was a funny one, and getting funnier,' said Miss Christopher. 'A great wanderer in the night, always taking off on solitary walks, never wanting any company, never saying where she was going or where she'd been. And so relentlessly gloomy! An oddball and no loss. Tell her precious sisters that.'

'Wandering in the night?' I said. 'You mean sleepwalking?'

'I mean slipping out after supper and hoping no one noticed,' said Miss Christopher. She had a particular way of drawing her double chin back into her neck and turning her mouth down at the corners. It was impressive as a means of conveying disapproval, but if she had ever seen it in her mirror she would not have done it again.

'And yet Miss Fielding and Miss Shanks had no concerns about her with the girls?' I said. 'She sounds not to be a suitable example to them at all.'

'We told you what a collector of lame ducks Miss Fielding was,' said Miss Barclay.

'Speak for yourself, Dorothy!' said Miss Christopher, chuckling again. Miss Barclay, realising what she had said, tittered too. Miss Lovage merely looked pained, and Miss Glennie did a fair impersonation of someone who has looked out of a train window, realised that she was hurtling along the wrong line and was plotting how soon she could get off again.

Miss Christopher wiped her lips and glanced at her wristwatch.

'Well, ladies,' she said. 'As you know, I like to have a good hour to myself before the lesson bell so I'll bid you all good morning.' She dropped her napkin onto her plate – not the discourtesy to the laundry maid it might have been had she not wiped up so assiduously with that piece of bread – and left the room.

'What time do lessons start then?' said Miss Glennie.

'Nine thirty sharp,' said Miss Barclay.

'As late as that!' Miss Glennie said before she could help herself, then she bit her lip and gave an awkward smile. It is never the done thing for a new girl to find fault with established routine, I supposed. Secretly, though, I agreed with her. Leaving the girls lolling around aimless until half past nine in the morning seemed rather decadent (and all of a piece with the heated pool and the cocoa). Still, it gave me time to do something useful beforehand.

All was quiet at the little wooden shack on the harbourside, the door locked, the blind drawn down and a cardboard sign proclaiming that not until noon would Aldo's be open again. I stepped around the side and threaded my way along the narrow alley, then I let myself in at the gate to the yard. If Joe was going to serve fried fish and chips to the masses at noon he would be here already, peeling his potatoes and stirring his batter mixture.

Sure enough, when I squinted in the back door, which was standing open and unobscured by any washing today, I could see him on his stool with the pail at his feet and the knife in his hand, but he was stock still.

'Mr Aldo?' I said, stepping inside. He started violently, sending the bucket of water whirling across the floor.

'Sorry!' I burst out, flailing after the pail and getting fairly well soaked for my trouble.

'I sorry,' said Joe. 'I lost in my thoughts today.'

I set the pail down firmly on the linoleum again and brushed the worst of the water from the front of my skirt.

'Sit,' said Joe. 'Good to see you. Very lonely here since Friday.'

'Yes, well, that's what I came about really,' I said. 'I spoke to Sabbatina. She's lonely too. Very unhappy. I think it would do her good to come down the hill and spend some time with you.'

'Sabbatina is lonely?' said Joe. 'Up in her school with all her friends?'

Only a fiend would have told him about the little space between his daughter and the other eleven girls at her dinner table.

'Well, sad, anyway,' I said. 'I know what you said about her staying away in case your wife came home again, but now that she knows she needs her father's comfort. You could comfort one another, couldn't you?'

'Sabbatina knows?' he said.

'I thought you told her.' I could see from his expression though that I was mistaken. 'Yes, she knows. Perhaps her mother telephoned to the school as well as to you?'

Joe stared at me for a long time before answering.

'Perhaps,' he said. He was nodding slowly and I very much hoped that he was not about to start bawling again.

'I wish my wife not leave me,' he said at last. 'I wish *I* saw her and her man friend that night when she go walking. I and not this stranger. I knock his head from his neck. I kick him over ten fields with my boot and then my wife is still here with me and my *carissima* Sabbatina not sad like now.'

It was my turn for silent nodding. He was beginning to whip himself up and I did not know how to stop him.

'Did he even try? This one who watches and sees and says nothing to me? Did he say, "Signora Aldo, why are you here with that man who is not the good Giuseppe?" Hah? No! Why he not speak up – one man for another man? Or why he not come to me and tell me – one man to another man?'

'Ah,' I said. 'It wasn't a man. It was a girl.'

'Hmph!' said Joe, emphatically if perplexingly. 'So. A girl. A bad girl to be walking outside when the night is dark, no? And a bad wicked girl who will come in here and laugh at me with her friends.'

'I don't think so, Mr Aldo,' I said. 'She's a nice sort of girl, really, despite the walks. She works for the police sergeant's wife and the boy she does the walking with is the constable. Couldn't be more respectable, really.'

'Hmph,' said Joe again. Then he cocked his head. 'Here is come my potatoes,' he said and as he spoke a boy in an apron appeared in the yard, struggling under the weight of a sack which looked to be full of pig-iron from its lumpy shape and the trouble he was having with it.

'There ye go, Mr Aldo,' he said, letting the sack drop onto the kitchen floor and straightening. 'One or two wee tatties for ye!' He stretched his neck first to one side and then to the other and wiped his nose with the back of his hand. Joe Aldo leapt to his feet and pressed a coin into the other hand, thanking the boy.

'Same again tomorrow?' the lad said.

'No, no, I come to the market tomorrow, same as for ever,' said Joe.

The boy looked rather crestfallen but then rubbed the coin on his shirtsleeve and flipped it up in the air with a grin.

'Better'n a poke in the eye,' he said and left, whistling.

'I made arrangement on Saturday morning,' said Joe. 'Delivery. Save me go to market in case Rosa come home and I gone. I forget to change. But now she gone and she not come home . . .'

'Life goes on, Mr Aldo,' I said. He was untying the neck of the potato sack but he turned and smiled at me, a smile with enough courage and sadness in it to melt my heart a little. 'You have your daughter and your cooking and believe me, there are many men who would be happy these days to have such a solid little business as this one.'

'I do fine here. Many people come. Not all the people, but enough.'

I thought about the throngs who had been there at luncheon time on Saturday and wondered at his mild grumbling. But then I supposed a real businessman would not be satisfied unless everyone in the town ate his dinner from Aldo's every evening and I had, it was true, heard more than one say they never went near the place.

'And I look out of my window at the beautiful sea and the sky and the green grass,' said Joe. 'I am a lucky man.'

'It's wonderful to hear you speak that way,' I said. 'To hear you a little more cheerful.'

'What business is your husband?' said Mr Aldo. 'You married lady, eh, *bellissima*? No way men not fight other men to make you married lady, eh?'

I willed myself not to simper, although it is hard to resist when a man with dancing black eyes and a smile as wide as the sea calls one '*bellissima*'. (For some reason, flirting in an Italian accent did not excite the outrage I should have felt had my admirer been the catcher of the fish, or digger of the potatoes, rather than the fryer of them.)

'He's a farmer,' I said, for this was what Hugh always said these days, now that his earlier answer (to wit: 'gentleman') was wont to meet with resentful glares or out-and-out guffaws.

'Ohhh,' said Joe Aldo. 'And he no mind you . . . detective, and not feed chickens and milk cows.' I was sure he was teasing, but it was impossible to take offence at him.

'Not at all,' I said.

'And you no want him help you . . . finger smudges and clues?'

'He is an excellent farmer,' I said. 'And I am an excellent detective. We're both happy this way.'

He straightened and gave me a more serious and very searching look.

'You happy,' he said. 'Good. *Bellissima signora* should be happy. I happy for *you*.'

A deaf dowager in her nineties would have blushed at that and I did not even try to disguise it. Indeed, my pink cheeks seemed to make him happier than ever.

'Well, I hope I shan't make you cross with me when I say this,' I said. 'Mr Osborne and I can't, in all fairness, keep searching for your wife now that we know she is alive and well. There's the body, for one thing.' He crossed himself and uttered a short prayer. 'And things are dreadful up at the school, with all the mistresses leaving and no one knowing why. We really can do much more good there than we can do for you.'

'Yes, yes, yes,' said Joe, some of his old spirit returning. 'You go – excellent and so charming detective – and your Mr Osborne too. I thank you.'

'I'm so glad you understand,' I said.

'Sì, sì,' said Joe. 'Rosa is gone – my heart is to break – but the poor dead lady need you and the ladies in the school too. Not my Rosa and me.'

I left then but could not help looking behind me with a fond smile at the place as I strolled back along the harbourside towards the town.

'Hoi! Dandy!' said Alec, leaning out of his bedroom window at the Crown. He was in his shirtsleeves and his hair was still slicked back wet from his bath. 'You look as if you've been walking in a bluebell wood with your true love,' he shouted down as I got closer.

'Alec, shut up, for heaven's sake,' I said. All around us people were turning to see what such a thing would look like and I hunched my neck down into my coat collar to avoid their gaze.

'Come up,' said Alec. At the next window along I saw the curtain move and was sure that the shadow there was the convalescent widow. Hands fussed their way out from behind the lace and brought the sash down with a sharp rap into its frame.

'Certainly not,' I said. 'Apart from anything else, if that was the quarter chiming then I need to hurry up to the school for the start of lessons. Come down and walk with me.'

He was at my side in less than a minute (oh, to have a man's toilet instead of my own, even with bobbed hair and zip fasteners and Grant to mix the lash-black), determined to solve the riddle of my shining eyes and the small smile I could not quite persuade to leave my lips.

'I went to see Joe to tell him we can't keep looking for Rosa,' I said.

'I'd have done that,' said Alec, handing me up the first and steepest of the cliff steps.

'I wanted to tell him how unhappy Sabbatina is too,' I said. 'Oof! Thank you, I'm all right on my own from here. She found out about her mother leaving and she's in low spirits.'

'Doesn't sound too enchanting so far,' said Alec. 'Why the bounce in your step and the broad grin?'

'Oh, too silly for words, but Giuseppe Aldo is such a flirt and I suppose I'm not quite beyond being flattered by it yet.'

'Not a flirt, Dandy,' said Alec. 'A charmer, I'd say. Don't forget how he had *me* hugging him in the street after a day's acquaintance. You have nothing to berate yourself with for being taken in.'

'Ah well,' I said. 'I daresay he won't be alone for long then. Any of the women round here who're used to fish guts and monosyllables might be happy to try hot fat and sweet nothings.'

'If he can pry his heart away from Rosa, anyway,' Alec said. 'But he might pine for ever.'

'Nonsense,' I said. 'His spirits are lifting already. He was talking about Sabbatina and the sunshine and sea breezes when I left him. I'm sure he does love his wife with that heaving Latin heart of his, but he's an India rubber ball and he'll bob back to the surface.'

'Anyway, thanks to you cutting the ties he is no longer our problem,' Alec said. 'So I feel no compunction in sloping off on the 10.05.'

'Sloping where?' I said. 'To do what?'

'Did you know that scholastic agencies open at eight o'clock in the morning?' he replied. 'And of course newspaper offices keep notoriously early hours, worse than bakers. I've done a day's work already. Oh, thank God!' We had reached the top of the cliff steps and come out on level ground. 'Twenty past nine, Dandy, let's sit a minute while I brief you. And I must say the revelations of life in a girls' school go on – nine thirty?'

'Oh, I know,' I said. 'I thought they'd be knee-deep in slide rules and conjugations by this time too. Anyway, the sloping?'

'North Yorkshire,' said Alec. 'It's a devil of a journey too unless

I catch this first train to Dumfries and hope for a tail wind. A very tight connection in Carlisle.'

I sighed and waited.

'Yes,' Alec said. 'Right. The Lambourne Agency popped Miss Blair's name right out as soon as I mentioned girls and cricket and apparently she's working at an establishment by the name of The Bridge House School for Young Ladies, which is somewhere out in the middle of the moors north of Pickering.'

'The agency just told you where she was?' I said. 'To help you poach her?'

'Well, she's none too happy about the moor, it seems,' said Alec. 'So she's still on the books, as it were. Anyway, north of Pickering, Dan. Not ringing any bells for you?'

I shook my head.

'The Forresters' house is less than twenty miles away.'

'Of course!' I said.

'And since Elf was a cousin of theirs, I think there's bound to be some leavening of the Lipscott loyalty with a little Forrester loyalty. Not to say in Aurora – but perhaps her husband? So I thought I'd stop in on them under some pretext or other and see what I can find out.'

'And you don't fear more dogs? Either at the school or the Forresters'?'

Alec laughed.

'I'd put on moleskin britches if I had them,' he said. 'But I told you yesterday, the farmer's wife actually *set* those dogs on me. I've never been snubbed by a dog of its own free will in my life. Plenty of cats, naturally, but dogs love me.'

'Strange way to offer bed and breakfast,' I said, then shook the thought away. 'What do you hope to learn from the Forresters anyway?'

'Well, the newspaper reports were very sketchy. Accidental death. Nothing to say whether he shot himself cleaning a gun or came off his horse crossing a ditch or anything.'

'How very odd. Go for Mrs Forrester senior,' I said. 'She's

always rather disapproved of Aurora and if you work up the current scandal with Fleur you might well loosen her tongue.'

'And what would you suggest as a method?' Alec said. 'Moral high ground? Flirting? Like Joe?' He gave me a sly look, still teasing.

'God, no,' I said. 'Fenella Forrester is a formidable woman of the old school – absolutely no nonsense about her. If I had to get her talking I'd go along the . . . good plain commonsensical route.' Alec looked puzzled. 'You know: it's all a bit of a mess and too silly for words so we'd better tidy it up before someone trips and turns an ankle.'

'I'm not sure I can pull that off,' Alec said. 'Not sure any man could.'

'I shall treat that as a compliment to my sex,' I said. 'No doubt wrongly. Also, if you do get hold of Aurora – and she's a much better bet than Pearl, which is probably why it's been Pearl who was delegated to speak to us; Aurora's far from bright and there-fore easier to winkle things out of – you should use a modified version of the same thing. All too silly and let's get it straightened out for poor Fleur.'

'And there's no way on earth I can pull off *that* one,' Alec said. 'Really, Dandy, I was feeling tiptop and all go until you started helping. Now I doubt whether it's worth the train fare.'

'Well, *I'm* not going,' I said, standing up and pummelling myself where I had been resting against the numbing stone of the parapet. 'I've got the third form for *Tam o'Shanter* any min—' I was inter-rupted by the clang of the lesson bell and immediately upon it came the now familiar sound of girls' feet tramping and girls' voices clamouring. 'And someone in this place must know some-thing about why the mistresses are scattering to the four winds and be willing to tell me.'

'Not to worry,' said Alec. 'I'm sure Miss Blair will have no hesitation in telling *me*.' With that he and I both sprang from our marks and set out to learn more and faster than the other, thinking only of winning and crowing and not at all of poor Fleur or No. 5 or any of the vanishing mistresses or putative murders.

One wonders at times whether this constant – or at any rate, frequent – immersion in crime and brutality is good for one. I was thankful that my two boys were going to be 'farmers' like their father and that neither of them would follow in my footsteps, for even amongst the constabulary of Portpatrick I could trace the path downwards from the open heart and clear head of a Constable Reid to the hard-bitten mien and flinty soul of a Sergeant Turner. Perhaps, I mused to myself as I followed the corridor to Fleur's classroom, here was the explanation for the nature of the sergeant which had always puzzled me: quite simply, it was the low point on the journey through the heart of darkness, inspectors having survived it and emerged on the other side and the lowly ranks having not yet reached its black depths.

I swung into the English classroom and saw twelve little girls staring down a heart of darkness all of their own. Twelve copies of Chaucer were open on their desks and twelve pairs of eyes looked lifelessly up from them as I entered.

'Good morning,' I said. 'Now—' but I had forgotten to leave time for the answering chorus, slow as a dirge.

'Good morning, Miss Gilver.'

'Yes, quite, thank you. Now, girls, close your books, please, and pass them along to the ends. We're having a change.' I swept into the book cupboard with the not inconsiderable pile of *Complete Works of Geoffrey Chaucer* and emerged again with the much more modest pile of *Complete Works of Robert Burns*. I suppose had he lived to see forty he might have run to a thicker volume, but I could not help but attribute my lighter load at that moment to his bonny nature rather than his sickly lungs.

'Open up to page one hundred and forty-three, please, girls,' I said. 'And . . . you there. Start reading.'

'Marion, Miss Gilver,' said the child I had picked upon. She fluttered the pages and stood up, clearing her throat.

'*Tam o'Shanter*,' she announced. 'When chapman . . .' She put her finger on the page and looked up. 'What does *chapman* mean, Miss Gilver?'

'An excellent question, Marion,' I replied. 'Does anyone know?'

There were blank looks all around. 'And what do we do if there's a word we don't know?' I continued, riffling hastily to the back of the book to check. 'We look it up in the Glossary, don't we? Look it up in the Glossary, Marion.' Not only did she but so did the rest of them, keen little scholars all, and the turning pages caused a breeze for a moment until they all found what they were looking for and their arms started to wave like ears of wheat. I nodded towards the nearest waving arm.

'Pedlar, Miss Gilver,' called out the child, as she shot to her feet and sank back down again. I could see that this off-the-cuff translation of Burns' Scots was going to be a good dose of healthy exercise for their arms and legs as well as their tongues and brains.

'Good girl,' I said.

'When chapman billies fill the street,' Marion resumed. 'And drouthy . . .'

The pages were fluttering again.

'Thirsty, Miss Gilver.'

'Splendid.'

'. . . neighbours neighbours meet.'

If this were all there was to it, I thought to myself, sitting back and almost enjoying the halting recital and the punctuating translations, then I was a marvellous teacher.

I thought too that I agreed with Giuseppe Aldo about his daughter's talents and not at all with Miss Shanks's dismissal of them, for when it came time for Sabbatina to stand and recite, she did so in a clear and pleasing voice and showed in her phrasing that she understood exactly what the words conveyed (unlike some of the girls who rumty-tummed their way through the lines regardless of their meaning). I was a little unsettled by hearing her describe Tam and the married landlady of the inn sharing their 'secret, sweet and precious favours', unable not to think of her mother and the nameless suitor who had charmed her away from her husband and home, dreading to hear one of the other girls whisper or giggle behind her hand. But either none of Sabbatina's classmates knew of the scandal, or they were too innocent to draw the grubby connection which sprang to my mind. Or, I allowed myself to think, they were too enthralled by the exciting material so skilfully chosen by their new favourite mistress.

By morning coffee time, however, when the girls went outside to run around for ten minutes, I was back on solid ground with my heels still ringing from how hard I had hit it. For the fifth form were lolling in a haystack with Piers Plowman as he dreamed one of his unfathomable dreams and while, to the casual glance, it was less terrifying than Tam's escapade with the ghosties and ghoulies it struck terror into me, for I knew not how to pronounce it, parse it, gloss it, or imagine what examination questions might have been set upon it or how in heaven I was ever to mark the answers to them.

'Um,' I had said in desperation, 'translate the next thirty lines, girls.'

'*Thirty*, Miss Gilver?' they had groaned as one.

I glanced at the gobbledygook stretching down the page.

'All right, twenty,' I said. 'And keep very quiet, on your honour, please. I've just got to slip out and see Miss Shanks about something.'

Thankfully she was not out on the cliff in her underclothes leading a class in callisthenics, or marking worn linen in a cupboard somewhere – I had not forgotten that she was a matron at heart (indeed, perhaps it explained why she was such a very peculiar headmistress, in a way) – but was sitting quietly in her study with fat ledgers open before her.

'Fielding always used to take care of the accounts,' she said, slamming a ledger shut with a sharp smack and a puff of dust. 'It's Greek to me.'

'School Certificate papers, Miss Shanks,' I said. 'I shall need to have a look at them if I'm to know what the girls should be swotting up – I mean, studying. And if I'm to be quite sure that I'm all set to mark them too.' I tried to make this second consideration sound very airy.

'Of course, of course,' said Miss Shanks. She stood and went over to a picture on her wall – an unfeasibly highly coloured print of cattle standing knee deep in a loch with glowering mountains behind them – unhooked it and set about opening the safe it was hiding with the largest of the bristling bunch of keys she wore at her belt.

'Now then, now then,' she said, stirring the papers inside the safe's modest chamber with perfect unconcern for their disarrangement. 'School Cert English . . .' She plucked a pale green sheet from amongst the mess she had made. 'And you might as well take the Higher Cert paper too, while you're at it.' A pale pink sheet joined the other. 'Bob's your uncle and Fanny's your aunt.' She lifted a knee to stop a small pile of letters from cascading out of the safe door onto the floor and managed to pin two or three to the wall. I shot forward and retrieved the rest. I shuffled them back into a bundle and exchanged them for the exam papers. Miss Shanks grinned at me, threw the letters back inside and closed the safe door with a clang.

'And when do you need the papers for the other forms?' I said.

'Oh, there's a whiley yet,' said Miss Shanks. 'Exams start in late June – along with the hay fever, you know. If we leave the doors open to the rose gardens half the wee souls have sneezing fits and if we shut them there's always one or two take to fainting. The examination hall was a ballroom, you know; faces due south, and was never meant to be used during the day.'

'Well, I'd better get back to my girls,' I said. 'Thank you for the papers. I assure you I'll keep them very safe and return them very soon.'

'Och, hang on to them if it'll help,' said Miss Shanks. 'I'm sure I can trust you with a wee question paper or two, Miss Gilver.' She gave me quite the most twinkling, glittering look I had yet seen from amongst her collection. 'Oh, and while we're on the fifth form – I want you to keep an eye on Clothilde Simmons. She seems a very bright girl. Might be worth some extra tutoring.'

'Has she just joined the school?' I said, puzzled as to how a girl could have reached the fifth form and only now be tapped as a scholar.

'No, she's been with us since she was an eleven-year-old with scraped knees and a lollipop,' Miss Shanks said. 'She's been hiding her light under a bushel, that's all. Naughty child!'

When I took in the jotters at the end of the hour I paid particular note to that of Clothilde Simmons, but could not see in the laboured and much rubbed-out and rewritten translation – all fifteen lines of it, since Clothilde was one of the handful who did not make it through to the end – any particular glow of brilliance. And leafing back through the pages that Fleur had marked I saw a great deal of red pencil and a progression of solid Bs and Cs. Perhaps she was a whizz at chemistry or something quite removed from English literature, hence Miss Shanks's prod about the coaching to round her out and tempt a university to give her a place there.

Piers Plowman, happily, was the low tide of that long first day. After lunch the lower sixth took to *Macbeth* with an almost unseemly relish, begging and pleading to be the witches, auditioning from their seats with much cackling and hunching of their lithe young forms into the twisted shapes of crones over a cauldron. Needless to say, *Rob Roy* was greeted by the second form like the Young Pretender arriving from across the sea: one girl threw *Silas Marner* into the air and shouted hurrah at the news that she need not read another word of it, and only the fact that she caught the book again, firmly, by its cloth covers and did not so much as crease a page saved me from delivering a lecture about the sanctity of the printed word in general and school property in particular.

Still, by the time three o'clock came – for such was the surprisingly early hour at which the St Columba's girls broke off from their short day of study and flooded back out into the grounds to take up their extra-curricular lolling – my head was awash with new names and old stories and my ears rang with piping voices clamouring 'Miss Gilver, Miss Gilver' so that the only thing for it was to take myself off all alone into the sea air and try to walk myself back to my own quiet thoughts and some semblance of tranquillity.

Besides, I had still not seen the cliff top along which Rosa Aldo, her fancy man, Cissie and Willie all had strolled on that fateful evening and from which Constable Reid was so sure No. 5 had tumbled, the cliff top which also led to Low Merrick Farm and the inhospitable farmer's wife who lived there. I was not sure I could summon the courage to follow Alec up its drive – for I, unlike him, could not vault a gate at a pinch – nor was I so conceited as to think I might find a clue at the castle that others had missed, but I could not help looking carefully at my feet and around the gorse and grass as I went along, with the ruin in view and the sound of the wheeling gulls replacing the girls' voices with their even more insistent cries.

Of course, there was nothing to be found: cigarette ends and flattened places in what Cissie had called 'the dips', corroborating her tale of courting couples holing up there; a few scuffed patches at the edge of the path which might have been places where someone lost her footing and fell, but might have been a hundred other things besides, and all more likely. There were no broken gorse branches where a murderer might have crouched, uncomfortably but discreetly, until a victim appeared; and there was nothing of any interest stashed anywhere either, just endless discarded sweet wrappers and matches, orange peels and apple cores as well as the grubby flags of wool which accumulate wherever sheep and gorse share a breezy headland and the equal weight (it always seems to me) of string and twine and sacking which farmers shed like snake skins in the course of their day.

At Dunskey Castle, I sheltered from the wind long enough to add my budget of match and cigarette end to the trove and then contemplated the journey back again. As is so often the case (but not often enough to inure one to the shock of it), turning around and facing the other way put the sun painfully in my eyes instead of comfortingly at my back. It set the wind against me too, making my nose run and my eyes water; gusting behind me, it had seemed a pleasant helping hand, urging me along. I sniffed, pulled my hat down harder over my forehead and looked about myself. There was Low Merrick Farm, a few fields over, just beyond a little railway bridge, and I knew that where there is a railway bridge (not to mention a farm) there must be a road. I had no desire, anyway, to scramble back over the tracks as I had had to do on my outward journey; although the trains, as Alec attested, were slow and few, the average passenger's wishes regarding speed and frequency are not those of a trespasser upon the lines and Hugh would never forgive me for being killed in such an unnecessary and bothersome (to the railway company) fashion. His sympathies whenever he heard of a body – be it human or bovine – falling onto a line were always firmly with the upset driver and delayed travellers, and there was nothing to spare for the flattened departed.

On the other hand, I had no particular desire to encounter the pack of ravening collies, but the prospect which *did* entice me was that of announcing to Alec that I had done so. I suppose, too, that a small part of me did not quite believe the tale of the mysterious arm and hand and the advance of the beasts. It sounded quite unlike sheepdogs, farmers' wives and in particular anyone who offered home cooking to paying guests.

I was decided, and set off across the sheep-cropped turf to the first of the gates with a swing in my step which belied the way my heart was thudding.

The first of the gates had latches and hinges, despite its share of barbed wire, and the second had hinges and not too nasty a knot holding it closed, so I made it to the last one without having to climb or wriggle. This, however, was a beast of a thing, tied in three places with baling twine and leaning into the field at an alarming angle. I studied it. And while I stood there, I saw something move from the corner of my eye. A dark figure was flitting up the farmhouse garden, racing towards the house. It disappeared around the corner leading to the yard and I heard a door bang. Sure that I was safe from the dogs, for no farmer's wife alive would let them into her garden, I squeezed through the gap between the gatepost and the wall and crept closer. She had been hanging out washing; a basket of linen sat in the middle of the patch of grass and a pair of underdrawers hung by one leg where she had abandoned them. Rather a splendid garment for a sheep farmer's wife, I thought, studying the satin waist-tape and the lace trim. And next to them on the line . . . I blinked.

'Never,' I said out loud. 'Preposterous.'

For next along the clothes line to the splendid underdrawers was a bandeau brassiere in the same white linen with straps of the same satin tape and no Scottish farmer's wife from Gretna Green to John o' Groats could possibly possess such a thing. Not only was it a bandeau instead of a chemise, but a bandeau of a texture and outline that was positively . . .

'Parisian,' I said, and I was over the wall and round the corner before any thought of a collie with ice-pick teeth could stop me.

'Mademoiselle Beauclerc?' I called out, banging on the door she must have gone through. '*Est-ce que vous êtes Mademoiselle Jeanne Beauclerc, la maîtresse?*' There was only silence. 'Miss Beauclerc?' I called again in an even louder voice, and this time I tried the handle. I heard the creak of a floorboard first and then saw a shadow behind the muslin of an open upstairs window.

'Who is this, please?' said a timid voice.

'A friend,' I said. 'An old friend of Fleur Lipscott and a friend of yours, too, if I can be of any assistance.'

The shadow moved again and at last she came into plain view, a pale young woman dressed in black.

'You came over the fields?' she said.

'From the headlands, yes,' I answered. 'Miss Beauclerc, *is* it you?'

'Of course,' she said. 'And you say Fleur sent you?'

'Perhaps you could come down,' I said. 'Or could I come in? I feel a bit like Romeo calling up to your window like this. It never seemed to me to be conducive to a proper discussion.'

She moved away from the window and from deep inside the house – Scotch farmhouses are extremely solid – I could hear the faint sounds of movement, receding along an upstairs passage, advancing down a staircase and then approaching a door near where I was standing. Bolts were drawn, keys turned and at last it opened.

'Where is it?' said Jeanne Beauclerc, looking past me.

'I'm sorry,' I said. 'I don't know what you mean.'

'Didn't you bring my luggage? Is Fleur bringing it? Are you coming too?'

'If I could just come in,' I said again and she drew back against the passage wall to let me enter. At the end of the passage, facing the sea view, was a sitting room of comfortable armchairs, reading lamps and low tables and from the walking guides, touring maps and picture magazines fanned out upon these tables I quickly surmised that this was the residents' lounge for Low Merrick's paying guests.

'So,' I said, perching on the arm of a chair, 'when you left St Columba's last week you came here?'

'And Fleur was supposed to pack a few things for me,' said Miss Beauclerc. 'If she could get away. But here I am with one change of linen and my toothbrush waiting and waiting and you haven't brought so much as a spare nightgown. And I can't stay here much longer.'

'Why not?' I said, puzzled by her air of grievance. Surely she did not mean to suggest that she was above the simple comforts of this pleasant farmhouse. 'Paying guests are quite the norm here, aren't they?'

She frowned and shook her hair back. She wore it in long loose curls, like a child.

'Mrs Paterson tells me she needs my room at the end of the week, for Parents' Day at the school. And they do not like keeping it secret that I am here. I shall not be sorry to go.'

'Why did you come here?' I said.

'We chose this place because it was right on the other side of the town from Miss Shanks but near enough to walk to, and very quiet. Hah! Quiet! First came the police and then a very strange young man – but I got rid of him.'

'I heard,' I said drily. 'Where are the dogs today?'

She ignored the question and the reprimand, although she had the good grace to blush a little.

'And now you!' she cried. 'What is happening?'

'Might one ask why you and Fleur were running away?' I said. 'In the middle of term, like two schoolgirls instead of two mistresses?'

'Hasn't Fleur told you?' said Miss Beauclerc, warily.

'Fleur, I'm afraid to relate, is gone,' I said. 'She left on Saturday.'

Miss Beauclerc was silent for a full minute, the blood draining from her face and her eyes widening and widening until I could see the whites all around. When she spoke again her voice was ragged.

'She left without me? She took her things and sailed away? Without me?'

'Sailed?' I echoed.

'*Oui*,' said Miss Beauclerc. 'This was our plan. We were to hire a little boat on Saturday, smuggle our things into it overnight – pretend to be ill and miss church if we needed more time – and set sail tonight on the tide. We even thought we might throw some of our clothes over the side to wash up and maybe people would think we had drowned and never look for us.'

'A boat,' I said. 'Of course.' The police had asked about trains and ferries and taxis, had even asked fishermen if they had had a passenger. They had dragged their minds into the twentieth century enough to ask at the garage if a young lady had hired a motorcar but it had never occurred to them to think that Fleur might have hoisted the mainsail of a little boat and taken herself away across the sea.

The worst of it was that, while one could forgive *them* – the police force of a small and traditional town where such modernity was unknown – I did not know how I was ever to forgive myself. I, who knew all too well of Fleur's love of boats and the sea, who had watched her playing at sailing ships in the lake and had read in Pearl's letters through the years that followed all about how marvellous Fleur had been crewing for this or that friend in some race or other. Even that summer when she was a baby of seven she had sat imperiously on her sandcastle that day at Watchet, a chicken leg in one hand and a spyglass in the other, watching the yachts out in the bay and regaling us all in her precocious way with where each crew had got its trim wrong and how differently she would have managed things if she were the skipper.

'I'd have shaved a good few minutes off that blue one's time, I can tell you,' she had said, taking her glass away from her eye and trying to spit out the mouthful of hair that had blown in before she took another bite of chicken. 'They don't have the first idea what she can do.' She tore a strip of chicken meat away from the bone with her teeth and put the glass back to her eye. 'A waste of a good wind, if you ask me.'

For the rest of the day, Aurora and Pearl took to calling her 'Cap'n Bligh' until Fleur pointed out with great dignity that Captain Bligh was a naval officer who would not have known a tiller from a teapot, and if they had to call her something of the like she thought Francis Drake was more of a sailor any day.

'Why did she go without me?' said Miss Beauclerc, bringing me out of my memories. 'And what am I to do now?'

'Well, if we're picking things over,' I said, 'why did you leave early and come to the Patersons'? If you were all set for today why did you bolt a week early?'

'I couldn't stay,' said Miss Beauclerc, not helpfully. She had bowed her head and muttered the words as though ashamed of them.

'Were you sacked?'

'No, I was not,' she said. 'I could not stay another minute in that place.'

'Yes, but why?' I said.

'How much do you know?' she asked. 'You said you are an old friend of Fleur's?'

'I know nothing about your business,' I told her. 'I don't know why Fleur left. I don't even know why Fleur *came*.'

'She came, as did I, because Miss Fielding was a wonderful, kind, compassionate and understanding person. Sadly deceived, too innocent and trusting to see what sort of woman she had fallen in with.'

'Miss Shanks,' I said.

'And so we decided to leave, Fleur and me,' said Miss Beauclerc.

'Just like Miss Blair and Miss Taylor and Miss Bell before you,' I said.

'Not the same thing at all. *They* were sacked. They were the lucky ones. We had to rip ourselves away and we knew that life would never be the same again. We did not care, we each had one true friend . . . Or I thought I did. I do not understand why she abandoned me.'

'Nor do I,' I said. 'I don't suppose I can strike a bargain with you, Miss Beauclerc. You tell me what Ivy Shanks did to you and Fleur and I'll fetch your things and arrange some mode of transport to take you away. What do you say to that?'

'I say no thank you,' said Miss Beauclerc. 'And I ask what sort of woman would bargain with me instead of just helping me.' I flushed then, for to hear it put that way was pretty shaming.

'The thing is, mademoiselle, that a woman's body washed up—'

'I know, I know,' she said. 'The policeman told Mrs Paterson, when he came. And Mrs Paterson said the man I saw off with the dogs had been talking about her to all the neighbours too.'

'And so I need to be sure that you know nothing about how she died before I could possibly think of helping you get away.'

'I?' said Miss Beauclerc. 'Why should I know anything about some poor drowned woman? I can tell you how it feels to seek that way out of life's cares, because I came close to it myself. Had it not been for Fleur *I* should have washed up somewhere with my face all nibbled and seaweed in my hair.'

'Did the police tell you that?' I said, sharply.

'They told Mrs Paterson, and she took great delight in telling me. But that is all I know and I can't understand why you would suspect me.'

'Just seems odd, that's all,' I said, rather lamely. 'You've run away to here and the police think that the body might have gone in from here.'

'And who is this woman I have killed for no reason?' she said. 'The wicked creature of depravity that I am.' She was getting very angry and yet, and yet, as I looked at her, her cheeks flushed and her eyes flashing, it was not offended innocence that I saw but something else entirely. And it occurred to me that no one running away in the night and shoving her belongings overboard in hopes of being thought drowned could be all that innocent anyway. She had maligned Miss Shanks but offered no details and although I too found the woman odd it could not be disputed that she was steering a very successful girls' school through a stormy passage with sackings, deaths and resignations threatening to capsize the vessel at every turn.

'No one knows who the body is,' I said. 'Fleur went to see and Miss Barclay did too and neither of them knew the woman.'

'And so why would you think she is anything to do with me?' said Miss Beauclerc.

'No reason at all,' I answered. 'Just that rather a lot has happened since I arrived, leaving no time to sort it all out and think it through.'

'Since you arrived where?' she asked me. 'Who are you, anyway?'

'I'm the new English mistress at St Columba's,' I said. 'Now that Fleur is gone.'

'And did Miss Shanks appoint you?'

'Sort of. Pretty much,' I said.

'Then you should be very careful,' she said. 'It must look like a lifeline to you just now. It isn't, believe me.'

'I'm going to ask you one last time, Mademoiselle Beauclerc,' I said. 'And then of course I shall fetch your things and bring them here to you whether you answer me or not. I'm not a monster. Now, once and for all, why did you leave St Columba's?'

'Because it is a place of great wickedness and it would have corrupted me to stay.' She must have known this was worse than useless to me, heavy on drama (and delivered most flamboyantly too, I must say) but lacking any actual content. Her voice softened a little as she went on. 'Fleur was happy here for five years and asked me to join her. I had one wonderful year with her and with Miss Fielding and the Misses Taylor and Bell too. But afterwards . . . We could not leave in the usual way – Miss Shanks's contracts are very binding – so we decided to leave in an *un*usual way.'

'But you bolted,' I said. 'And then Fleur bolted. And Fleur left you stranded.'

'And then you came and now you will help me.'

'And where will you go?'

'I don't know,' said Miss Beauclerc. She did not wring her hands exactly but she clasped them together so hard that her fingers whitened. 'We were supposed to go away to Fleur's home.'

Of course, I thought. Pereford. Where else would she go? There had been times in my own life when I had dreamed of going back to Pereford for succour, and I had never really lived there.

'But I can't go there without her, can I?' Miss Beauclerc was saying. 'I have no money left and no family who will own me. I – I – I . . .'

I would love to report that what I said next sprang from pity for her, so far from home, friendless and without a change of clothes, sitting there hunched in her chair and staring at an impossible future of lonely destitution. Honesty forces me to admit, however, that I wanted her safely stashed where I could easily find her again. It was out of my mouth before I could catch it and swallow.

'If I bring your things this evening can you catch a late train?' She started to interrupt me. 'And you can go to Perthshire. To my home. And stay there until things here . . .'

'Be a guest?' she said. 'In your home?'

Belatedly, my common sense began to rumble into gear as I imagined what Hugh would make of me sending strangers – nay, foreigners – to live in his house while I was out of it.

'Can you sew?' I said. 'Or anything? You could help my maid, Grant. She'd love to quiz an honest-to-goodness Frenchwoman on the subject of clothes.'

Miss Beauclerc drew herself up a little and her voice shook as she answered me.

'You think of me as a servant?' she said. 'Or worse, *possibly* a servant, if I can tell you that I am able to sew?'

'You're a working woman,' I protested. 'I don't see why you should take it *that* way.'

'My family,' said Miss Beauclerc, 'is of the most ancient and exalted line. The Beauclercs have been in the Dauphiné since—'

'But they, my dear mademoiselle, have disowned you,' I said. 'And you were a schoolteacher, which is not so different from a governess, who is almost a servant. I'm sorry my suggestion offended you and I withdraw it.'

'I am a scholar,' she said. 'I have a degree, from Grenoble. I wrote an article published in the—'

'I am offering refuge, Miss Beauclerc,' I said. 'If you cannot sew then my maid and my husband will both wonder what you are doing there. I've done it myself before now, you know. Pretended to be a servant to earn my place in a household where I needed to be.'

She stared at me and breathed rather hard while she thought it through.

'I can sew,' she said at last. 'And I can embroider too and even make lace, if I have to. Thank you.'

One did not wear much in the way of embroidery any more, thankfully, but if that was her handiwork pegged out in the farm-house garden then her place in Grant's heart was assured, for my maid deplored modern, factory-sewn underclothes above all things and her distress at my thrift in banning the beautiful garments I used to order by the dozen before the war had been piercing. They had been made by silent nuns somewhere in the Alps, and if my geography were not deserting me Grenoble was near enough the Alps to put a smile on Grant's face that might last until Christmas.

'I shall return after nightfall with your luggage,' I said, 'if you'll tell me where you think it might be.'

On my way back to St Columba's again I stopped at the harbour and shook my head in shame to see the little hut with its painted sign: *Fishing & touring boats for hire. By the hour & by the day. Enquire within.*

Knocking on the door, I roused an ancient mariner with a leathery purple complexion and a demeanour which made the driver of the railway station dog-cart appear like the doorman at the Savoy.

'Aye?' he barked at me from around his pipe, glaring out of small, red, swimming eyes. 'What do ye want? I'm in no mood for women today.'

'A question for you,' I said, taking a step back away from the combined exhalation of tobacco and whisky. 'Did you rent a boat to a young lady on Saturday past?'

'Aye!' he bellowed, bridging the distance between my nose and the fumes. 'And if you've come wi' a pack o' excuses fae the besom, ye'll can get straight back and tell 'er fae me that she's a wee b—'

'Before you say something you might come to regret,' I said, 'let me assure you I have no idea where the lady went to and I had no advance notice that she was going to steal your boat.' My plain speaking mollified him somewhat, and his next speech was grunted rather than boomed.

'One pound ten shillings and sixpence she paid me,' he said. 'And she owes me another fifteen guineas b'now.'

'That seems a little steep for a week's boat rental,' I said.

'That's a fine, no' the rent,' he said.

'Have you reported the matter to the police?' I asked. 'Or the coastguard?'

'Aye well,' he said. 'Well, no' just yet, like.' Which I took to mean that he feared a report would lead to a return and the mounting fine would then stop accruing. He preferred, I surmised, to fester and whinge and think of the total growing greater every day.

'I take it you had a proper contract?' I said. He nodded. 'Might I see it?' He nodded again and, reaching behind him into the hut, he unhooked a board from a nail beside the door and showed it to me.

There on the yellow form, as large as life, was her signature: *F.D. Lipscott.* While I stared at it, a crabbed and yellowed finger threaded in under my arm and tapped the form, the thick black nail – hideous to behold – like a scarab.

'Late fees,' he said. 'All set oot there and she's got a copy o' it.'

'Nevertheless I think you should tell the coastguard,' I said. 'And the local bobbies too.' I thrilled to think of Sergeant Turner's blush when he realised as I had that Fleur had got clean away from under our noses and that all the jostling boats in the harbour, their chugging engines, the snap of the dinghies' sails and the clink of the painters had not jogged our brains at all in two long days.

8

'You are a brick, Miss Gilver,' said a guileless child by the name of Jessie or Tessie or possibly Bessie, over dinner. 'I've had the most enormous crush on Rob Roy Macgregor since I was a tiny child.'

'How can you have a crush on someone in a book?' said another. There were general snorts of derision from all around her and one dainty little miss went as far as to roll up a piece of bread into a missile and throw it at her.

'Petra lives for chemistry,' one of them explained to me. 'She'd only have a pash for—'

'Mendel,' said a child at the end of the table, provoking gales of laughter. Petra was unperturbed.

'Gregor Mendel was a *biologist*,' she said. 'You mean Mendeleev. Now, the fascinating thing about Mendeleev—'

'Oh, shut up!' said Bessie or Nessie, as Petra underwent another hail of bread pellets.

'Girls, really,' I said, a little too mildly and a little too late. I was watching out of the corner of my eye in case one of the real mistresses were about to storm over and effect a coup.

I had decided I could not justify more time spent on the sixth formers, who had told me all they were ever going to, and I had swapped places with Miss Christopher. These little ones, however, were so much more boisterous at table than they had been in the classroom and so very much more boisterous than Stella and her crew, unfettered as they were by any desire to be thought languid, that I was beginning to feel overwhelmed. And we were only at the soup.

'I like David Copperfield,' said another.

'Or George IV,' said the first bread thrower. 'From that history book The Maid used to use. He always seemed like great fun.'

'Ugh! Angela, you're horrid even to say it as a *joke*. George IV with all that clay in his hair and never bathing. You'd be sick.'

'Girls, really, please,' I said. 'No more talk of pashes and crushes.' Was I ever this frivolous, I wondered? Certainly not in front of grown-ups.

'Oh, Miss Gilver, don't get like Juliet!' said Petra. 'All that great sweep of literature and she wouldn't let us read a word that would give her broken heart a pang.'

'Silly little girls,' I said. I drank some soup and while I did their words caught up with me. 'What broken heart?'

'Oh Romeo, Romeo!' said a pair of them in chorus. 'Of course she had a broken heart. She displayed all the symptoms – solitary walks, pale cheeks, endless trips to church even when there wasn't a service. We think he must have died, don't we, girls? She was too woebegone for someone who'd been jilted.'

'Stop it, you dreadful children,' I said. Of course, the exasperation was all an act; I could not wait for dinner to be over and for Alec's expected telephone call to ask him what he thought of the theory. Slowly, I became aware that the girls were giggling in that stifled way which only produces more giggling than if they had let their laughter go. Clearly they could tell that I was thinking over their words in a most undignified way.

'You think we're right, don't you, Miss Gilver?' said one.

'Enough!' I said. 'On pain of *Silas Marner*, you are not to talk in that disrespectful way of Miss Lipscott any more.'

'In your hearing, Miss Gilver?' said Petra. 'Or at all?'

'At all, you little monkey,' I said. 'I'm putting you on your honour.' And it was wonderful to see how this subdued them. How long would it last that their untarnished honour was as a line drawn, uncrossable, in the sand? I hoped for some of them it would endure their whole lives through.

There was time before Alec's scheduled call for a short trip to the little flower room downstairs where Jeanne Beauclerc had told me the mistresses kept their luggage. I had my own suitcase as my excuse for wandering, but it did not take long for me to realise there was no way I could manhandle it down the stairs on my own. (A new-found respect was born in me for Grant, far from hefty, who threw the thing around like a beach ball, and for all the station boys and elderly porters who had shouldered cases and trunks in and out of boots and guards' vans, full of clothes, in my travelling years.) I dragged it back to my room and set off with a hatbox and my overnight case instead, worrying a little about how I would manage Miss Beauclerc's suitcase if it were as large as my own.

Unfortunately I was only ten paces from my door when I was waylaid.

'Miss Gilver?' It was one of the maids. She bobbed and then stared at my bags.

'I was just looking for somewhere to put these where they won't be in my way,' I said.

'The mistresses don't put their bags in the attic, Miss Gilver,' she said, and before I could stop her she took the bags out of my hands. 'You wouldn't believe the pandemonium at the end of term and a nice leather case like that would get scuffed away to bits in the scrum, for sure.' She was retreating and I sped after her. She had reached the head of a small casement staircase and shot down it with the light steps of youth and daily practice. I shot down after her, tense with the knowledge of my greater years, greater weight and lack of acquaintance with what characterful traits this stairway might have to its name.

'The mistresses keep their cases in the wee luggage room by the side door that used to be the flower room,' she called over her shoulder, as she descended. 'Nicer for them not to be jostled in with the girls.'

'Ah, I see,' I said. The stair spat us out in a corridor of the ground floor I had not encountered before, somewhere in the kitchen wing at my best guess, and the little maid barrelled along it at the most amazing speed. If she had been up since six scrubbing and sweeping, her energy at seven in the evening was a thing of wonder.

'You don't need to come, Miss Gilver,' she said, showing a concern for the elders of St Columba's that I had not seen before.

'Well, yes, but just in case I need to lay hands on it,' I replied. 'Best if I know where things are. That hatbox still has the hat inside, for instance – nowhere better to keep it, don't you know, but I might need it for Parents' Day.'

'Oh, uh-huh?' said the maid. I could not be sure if she were being politely interested in my remarks or if they had raised suspicions in her.

'It's rather swish, if I say it myself,' I said. 'And I don't know the form, you know? Wouldn't like to upstage the mothers or the headmistress or anything.'

She gave a longing look at the hatbox in her hand, perhaps taken with the idea of a swish hat (for while maids seldom have the means of acquiring much finery nor the occasions which call for it, that does not mean they feel any less the desire, as witness Grant's frustrated attempts to indulge it vicariously through endlessly disappointing me).

'Here we are,' said the girl, turning into a room at a bend in the passageway. 'It's not locked, since everything's empty that's stored in here.'

There were many trunks around the walls, and several hatboxes and small cases on the slatted wooden shelves where once flower bulbs might have been set to dry over winter. In fact, I could not immediately see where on the shelves I could squeeze my bags in.

'I'll just stack them up a wee bit and make some space,' said the maid. 'There's no need for this lot to be all set out in a row . . . That's funny.' She was tugging at a small case on a low shelf. 'It's kind of heavy.' I bent to see.

There were two stout cases side by side, strapped shut, and two small bags wrapped in mackintoshed cloth as though to withstand more weather than their manufacturer had had in mind. Weather, I thought, or possibly sea spray. Did all four belong to Miss Beauclerc? It was possible, and yet there was a symmetry and neat modesty about the two large cases and the two small bags which put me in mind of lockers and bunks and sailors' duffel bags, and of the smallness of Hugh's army kit when he went away to war.

If there were any further doubt in my mind the maid removed it.

'Thon's Miss Lipscott's bag,' she said, pointing to one of the two larger cases. 'And this other one's Mam-wazell B's. She's a proper lady like yourself, miss, and she's got the most beautiful things. I'd know her bags anywhere.' She put her hands up to the sides of her face and turned to me.

'Miss?' she said. 'They said that poor soul that fell in the sea was a stranger.'

'She was,' I said.

'But there's their traps. Both o' them. Where have they gone with none of their things, miss?'

'The body,' I said, 'can't have been Miss Lipscott, for I was there when she went to look at it. The body was dead by Wednesday at the very latest. And Miss Lipscott was here until Saturday morning.'

'But Mam-wazell!' said the girl. She kept looking back at the cases and her teeth were beginning to chatter.

'It wasn't Mademoiselle Beauclerc,' I said, firmly, wishing I could tell her (but knowing I dared not) whence the firmness sprang. 'That poor dead woman was nothing to do with St Columba's at all.' The girl looked at me with a great deal of troubled doubt in her young eyes. 'Trust me,' I said, hoping that I was to be trusted. For even though No. 5 predated Fleur's departure, I had seen Jeanne Beauclerc with my own eyes and Miss Blair was apparently bringing cricket to the schoolgirls of North Yorkshire, there were still two mistresses unaccounted for. And if it were too much of a stretch to imagine that Miss Taylor or Miss Bell had revisited her old stamping ground and been drowned there, there was still a world of other ways the body could have something to do with the school. In fact, it offended all reason to think it did *not* have something to do with the school. For starters, as my sons were wont to say, *there* were women who dressed plainly in dark garments and went about their lives unprotected by husbands and *here* was a woman's body dressed plainly in dark garments which seemed not to have any abandoned husband searching for it. Besides that, the headmistress (of a school I had heard called evil and corrupting) had immediately thought when she heard of the body that it was one of her girls or one of her staff. Not to mention the fact that a mistress had taken one look at the thing and promptly fled, leaving her plans, her friend and her very luggage behind her. There had to be a connection somewhere, even if I was without the merest hint of what it might be.

'No,' I said again. 'Nothing to do with St Columba's. Now, what's your name, my girl?'

'Maureen,' said the maid.

'Well, Maureen, you run along and don't give these bags another thought. I'll take care of getting them sent on after Miss Lipscott and Miss Beauclerc. And Maureen? Best not mention them to anyone, eh? It *is* a bit odd and we don't want to cause a lot of worry.'

There was no way of knowing whether she would heed my words or scurry back to her bedroom to regale the rest of the maids with the news. She bobbed silently, still looking anxious, and was gone, leaving my hatbox and case in the doorway and leaving me the problem of just how this 'taking care' was to be effected.

What I wanted to do was wrest open Fleur's bags with a chisel to see if they yielded any clues as to where she had gone but, thinking calmly, I could see that if her plans had changed to the extent that her bags had been abandoned in the flower room this way her destination might well have changed too. What I should do, of course, what honour bound me to do, was take Miss Beauclerc's bags to her as I had promised.

The sound of a door opening somewhere close by in the house jogged me at last into action. What I could *not* do was stand here staring at the luggage, waiting for someone to find me. I shoved my own bags onto a low shelf and grabbed those I judged to be Jeanne Beauclerc's – they were indeed of very buttery pigskin and had her initials, rather an impressive string of them, tooled in gilt (somewhat vulgar, but then perhaps they did things differently in the Dauphiné). Taking them with me, I shut the door on Fleur's. They had sat there undisturbed for two days and two nights and there was no reason not to think they would sit there a little longer. I would take these to Low Merrick Farm, return for the other two, smuggle them to safety and ransack them at my leisure.

I made it almost all the way to my room to fetch my outdoor things before my plan started to unravel. The corridors were quiet, all the girls at rest, I supposed, and all the mistresses hard at work in their studies as usual, and in the echoing silence it was impossible not to hear the cry when it began.

'Miss Gilver! Miss Giiiiilverrrrr . . .'

It sounded like Ivy Shanks, that peculiar playful way the words were sung out that made me think of the big bad wolf and his sing-song call of 'Come out, come out, wherever you are!' I looked desperately around for some curtained niche or blanket chest where I could shove the bags, and seeing nothing I stepped lightly up the nearest stairway.

'Miiissss Giiil-verrrr!' sang Miss Shanks's voice again.

Making no effort to be quiet this time I turned around and came back down the stairs.

'Miss Shanks?' I said, stopping a few steps from the landing and peering down. 'Did you need me?'

'Ah, there you are!' said Miss Shanks, tripping along to the bottom of the steps to meet me. 'What are you doing up there?'

'I was taking these to the attics,' I answered, indicating the bags and trying not to look like a liar. 'I won't be a tick.'

To my immense relief, Miss Shanks gave my burden barely a glance, but just wound her arm round and round as though reeling me in on it and started walking back the way she had come.

'Leave them just now, Miss Gilver, you're wanted on the telephone.'

'I see,' I said, hurrying after her. 'I'll just . . .' I opened my door on the way past and practically threw the bags inside. 'Thank you for coming to fetch me, Headmistress. Is it . . . Did the caller say . . . ?' A sudden enormous worry had bloomed in me like ink dropped into water that if Miss Shanks herself had run to find me, perhaps it was a telephone call of grave import. Perhaps it was Hugh. Perhaps one of the boys was in trouble. I did not quite like to mention my husband and sons out of the blue to a woman so deep in the fiction of my spinsterhood that she seemed to have forgotten it was not true.

'It's that nice young man of yours,' said Miss Shanks with a twinkling look over her shoulder. 'Can't take himself off to his bed without the sound of your voice.' She grabbed the handle and threw her office door wide.

'There ye are, make yourself at home and I'll wait in the staff-room.' She beamed at me, shooed me inside and closed the door again.

'Alec?' I said, sitting down in the chair at the desk. It was an oak and leather affair, one leg and four little castored feet, and it was set very low to the floor for Miss Shanks's short stature. I twirled it round and around a few times to make myself comfort-able and by the time I had undone the ensuing tangle with the telephone cord, Alec had roused himself and was talking.

'Dandy!' he said. 'What a day I've had. I hope that woman isn't angry I rang you.'

'No,' I said. 'She doesn't seem the least bit put out. She's shown me into her own office and gone to camp out in the staffroom until I'm done. Now, listen, Alec.'

'I found Blair,' Alec said.

'*I* found Beauclerc,' I said, unable to resist it. There was a short silence.

'We'll get to you in a minute,' Alec said, eventually. 'I also found out something very interesting about Elf. His life, I mean. Not his death, exactly.'

'He was Fleur's lover?' I said. 'I thought as much.'

'Well, aren't you clever?' said Alec, bitterly. 'Fine. Tell me about Mademoiselle Beauclerc then.'

As succinctly as I could, for I instantly regretted taking the wind out of his sails that way, I related the discovery of Jeanne Beauclerc in the Patersons' farmhouse, the tale of her and Fleur's planned escape, the evidence of the rented boat never returned and the two sets of waterproofed luggage sitting in the flower room.

'My word,' said Alec, with the understatement he always affects when he is more impressed than he cares to admit. 'At Low Merrick, eh? And you interviewed her.'

'And found out precisely nothing,' I reminded him. 'She gave no hint about why she and Fleur were taking off, nor why she suddenly bolted almost a week early. She's in a bit of a fix now, of course, but still admirably – well, lamentably – close-lipped about the whole thing. So, tell me, Alec, what do you think of this idea?' Quickly I described my arrangement that she should travel to Gilverton and lie low there.

'It would certainly be nice to have her safely stored until we can give her our full attention,' he said.

'My thoughts exactly,' I said. 'So that's *my* miraculously reappearing mistress. How about yours?'

'No, no,' said Alec. 'You carry on and tell me the rest. How did you guess about Elf?' I could hear the rustle and click of pipery going on and knew that he was determined to cap me one way or another.

'Well, I didn't really until you hinted,' I said. 'I was just being a pest. Only the girls at supper did a lot of silly giggling about the idea that Fleur had a lost love – a dead lost love. Goodness knows how they cottoned on to it but they seemed pretty sure. *That's* why they called her Juliet, apparently.'

'Not a happy precedent,' Alec said. 'Right then, to me. I got to The Bridge House in time for tea – not that I was offered any, mind you. They viewed me as rather a fox in the hen coop, quite unlike St Columba's. But Miss Blair came out to speak to me and we tramped around the playing fields in the freezing cold and driving rain for a while.'

'And?'

'And she was pretty forthcoming about life in Portpatrick, eventually,' he said. 'Oh, at first she tried to make out she had resigned, only she wouldn't say over what, or why she had left in the middle of term or what possessed her to give up the fresh sea breezes for this moor and the hacking cough she has had since she got here. Eventually, though, as I say, she broke down – a chest infection is wonderfully weakening to the spirit – and vouchsafed to me that she had been sacked. Her eyes watered as she told me and I don't think it was just from coughing.'

'You are a meanie, Alec,' I said. 'You might have taken the poor woman to a tea shop if they wouldn't let you inside the school.'

'Tea shop?' he cried. 'Dandy, I don't think you quite appreciate the scope of this moor. You might as well say I should have taken her to a bull fight or a cancan show. The North York Moor makes Perthshire look like Biarritz!'

'All right, all right,' I said. 'She was sacked. Why?'

'*I'm* still shivering a little,' Alec said, then at last he resumed the tale. 'She didn't know why. And I have to say I believe her. She was still very hurt and completely bewildered. She said she had known Miss Fielding from some place they had both worked at before and that Miss Fielding had written to ask her to join the staff of St Columba's while it was still at the planning stage. All was well for five years or so and then Miss Fielding died. Before she was cold in her grave, Miss Blair said, Old Hammy Shanks had sacked her. Just told her her services were no longer required and could she push her key through the letter box as she was leaving. Along with a Miss Spittal who taught riding on a monthly contract, Miss Mount the swimming instructress who used to travel in from Stranraer in the summer term and a pair of sisters from Portpatrick village who took the little ones for ballet and taught the big ones a spot of waltz and rumba.'

'And Miss Taylor and Miss Bell?' I said.

'They were still in post when she left,' said Alec. 'And since – quite understandably – she didn't keep up a correspondence with a place which had used her so ill, she doesn't know what became of them afterwards.'

'And you think she's being quite honest, you said?'

'Oh yes indeed. She's horrified by having been sacked, Dandy. A spotless record up until that point, apparently, and now she feels all tarnished and sullied and doesn't want to make friends so that she never has to tell anyone. I felt quite sorry for her, in spite of everything.'

'What everything?'

'Oh, you know,' said Alec. 'Cricket! And you should have *seen* the creature.'

'Poor woman,' I said. 'We can't all be . . . bathing beauties.'

'Bathing . . . ?' said Alec, laughing to mock me, but only a little. 'The very thought of Miss Blair in a bathing suit!'

'Speaking of bathing, though,' I said. 'It seems odd that a school would sack its swimming instructress and then build a new pool.'

'Didn't you say it was endowed or donated or whatever?'

'But I think the parents just stump up the cash, don't they? I don't speak from experience, obviously. Doesn't the school choose what to lash it out on?'

'Anyway,' said Alec, 'so much for Miss Blair, alive and kicking and sacked in a very peremptory way in February of 1926. *Not* one of the four bodies, which four murders would have brought into play.'

'Speaking of which,' I said.

'Ah yes, indeed,' said Alec. 'Speaking of which. Well, I left The Bridge House and shivered and shook in my rented motorcar all twenty godforsaken miles, reaching Goatland Priory just in time for drinks. And this time, I'm glad to say, I got one. They must be pretty desperate for visitors up here – welcomed me with open arms and barely a thought of who I was and why I had come here.'

'Here?' I said. 'You're still there?'

'I am,' said Alec. 'Sitting in a lovely warm bedroom in front of a roaring apple-wood fire with an enormous brandy and a tummy full of mutton. I like Forrester, I must say.'

'And was he as forthcoming with stories as he is with meat and drink?' I said.

'Not exactly,' said Alec. 'I've had to tell rather a lot of whoppers, in fact. So I'm going to make the most of my comfortable night, because once I go and they get a chance to discuss me with mutual acquaintances they're never going to let me darken their door again.'

'Go on,' I said. We had a slight hiatus while the exchange confirmed another three minutes and then Alec resumed.

'Well, I told them who I was, naturally. Thankfully Aurora wasn't around at this point, just Forrester himself, his mother and an aunt who it turns out is a closer relation to the departed Elf than this branch – spot of luck, I thought. Anyway, we managed to find some names to fling back and forth – I was at school with the son of another aunt and one of this aunt's husband's sister's children is married to a girl who was a bridesmaid at a wedding in Hampshire where I was a pageboy.'

'God Almighty,' I said.

'I know, but it helped in the end to have them think they knew me. And yet the connection was so slight that I felt unencumbered when it came to concocting my history. I said I'd been visiting my daughter at The Bridge House – cue lots of chatter about what sort of place it was and I came out with my sorry little story that its chief attraction for Belinda, that's my daughter, was that it was a long way from Dorset and a very long way from the sea. I said she had got a sort of a phobia for the sea since her mother drowned.'

'Oh, Alec!'

'And so they asked, as you would, whether it was a boating accident and I mumbled a bit about my wife always having been very unhappy and something about a brother lost in battle and a baby son who only lived a—'

'Oh, *Alec*!'

'And Forrester himself, as you can well imagine, couldn't get out of the room fast enough. So he popped off to his office or somewhere and that was my cue to rouse myself from my pit of gloom and apologise with much hand-wringing about the unburdening. Couldn't account for it, no idea why I suddenly let go in a rush. All that. And it was at that point that Mrs Forrester and Aunt Nadine – Mrs Walters – came over all maternal and rushed to assure me that these thing happen in the best of families – i.e. their own – and that's when they told me about Elf.'

'Where did you get the nerve?' I asked him. 'You just rolled up at the house, dropped into an armchair and started spouting about suicide!'

'Hardly,' said Alec. 'I emptied my petrol tank out onto the moor and plodded up the drive with a five gallon can. And I put in a good two hours of work with the women talking about the school – very careful groundwork: you'd have marvelled at me.'

'Oh, you can always get women talking about schools,' I said. 'It's just like servants.'

'The poor widower Osborne has had his troubles there, too,' said Alec. 'I really set to and wooed them. By the time they were telling me about Elf we were old friends, the three of us.'

'And what *about* Elf?'

'Yes, well, it was drowning with him too, if you remember.'

'Vaguely,' I said. 'Now that you remind me.'

'Off a cliff, on the coast, by Pereford. He had gone for a walk and I'll give you one guess who with.'

'No!'

'Oh yes. They had been spending a great deal of time together that summer, lots of walking and rowing about in a little boat and there might even have been some poetry.'

'Written?'

'Not as bad as all that, I don't think,' Alec said. 'Read out, though, in the rowing boat.'

'Dear me.'

'And so Elf's mother – Mrs Franklin—'

'Marigold,' I said. 'For her sins. I always felt a kinship.'

'Anyway, Marigold did some Lady Bracknelling about, seeing what she thought of Fleur as a daughter-in-law. She didn't go as far as to ban the nuptials, but she wasn't too keen.'

'Why not?

'Just wait, Dandy,' said Alec.

'I know Fleur had a wildish spell after the war although I don't know the details. But there were no babies and nothing in the papers and she had *such* a lot of money.'

'All will be revealed,' Alec said. 'So this day Fleur came back to the house at Pereford without Elf and looking very white and strained and collapsed in a heap on the hall carpet.'

'Marble,' I said. 'The carpets were rolled up and stored in the summertime.'

'Poor girl, then,' said Alec. 'Anyway, as she was coming to, she said quite plainly in the hearing of Marigold Franklin, as well as Fleur's own mother and sisters, that she had told Edward again and again that she wouldn't marry him and that he just wouldn't take no for an answer. And she said, "I'm so sorry," and fluttered her eyes and that was it for four days.'

'That was what?'

'Catatonic shock, the doctors said. By the time she came round the second time Elf's body had washed up and the inquest had been ordered and Fleur claimed she couldn't remember a thing. Couldn't remember the walk or coming back to the house and saying what she had. She stuck to that story like glue and wouldn't budge. Her mother and sisters seemed to believe it and they closed ranks and wouldn't let anyone – not Marigold, not Elf's father, and certainly not the police – talk to her. They bundled her off to a nursing home and the Franklins seem to have taken the view that nothing would bring him back and that since the two families were already connected through Aurora and Drew (and their baby son) any scandal would end up tainting the whole lot of them, so they went along with the theory of an accident. Witnessed by Fleur, who was Elf's betrothed and who had suffered some kind of hysterical amnesia from the shock of it.'

'Golly,' I said. 'They really just told you all this?'

'I told them my daughter witnessed my wife's suicide and that I was a lonely widower despairing of an end to my solitude with this millstone of tragedy and shame around my neck. And I think there are a few Franklin nieces who're in their thirties and looking set to wither on the vine.'

'Alec, you do say the most hideous things sometimes.'

'Here in Yorkshire,' Alec said, 'we call a spade a spade. And I'm a bit drunk too, I think. Anyway, I'm sure Aurora hasn't told anyone in the household about the new chapter of scandal with Fleur. The ladies were speaking as though of ancient history.'

'And where is Aurora?' I said. 'Has she dashed off to be with Fleur somewhere?'

'Oh no, she's here,' Alec said. 'She appeared for dinner. A slightly sticky moment when she heard my name and asked me if I was the Mr Osborne from Perthshire. I did a marvellous job of looking like someone who'd never heard of the place and then her own mother chimed in with 'No, dear: Dorset' and the moment passed. She's not the shiniest button in the box, as you said yourself, and so she was quite placated with the story of my daughter at school nearby and seemed to settle on the idea that I've been here a lot and we might have run into one another at things with ponies. Her daughters, apparently, spend a great deal of time walloping around the heath on horseback and they meet the Bridge House girls all the time.'

'Right.' I was thinking back over all that he had told me. 'All has not been revealed, though,' I said at last. 'Why did Marigold Franklin not want Fleur as a daughter-in-law when she looked into things, Bracknell-style? As you say, the two families were already connected.'

'Because,' said Alec and his voice had a drum roll in it, 'simply because Fleur had been secretly engaged once before.'

'So what?'

'And the reason she hadn't married – or even got as far as the engagement being announced – was that her then lover died before the wedding. In other words, he was No. 3.'

He waited.

'Dan? Are you still there?'

'I am,' I said. 'Too stunned to speak. I've never heard any of this.'

'It was pretty successfully hushed up by the Lipscotts,' Alec said. 'But the Forrester-Franklin contingent – being in the family, as it were – were able to find out all about it. It happened in 1919. A car crash this time, although no one saw it happen. Fleur walked away from it and the fiancé was burned to a crisp.'

'I can't believe it.'

'After which Fleur spent the late winter and spring in the usual nursing home and had only just got back to Pereford from *that* rest cure when the Franklins arrived for their ill-fated visit.'

'And Fenella and Marigold just told you all this?'

'Well, Marigold is a born gossip and she's quite removed from the scandal really. Only a nephew married to a sister of the wicked girl.'

'And Fenella?'

'She's getting on in years,' Alec said.

'What does that mean?' I asked him, sincerely puzzled.

Alec cleared his throat.

'It means I'm not entirely sure she understood just who I was,' he said. 'In fact, I rather think she took me for her late husband.'

'Oh, Alec,' I said. 'Don't tell me you really took advantage of a poor old lady wandered out of her wits! Goodness, it must have been years since I saw Fenella Forrester – it's hard to imagine.'

'It did her no harm,' said Alec. 'She was glad to see him, if anything; must have been a love match. And anyway in this case the ends more than justify the means. Three of them now, Dandy. The lover of 1919 makes three.'

'And how will you set about learning any more of him?' I said. 'Can you winkle it out of the ladies? Is there anything that could get you started on a hunt through the newspapers? How many fatal car crashes can there have been in that year? If you were to restrict yourself to Dorset and London.'

'Sh!' said Alec. 'Someone's coming.'

I pressed the earpiece so hard against my head that my ear smarted from the pressure and I was rewarded with the sound, coming down the line, of a door being wrenched open and an angry voice, almost shouting.

'Alec Osborne!' the voice said. 'Alexander Osborne! Yes, from Dorset, granted. But not any more. And you just marched in here and tricked my poor mother-in-law like a common con artist from the gutter.'

'Is that Aurora?' I asked, but Alec did not answer.

'Mrs Forrester,' he said and I had to strain very hard since he was no longer speaking towards the instrument. 'What do you know about the young man of your sister's who died in 1919? Not the one who died in 1920, you understand. The first one.'

'Might *not* be the first one,' I reminded him.

'How dare you!' said Aurora. Her voice was trembling with suppressed emotion. 'We sacked you. You have no right to be asking these beastly questions.'

'I'll speak to her,' I said.

'Who are you talking to on that thing, anyway?' Aurora said.

'It's Dandy,' said Alec. 'Would you like a word?'

'She was our *friend*,' Aurora said, sounding tearful now.

'She still is,' said Alec. 'And so am I. We're both trying to help.'

'Get out,' said Aurora. I could hear the muddled sounds of movement. 'Get out of this house and don't ever come back.'

'You can't throw me out onto the moor in the dead of night,' said Alec. 'Don't be ridiculous! What will your husband say? I mean, I take it he knows nothing of this latest death?'

'Shut *up*,' said Aurora, collapsing into sobs. 'And get out. My husband . . . My husband will chase you off with a shotgun if I tell him how you tricked us all.' Alec came back to the mouthpiece and sighed down the line.

'I'm not sure I believe her, Dan, but I'd better go,' he said. 'I'll be at the Horseshoe in Egton if you need me.' He laid the earpiece down, without hanging up, and I could hear more movement and then silence. I waited. After a moment there were some swishing noises as someone moved closer and then Aurora's voice came down the line.

'Is anyone there?'

'It's me, darling,' I said. 'Alec told you.'

'That was a rotten trick to play,' she said. 'Fenella doesn't know who she's talking to these days. What did she tell him?'

'About Elf's death, and about his predecessor.'

'Oh, Dandy, it's not how it seems, please believe me. Poor Elf and poor Charles and poor, poor darling Fleur. It's not at all the way it must sound. And she's been absolutely wonderful for years and years now.'

'Yes, eight years is a good stretch,' I said. 'It held until last Tuesday or Wednesday and now there's another corpse and Fleur's disappeared again. Where's this nursing home she usually goes to? Have you bundled her off there for a third time?'

'Stop it! Stop it!' said Aurora. 'We don't know *where* she is. You've no idea, Dandy, what we go through when we don't know where she is, Mamma, Pearl and me.'

'The truth will out, Aurora my dear,' I said. To my surprise she snorted.

'Hark at you, talking about "truth" like that,' she said, 'when both of you are just as twisty as corkscrews. I don't think for a minute that you want to look after Fleur, any more than I believe Mr Osborne just happened to run out of petrol right by our front gate *or* that his wife killed herself jumping off a cliff. Why ever in the world he's sent his daughter to school all the way up here, it wasn't for that.'

I did not correct her. She would only have felt foolish and got even more angry. Instead, I rang off and immediately asked the exchange to put me through to the telegraph office.

'"Name was Charles. Stop. Shiny Button told me. Stop,"' said the operator. 'Have I got that right?'

'That's it,' I said. 'Osborne at the Horseshoe Inn, Egton Bridge, Yorkshire, please.'

Surely there cannot have been too many young men called Charles who had died in crashes in 1919, I thought, hanging up again. In fact, I almost fancied there was a faint memory stirring in me at the thought of it. Alec would be able to turn up something in the morning if he could get to a newspaper office or a library somewhere.

As for me, I had go to Paterson's farm again and take Miss Beauclerc her things. Then, I supposed, I should have to forewarn Hugh of her arrival. In fact – I looked at the telephone sitting there on Ivy Shanks's desk – since I was right here . . .

'Gilverton, Perthshire,' I said to the woman on the exchange and then, 'It's me, Pallister,' when the telephone was answered. I could picture him standing in the passageway just our side of the green baize door and glaring down his nose at the mouthpiece. Pallister does not approve of telephones, or of his mistress, either, these days.

'Madam,' he replied.

'Is my husband there?'

'Of course, madam,' he said with affected surprise (the point being that decent people were *all* blamelessly at home, and only the very depraved were ringing from goodness knows where). 'I shall alert Master and have him pick up the telephone in the billiards room.'

'Who's there?' I asked Hugh when he answered a few minutes later, for he never practises billiards alone and so is only ever in the room when there is someone to challenge to a game or two.

'Ah, Donald,' he said.

I sat up very straight, very fast, in Miss Shanks's chair, causing it to catch me in the small of the back as it tipped forward.

'Good God, he's been expelled!' I said. 'What for? What did he do?'

'Marvellous that you have such faith in the boy, Dandy,' said Hugh. 'He has a weekend pass for the half-holiday and decided to come home.'

'Right,' I said. I had forgotten it was half-term time even as the rumblings about Parents' Day at St Columba's reminded me. 'He'll spend it all on trains but for a day,' I went on, blustering a little from shame over my outburst. 'What about Teddy?'

'Thankfully he's been invited out with a friend,' said Hugh. 'Sewell. So you have no reason to be feeling guilty.'

I had not been, to be honest, and resented the veiled implication that I should. All the same I would send a letter and a ten shilling note to the Sewells; I knew that Teddy would rather have a tip than a visit from me any day.

'Now then, Hugh,' I said. 'I have something to tell you.'

'I should say you do,' said Hugh very drily. He covered the mouthpiece with his hand but I could still hear him talking to Donald. 'Could you run along and fetch my diary from my business room desk, old chap? Thank you.' I rolled my eyes; Hugh only old chaps the boys when he is trying (sometimes quite ostentatiously) to look like the perfect parent in comparison with me. 'I've had the most extraordinary letter, Dandy.'

'Who from?' I asked.

'From whom is a question I cannot answer,' Hugh said. I did not miss the little dig at my grammar, but I rose above it.

'Illegible signature?'

'Anonymous,' said Hugh. 'Asked me to reply by return to a poste restante. Like a penny dreadful.'

'What does it say?'

'It tells me nothing I did not already know,' he replied. 'That you are living there (Portpatrick, one surmises) with a man who is not me and passing yourself off as—'

'I am not!' I said. 'We stayed in the same pub in separate rooms for one night and since then I've been living at the girls' school.'

'Passing yourself off as a schoolmistress,' he finished. '*Miss* Gilver.'

'Oh, for heaven's sake,' I said. 'I know exactly who sent it. "Here" is the Crown and it was written by a very nosy and thoroughly unpleasant woman who's holidaying there also with her companion. She witnessed Alec and me doing such shocking things as eating breakfast and standing on the street talking. Throw it on the fire, Hugh, and forget about it.'

'I threw it on the fire within a minute of opening it,' Hugh said. 'Revolting thing.'

'And it's nothing to do with what I have to tell you anyway. The thing is, you see, that someone is coming to stay. At Gilverton. Probably tomorrow.'

'Someone we know?' said Hugh. There was an ominous note in his voice which I ignored.

'No, a stranger,' I said. 'A Frenchwoman by the name of Mademoiselle Beauclerc. One of the Dauphiné Beauclercs.'

'The who?'

'She's actually been working as a French mistress here at St Columba's.'

'Where?'

'Oh Hugh – the school where I'm working on the case. You never listen.'

'Convent school, is it?' said Hugh, the mention of a saint clearly setting all sorts of alarm bells ringing.

'Perfectly ordinary girls' school, chapel is the local kirk,' I said. 'In fact Basil Rowe-Issing's girl is here. And one of the Norton daughters too. I had her reading Macbeth this morning. Anyway, I *had* thought Mademoiselle Beauclerc could have a bed in the servants' wing and help Grant but those attic rooms are horribly draughty. She could always go to Dunelgar instead. Or she could go to Benachally and look at the hangings. She said she could embroider like anything.'

'And is she in hiding from the police, might one ask?' said Hugh. 'Or is there more likely to be a ne'er-do-well hot-footing it after her?'

'Neither,' I said. 'She needs somewhere to be, out of the way, while matters settle.'

'While matters settle,' he repeated. 'Very well, Dandy. Tell me when she's arriving and I'll send the car. If some old French nun can fix those hangings without it costing us, I should be perfectly happy to put her up for a while.'

'It's not a convent,' I said again. 'And I've never asked but judging by appearance I'd say Mademoiselle was about twenty-five.'

There was a short silence, whose source and whose journey I could not fathom.

'She'll be able to walk from the station then,' said Hugh.

I did not answer for I was thinking not about Jeanne Beauclerc walking from the station but about me trying to find the farm track again; thick clouds had turned this May evening as dark as December and the wind was blowing hard. On the other hand, I could hardly leave her thinking she had been abandoned a second time. On a third hand, my luck in being left alone to make these telephone calls was surely running out by now. 'Can I ask you a favour, Hugh?' I said at last.

'You may,' Hugh said, annoyingly.

'Could you ring her up and tell her she can't have her luggage tonight? It's the wilds of nowhere where she's staying, and Alec's away. If you could just ring up Paterson of Low Merrick Farm, Portpatrick and tell Mademoiselle Beauclerc that I'll bring her bags before breakfast tomorrow and that she should get herself to the station and take the train to Dunkeld—'

'Why don't you just take her stuff to the station?' interrupted Hugh.

'Of course!' I said. 'Thank you, dear.'

'Seems like the obvious thing to me,' he said, milking his little triumph now. 'My goodness, Dandy, if that's an example of your canny detective's brain at work! I daresay the whole puzzle isn't really all that puzzling at all if you had a methodical mind tackling it.'

'You don't know the first thing about the case!' I said.

'Precisely my point,' said Hugh.

'There have been five murders,' I said.

'Since Friday?' He sounded suitably astonished.

'No, one last Tuesday or Wednesday and two more in the preceding decade.'

'That's not five, my dear Dandy,' he said.

'And there are five missing persons,' I said, flushing but ignoring him. 'Well, actually we've found two. But lost another one. And actually another. Yes, five.'

'Perhaps I should come down there and sort it all out for you,' he said, in a condescending tone that made me wish he *were* there so I could kick him.

* * *

Finally, I settled the telephone back in its cradle for the night and rubbed my ear hard with the heel of my hand. Then I twirled Miss Shanks's chair back around to its usual setting and stood to leave.

Coming round the desk, though, I spied something upon the carpet just inside the door which certainly had not been there when I had entered and sat down.

A note, a folded piece of lined paper torn from a jotter. Written in pencil on its outside: *Miss*. Now, obviously Miss was Miss Shanks, for this was her office; and just as obviously there was no justification in the world for looking at a letter – even one not inside an envelope – addressed, however cryptically, to another person. (Indeed it had been one of the lessons most fiercely drummed into me by my mother and Nanny Palmer, working for once in tandem, that personal letters never *were* sealed into their envelopes. I had thought as a child that that was to show how much one trusted one's servants and the Post Office employees and the servants of whoever one was writing to. It was only later that I twigged: one never sealed a letter for to do so was to imply that there were matters in one's life unsuitable to be known by all.)

Be that as it may, I unfolded the sheet and read it quickly. Ivy Shanks's life certainly had matters unsuitable to know and that was precisely the reason I wanted to know them.

Of course, it was a bitter disappointment.

I would like leave to go home tomorrow on a visit, please, it said. *I am very unhappy and need to see my father.* Poor little mite, I thought as I read the signature. *Betty Alder.*

A poor little mite indeed. I refolded the paper and let it fall for Miss Shanks to find when she returned.

Walking along the passages to the staffroom, though, I could not get the girl out of my mind. Part of it was worry about Donald, I supposed, in a funny sort of way, for there was something behind his sudden decision to trawl all the way home and all the way back again. I only hoped that he had not made the journey hoping for my ear and shoulder only to find himself stuck with Hugh and unable to get away again. Donald was never one to hurt our feelings and was always confident that we both – even Hugh – had them.

There was so much sorrow in that little letter. I could not leave the child to the sympathy of Miss Shanks, who had been cold even in referring to her and could not be expected to be warm when faced with her asking for dispensation. I put my head around the staffroom door, meaning to tell Miss Shanks that her room was her own again. She was not there and that decided me. Sabbatina Aldo needed comfort and needed it now. If Miss Shanks had gone to bed she would not see the note until the morning.

But how to find her?

'Mrs Brown?' I said. That lady was sitting planted four square in her tub chair by the sideboard. She looked up from her knitting and regarded me with some surprise. 'Do you have a room list of the girls?' She frowned. 'At least that's what they called it when I was at school. A chart of who's where with all their names. It's the names I want really, not the places, but I thought that would be where they were all written.'

'Don't you have class lists?' said Mrs Brown. She, Miss Barclay and Miss Christopher were all looking at me very oddly now.

'I haven't come across any,' I said. 'Perhaps Miss Lipscott put them in an out of the way corner and I haven't turned them up yet.'

'You mean you haven't been taking the register?' said Miss Christopher.

I smiled what I hoped was an ingratiating smile, secretly thinking that I had done rather well getting to Monday evening before my first big gaffe came to light.

'Oh, I'm sure the other girls would have mentioned it if one of them were missing,' I said. 'But that's even more reason to get my hand on these room lists, Mrs Brown. I'll make up a register for tomorrow.'

She shared another look with Miss Christopher and Miss Barclay and then jammed her knitting needles into her ball of wool and hauled herself to her feet. As I followed her to the housekeeper's room I wondered again about Hugh's jibe. Was there an easier way around this too? Should I have been able to find out where Sabbatina Aldo might be without these convolutions?

Convoluted or not, though, my method worked. Mrs Brown handed over a paper ledger of reddish brown, stuffed with health certificates, notes of doctors' visits and a plan of the house with the girls' names printed out in pencil against their dorms.

'Thank you,' I said. 'I shall take very great care of it and return it to you as soon as I can.' Then I hurried off, already flipping through its pages, and had found ALDER clearly marked against a dorm on the west side of the house before I had turned the first corner.

It was a pleasant enough room. The afternoon sun had warmed it, and with the four bedside lamps lit and a large white radiator emanating more heat it almost managed – linoleum floor and metal bedsteads notwithstanding – not to seem too much like a hospital or (I imagined) a prison. The girls had covered their dresser tops with pictures of their families and pets and on three of the beds there were brightly patterned quilts and coverlets over the brown school blankets. The fourth was covered with a white bedspread of fine pulled stitching, edged with crocheted scallops in wool as light as spiders' webs; and on it Sabbatina was sitting, the very picture of woe.

'I came to see if you're all right,' I said.

'No,' said Sabbatina. 'I'm not.' And then the tears began to pour out of her, as though pulsing from some internal pump of efficient design, as she hugged herself and rocked back and forth. I sat down beside her and stretched out one hand to rub her back, half-expecting a rebuff. Instead she turned, threw both her arms around my middle, buried her head in my breast and sobbed as though her heart would break, gulping and sniffing and simply howling, on and on.

I had no daughters and my only sister did not particularly like me, so it had been years since someone had engulfed me in a hug and bawled, and Sabbatina Aldo was much bigger than the boys had been the last time they had broken down over the death of a pony or a whipping from Hugh. This was very different and I felt rather panicked as I patted and shushed and smoothed back her masses of hair (this last was not exactly comfort, but more to get it out of my face and stop it tickling me).

'I know I've got to go and live at home now,' she said eventually, in a voice muffled by being buried against my shirt and made nasal by the inevitable accompaniment to all those tears. 'But I don't want to leave St Columba's. And I don't want to stay either. I don't fit anywhere and there's no one to help me.' She was seized by another storm of weeping and by the time this one had passed her breath was coming in hiccups.

'What about your father?' I said, trying to set her back from me a little without seeming as if I were doing so. Her note had pleaded for permission to visit him. 'Can't you and he help one another?'

She did sit up a bit then, and she blinked and sniffed and went searching for a handkerchief to begin to mop herself up.

'I don't want to see him,' she said. 'Everything's changed.'

'Oh, Sabbatina,' I said. 'There are always two sides. At least two.'

'I know I shall have to forgive him in the end but I just can't imagine it now.'

Which I thought was a bit thick. Joe Aldo was quite the most loving, affectionate and proud husband and father I had ever encountered (certainly I had never seen his like in my own family) and if anyone were to be shunned and then grudgingly forgiven it should be the minx of a wife who had abandoned him and left this poor wretched child to cry herself hoarse with a stranger. Very probably the psychologists could explain the muddle, but it was beyond me.

'Well, then,' I said, 'I think the best thing for you to do is work hard at your lessons and visit on Saturday as usual. I mean, not *as usual*, obviously, but . . .'

'It's the Saturday after Parents' Day,' Sabbatina said, and she started to sniff again. 'Parents' Day! They'll all be here taking the girls out for tea. I wish I could just run away and never come back.'

'Now, now, don't even talk about that,' I said. 'Gosh, the last thing anyone needs is you running away too. You know how awful it is for those left behind. Hm? Now, promise me?'

She rubbed the tears which had just started to form and fall, and nodded.

'I promise.'

'Good girl,' I said. 'Now you go and splash your face and clean your teeth and I'll turn down your bed for you. An early night will do you a world of good.'

'No!' said Sabbatina, then she bit her lip. 'Please don't— I mean, please don't take my cover off, Miss Gilver. I'd like to keep it on tonight.' She had clutched a fold of it in her hand as she spoke but she smoothed it out again now. I smoothed my own hand over it too, studying the tiny stitches and the intricate knots and webs of the pattern, and decided to let her have her way, although it offended every nursery rule ever written not to take off a counterpane at bedtime.

We parted company outside the bathroom door and I descended the nearest staircase, meaning to take the ledger back to Mrs Brown. Finding myself, however, at one end of the corridor leading to the flower room, I decided that instead of risking another trip to fetch Fleur's bags tomorrow I would go now while the house was quiet. I took a look both ways and then set off on quick light feet with the ledger under my arm and my ear cocked for the sounds of unwanted company.

I met no one on the way, however, and opened the door congratulating myself on the decision. Hugh was quite wrong: I did not make difficulties for myself at all. I closed the door softly, clicked on the electric light and turned around.

The bottom shelf was clear. The bags were gone.

I scanned the shelves and looked behind them, even shifting a few bulky items to make doubly, triply sure. There was no doubt of it, however. They had lain undisturbed since Saturday afternoon and I had had a fine chance to nab them. Stupidly, I had taken the bags which would tell me nothing (the bags of a woman already found) and left those which might yield some clue of the woman vanished. And who had taken them? I had been speaking on the telephone for quite a while, but the Misses Barclay and Christopher had had a very settled look in that staffroom of theirs. Mrs Brown, too: she had got up out of her armchair like the sword from the stone. Ivy Shanks! Of course. She had said she was going to the staffroom, but she was not there. And she had seen me with what she thought was my luggage searching for a place to store it. Perhaps she had only then thought to wonder what had become of Miss Lipscott's things or the mademoiselle's.

Then another thought struck me. Had she really believed those bags were mine? Taking my own with me this time, I sped upstairs to my room and shot inside almost expecting that luggage to be gone too. There it was, though, shoved just inside the door where I had left it. I opened my large case – glad now that I could not lift the thing – stowed Jeanne's more modest-sized one inside it and closed it tight, strapping it and locking it and putting the key in my pocket. I locked her overnight bag in my wardrobe. I smoothed my hair, tried in front of the glass to bring my face back to the look of serenity bordering on weariness that one would get from making up register lists, and headed back to the staffroom with Mrs Brown's ledger.

She was re-established in her tub chair and her knitting had grown another inch or so. Miss Barclay and Miss Christopher were as they had been too, at either end of their empire sofa, and Miss Shanks had reappeared. She was looking rather ruffled. From exertion, I wondered? From barrelling around the passageways with a heavy bag in each hand? She did not have the build for it. Actually, though, the dominant look about all of them was one of arrested movement; as though they had been stopped short in the midst of some animated exchange.

'Your ledger, Mrs Brown,' I said, setting it down again on the table at her elbow. 'I've got my class lists all drawn up now. Thank you.'

'Have you then?' said Mrs Brown. 'Have you indeed?' She gave quite the most horrible imaginable look out of the corner of her eye towards the other three, sliding her gaze right to the edge of her eye sockets so that only the white showed and not moving her head even an inch.

'Yes,' I said, trying to sound offhand. I took a breath to say more.

'That's clever of you,' said Mrs Brown. 'Seeing as how the forms aren't listed here.'

I recovered fairly quickly.

'Well, there are only a hundred, aren't there? I just made one big alphabetical list and I'll do the rest with coloured pencil. A code, you know. Yes, a code.'

Mrs Brown raised her eyebrows very slowly until her forehead was a rack of wrinkles, then just as slowly she turned her head and gave a hard stare towards Miss Shanks. Miss Shanks heaved an enormous sigh made up of grievance and self-pity and then plastered a more than usually sickly-sweet smile on her face.

'I wonder if you would come and have a private word with me, Mrs Gilver,' she said.

'Mrs Gilver again, am I?' I responded, startled.

'In my office, nice and private,' said Miss Shanks.

'Oh Ivy, you're no fun,' said Miss Barclay and she gave me a greedy look with an unpleasant reptilian glitter about it.

'What's going on?' I said. I had had a long and exhausting day full of other people's emotions and perhaps it had worn me out. Certainly I was feeling most peculiar standing here. The way they were all looking at me made me want to feel behind myself for the door handle to be sure that if I had to I could easily get away.

'What's going on, she asks!' said Miss Shanks, with a good measure of glee. 'Well, you've been disappearing, haven't you? Wandering the village when you should be at prayers, tramping about the countryside instead of supervising prep, you've made very free with my telephone and you've done a wee bitty too much skulking around the house too.'

'Not to mention not taking the register,' put in Miss Christopher.

'And your discipline in the refectory is abysmal,' said Miss Barclay. 'Giggling fits from start to finish and you just sit there and let them.'

'And to cap it all,' said Mrs Brown, 'you go drinking in pubs. Don't think you kept that one quiet.'

'Rather difficult to keep anything quiet when there's a member of the Brown family to hand,' I said coolly. My face did not feel cool, for when they set out my last few days like the sweets stall at a bazaar they made pretty rich pickings.

'I've done a wee tate of checking up on you,' said Miss Shanks. My heart was hammering now. 'And do you know what I found?' I shook my head, dreading the answer.

'I can't find the Gilver and Osborne Agency listed anywhere. I rang the number on your wee card and all I got was some hoity-toity fellow-me-lad who wouldn't give his name and had never heard of it.'

Pallister, I thought, not knowing whether to bless him or curse him. His wilful determination not to countenance the existence of my career had no doubt cost me a case or two in the past (and I thanked the gods that most requests came by written letter) but at least he had not regaled Miss Shanks with the news that Gilver and Osborne were detectives.

'So we've been having a wee confab to ourselves,' Miss Shanks went on. 'And we reckon you're no more an English mistress than I'm a kangaroo.' I kept my gaze level and waited. 'We reckon you were just chancing your arm slipping in here when you knew your pal was slipping out, looking for a roof over your head and three square meals a day.' Still, I made my face remain impassive. Was it possible that they had, in Teddy's phrase, rumbled me as a counterfeit schoolmistress and yet completely missed the truth?

'So we're all agreed?' Miss Barclay said, looking round.

'I've been saying it since Friday,' said Mrs Brown.

'We're all agreed,' said Miss Shanks. 'We'd like you to leave, Mrs Gilver. Anderson will take your things down to the Crown directly.'

'What about the girls?' I said. 'Who's going to give them their English lessons?'

'I'm sure Miss Glennie will oblige,' said Miss Christopher. 'And it's really none of your concern anyway.'

'So I'm being sacked,' I said, 'for using a telephone I was invited to use and for going on walks no one told me not to go on and for spending time in a village inn that you knew I was staying at when you employed me, because you visited me there.'

'You're being sacked,' said Miss Barclay coldly, 'for perpetrating a fraud.'

'Och, come on away!' trilled Miss Shanks. 'No need to get so het up.'

'I'll make my farewell then, ladies,' I said. 'I wish you well and give my regards to Miss Lovage and Miss Glennie.'

I bowed my head briefly and left them. Part of me was glad to be released, I thought on my way upstairs again, for now I could investigate the case instead of reading stories with school-girls and letting Alec have all the fun. Another part of me, however, could not bear the thought of leaving this strangest of places before I had discovered what was going on here. A third part of me, despite the fact that it was happening with depressing regularity these days, still felt that the touch of a boot to the seat of my skirts made rather a dent in my dignity.

But there was no time to nurse it. Before I left St Columba's for ever there was something I had to do.

9

'Miss Glennie?' I said, opening the door in response to the timid invitation to enter.

'Miss Gilver,' she said. 'Again.' She was hunched over her desk with a great number of sheets of paper spread around, but looked up as I entered.

'I've come to warn you,' I said, closing the door behind me. 'I know you've only just arrived but if there was another opening you turned down in preference to this one, I'd urge you very strongly to see if it's still there.'

'There wasn't,' Miss Glennie said. 'Lambourne only sent me this one and I was lucky to have that. And then Miss Shanks has been very kind to me . . . most accommodating. Bent over backwards, actually.'

'No doubt,' I said, thinking of the way Ivy Shanks had given over her study to me and allowed Alec to visit me in my room until her swift volte-face and my even swifter sacking. 'And do you know she's expecting you to teach English as well?' I saw from her quick frown that this was news. 'I've been given the boot, you see. And I want to help it not happen to you.'

'I—' stammered Miss Glennie. 'I'll very happily take on English if there's time. I mean, the other mistresses help out in areas not their own, don't they?'

'Well, then, at the very least, if there's any way that you could . . .' I fell silent. This next bit was rather difficult to work one's way round to. 'If you had said anything, out of nerves perhaps, over-egging or maybe even slightly exaggerating your curriculum vitae, I think it would be a good idea to see if you could perhaps tone it down a bit. Rescind, if possible. Recant. Miss Shanks can be a bit capricious when it comes to . . . she might seem to have countenanced something that she later will pounce on. You might not even know why.'

'What are you talking about?' said Miss Glennie. She looked baffled; no sign that she had caught even a wisp of my meaning.

'Well, if you didn't want her to know that you'd been without a position for a while and you said something . . . unlikely . . . that you regretted.'

'My last position?' said Miss Glennie, cottoning on at last. 'She's been nothing but sweet about that. And I didn't tell her. Lambourne told her.'

'You told them, presumably,' I said, thinking she was rather splitting hairs.

'I think they knew anyway,' said Miss Glennie. 'They hinted as much when they rang me. I was . . . very surprised.'

Not as surprised as me, I thought, staring at her. Could it be true after all that this awkward woman really had been a member of the royal household? How did she come from that to Miss Shanks's school? Or even to a scholastic agency? Would she not be desired by every family in the land to teach their little ones the French she had taught to the princes and the princess there?

'Naturally, I hadn't said a word,' said Miss Glennie. 'But one of the Lambourne ladies is Aberdonian and maybe there was a domestic connection.'

'Very possibly,' I said, thinking of the Browns and how they ran the Crown, the Post office and St Columba's amongst them. 'And very commendable of you, Miss Glennie, I must say, not to trade on your illustrious acquaintance. It must make you uncomfortable that Miss Shanks is so much less circumspect, eh?'

'I'm in no position to complain,' Miss Glennie said. 'Thankful to have a job and to be accepted by these good people.'

Almost as though, I thought to myself, it was something of which to be ashamed. A very odd position to take, unless one had fallen in with Bolshies, which Miss Shanks and her mistresses were not.

'Well, I've said my piece,' I concluded, 'and I wish you all the very best, in spite of it. I hope you will be happy here.' Miss Glennie gave a pained smile, although whether to indicate that she doubted it or simply that she had had enough of this odd woman bothering her was hard to say.

'You seem to have settled in anyway,' I said, waving a hand around at the watercolours hanging on walls which had been bare the day before and the crowd of photographs on the chimneypiece. I am ashamed to say, I even sidled towards these to see if among them were any of the exalted household; for governesses, like nannies, were much given to mementoes of their charges. To my disappointment, if not my surprise (for I still did not quite believe the Balmoral angle), the photographs in their ornate frames were two ancient ones of a couple dressed in high Edwardian style, and a enormous number of just one child from infanthood to the army.

'My parents and my brother,' said Miss Glennie.

I knew better than to ask about the brother, for when the photographs stop with a young man in uniform one knows exactly what it means.

'And are your parents . . . gone to their rest?' I said. It was Grant's phrase and I had not employed it before.

'No,' said Miss Glennie, her face tightening.

'My mistake,' I said. 'Awfully sorry.' And since there is nothing much to say after one has suggested that a person's entire family is dead and been corrected, I bade her goodnight and withdrew. Well, what did she expect? I asked myself crossly as I returned to my own room. She should have a snap of them all white of hair and gnarled of knuckle at their cottage gate if she wanted people to know they were still living.

'Ah, there ye are,' said a gruff voice as I turned the last corner. The sound of it was startling in this place where femininity reigned. It was Anderson the handyman.

'Here to see me off the premises?' I said.

'Just to give ye a lift wi' yer bags, miss,' he said, and his eyes, it is true, were kindly enough. He might be Miss Shanks's servant but he was not, I thought, her henchman.

'Lots of coming and going, eh?' I said. Anderson raised his eyes to heaven and whistled. Meanwhile I opened my suitcase, standing with my back to him and hoping to cover my movements. I took out Jeanne Beauclerc's case and immediately sat my hat on top of it. I opened my wardrobe, extracted the small bag and dropped my mackintosh over it. Thus I tried to hide the initials, which had winked at me in the lamplight.

'And now I just need to throw some things in here,' I said, nodding at my own case.

'I'll go down and get your trunk,' he said. 'I thought ye were packed and ready.'

'Oh, I don't have a trunk,' I said, flinging open drawers and tossing underclothes into the open suitcase. Anderson looked everywhere except at the flying stockings and vests. I scraped the heap of brushes, papers, cigarettes and powder tins in on top and shut the lid, stuffing in the escaping corners of garments until the latch caught and I could lock it.

He lifted it without effort and made a move towards the larger of Jeanne Beauclerc's cases too.

'I'll take those, Anderson,' I said, working my hands in under the hat and coat and grasping the handles.

'Away,' said Anderson. 'I'll manage them fine. One under ma oxter and the other in ma hand.'

'No, no, really, I insist,' I said.

'I'm mebbes nearly seventy but I'm no' that clapped out just yet,' he said, setting his jaw at a mulish angle.

'Oh God,' I said – which shocked him more than my proposal to carry my own bags – and lifted the hat and coat. He was looking me right in the eye as he tucked the overnight case under one arm, but he glanced down as he grasped the other handle and his eyes widened. *J.A.deV.B.* glinted unmistakably there. I considered for just a second trying to convince him that these were the initials of my maiden name, but the notion passed without making its way as far as my lips.

'You must be wondering about that, Anderson,' I said. But he surprised me.

'I keep my head down and my trap shut,' he said. 'This job comes wi' a house and there's a fine big stretch o' garden.'

Now *my* eyes flashed. What did he keep his head down to avoid seeing? What did he keep his trap shut about? Before I could ask him, we were disturbed by the sound of someone approaching. Not Miss Shanks for once, I thought, even before the figure appeared at the bend in the passageway. It was Miss Barclay, holding herself very rigid and with a thin smile of untold meanness on her mouth. She held out a brown envelope to me.

'One day's pay, Miss Gilver,' she said. 'So there'll be no need for you to come back for anything once you've gone.' She glanced at Anderson and I was surprised and delighted to see that he had turned the case, so that its initials were hidden against his corduroyed leg.

'Miss,' he said, giving a nod.

Miss Barclay gave exactly the same nod back to him and, with her mouth even tighter and yet even more amused by it all, she left us.

I followed Anderson in silence to the side door, where he loaded my bags onto a small handcart, lit a lantern which swung from a pole at its prow and started pushing it up the drive.

'It's a jolly long way,' I said, trotting after him.

'Safer than the cliff steps, though but,' said Anderson.

'And it'll give us a nice chance for a chat,' I said, hopefully.

'We've got space for ten chickens and we can fatten a pig,' said Anderson, returning to his previous topic. 'And there's a good apple tree and a fine patch o' rhubarb and brambles all over the bank.'

'And I would do nothing to put any of that in danger of being snatched away,' I said. 'If you have anything to tell me I shall think of some way to make it seem I found out from an entirely different quarter, you have my word.'

'Oh, it's no' that,' said Anderson. We had emerged from the drive now and were making our way along the top road towards the row of villas. 'Just if St C.'s gets shut down what's to become of Maidie and me? Our laddie has six o' a family in a two-room house and our lass is in service. I dinnae fancy the Parish – would *you*? – so I keep my head down.'

'And your trap shut, yes,' I said. So whatever it was would close St Columba's down, would it, if it ever came to light?

'Anyway, nae harm done,' said Anderson.

'I'm not sure Mademoiselle Beauclerc would agree with you,' I said, crisply. 'Or Miss Lipscott.'

'Eh?' said Anderson. 'They're off an' out o' it. They're all right now.' I made the mistake of looking as interested as I felt in this cryptic remark and by the light of his lantern he saw me. He shut his mouth as though he meant never to open it again in his life and put his head down like a bull, pointing the way with his lowered brow. I got not another syllable until he lifted his cap at the door of the Crown and said farewell.

The landlady of the Crown was in her dressing gown and curling papers with vanishing cream in a thick layer all over her face, but she had me sign the guestbook without making too much of a murmur – after I named a lordly new rate for the same room in which I had spent that first night – and she unbent so far as first to shout for her husband to carry my cases and then to ask me if I had had my tea or would I like a drop of soup brought up to me.

'The parlour fire's banked for the night, madam,' she said, 'so you'll be cosier in your bedroom with the gas on.'

It seemed a long time since dinner with those silly little girls but I rejected the offer. I know that the leftover soup from a Scotswoman's kitchen is not for the fainthearted, given its starting point of rib-sticking heft and the nature of the inevitable barley which works away long after the actual cooking is done, so that sometimes second- or (I have heard tell of it) *third*-day soup can be just as easily eaten with a fork as with a spoon.

A door across the landing cracked open as the landlord – hastily bundled into his trousers over his nightshirt – set my bags down inside the door of my room and in the space I saw the gleam of more vanishing cream and the wink of the landing light glancing off spectacle lenses. The landlord stumped off to the back stairs.

'Can I help you?' I said with cold grandeur, at which the convalescent widow opened her door and attempted to stare me down.

'He's not here,' she said. 'He left this morning.'

'I do not have the pleasure of understanding you,' I replied.

'Oh, very dignified,' she said, 'with your chin in the air and your head high!' Her lip had curled. 'I wouldn't live that grubby, scrabbling life of yours for a king's ransom.'

There could be no doubt of her meaning and I should have been able to sneer back, shrug and shut my door but I was possessed of some devil all of a sudden. I could not help thinking of all the girls who would hang their heads in the face of it. I saw Jeanne Beauclerc's drooping head in my mind's eye and remembered her saying her family did not own her. I saw Fleur's pinched, pale face and her fathomless reserve. I saw the scared eyes of Miss Thomasina Glennie as she huddled over her papers, shrinking away from me. I could picture too Miss Blair's look of hurt and bewilderment, as Alec had described it, and I wondered what we would see in the faces of Miss Taylor and Miss Bell if we should ever find them. Something – some idea, vague and shapeless – shifted deep inside me like a shipwreck dragging across the ocean floor when a current catches it broadside.

I blinked and the widow came into focus again.

'Gossip is a nasty habit, my dear madam,' I said, 'but slander is a crime. Or is it libel when it's written? I can never remember. And lying is a *sin*.'

'I don't know *what* you mean!' she said, thoroughly ruffled.

'And the poison from a pen travels up the arm more readily than it does onto the paper,' I went on.

'What are you talking about?'

'Imagine if you died tonight. And met your Maker.'

'You're not right in your head!' she said. 'I shall go to the police tomorrow and tell them you've threatened me.'

'You do that,' I said to her, smiling, 'and see what they say.'

I allowed her to turn, with a swish of her shiny dressing gown, and slam her door. It would have been very satisfying to beat her to it and leave *her* standing there, but I wondered if the idea would come back and take form if I kept still and let it return to me. I was still waiting motionless, when the electric landing light, set on a timer I supposed against the profligacy of the guests, clicked off again and left me in blackness.

Inside my room, I set Jeanne's cases by the door for the morning and began the dreary task of unpacking the jumble of belongings I had swept into my own. A box of powder, improperly clasped, had burst open and liberally doused the top layer of items. I banged my hairbrush and blew the worst of it off my sleeping cap, then I lifted an untidy heap of papers and shook them like maracas. One green sheet drifted free and eddied to the floor. Oh Lord, I thought, as I dumped the rest of them down and bent to retrieve it. It was an examination paper. In all my muddle I had not returned it to Miss Shanks and in all hers she had forgotten to ask for it from me. But should I burn it or send it back to her in the morning? I sat down on the low fire stool and started leafing through the rest of the pile – newspapers, scribbled notes on the case, scribbled notes on my abandoned lessons – for the other one. Halfway through the heap, I caught a glimpse of the pink paper I remembered taking from Miss Shanks's hands. And there on top of it was something else. Something I could not understand coming to be there.

It was a letter, a pale mauve envelope, and the address, written in blue ink with a thick pen, was *Miss I. Shanks (Headm.), St Columba's School, Portpatrick*. I picked it up and stared at it, then I ran over the scene in Miss Shanks's office in my mind: she opened the safe and stirred the disorder of papers inside it. Aha! Yes, she had stopped a small landslide with her knee and shoved the things back. She had handed me two sheets, and this envelope must have been caught between them.

It had not occurred to me then but it struck me as very odd now. No one kept letters in a safe, did they? One kept examination papers (if one ran a school), deeds, bonds, cash, jewels, one's chequebook if one were the cautious sort. But not letters, unless it were that one happened to have an autograph letter from some great man – the Duke of Marlborough on the eve of battle, say. And yet Ivy Shanks had had a heap of them, and great men did not write on the eve of battle using blue ink and mauve paper.

I turned the envelope over and lifted the flap with not even a moment's hesitation. The sender was a Mr Thos. Simmons. His name and address (The Rowans, Moffat) were embossed on the paper along with a reproduced etching of his house in a little oval lozenge, two dark patches on either side representing the eponymous rowans, one supposed.

Dear Miss Shanks, the letter began. *Thank you most kindly for yours of the seventeenth. My lady wife and I will most certainly look forward to seeing you on 'Parents' Day' at St Columba's and are already anticipating with eagerness getting down to the 'nitty-gritty'. Ship ahoy! Or as it might be – Tally-ho! We are delighted to hear that Tilly is 'doing so well'. Yours most faithfully, Mr & Mrs Thos. Simmons.*

Of course, I thought. The name of Simmons had rung a bell. 'Tilly' who was 'doing so well' (why the quotation marks there? Who could say?) was Clothilde Simmons, to whom Miss Shanks had alerted me during my one and only day as English mistress. That one part of the letter made sense to me: the rest of it was a mystery. Tally-ho? Ship ahoy? Nitty-gritty? And had Miss Shanks really written a letter to every pair of parents inviting them to the Parents' Day, which must come around with foreseeable regularity every year? If she had found the time for such a pointless gesture, why on earth was she keeping their replies in the safe?

Thoughtfully, I folded the letter and returned it to the envelope, then I tucked it and the examination papers back into the gloves pocket of my bag. The letter was a crashing let-down when it came to the puzzle of Ivy Shanks and the greater (if more nebulous) puzzle of St Columba's in general, but it was good to have some reason to go back there should the need arise, if only because that little brown envelope of money from Miss Barclay showed me how very much they hoped I would not do so.

I finished my rough unpacking, paying less and less attention to the removal of powder as the task went on, and then crawled, exhausted, into my little bed in a dusty but sweet-smelling nightgown and was dead to the world before the midnight high tide came crashing and booming into the harbour.

I was up and off long before the landlady had started frying bacon the next morning, and all was quiet behind the convalescent widow's bedroom door. The station, in contrast, was greatly a-bustle, fish crates stacked under sacking waiting for the goods train to take them to town and enough housewives in their good coats and farmers in their good trousers to imply that today was a market day somewhere and a train bound for it was due along soon. Checking with the ticket-master, I decided to wait instead of dropping off Miss Beauclerc's bags and was rewarded less than a quarter of an hour later when a figure in a bulky checked overcoat of an unlikely blue and with a headscarf pulled far forward and tied on the chin so that only a sliver of face was showing, and that in shadow, stopped in front of me and cleared her throat. The slim legs and narrow, hand-stitched shoes did not go with the garish coat and dowdy headgear and when I looked up it was into the face, pale and stark, of Jeanne Beauclerc.

'Thank you, Miss Gilver,' she said, sitting down on the bench beside me. 'Your good husband rang me last evening and he has told me I will be met at your little station. He has told me that I am to be a guest in your house, not a servant after all.'

'Not at all,' I said. 'Glad to help. We'll find Fleur, and as soon as we do I shall ring home and let you know.' She nodded and bit her lip. 'I don't suppose, now you're on your way, that you'll tell me any more of what's going on?' She shook her head. 'I thought as much, but I had to try. Well, can you tell me this? My husband asked me and I assured him, so I'd like you to assure me. You're not mixed up with any rascals who're looking for you, are you? Or in trouble with the police?'

'There will be no rascals,' said Miss Beauclerc and for the first time I thought I could hear a smile in her voice. 'Your husband is in no danger.'

'And no police? I know you must be in some kind of trouble to be planning, as you were, to run away.'

'No police,' said Miss Beauclerc. Then she ruined the reassurance completely. 'I was acquitted.'

'Of what?' I said, sitting up and peering round the corner of her headscarf to look into her eyes. 'My son is there too, you see. Young and innoc— Well, impressionable anyway.'

'Of everything,' she said calmly. 'If your son is there perhaps I can make myself useful instructing him. I am a French mistress more than I am an embroiderer, you see.'

I quailed to think what a Frenchwoman of twenty-five whose family had disowned her, acquitted or no, could teach Donald, but before I could say anything everyone turned their heads in unison as the train whistle sounded just out of sight.

'I'll be in touch very soon,' I said. 'You'll probably only need to be there a day or two.' I was comforting myself now. 'But, I say, I tell you what you could do for me. My dog – Bunty – dear old thing. You could cuddle her and spoil her. Hugh would never be cruel but he neglects her most fearfully when I'm away. I've come back before now to find her billeted in the stables, the poor darling. If you like dogs, that is. I'd be very grateful.'

'I adore little doggies,' said Miss Beauclerc. 'What kind is she?'

'A Dalmatian,' I said. 'Not so little. Do you know—'

'But of course. With the polka-dots like a pretty dress. Such beautiful creatures. I shall give her all your hugs and kisses and tell her of your love.'

With that the train was upon us, snorting and steaming like a beast from mythology in that terrific way that trains always seem to do when they arrive in very quiet country stations (in comparison with great metropolitan stations where amongst the other noise and bustle the trains seem quite tame creatures). Jeanne Beauclerc stood, kissed me once on each cheek, and stepped inside the first-class carriage.

Acquitted of everything, was all I could think of as I made my way back to the Crown. Should I ring Hugh and tell him? I am sorry to say that the thought of Bunty being showered with kisses won the day and I decided that Hugh and even Donald were big boys now and could cope with whatever a Mademoiselle Beauclerc might bring. So I turned my mind to the case again, the great sprawling tentacled monster of a case, still growing and still eluding my grasp with every flex of its muscular form.

'Sacked?' said Alec, cackling down the line. 'Dear goodness, Dan. So where are you?'

'Back at the Crown,' I said. 'Much to the disgust of the widow.'

'Poor you,' Alec said. 'The Horseshoe at Egton is a delightful billet. I reckon I could put up here for a good three weeks until I'd eaten my way through their supper menu and the breakfast I've just polished off – words fail me.'

'Good,' I said, but he had been speaking metaphorically.

'I had this stuff – a kind of sausage, I suppose – that goes by the name of black pudding. Have you ever had black pudding, Dandy? It's a little like boudin noir, only—'

'It's a great deal like boudin noir, you goose,' I said. 'It *is* boudin noir!'

'Really?' Alec said. 'I failed to recognise it in the midst of the general fry-up, I suppose.'

'There really isn't time for—' I said.

'Speaking of fry-ups,' said Alec, 'what of Joe?'

'I don't think you fully appreciate just how busy I've been at this end,' I said. 'I haven't had time to hold Joe's hand as well as everything else. I've made our apologies and he's on his own. Literally. Poor Sabbatina is so angry with him, she can't look him in the eye.'

'Angry with *him*?' said Alec.

'I know, it's terribly unfair,' I said. 'But it's very hard to be angry with someone who's gone. And one can't help but wonder . . .'

'What?'

'Oh, if all the lovey-dovey stuff is genuine or if it was for our benefit, after the fact,' I said. 'I mean, he charmed me and he charmed you. His own daughter is most likely of all three to have a clear view of the man. And his wife did leave, after all. Anyway, never mind that. Now I'm released from servitude again we can apportion the tasks a bit more equally.'

'As long as I don't get stuck with the donkey work now that you're available,' said Alec.

'You choose first then,' I replied. 'I'm just happy not to be reading Milton. Except, clearly, it makes sense for me to talk to the Portpatrick police.' I heard him drawing breath to ask what about, so I told him. 'The news that Fleur's bags were left behind makes me much more worried that she didn't just take off. And knowing that she had a plan and abandoned it only adds to the concern. They need to put a lot more effort into finding her, if you ask me.'

'Agreed,' Alec said. 'And agreed also that you should do that since you're there. As far as I can see, the other tasks are finding out about the car crash that killed Charles – thanks for the telegram, by the way; it raised my stock no end with the serving wenches. Got me a sandwich at bedtime. The other thing we need to do is find out what happened to the Misses Taylor and Bell.'

'And I only hope that one thing or another jogs the whole mess back into gear somehow,' I said. 'I'm convinced there's a pattern there somewhere if I could catch hold of the ends . . .'

'My dear, your metaphors,' said Alec. 'But I know what you mean. It's a veritable hydra this one, isn't it?'

'Exactly what I was thinking,' I said. 'Even if we excise your case from the tangle – ignore Joe, ignore Sabbatina, ignore what Cissie saw – there's still Fleur and Jeanne and Miss Blair and Miss Taylor and Miss Bell.'

'And No. 5 and Elf and Charles and another two murder victims somewhere,' said Alec.

'And Miss Shanks and Barclay and Christopher and Lovage,' I said.

'And the new one,' said Alec.

'Miss Glennie,' I said. 'But she doesn't go with them. She's another like Fleur and the mademoiselle.'

'What does that mean?' said Alec. I thought very carefully before I answered him.

'I don't know,' I said, at last. 'Just a hunch. One of those wispy . . .'

'Oh, one of *them*,' Alec said, teasingly. 'Well, I suppose they've led you to a solution more than once before now.'

'They've led me up the garden path a lot more often, though,' I said. 'And to complete our list there's "The School". I almost wish I had managed to stick it. At least until Parents' Day.'

'What's that?' said Alec. 'Sort of a Speech Day thing?'

'Yes, and I found the most peculiar letter from a parent accepting the invitation to it.'

'Oh?' said Alec. 'Peculiar how?'

'Well, Miss Shanks had it under lock and key for one thing. And it said how pleased the father was with his daughter's form place and how much he was looking forward to coming for a visit. And it said "Tally-ho" for no good reason I can see.'

'Well, call for the police,' said Alec. 'Tally-ho, eh?'

'You'll be sorry you mocked me when the dread deeds come to light,' I told him. 'So, Taylor and Bell for you? Or Charles and the car crash?'

'Oh, Taylor and Bell, I think,' said Alec. 'The girl on the desk at the Lambourne Agency is my old friend, remember. I've got a head start with her. And anyway, I'd rather telephone than drag myself to a library. It's fish pie for lunch at the Horseshoe.'

'Don't forget the Somerville College possibility if the agency can't help you,' I said. 'Until later then.' I rang off and remained seated in the little alcove, thinking it all over and planning the course of my day until I grew aware that someone was watching me. Suspecting the widow, I turned with a cold look on my face, but it was only the maid.

'Are you finished with the telephone, madam?' she said. 'Only I've to sweep the hall.'

'It's Miss Brown, isn't it?' I said.

'Mary, madam,' she said. 'I'm only a parlour maid.'

'But it's Mary *Brown*,' I persisted.

'Yes, m'm,' she said.

'Well, Mary, I don't know how much of my conversation you overheard while you were standing there,' I said, 'but make no mistake, I shall take a very dim view if any of it gets up the hill to your aunt at the school.'

'Oh no, m'm,' she said, colouring deeply and clasping her hands in front of her.

'I shan't scruple to inform your employers and I shan't be content until I know you're not in a position to carry tales again.'

'No, no really, m'm,' she said. 'It's not me. I mean, yes, Mrs Brown is my auntie, but it's my sister, you mean. Kitchen maid. Her and Auntie Belle are as thick as thieves. I'm not— I mean, it's Elsie you mean and I don't tell her nothin'.'

'Glad to hear it,' I said, and with one last bob the poor girl scuttled off into the back regions, presumably to fetch her brushes. I stood and stretched and made for the foot of the stairs, but was arrested by the sight of the widow, with her companion beside her, halfway up the first flight, looking down on me. She was holding the younger woman back with one arm thrown out.

'Threatening the little maid now, is it?' she said. 'You need a doctor, not a policeman.'

'I see that your companion has more breeding than you, madam,' I said, nodding at how the widow's arm was blocking the way. 'She clearly understands that one should make one's presence known when one intrudes upon a private conversation, not lurk at the turn in the stairs, eavesdropping.'

'And would you say eavesdropping,' said the widow, flushing, 'is a bad habit, a crime or a *sin*, Mrs Gilver?' She half-turned to the other who was squirming with embarrassment. 'I told you, Enid. She's without any shame.'

'Eavesdropping,' I said, 'is a window on a flawed moral character but too tawdry to dwell upon. Blackmail, now . . . Blackmail is much more serious.'

'Blackmail!' said the widow.

'Strictly, I suppose, just the first careful step towards it.'

'Are you threatening me?' said the widow, while her companion shifted from foot to foot and whimpered ineffectually at her elbow.

'Only with exposure,' I said. 'Do you deny it?'

'Blackmail now!' said the widow. 'Slander and libel and lying and blackmail. You're not safe to be out amongst decent people! Come on, Enid. Let's go. I need some fresh wholesome air.'

At the police station, to my disappointment, it was Sergeant Turner who came to see who had crossed the threshold and caused the bell to ring.

'Mrs Gilver,' he said, in the tone one would use to say 'burst water mains' or 'flat tyre'.

'Sergeant Turner!' I said, trying to sound as one would saying 'rising stock prices' or 'sunshine forecast'. 'I was wondering if there was any news in the hunt for Miss Lipscott. I have some evidence to add to what we know of her disappearance.'

'There you go again, madam,' he said. 'We-ing. *We*, the police, might not choose to share anything *we* know with *you*, the general public.'

'Well, Sergeant,' I said, after a swift review of whether there was any reason not to tell him, now that I had given up trying to pass myself off as a mistress at St Columba's, 'we – Mr Osborne and I – are not the general public, exactly. We're private detectives. And we've worked with policemen before.'

'Private detectives?' said Sergeant Turner and, if I had to supply another phrase to suit the tone *this* time, 'amoebic dysentery' would be near the head of the queue.

'Two things, Sergeant,' I said, sailing on. 'Miss Lipscott did not take her bags with her when she left. They were packed and yet she didn't pick them up. If she left of her own accord and under her own steam it's safer to say that she *fled* than simply moved on.'

'Thank you,' said Sergeant Turner and did not utter another syllable.

'Also,' I said, 'I can tell you now with complete certainty that the body at the cable station – or wherever she is now – is not Jeanne Beauclerc.'

He dearly wanted to issue another bland thank you such as the police give to the general public who offer information, but he also wanted to disparage my contribution and after a struggle that urge won.

'We knew that,' he said. 'Two mistresses from the school said it wasn't her.'

'Still,' I said, 'a faceless handless corpse . . . whereas I can confirm it for sure.'

'How?' said Sergeant Turner, after another brief struggle.

'Oh good, let's share our information after all,' I said. 'Good show.'

What, I wondered, was wrong with me this morning? I had gone after the poisonous widow like a Jack Russell terrier and now here I was antagonising the police sergeant too.

'It's not a question of sharing, Mrs Gilver,' said the sergeant. 'It's a question of withholding – unless you answer my question. And withholding desired information from the police is a very serious matter.'

'And is it desired, Sergeant?' I said. I could not seem to help myself. 'I thought you knew already that the body wasn't Miss Beauclerc. What information do *I* have, to withhold or not?'

He glared at me for a moment and then looked over his shoulder and barked for the constable. Reid popped his head out of a door.

'Deal with this, laddie,' said Turner. 'I've got more to be doing than wasting time with a lot of . . .' He waved a hand and withdrew into the back premises well away from my nonsense. I turned down the corners of my mouth and flashed my eyes at Reid but he regarded me with a very stony expression.

'What is it?' I said.

'What's what?' said Reid.

'Something's wrong,' I said.

'Nowt wrong wi' me,' said Reid, but like his sergeant he lost the struggle with his better self. 'What did you say to—' He looked over his shoulder and dropped his voice. 'What did you say to Cissie on Sunday?'

'Many things,' I replied. 'What do you mean?'

'She's sent me a wee note this mornin' wi' Tam Ramsay the baker, sayin' she won't see me tonight.'

'Of course,' I said. 'It's Tuesday, isn't it? Your night for walking and – em – sitting. Well, possibly Cissie doesn't feel the same about the Dunskey Castle cliffs since she had to think about someone plunging off them.'

'Aye but it's no' just that she doesn't want to go a walk,' said Reid. 'We sometimes go to the Empire in Stranraer. She disnae want to see me at all. What did you say?'

'Nothing.' I thought hard about our conversation. 'I swear to you, William. Absolutely nothing. I'm sure all that's wrong is that she's unnerved by the talk of bodies and strangers and people watching. She'll come round again. But listen, I've come to ask how the search is going for Miss Lipscott and also to tell you something.'

Quickly, I rehashed the tale of Fleur being packed and ready to go and yet leaving her bags behind her. He stared at me for a moment and I thought he might say another quelling thank you just as the sergeant had done, but he was made of finer stuff and had a sharper wit any day.

'Why were her bags packed?' he asked.

'Because she had been planning to go already,' I said. 'Quite elaborately planning. She and Miss Beauclerc were going to go together. Only Beauclerc fled too. A few days before the plan was ready to be executed.'

'And how did you find all this out?'

'I found her,' I told him.

'You just asked me how the search was going—'

'I found Miss Beauclerc,' I said. 'She was hiding at P— Well, in a local guesthouse, waiting for Miss Lipscott to send word to her.'

'Paterson's farm!' said Reid. 'I chapped their door on Saturday asking all about did they see the corpse go in and did they ken where Miss Lipscott was.'

'They didn't, to be fair,' I said.

'Splittin' hairs, that! Right, well, I'd better get round there and talk to her. There's somethin' gey queer about all this runnin' away.'

'Ah, well, as to that,' I said. 'She's not there now. She was only waiting for Fleur and when I told her Fleur was gone, there was no reason for her to hang around any more.'

'That's a pity,' said Reid very sternly, quite obviously blaming me for her departure. (If he knew that I had fetched her bags, he would have a fit. If he knew where she was going, he would have a heart attack.)

'But to be fair,' I said, 'she knew nothing of No. 5 or of Fleur's change of plan or where Fleur might have gone.'

'She must ken where they were both headed to begin wi',' he said.

'Miss Lipscott's family home,' I said. 'But unless her family is lying, Fleur's not there now.' I was determined not to tell him where Jeanne Beauclerc was off to; I had assured Hugh there would be no policemen following her there.

'Aye, you're doubtless right,' said Reid. He reached under the counter and drew out his hat. 'At least, I can come and get her bags. Eh? Might be something in them, like a wee clue.'

'Ahhhhhh,' I said. 'Yes, Miss Lipscott's bags, actually, are gone.'

'Gone?'

'Yes, I um, yes.'

'But you found them. Where did you put them?'

'I left them where they were,' I said. 'Yes, I let it be known that I was sniffing around the luggage room where the bags were sitting and then I just left them there. Someone – Miss Shanks is my guess – must have spirited them away overnight. Not my finest hour, I'll grant you.'

'But why would anyone want to hide the bags except for to make it look like somebody left when really she's—'

'In a barrel of brine in the larder?' I said. 'Or hidden under a pile of coke in the boiler room?'

'If I was a sergeant and had ma own say-so I'd be up there with a warrant. Ask that wee Shanks woman what the devil's goin' on.'

'You couldn't persuade Sergeant Turner?'

The noise Reid made was expressive if rather sickening.

'Him!' he said. He took his hat off again and threw it under the counter. 'He cannae see there's anything to bother about. Even though I've never smelled a rat like it since the Pinminnoch Burn flooded and one the size o' a dog washed in tae ma Auntie Margaret's privy.'

'You paint a vivid picture,' I said, shuddering. 'Cissie will return to you for your silver tongue if nothing else, I'm sure.'

And so to Stranraer library, to sneeze and itch my way through a morning with the newspapers of nine years before looking for the death of 'Charles' who was auditioning for the part of No. 3.

It was not one of Andrew Carnegie's bequests, but was easily as solid and massive as if it had been, heavy with pillars and porticoes without and even heavier with marble and gilt banisters within, and I swept into the reference room blithely confident that they would have exactly what I was seeking.

The woman behind the reference desk, however, soon took the wind out of my sails.

'*The Times*, madam?' she said. 'The London *Times*? The English one? No, there's no call for that here.'

'But it's . . .' I said, and stopped myself before saying that it was *the newspaper*. A reference library not keeping *The Times* was like a cheese shop which did not sell cheddar. 'Which national newspaper do you carry?' I finished.

'*The Scotsman*,' said the librarian and dared me to comment on it.

'Ah, excellent,' I said, not convincing her for a second. 'Could I see *The Scotsman* for 1919, please?'

'Which month?' she asked, drawing a slip towards her and raising her pencil.

'All of them,' I said, as she well knew.

'Let's start with Jan to Mar,' she replied, scribbling, 'and we shall see.'

This remark, impertinently hinting that I had no sticking power, made me determined to read every issue of the damned thing from New Year's Day to New Year's Eve, even though I had been quietly wondering how newsworthy a motorcar crash (even one in which a fine young man was burned to a crisp) could possibly be. Would such an event in Dorset or London trouble the doughty *Scotsman*?

As the porter was summoned and sent to fetch the first volumes, I turned back the cuffs of my coat and tied a silk scarf over my hair (I am without vanity when it comes to old newspapers these days, after many a mite and a ruined shingle) and when they were plonked down on the table in front of me with a puff of musty dust which would not have put a conjuror to shame, I was ready for them.

The first few took an elephant's age as ever, until my eyes adjusted to the type and I began to see the pattern in the pages, the classified advertisements giving way to the political news, the society pages, the sporting triumphs and tragedies. By the time I was halfway through February I was so adept at finding the pages where such human interest snippets as a motorcar crash might be that more than once the librarian looked across and lowered her spectacles at me, concerned for the paper as I whipped it through my fingers in a blur.

And so, slowing down, I started to see the news I had been ignoring: the brand new National Socialist Party in Germany gathering steam even as the Treaty of Versailles lumbered towards its signing; the first reports of Herr Hitler's Italian counterpart – the one whose name I always thought sounded like some new delicious pudding – joining him at his game. Hugh's voice sounded in my memory again and, at least partly to silence it, the pages picked up speed once more. I turned aside a little to avoid the librarian's eye.

It was not until almost the end of March that I spotted something to arrest my progress and when I saw the headline – TWO KILLED AT LOCH BROOM – the faint bell which had rung when Aurora said the name 'Charles' clanged again, this time more clearly.

I remembered that young man dying, although I could not have produced his name before the newspaper reminded me. As far as I could recall, he was a youngster who, after a riotous party, had attempted a Highland road in a borrowed and unfamiliar motorcar and had driven it into a forest of pine trees where it had burst into flames. *The Scotsman* said as much and not a great deal more, in its sober way.

In the early hours of Sunday morning past on the road at Corrieshalloch Gorge, Charles Leigh, 23 yrs old, and his fiancée Leigh Audubon, 18 yrs old, were instantly killed when their borrowed motor collided with a tree trunk, which happening caused an engine fire. The victims were identified by means of their pocket watch and cigarette case respectively. The motorcar, a Bugatti of racing type, was destroyed. No one else was hurt.

I shuddered, reading it, remembering the cigarette case and watch now that I had been nudged; everyone regaling everyone else with that detail in horrified delight or genuine horror according to disposition.

So this could not be the Charles Aurora had meant. For one thing, his fiancée had not killed him and become a schoolmistress: she had died with him, leading some hard-hearted sorts to murmur that perhaps a lifetime of being called Leigh Leigh was worth escaping.

On the other hand, Corrieshalloch Gorge was less than fifteen miles from Ullapool and across the sea loch from Ullapool was the Major's hunting lodge. If Mamma-dearest had not sold it after his death (and why would she?) then that was a striking coincidence. Also, now that my memory was oiled and turning, I recalled a conversation with Hugh, relayed from George at the club, on the subject of this engagement which only came to light after the deaths. There had been some smirking, apparently – fiancée, indeed! – until the thought of the watch and cigarette case turned everyone solemn again.

I stared at the page until the tiny print and the yellowed background began to dazzle and I had to blink several times to clear my eyes again. Was I really going to ask the librarian to ask the porter to bring me Apr to Jun, Jul to Sep and then Oct to Dec, in hopes of another Charles who better fit the bill? I closed the March volume, and left the library, wiping the book dust from my fingers with a handkerchief.

There was no point in telephoning to Pearl again to find out any more, I considered, walking with measured pace along one of Stranraer's main streets. Most assuredly there was no point in telephoning to Aurora. That left Mamma-dearest. Did I dare? She was a woman of fathomless tranquillity and the thought of disturbing it was unpleasant. Besides, if her other two daughters had managed to keep the news from her that Fleur was missing again, I did not relish being its bearer. There was also the consideration that even at my advanced middle age, Mamma-dearest Lipscott – being one of the most striking characters of my youth and never seen again since then – was still 'one of the grown-ups' to me. Quite simply, I shrank inside at the prospect of interrogating her, even gently quizzing her, as though she could still if she chose write to my mother to tell of my shortcomings so that the visit was spoiled with the dread of returning home.

To be fair, though, that had never happened at Pereford. I had not given my poor mother a thought the whole summer long, beyond sending her a picture postcard from Watchet and choosing a hideous commemorative china basket of roses with Dorset written on it in loopy gold writing. I do not think that I picked it out deliberately to offend her taste but when I saw her open the tissue-paper package, in her own sitting room surrounded by her hand-hewn oak furniture and her verdigris obelisks, and saw too the sudden wince as though she had bitten down on a boiled sweet with a bad tooth, I knew my mistake. There was no sign of it anywhere when we tidied her things after her death, certainly.

I could not help but contrast Mamma-dearest's placid adoration of her own children's efforts; her almost voluptuous joy in the pipe-cleaner and pine-cone families Fleur made for her, the tears she shed over Aurora's piano-playing, claiming that she had never heard the *Lieder* sound more lovely. When Pearl painted her a watercolour rendition of the Major's last battle, Mamma-dearest shot to her feet and rang a framer in Weston to get it behind glass immediately for preservation. It was a pitifully amateurish picture too, the paper bubbled with too much water and the bloody battle so tastefully toned down that, if one did not know, one would imagine those men in their bright clothes to be having a round of golf on that green hill. Still, the painting hung in her bedroom, the pine-cone family sat on her writing table and Aurora was invited to play Schubert at every party, while Mamma-dearest sat misty-eyed and seemed not at all to notice the other guests squirming.

I had walked as far as the station, and remembering Signora Aldo's choice of kiosk from which to inform her husband she had left him, I thought I might as well make use of a telephone there. The privacy at the Crown was far from perfect, between the blackmailing widow, poor Enid at her elbow and the sisters Brown. I went to the newspaper-stand to buy a bar of chocolate and get some change (libraries, where even a peppermint is cardinal sin, always make me ravenously hungry) and then stood in one of the kiosks exhorting myself to courage, practising the opening line and casting around with mounting desperation for an excuse to abandon the plan. The tension was beginning to make my head ache (or perhaps I had tied the scarf over my hair too tightly) and when the operator demanded instructions I heard myself asking, instead, for a trunk call to the Horseshoe.

In the five minutes I was told it would take to string together this inordinately long line of connections, I wandered the station, noting the travellers reeling out of the boat train, still rather green about the gills, and the many passengers who seemed to be arriving with great heaps of luggage to cram onto a short train which sat pawing the ground and ready for the off.

'You getting on the 10.15, madam?' said a porter.

'I'm not,' I replied. 'I'm in the minority, eh? Busy little train.'

'Oh, she's a wee beauty,' said the porter. 'Here to Glasgow for the Flying Scotsman.'

'The Flying Scotsman starts at Edinburgh, doesn't it?' I said.

This was one of things one knew about the railway even if one knew nothing else. The Flying Scotsman left King's Cross at ten in the morning and left Edinburgh Waverley at one in the afternoon.

'She does not!' said the porter. 'The Flying Scotsman starts in the fair city of Glasgow. Edinburgh is just one o' the stops.'

'Golly,' I said. I had never known a porter so bursting with pride, and although I had no luggage and was not even boarding, I tipped him for his sheer *joie de vivre*. Then I checked the platform clock – it was just gone ten and my five minutes' wait was up – and returned to the kiosk.

'You sound as though you're in a barrel of nails, Dandy,' said Alec's voice. 'What a terrible line. Where are you?'

'Stranraer station,' I said. 'Yes, you're a bit gravelly too. How did it go?'

Alec began a tale which reached my ears as a series of clicks and buzzes with the odd word sticking up out of the noise like church spires in a low fog.

'No use, darling,' I said. 'I can't hear you. I said, I can't hear you!'

There were more clicks and buzzes and all I heard was my name.

'This is pointless,' I bellowed into the mouthpiece and then some kind of madness came over me, I think. I slammed down the telephone (such an ungrateful wretch after the exchange had put the connection together for me so quickly), glanced at the clock – ten past ten – and went to seek my porter friend again.

By *fifteen* minutes past ten, I had sent another telegram to the Horseshoe with detailed instructions of what I wanted Alec to do, purchased a ticket, asked the Crown to hold my room and was sitting in the last first-class seat in the only first-class carriage on the little train, with the fire dying down to grey embers in my belly and the list of essential items I did not have with me growing in my head. Hairbrush, toothbrush, underclothes, warm coat, the comfort of knowing that my husband knew where I was and what I was doing, the comfort of knowing myself why I was doing this . . . What I *did* have was an almost new notebook, a couple of sharp pencils and hours and hours of luxurious time to organise my thoughts and discoveries so that I could fathom out this maddening case before its waters met over my head and it drowned me.

10

When I stuck my head out of the window at York where we had a half-hour break for tea, Alec hailed me in great high spirits, waving a brown paper bag at me like a backbencher with his ballot papers.

'What's that?' I asked him. 'Hello, darling.'

'It's for you,' he said. 'Toothbrush, toothpaste and a few delicate garments I got in a ladies' outfitters.'

'You went into a ladies' outfitters and rifled through—'

'Of course not,' he said. 'I just murmured to the girl in the shop – something about my wife's lost luggage, you know – and she picked everything for you. No idea what size, though. I said you were "average".'

'How flattering,' I said. 'Hairbrush?'

'Ah,' said Alec. 'Well, you can borrow one of mine.'

'And Nanny Palmer turns in her grave once again. But thank you, thank you and a thousand times thank you. Now we can use our teatime to have some tea.'

'Better tea on the train,' said Alec, displaying yet again the new concern with his own stomach which had been so very much to the fore in Joe Aldo's and at the Horseshoe.

'But at such close quarters one can't talk freely,' I said. 'Come on, to the platform buffet with you and then we can go straight to the smoking lounge when the train sets off.'

We found a quiet table (or what passes for one amidst the hiss and clatter of the tea-making and plate-clearing which always go on apace in these settings) and over strong Indian and a plate of buns, I tried to explain to him what had come over me.

'Demob fever after being sacked, perhaps. It's lucky I'm not sitting on a sailor's lap drinking stout from the bottle. No, in all seriousness, I think Pearl is too much of a hard nut for us ever to crack her. You possibly went a little tiny bit too far the other way with Aurora. So like Goldilocks we need to try the third one and steer a middle course. And I need to go back to Pereford where it all began. Something happened there, Alec, to turn Fleur from the child she was into the girl who became the woman she is now. And Mamma— Mrs Lipscott doesn't know she's missing. Pearl and Aurora are protecting her from the pain of it.'

'But you think the pain might be useful if it joggles her into an explanation?'

'Rather a brutal way to put it but . . . yes. Now, tell me about Taylor and Bell. I didn't catch more than one word in ten on that nasty trunk line.'

'Ah yes,' said Alec. 'Well, I'm more than happy to have done with the dread contraption for a while myself, actually, because I was fairly finely grated by various parties this morning.'

'Oh?'

'I tried Lambourne first. Charming enough to bring the birds down out of the trees, if I say so myself, and got short shrift. I reminded the girl who answered the telephone that she had helped me earlier with Miss Blair and I asked – all chummy: I even remembered her name, which was Beverley – if she could work her magic again and put me in touch with the other two. She instructed me to wait and the next thing I knew some dragon was breathing fire down the line, demanding to know who I was and what I was up to and whether I wanted the police after me.'

'Really?' I said, arrested with a bite of bun halfway to my mouth. It fell off my fork and landed icing side down on the doily. 'Why the dramatic change?'

'I think Beverley must have casually mentioned my first enquiry and the dragon knows more about what's going on at St Columba's than she wants anyone else to find out.'

'You could be right, you know,' I said. 'Miss Glennie did say that Lambourne positively courted her. That's not how scholastic agencies usually go on.'

'I suppose not. So Beverley must have been well warned what to do if I ever rang again and she did it.'

'So what did *you* do?'

'Well, in for a penny in for a pound. I just plunged on and asked the dragon about Taylor and Bell anyway – hoping she'd say something useful if I rattled her – and I told her I didn't mind if she called the police. In fact, maybe *I'd* call them to see if they could help me. And guess what?'

'I give up.'

'She slammed the telephone down. And when I got the girl to try the number again it was engaged and it stayed engaged from then until I left the Horseshoe.'

'Hmph. So Taylor and Bell remain a mystery. Oh well.'

'No, no, not at all,' Alec said. 'I did as you suggested, Dan, and got on to Somerville College. Stirred up a secretary.'

'In a falsetto voice?' I asked. 'Pretending to be an old girl? I wish I'd been there to hear it.'

Alec blew a raspberry at me, attracting the glaring attention of a very respectable family at the next table who were eating ham and eggs as though stoking a boiler for a cold winter's night.

'No, I said I was writing an article on pioneering female scholars for a scientific journal and I particularly wished to speak to any of their early scientists.'

'Which one was the science mistress?'

'Tinker Bell,' said Alec. 'Do you know that was her nickname at Somerville too? So I was expecting some delicate little thing. Her voice down the line when I finally got through to her almost knocked me flat. I haven't heard a pair of lungs like it since a fairground tout who made me drop my lolly when I was six.'

'Down the line?' I said. 'You mean you actually spoke to her?'

'And she's still good pals with Miss Taylor too,' said Alec, with a triumphant wiggle of his eyebrows. 'But look, let's powder our noses and get back on board, eh? I'll tell you everything else on the way to London.'

'Everything else', though, did not get us much past the northern suburbs of Doncaster. We chose the smoking lounge in hopes of finding fewer ladies in there and in recognition of the shaming fact that gentlemen are less interested in others' concerns and would not listen, and were so lucky as to find no ladies at all and only two gentlemen, both at one end of the car, both elderly, both reading, and both swaying with the movement of the train in a way that suggested they would soon be asleep. We settled ourselves into armchairs at the other end. Alec rummaged in his pocket and drew out not the usual equipment but a paper bag which he held out to me.

'Pontefract cake?' he said.

'I've just eaten a bun,' I replied. 'And you ate two!'

'They're not really cakes,' said Alec. 'Pastilles, liquorice. A local delicacy. I got them while skulking outside your underclothes shop.'

I glanced at the two gentlemen but they were paying no attention.

'Not bad,' I said, tentatively rolling a pastille around my mouth. 'Now, Alec, what of your two mistresses?'

At that, I rather thought one of the old gentlemen *did* stir. Laughing gently, Alec resumed his report.

'Miss Bell is at St Leonards now,' he said. 'The secretary at Somerville was quite happy to tell me, and I caught her between breakfast and chapel which was handy.'

'St Leonards, eh?' I said. 'Pretty hot stuff then, this Miss Bell. What was she doing in Portpatrick in the first place, one wonders?'

'One wouldn't have to if one would shut up and listen,' said Alec. 'She and Miss Fielding and Miss Taylor were at Somerville together.'

'We knew that.'

'And she and Miss Taylor agreed to join the staff of Miss Fielding's new enterprise . . . not quite for old times' sake, but certainly not for the advancement of their careers. The way she spoke made it sound like a kindness to an old friend.'

'Quite a considerable kindness,' I said. 'How long would they have stuck it if Miss Fielding hadn't died?'

'Who can say, but Miss Taylor has returned to academia

proper since she left St Columba's. She's currently in Greece getting excited about the deflation of the coinage in the ancient empire.'

'Takes all kinds,' I said. 'So they what? They felt their loyalty was to Miss Fielding personally and dropped poor Ivy Shanks like a brick after the funeral tea?'

'Again, if you would let me tell you,' Alec said. 'No. At least, they might have felt that way but they are both women of the stoutest ethical fibre and they would certainly have devoted as much more time as was wanted.'

'But?'

'It turned out that what was wanted was about six weeks. Six weeks after Miss Fielding died, they were both handed their pay packets and told to leave.'

'Odd.'

'Miss Bell said she assumed Ivy Shanks was in a fluster about money – she and Miss Taylor were on salaries commensurate with their great learning – and they offered to take a kind of furlough or whatever you would call it, while Miss Shanks got herself sorted out. Miss Taylor even offered to be a sort of acting headmistress and do the accounting. But no – they were thanked kindly and shown the door.'

'In the middle of term?'

'It seems so.'

'And they just left their budding scholars and university hopefuls in the lurch?' I said. 'They could at least have stayed on in the village and given some extra tuition.'

'I never thought of that, and Miss Bell never mentioned any guilt about the girls, actually. That's odd too. In fact, she went as far as to say that she and Taylor – that's how she referred to them both: Taylor and Fielding, like the army! – anyway, she said that she and Taylor felt a measure of relief that they were no longer to be stuffing Newton's apple and the House of Tudor into the heads of a lot of farmers' daughters who forgot it all every day over tea.'

'Academic snobs,' I said. 'Some of the St Columba's girls are really quite bright indeed. Thank goodness, in a way, that I didn't get a chance to ruin them.'

'So I'd say that Miss Shanks made a blunder in offloading the two of them,' Alec went on. 'But it wasn't the fevered and frantic business of running away and scrabbling for an agency stand-in that it's since become.'

'Odder than odd,' I said.

'Passing strange and far from wonderful,' agreed Alec. 'But here's something Miss Bell did say that's interesting, Dandy. When I told her about Miss Glennie – late of Balmoral, as you say – Miss Bell said something like "maybe Fielding's ways had rubbed off on Shanks after all".'

'What did she mean? Did you ask?'

'I did, but all she said was that they had never blamed Miss Fielding for wanting a nursing matron she knew right there on the spot but they had always thought it a great lapse of judgement to make Miss Shanks an equal partner.'

'I agree,' I said.

Alec crossed his eyes and blew a big breath out of his puffed cheeks.

'The more I hear the less I know,' he said. 'Anyway, the point of tracking them down was to make sure they're not No. 5 and I've done that.'

'Have you? Absolutely? Can we be sure Miss Taylor didn't come back from Greece and drown?'

'Yes,' Alec said. 'Miss Taylor apparently is fair-haired and five-foot-three. So No. 5 remains a mystery. How did you get on with No. 3?'

I told him the brief facts: the proximity to the Major's lodge and the boy being the right sort of age and class to have been Fleur's lover, but I told him too of the complicating factor of Leigh Audubon, the dead fiancée.

'But you think no one knew about the engagement until after the deaths?' Alec said. 'Well, then. The Audubons would be more than happy to have it put about that the girl was engaged to him, considering she was alone with him in a car at after midnight, especially if they weren't heading towards her home. And you say it wasn't Charles Leigh's Bugatti? And presumably it wasn't Miss Audubon's either, or they'd have said so. If it turned out that this car belonged to someone who can connect them with Fleur . . . or if Fleur was at the party . . .'

'Let's hope Mamma-dearest is in the mood to talk,' I said.

'You sound very scathing when you call her that,' Alec said.

'I don't mean to,' I replied. 'It's what the girls always called her. Maybe I'm getting cynical about them all and a note is creeping in.'

The steward came along just then, asking us if we would like the curtains drawn over since we were on the west side of the carriage and whether I would care for a foot-warmer and what we would each like by way of a drink before dinner?

'We should do more of this, Dan,' said Alec when the man had gone to fetch a whisky for Alec and a sherry for me. 'Beats rocketing around in that little Cowley.'

'Wait until we've got to Taunton,' I said. 'See if you still think so. One always forgets that the West Country isn't just round the corner from London.'

'Speak for yourself,' said Alec. 'I spent my childhood on the Cornwall sleeper getting to school and back again. It holds no secrets from me.'

He was, however, looking shattered and grey (as one always does after a night on a train) rather than pink and refreshed (the way the people look on the railway posters) when we arrived, with the milk, in Somerset the next morning. I had already had more than enough by King's Cross and would have welcomed a night in an hotel, but there was no stopping Alec: he had bundled me into a taxi and we were at Paddington before I could object, then there were two good first-class sleeper tickets still available, which made it seem meant, and now here we were, flat of hair and gritty of eye, standing in the yellow mist of an early summer morning, wondering how best to get to Pereford and beard Mamma-dearest in her den.

'Better to hire a motorcar here,' I said, 'than get to the nearest station and then find out they haven't got one.'

'We're not in Scotland now, Dandy,' Alec said. 'We're back in the civilised world. Of course they will.' It should have been touching to see how he drew down deep lungfuls of the air, as though it were his first proper breath since last he was this near home, but after my short and dreadful night's sleep it was only irritating and I took a mean pleasure in hearing the porter tell him that there were no trains north for a good hour or more and Sir would be better in a motorcar if there were any kind of hurry about it.

'Marvellous,' said Alec. 'Just the kind of cheerful helpfulness I've been missing. Not like that old misery on the Portpatrick dog-cart, eh?'

I decided not to tell him that a porter at Stranraer carried the whole timetable of his beloved railway in his head, but only nodded and followed him meekly to the hiring garage to let him pick.

Pereford. I had expected to find it changed; smaller-seeming, perhaps, or even run to seed in some way. I had fully anticipated that I would be forced to smile at my eighteen-year-old self and her besottedness with the place as the humdrum reality quenched the golden remembering. So when we turned off the Dunster road and swept between the gateposts, I steeled myself for disappointment. The avenue was the same, the branches just meeting over our heads and the new leaves exactly the yellow-green of the shoemakers' elves' little caps in the book I had read to Fleur at bedtime.

'It's just round this corner,' I said to Alec and then as we turned it I gave a cry.

The roses were blooming, tumbling and scrambling all over the pillars of the verandah, and the path was carpeted with their petals. The lawns, their nap like velvet, rolled away to the edge of the trees and the marks from the gardener's broom brushing off the dew could be seen in swathes. The pink-painted stone of the house was, as it had always been in early-morning sun, like the inside cheek of a seashell, blushed with peach; and at the windows, already open for the day, cream linen billowed out like the train of a wedding gown so that it seemed the house was waving a welcome at us as we slowed and stopped at the front door.

Our pull of the bell was answered by an elderly and rather stooping butler, who smiled with kindly enquiry.

'We've come to see Mrs Lipscott, with apologies for the hour,' I said. 'But if you tell her it's Mrs Gilver – I'm an old family friend.'

'Of course you are, Mrs Gilver,' said the butler. 'Or Miss Leston, as you'll always be to me.' I squinted at him, felt the flicker of recognition and quarried deep and long for his name.

'Higson?' I said, at last.

'Hinckley, madam,' he replied, 'but well done after all these years for getting that close! So Mrs Gilver and who shall I say, sir?'

'Mr Osborne,' said Alec.

'Of Dorset?' said Hinckley.

'Bill Osborne is my brother,' Alec said, visibly impressed.

'If you would care to come into the morning room,' Hinckley said, 'I'll tell Mrs Lipscott you are here.'

We followed him across the marble of the hall where more of the pink and yellow roses from outside were gathered together in bowls and in pots on pillars. Their scent – warmed by the light from the cupola floors above – was as sweet as honeysuckle already. I gazed about myself with growing rapture. There was the Fragonard (disputed) which we had all loved with girlish devotion. There was the Staffordshire pig with her ten little pink piglets which stood on the round table in the middle of the hall and under which we used to tuck the edges of notes to stop them blowing away. There were the three sketches of the house done by the three daughters the summer before I came to stay and framed as a triptych to stand on top of the library door.

Alec was in the morning room and had turned to face me.

'You have a very misty look on your face, Dandy,' he said.

'The chairs!' I cried. 'The same chairs!' I rushed over to the ring of armchairs grouped around the fireplace – four of them – where Lilah, Mamma-dearest, Pearl and I would sit, with Fleur on someone's lap and Aurora, as she preferred it, sprawled on the rug waiting for the carriage to be brought when we were going out for the day.

'Why shouldn't they have kept their chairs?' said Alec. 'Do you think Mrs Lipscott will receive us or just send a response? I don't fancy having to get firm with that sweet old butler.'

'Oh, she'll come,' I said. 'Of course, she won't be up yet. If it were just me I daresay I'd be taken to her bedroom and have to sit amongst her letters and kittens the same as ever, but I suppose she'll put on a dressing gown and come downstairs since it's you too, darling. Alec?'

He was standing with his back to me over by a side-table.

'Alec?' I said again.

He turned and I saw that he was holding a photograph frame in his hands. He held it out towards me and I walked over. It was Fleur, grown-up but not yet grown sombre. She was standing with her foot up on the running board of a motorcar and her head flung back, laughing. Her hair was short already and had ruffled up in the breeze so that it was a blur around her.

'I'd guess that would be about 1918 or so,' I said. 'Before.'

'Oh, it's certainly before,' Alec said. 'Look at the car, Dandy.' I looked but shook my head. 'It's a Bugatti,' he told me and our eyes met. He was breathing as though he had been running. Perhaps, like me, he had not really believed any of it until now.

'Dandy?' said a voice behind us. We turned and I could not help going over with both hands out to clasp those of the woman who had just entered the room. Mamma-dearest was probably older-looking to anyone who could look with an objective eye, but all I saw was the same mass of hair held up in a kind of hammock of net for sleeping, and the same pink flannel nightgown and pink silk dressing gown (cosy for bed and just a hint of decency in case I'm out in the garden and the vicar calls, she always used to say). 'Dandy, my dearest darling.' She wrapped me in a hug, smelling of lily-of-the-valley scent and mint toothpowder. 'What on earth brings you down here?' Then she held me at arm's length and beamed at me. I simply could not bring myself to say any of the things I should have said. Nor could I bear to soften her up with small talk and family news then turn the conversation later. I simply gave a dumb look at Alec.

He walked over and put the photograph between us, right under Mamma-dearest's nose.

'We're here to talk about Charles Leigh,' he said.

Any hope I had held that we were wrong drained out of me, just as the blood drained out of Mamma-dearest's plump cheeks.

'But . . . Charles was nine years ago,' she said. All the colour was gone from her voice too and she spoke in a bleak near-whisper.

'And Elf was eight years ago,' said Alec. Mamma-dearest squeezed her eyes tight shut.

'And – I'm so sorry,' I added, 'but someone else died last week and Fleur . . .'

'Has she gone off the rails again?' said Mrs Lipscott, opening her eyes. 'Do the girls know? They haven't told me.'

'They wanted to spare you,' I said.

'Did they send you to tell me?' she asked. I started to answer no but Alec cut me off.

'What happened with Charles Leigh, Mrs Lipscott?' he said, shaking the photograph a little to make her look.

'She bought it with her own money,' said Mamma-dearest, hugging herself, putting her hands right up inside her nightgown sleeves. 'On her eighteenth birthday when she came into what the Major had settled on her. I knew it was too young to settle money on them, but of course . . . And you can see how she loved it, can't you?'

'And the crash itself?' I said. 'What happened?'

'I don't know,' she said, miserably. 'No one knows except Fleur.'

'Tell us what you do know,' I said gently. 'Perhaps we can piece it together from there.' She walked slowly over to one of the armchairs and dropped down into it. We followed her.

'Well, after . . .' she began, and then she cleared her throat and started again. 'At the age of about seventeen, of course, Fleur took a great shine to the lodge. Ironic is the word, I think.'

'Ironic how?' I asked. Mrs Lipscott opened her eyes very wide in an innocent way and for the first time I did see that she was older now.

'Oh, you know,' she said. 'It was as unlike Pereford as chalk and cheese and it was the Major's house and Fleur never even met the Major.' She turned to Alec. 'My husband died in Africa when Florrie was a little baby,' she said.

'So she was at the lodge when Charles Leigh died,' Alec said.

'Why do you want to know all this?' said Mrs Lipscott. 'And Dandy, why do *you*?'

'Was she at the party with them?' Alec said and I found myself wondering if he was always this brusque, if I was too when it was a stranger I was grilling, whether I only saw it now because Mamma-dearest awoke every tender feeling in me and made me see Alec's manner in a new and unflattering light. It could not be denied, however, that it was working.

'Yes, she was at that wretched party,' Mrs Lipscott said. 'The party Charles and Leigh went racing away from. You see, the thing about the lodge was that she could get up to all sorts of mischief unwitnessed; it was such a long way for us – the girls and me – to haul ourselves up there. Even if we heard tell of her escapades, which usually we didn't. It's quite out on its own.'

'Well I remember,' I said. 'Hugh used to shoot with one of the neighbours. Highland neighbours – seven miles of bad road away. He insisted on dragging me along, naturally.'

'Well I sold it in the end,' said Mrs Lipscott. 'After the accident – one of these anonymous bidders who buy up everything these days – and I've never missed it.'

'Getting back to the night that Charles Leigh died then,' I said. '*Was* Fleur engaged to him, as the Forresters think? Or was Leigh the fiancée, as reported?'

'Oh, you've spoken to the Forresters, have you? Was it Aurora who asked you to come and speak to me?'

'No,' I said, crossing my fingers and hoping she would assume it was Pearl. 'Was she?'

'Well,' said Mrs Lipscott, 'I don't suppose he was actually

engaged to either of them. But since he was dead and would be marrying no one, the poor dear sweet boy, and since poor darling Leigh died with him, what would have been the use of exposing her to censure and Fleur to ridicule?' Alec had been right then.

'More than ridicule, Mrs Lipscott,' Alec said. 'If she killed them.'

'She didn't! She couldn't have.'

'How can you be sure?' I said. 'What do you know?'

'Only that they were all together at the party, and that Fleur didn't turn up at home until six in the morning and she was very bedraggled and smelling of smoke.'

'Smoke?' I said. 'Cigarette smoke?'

Mamma-dearest gave me a look of fond pity. 'Filthy black oily smoke, Dandy my love.'

'And what did she say about it?' said Alec. 'That she remembered nothing?'

'No, Mr Osborne,' she said in the crispest tone I had ever heard her use. 'She said she had killed them both. She said she was guilty of another two murders and she wanted to tell the police and go to court and be hanged.'

Alec had the grace to lower his head and after a quiet moment she spoke again.

'But it was nonsense, of course. Apart from anything else, how could one person out of three make sure she survived an accident that killed the others? Anyway, we sent her away to rest and before too long she was better again.'

'But not her old self,' I said.

'No,' said Mrs Lipscott. 'She hadn't been her old self for a while, but she wasn't even her new self after Charles. She was . . .'

'I saw her last Saturday,' I said. 'I know.'

'Oh, my poor naughty little sprite,' said Mrs Lipscott. 'My cherub, my little pixie. Do you have children, Mr Osborne?'

'We really don't want to upset you,' I said to her before Alec could answer, acknowledging with a rueful smile that we were a little late to avoid it now: her eyes were swimming with unshed tears and her hand shook as she put it to her throat. 'But I must just ask one more thing. Fleur said on Saturday that she had killed five people. Charles and Leigh are two, Elf makes three and this last one is four. You yourself just said, of the crash, "another two murders". So, who was the first?'

'We know *when* it was,' said Alec. I nodded and tried to look wise, even though I did not know what he meant. 'It happened when she was seventeen, didn't it? When she started staying away from home? And it was afterwards that she bought herself the motorcar and turned into a bit of a scamp by all accounts. That was what made her "her new self", as you put it.' I was nodding more eagerly now. 'But who was it, Mrs Lipscott? Who did Fleur kill when she was seventeen?' Mamma-dearest was shaking her head and her tears had dried again. 'If we look through a year's worth of newspapers,' Alec went on, 'will we find another death notice of a family friend? If we spoke to her acquaintances from that time and asked them if someone died unexpectedly, what would they tell us?'

Mamma-dearest was almost smiling now as she continued to shake her head.

'My daughter killed no one,' she said.

'You're very sure considering you don't know the first thing about this latest corpse,' I put in, and her smile was gone.

'She didn't, Dandy,' she said. 'Tell me it's not true. Tell me that you don't understand why she's claiming any such thing and you can't see how it was done.'

I glanced at Alec and although he told me, with a tiny shake of his head, to refuse to comfort her, I could not oblige him.

'That's more or less true,' I said. 'I mean she could have done it, but we don't have the first inkling as to why. We don't even know who it was.'

'She didn't do it then,' said Mrs Lipscott and she sat back with a great rush of relief. 'So is she still teaching? Or has she gone to rest for a while? It's always so very upsetting for her.'

'She's . . . um . . . yes, she's taken off for a bit,' I said. 'I gather you don't speak every week on the telephone then? Or exchange frequent letters?'

'I have had to let my little bird go, Dandy,' said Mrs Lipscott. 'I stand with my arm outstretched and my hand open and I pray that one day she'll come flitting back again. It's the hardest thing any mother ever has to do. To love and love and know that her child is alone and scared and won't take comfort.'

'It sounds absolutely unspeakable,' I said. Not that my boys ever took much in the way of comfort anyway and if they knew that they were 'loved and loved' from near or from far they would make sick-noises and laugh at me; but sometimes in the night, when I could not quite silence Hugh's voice in my head, I imagined one or both of them not in their dorm at school but in khaki in a foreign land with the sound of shells going off. Then I would remember the soldiers in the convalescent home – the ones who sat frozen, staring ahead (the ones who cried and accepted soothing words and pats on the arm were easy). I could rattle myself so badly that I would have to get up and go into their bedrooms and remind myself from all the model aeroplanes and frogspawn and cricket bats there that they were children, not soldiers, not yet; and since Hugh was wrong, not ever.

'And now you must excuse me,' said Mamma-dearest. 'I am going to go to my room. I've just enough time for a good cry before breakfast. Nine-ish, Dandy darling, as ever.' I had risen to my feet and made some ineffectual noises. 'No, certainly not,' she said. 'A woman my age weeping is not a pretty sight. Take a walk in the garden, hm? The roses are lovely just now.' She stood. 'Of course, last week they were lovelier but that's the way of it with roses.'

We did, in fact, step out of the french windows of the morning room and walk over the brushed grass to the rose garden. We went in silence but once we were through the arch in the yew hedge and strolling up and down the paths drinking in the scent, Alec started again.

'Of course you could walk away from a crash that killed two,' he said. 'Drive the car quite gently into a tree and set light to the petrol tank with the others still in it.'

'Oh, stop,' I said. 'I feel unspeakable, Alec. She obviously thinks her daughters sent me to help.'

'You've investigated acquaintances before,' Alec said.

'These Lipscotts aren't acquaintances,' I told him. 'They're my dear, dear friends. And this place is . . . I can't explain it, but I feel as though I'm trampling something precious underfoot.'

'Best concentrate on the case then,' Alec said. 'Take your mind off it. Do you agree that Fleur could have caused the crash?'

I sighed. Of course, he was right.

'Why wouldn't Charles and Leigh just get out?' I said. 'They'd have to be drugged or extremely drunk.'

'And of course no one ever leaves a party that way,' said Alec. 'I wish Mrs Lipscott would just tell us what she knows about No. 1, don't you?'

'I do. Then at least I could stop poking her with a stick and feeling as if I were baiting a wounded bear.'

'Dandy,' said Alec, in warning.

'Yes, all right. Good work for knitting together all those little half-hints and catching her out that way. I knew something must have happened to turn Fleur into the little minx I saw at the party on Armistice night.'

'Sh,' said Alec, cocking his head. 'She's coming back. Maybe she's changed her mind.'

But the woman who came round the corner was not Mamma-dearest, the same as ever in her pink flannel nightie. It was a woman of great age and great dishevelment with long grey hair hanging down her back in rats' tails and an outfit composed of men's twill overalls with a bathing suit underneath and down-at-heel dancing slippers on her feet.

'You!' she said. 'You're back. They've all gone now.'

'Lilah?' I said. 'Batty Aunt?' She gave me an enormous grin. Quite terrifying, since her teeth were few now and those remaining were not the teeth of which dentists dream. Her face was purple and pouchy with a wattle under the chin and fat yellow bags under each eye, and it occurred to me for the first time that she might not have been batty all those years ago, but sozzled. She was steady enough now, however, as she trotted up to us in her slippers and held out a hand to Alec.

'Aunt Lilah,' she said to him. They shook and then she clasped me to her and planted a kiss on my cheek which I could feel drying there and which made me itch to take out my handkerchief and scrub it away.

'So what brings you back down here?' she said. She had been fishing in the bib pocket of her dungarees and now she drew out a pair of secateurs and set to on the nearest rose bush. She was not exactly deadheading, since the blooms she snipped off were not at all faded. But neither was she gathering flowers for the house in any way that made sense, since the heads were let fall to the ground and then kicked away.

Alec waved his hand to get my attention and then gestured to Aunt Lilah in a very urgent-seeming way. I shook my head vehemently, determined that I would not grill this wandered (or drunk) old lady for secrets while her niece and protector was out of the way.

'We came to talk about Fleur,' I said and ignored Alec's scowl. That was as far as I would go.

'Oh, Fleur!' said Lilah. She moved on to a second bush and attacked it with zeal.

'Should you be doing that?' I asked mildly.

'She's gone,' said Lilah. 'She left long, long ago.' Then she held her secateurs up high in the air and snipped them together a few times before putting them back in her pocket and turning round. 'She killed her father, you know.' This was delivered in the blithe tone of someone imparting news that a friend had moved to town, or got a puppy, then she took off around the corner of the path, leaving us in dumb silence. After a moment the sound of snipping started up again. Slowly, Alec and I followed her.

'Fleur killed her father?' I said. 'The Major?'

'That's him,' said Lilah. 'Johnny Lipscott. Yes, he died.'

'But Fleur was a baby,' I said.

'Yes, a little baby girl,' Lilah said.

'And the Major died in Africa in the war,' said Alec.

'Oh, you knew that too?' said Lilah, glancing round. 'Yes, he did. Terribly dangerous place, Africa. You wouldn't catch me there even for the elephants.' In the distance the glockenspiel sounded its trill of notes. 'Breakfast!' she cried gaily, and again put her secateurs away. 'Hope there's some kedge.' She left the way she had come.

'What a very unsettling person,' said Alec. 'And what on earth did she mean?'

'Let's go and ask Mrs Lipscott,' I said. 'It does make sense of one thing though – why it should be "ironic" that Fleur took a shine to the Major's hunting lodge.'

'But he died in battle,' said Alec. 'That's not the kind of thing you can make mistakes about.'

'What if he was missing, or if his body was misidentified and he made it home and lay low and years later . . .'

'I've been in the army, Dandy. If they list someone as dead, he's dead. Let's go and see what his widow has to say.'

They were in the little breakfast room with the Chinese wallpaper of yellow pears and blue doves, and there was indeed kedgeree into which Batty Aunt Lilah was tucking with enormous relish.

'Coffee, eggs and things . . .' said Mrs Lipscott waving a vague hand. 'Are you staying, Dandy? Would you like your old room? And you, Mr Osborne?' She blinked. 'I haven't quite accounted for you yet, I must say, but you're very welcome, naturally.'

I poured myself a cup of coffee and sat down opposite her. Again her hand fluttered at her throat, nicely dressed in pearls now above a very pale pink jersey of soft wool. She was right about the crying, though: her face was sodden and crumpled and looked ten years older than it had when we arrived, no matter the soft pink wool and pearls chosen to help it.

'Batty Aunt Lilah just told us something quite surprising,' I said. Lilah dropped her fork with a clatter, but Mrs Lipscott leaned over and patted her arm, giving her a warm smile.

'Don't worry, Aunt,' she said. 'You could never say anything that would make me cross with you, my darling.'

'Try this,' said Alec, rather grimly. He had not even taken so much as a cup of coffee, I noticed. 'She told us that Fleur killed the Major.'

'I'm going to finish this in my room,' said Lilah, picking up her plate and her cup of milk and beetling off at top speed.

'I'm not angry with you, my batty old aunt,' Mrs Lipscott shouted after her. Then she turned back to Alec and me. 'And so now you see how I can be sure she didn't kill Elf or Charles or Leigh or this new one either.'

'I don't know about you, Dandy,' said Alec, 'but I don't see that at all. Perhaps, Mrs Lipscott, you would care to explain.'

'You're terribly earnest for an Osborne,' she said. 'I was at a hunt ball with your father once – before he married your mother – and he was much more fun.' She gave her dimpled smile a good airing in Alec's direction but, when it was met with a blank look, she sighed and held up her hands in a gesture of defeat.

'All right,' she said. 'Here's what happened. When Aurora was due to be born in '84 the Major was in India and he wanted to go to Egypt to join in the fun, but he came back for the birth of his son and organised bonfires on all the headlands and a huge party for the staff and the village, and of course no son came along. The bonfires were dismantled and the staff were told to go back to work and the Major returned to India. In '87 when Pearl was born the whole thing happened again. He sailed home, built bonfires, organised parties and then took one look at her and went to Plymouth to get on a ship. Now in 1898 when I told him a third child was on its way, he refused to come back. He stayed put in East Africa where he was stationed, saying if it was the longed-for son at last he'd come home and if it was another benighted daughter he was off to fight the Boers in the South. He was long past the age where he had to keep his commission by this time, you understand, so it was his path to choose.'

She paused and looked at us as though expecting comments. Since the only one I could think of was that if he had not kept storming back off to the army in a huff at every daughter there would have been a higher count of babies in total and he would no doubt have got his son in the end, I said nothing.

'So I sent word that it was another darling beautiful little baby girl and he promptly departed for the war and got himself killed there. After that the four of us and – and after Lilah came, the five of us – were just as snug as an infestation of bugs in a rug and all was delight and merriment.'

'After your grief subsided, of course,' said Alec, not liking – as a soldier himself – to hear that the Major was not mourned by the women he gave his life protecting.

'Oh well, you know,' said Mrs Lipscott. 'Anyway, Fleur was always the most fanciful little thing in the world, wasn't she, Dandy? And when she was getting quite big and almost finished with lessons she started thinking about coming out and getting engaged and getting married and all that and she became quite sorrowful at the thought of having no father to give her away. She started imagining it must have been dreadful for me to have no husband and I said that she shouldn't think that for a moment and that I would rather have her than my silly husband and some silly son. I wasn't thinking. She asked what I meant. And I told her. All I had in my mind was that if she heard what a ridiculous man her father was she would stop missing him and stop fancying that I missed him. Of course that's not how she took it at all. I remember it as though it were yesterday: her standing poker-straight and as white as a sheet in my bedroom and staring at me with those beautiful eyes. "Do you mean to tell me," she said, "that I killed my father by being born?" "No!" I shouted. "An Orangeman with a bayonet killed your father by sticking him in the tummy." But there was no consoling her.'

'And that's when she started her wild years?' I said.

'The Bugatti, Charles Leigh – who was very fast – frocks so short you'd think she'd forgotten to put one on. All those horrid parties with everyone smoking nasty things and being sick. She had decided she was a wicked girl and so she thought she'd jolly well behave like one.'

'And why didn't you just tell us this?' said Alec.

Mrs Lipscott gave a carolling little laugh. 'Oh, Mr Osborne, no one likes to say there's *that* in the family.'

'That what?' I said.

'Mania, madness, whatever they're calling it now. I didn't want anyone to know that one of my girls wasn't right in the head.' I frowned and shot a quick glance to the door where Batty Aunt Lilah had exited with her kedgeree.

'Oh, but Lilah's a connection by marriage,' said Mrs Lipscott. 'My uncle's wife. No blood relation at all to me. I couldn't bear the thought of Florrie-mittens being called nasty names and having to go to some dreary hospital somewhere.'

'Although it came to that in the end,' I reminded her gently. 'More than once.'

'She wanted to turn herself in, Dandy,' said Mrs Lipscott, leaning forward in her chair to look pleadingly into my eyes. 'After Charles, I mean. After Elf we couldn't take the chance.'

'So, she's never run off exactly like this before then?' I said. She sat up and opened her eyes very wide. 'We slightly overstated it when we said she had gone to recuperate. We don't actually know *where* she is. No one does.'

'She'll go to the police,' said Mamma-dearest, standing up and letting her napkin fall to the floor. 'She'll give herself up and be put away.'

'I don't think so, Mrs Lipscott,' said Alec. 'The police were right there when she disappeared. Almost as though it was them she was running away from.'

Mamma-dearest was shaking her head in a distracted way, fast enough to make her pearls rattle together on her neck.

'No, no, you don't understand Fleur,' she said. 'If she thought she'd done it she'd never try to duck out of it. Her whole life since Charles and Elf has been one long act of atonement. Taking herself away from men and from her family and living like a nun in that dreadful school. She said she was trying to keep as many girls as possible on the straight and narrow path.'

She went towards the door and paused before going out of the room.

'Aurora and Pearl know about this, you say? I'm going to telephone to them now. We must find her. I shall never forgive them for keeping all of this from me.'

'We're for it, when the other two find out we came down here,' Alec said once we were alone.

'Unless Mamma-dearest talks them round,' I said. 'What did you make of all that?' Alec went to the sideboard and began heaping rashers of bacon onto a slice of toast. He squashed the heap down with another slice, picked up this ungainly sandwich in one hand and rejoined me.

'I'm relieved to hear what counts as "murder" in Fleur's book,' he said.

'Yes, she might well be no more responsible for bodies two to five than she was for the first one. She's ill, not wicked.'

'Although we can't be sure,' said Alec through a thick mouthful of bacon and bread. 'Perhaps her being mad – and she does sound mad, doesn't she? – makes her more likely to have killed, not less.'

'Killed all of them?' I asked him. 'After her father, I mean.'

'Perhaps,' said Alec. 'Or given that what she heard about the Major was no more than an upsetting revelation, and even if Charles and Leigh were an accident – if, mind you, *if* – by the time she was out walking on a cliff edge with Elf she already thought of herself as a murderess. And her mother just said it herself: she set out to be the wicked girl she believed she already was.'

'If only we knew who No. 5 *is*,' I said. 'I mean, Fleur must have known her, agreed? How can no one have missed the woman?'

'We need to find Fleur and ask her,' said Alec. 'And here's a thought, Dandy. Since the police know they're looking for a particular boat now, they've probably found her, or traced part of her journey. Every harbour has a harbourmaster, after all. What is it?'

Clearly, my face was reflecting the sudden sick feeling I had inside.

'I don't think I told them,' I said. 'Sergeant Turner was being beastly and I know I didn't tell *him*. Then Reid was flapping about Cissie and I told him about finding Fleur's bags and losing them

255

and about finding Jeanne Beauclerc and about them planning to run off and then Jeanne bolting too early and . . . that's it. I didn't tell them about the boat at all.'

'But the chap who owns it . . . ?'

'No! That's the thing. He's got his eye on the endless mounting up of the late fees. He'll never tell them. Oh God, what a chump I am.'

'Do you think Mrs Lipscott would let us use her telephone if we say it's to help Fleur be found?'

'Not after she's spoken to Pearl,' I said. 'And think of who we'd be asking to find her!'

'Could we go to the local bobbies here? Or the coastguard? Nearest harbourmaster?'

'We could try,' I said. 'But would they care? Do you think Fleur's description – her lines, Reid called it – was broadcast all the way down here?'

'Doubtful,' Alec said.

'I think we need lay it all out for Constable Reid,' I said.

'Another trunk call?' he asked. 'Let's hope for a better line.'

'Perhaps we'd have more chance if we go back and tug his sleeve until he listens. And it's not as though there's any tearing rush, is there? She's been gone since Saturday. If she were going to kill herself she'd have done it by now. If she went and holed up somewhere she'll still be there for the police to find her.'

Just too late I saw Alec's eyes flash and I turned around to see Mamma-dearest standing in the doorway. Her face was whiter than her pearls.

'Have you any idea how you sound?' she said to me.

'Mamma—' I began, but her eyes narrowed. 'Mrs Lipscott,' I said, 'you weren't supposed to hear that.'

'I thought you were our friend,' she said. 'I've just been defending you to Pearl even though you tricked me into thinking she'd sent you.'

'Not exactl—' I said.

'*If* she killed herself, or *if* she holed up and can be caught by policemen! As though it's a game.'

'We speak very matter-of-factly when we're trying to get a hard job done well, Mrs Lipscott,' said Alec. 'It doesn't mean that we're not desperately concerned to see a just outcome.'

'A just outcome!' said Mamma-dearest. 'No matter who gets swept away by it. I think you should leave now, both of you. Just leave us alone.'

As we hustled and jumbled ourselves out of the breakfast room, through the hall and onto the doorstep, and heard the front door slam firmly shut behind us, Alec was almost laughing; but I felt a bulge of misery inside me that I could not bear. To have been thrown out of Pereford and told never to return! To have been cast off by Mamma-dearest with such disgust for me in her face and voice!

'Don't look like that,' Alec said. 'It's not the first time we've ruffled feathers, not by a long chalk.'

I nodded glumly, but he did not know what I had lost if I had lost the Lipscotts. I bowed my head as the hired motorcar wound down the drive past the roses and brushed lawns and into the avenue, fearing that if I looked I would see a bench or pond or summerhouse and remember a sunny hour spent there with the closest I had ever come to sisters (except my real sister, who fell far short of my imaginings), being told I was clever and beautiful and funny and that my life would be a happy charm. I dreaded the prospect of rewinding our yesterday's journey all the way, Taunton to London, London to Scotland, those endless empty hours ahead of me for the miserable thoughts to outwit my attempts at control and send me into a fit of self-pity and weeping.

Thankfully, the after-effects of a night on the sleeper descended within minutes of the first train moving and it was not until we were slowing at Paddington that I lifted my head from Alec's shoulder and wiped my mouth with the back of my hand.

'Thank God,' he said. 'My neck seized up at Frome but I didn't like to disturb you. Are you feeling any better?'

'No,' I croaked. 'Worse.' I sat up and stretched. 'And the only thing to be done about it is to solve the case and restore poor Fleur to her family.'

'And if solving the case sends her to the gallows?'

'Let's cross our fingers that it won't,' I said. 'There's nothing else for it.'

So on the Flying Scotsman, once the pudding plates were cleared after luncheon, I took out a notebook and spread it on the tablecloth beside my coffee. I ignored Alec's groans of protest.

'Yes, I know what you think,' I said, 'but it helps me organise things.'

'No wonder you took to the classroom with such gusto,' he said. 'What things are you organising anyway? Nos. 1 to 5?'

'You do the corpses,' I said, opening the book to the middle and tearing out a double sheet from around the stitches. 'I'm going to concentrate on the mistresses.'

'What about them?' Alec said. 'Beauclerc, Blair, Taylor and Bell are accounted for. Do you mean Fleur?'

'I don't know what I mean,' I said. 'And I hate that. Now, keep quiet and let me think, please.'

'I will in a minute,' Alec said. 'But when you say "do the corpses" what do you mean? Do what with the corpses?'

'Tabulate,' I said. 'Cross-refer. You know . . . organise.'

Miss Fielding, I wrote in my book, *Miss Taylor* and *Miss Bell*. Three members of Somerville College. *Miss Fielding* and *Miss Shanks*, two friends who started a school. *Miss Lipscott* and *Miss Beauclerc*, whom Miss Fielding employed and who stayed for some time after her death. *Miss Blair* whom Miss Fielding employed and whom Miss Shanks sacked. *Miss Barclay* and *Miss Christopher* whom no one sacked. *Miss Glennie* whom Miss Shanks employed and had not sacked yet, unlike Miss Gilver who found favour and lost it again in a day. And *Miss Lovage*, with money invested. And *Anderson* the handyman, who wanted to keep his cottage. And *Mrs Brown* the housekeeper and cook, friend of Miss Shanks and known to Miss Fielding, who was very solidly still there and going nowhere.

I stared at the list of names.

Who employed Miss Barclay and Miss Christopher? I wrote. I did not know but I made a private bet with myself that it was

Ivy Shanks who introduced them. They, like she, were comfortable and happy there. Mrs Brown was too. Miss Glennie was not and to say that Fleur and Jeanne had been uncomfortable was rather understating matters.

Waifs and strays, I wrote. *Glennie, Beauclerc, Lipscott.*

Independents, I wrote. *Lovage, Taylor, Bell. Blair? Brown?*

I turned to a fresh page and set down in thick capital letters the central puzzle of St Columba's School. IVY SHANKS. And the floodgates were opened.

Why does IS keep letters in her safe?

Why did IS employ DG and then sack her?

Why is IS not suspicious of Miss Glennie's supposed history?

Why was IS in a tizz about French and not about science or history (or English)?

For she had been. That first night I met Miss Shanks on the terrace she had been beside herself over the emergency of finding a new French mistress and there was Fleur Lipscott who spoke perfectly good French and knew how to teach. Why could she not take over 'double duties' as Miss Lovage called it, just as Barclay and Christopher had had to do?

Questions beginning with 'why', however, were not the sort which could be cracked on a train with paper and pencil. Organising was no good for why.

Order of departure, I tried next. *Fielding, Blair, Taylor/Bell, Beauclerc/Lipscott* (planned), *Beauclerc, Lipscott* (actual).

The order of arrival I did not know.

How about subjects? Latin was lost when Fielding died. Science and history and PE with the first round of sackings. French and English with the hasty departures. Geography and maths had suffered no interruptions at all. I put down my pen and stared out of the window at the rolling green hills sweeping by.

What had I seen and forgotten at St Columba's? What had struck me in the subconscious when I was thinking of other things and was now lurking unobtainable in some dusty corner of my brain?

I picked up my pencil again and began a list of oddities, hoping that one of them would snag the memory and bring it to the surface again.

Grace, bathing pool, cocoa, late start, supper in dorms, loafing around in gardens, teachers making own beds. In fact, teachers appearing to work a great deal harder than any of the girls, as far as I could see.

'Good grief, Dandy,' Alec said. 'Do you know you're huffing and puffing like a hippo in a mud wallow?'

'How are *you* getting on?' I asked him.

'Dreadfully, I think,' Alec replied. 'Although since I don't know what I'm supposed to be achieving, perhaps I'm getting on quite wonderfully.'

'Well, what have you got?'

'I've set out cause of death, characteristics of victim, relation to suspect and suspect's reaction,' he said. 'For instance, battle, fire, fire, drowned, drowned. Man, man and woman, man, woman. Is this the sort of thing you mean? Father, lover and friend, lover, who knows.'

'Suitor not lover,' I said. 'For Elf.'

'Off the rails, threat to confess, claim of amnesia, flight. If there are patterns there I can't find them.'

'Africa, Highlands, Somerset, South of Scotland,' I added.

'Well, Irish Sea,' said Alec. 'There's nothing there, is there?'

'Not much,' I admitted. 'Except you didn't really go far enough with Fleur's reaction to events. When she heard about the Major she went off the rails, that's true. When Charles and Leigh died, drunk in a fast car after a fast party – a very off-the-rails death – she went back to her family. Elf died while she was with her family and she left them, went to where there were hardly any men at all and no chance of romantic entanglements, and when No. 5 happened there . . .'

'She went somewhere we don't know,' Alec said. 'Not back to her family – that didn't work last time. And presumably not to another girls' school since *it* didn't break the curse either. And she's hardly likely to go on another bender like a flapper girl. Not at thirty. By golly, Dan, I think I'm beginning to see the point of this. It does help one . . .'

'Organise?' I said, trying to make my smile not too smug.

'So where would she go to be even more safe and cloistered than she was at St Columba's?'

'Cloistered. Hm,' I said. 'An out-and-out nunnery? More Ophelia than Juliet, after all?'

'I wonder which heartbreak it was that earned her the nickname,' Alec said. 'Charles or Elf?'

'Sorry?' I said. 'Listen, darling, I'm thinking. I know I was very offhand about suicide – God, I'll never forgive myself for Mammadearest hearing me! – but something's occurred to me. She fled.'

'Yes,' Alec said.

'She took flight. She's never done that before. I mean, removing herself from her family's care and starting her wild time must have been a gradual thing, mustn't it? She didn't go to bed a good girl the night she found out about the Major and wake up a bad girl in the morning. And she went to a sanatorium after Charles and after Elf. Presumably she took a bit of time deciding to be a schoolmistress too and did some rudimentary preparation for it. This time, though, new future planned, all set to take Jeanne Beauclerc home to Pereford (I wonder why she didn't tell her mother?), she abandoned everything and simply *fled*. That can't have been guilt.'

'Fear of discovery?' said Alec.

'What discovery?' I said. 'No one knows who No. 5 is and we haven't been able to come up with a single scrap of evidence that Fleur had anything to do with her murder. She can't have felt the noose tightening.'

'But scarpering like that and leaving Jeanne Beauclerc in the lurch does look like fear,' Alec said. 'So if not fear of discovery, arrest, conviction and hanging, because she didn't really kill No. 5 in the legal sense, then what?'

'Not in the legal sense, no,' I said slowly. 'But if she felt that she killed her father purely by being born, she might have felt that she killed No. 5 because she put the woman in harm's way quite inadvertently.'

'Yes, of course!' said Alec. 'Which makes perfect sense of her saying "Five" like that when she saw the corpse!'

'Oh, hallelujah! At last!' I said. 'She *already* felt she was putting this person at risk of harm and when she saw the corpse she knew that the harm had come.'

We beamed at one another.

'But we've got side-tracked. What did she fear? Why did she run away?'

'Perhaps,' said Alec with a quiet thrill of triumph in his voice, 'because she knew where the harm had come from. *She* didn't kill No. 5 any more than she killed No. 1, but—'

I joined him and we spoke in chorus.

'*She knows who did.*'

'And,' continued Alec, 'she thinks she's next.'

'So she didn't dare take Jeanne Beauclerc along.'

'We have to find her,' Alec said. 'And it *is* pretty urgent, after all.'

I I

We did not, however, get off at the next station and try to tell all of that to Sergeant Turner on the telephone. Even if he had let us speak to Constable Reid we might have been struggling to unwind the plaited threads of poor Fleur's history and convince him. Instead we spent the rest of the journey devising the plainest, clearest report into which such a twisty tale could be straightened out and when we finally fell out of the little train at Portpatrick again some thirty-six hours after we had left we went straight to the police station.

Constable Reid was on the back shift and we found him in the office all trussed up with his tunic closed and his hat on, ready to go out and make one of his rounds. Since the weather was so filthy, though – it had started raining almost precisely at the border on our journey north and sheets of water were coursing down over the sea, turning even this summer evening as black as January – he took little persuasion to abandon the plan and give us his ear.

'Nobody'll be out causin' bother on a night like this,' he said. After that his contributions dwindled.

'Uh-huh, uh-huh, uh-huh,' was all he offered as we laid it out for him, and he stopped taking notes a little way in. By the end, he had his hat off and his head in his hands.

'So . . .' I finished, 'if you can at least find the boat you'll know which way she went and then you'll know which police force to ask to look for her. Or however you do it. Obviously you know best.'

'The boat,' said Reid. 'That you knew about on Monday afternoon, and here we are on Thursday night.'

'Yes, sorry about that,' I said. 'But you know now and so you can get started.'

'I cannae start somethin' like that,' said Reid. 'It'll need to be the sarge and he'll need to ask the inspector and even he'll mebbes need to go right to the top.'

'I see,' said Alec.

'And that's fine by me,' said Reid. 'I'll go straight up to his house right now and tell 'im.'

'Won't he be angry if you bother him at home?' I asked. 'I'd rather wait until the morning and have it done than antagonise the sergeant tonight and get nowhere.'

'I'm no' carin',' said Reid. 'I want to see Cissie. She answers their door, you know.'

'She still hasn't forgiven you?'

'Not a word since she said she didn't want to see me Tuesday afternoon,' Reid said. 'I've left two notes in our wee place and she's taken them out but no' answered.'

'Well, she can hardly avoid you if you turn up on the doorstep,' I said. 'Shall we come too?'

'I'll manage fine myself,' said Reid and he shooed us out of the little police station so that he could lock it behind him.

Portpatrick was battened down, either for the rainstorm or just for the night, with windows and doors closed, no washing left out to catch the warmth of the fading day and no one leaning on the harbour wall or sitting on the bollards outside Aldo's. In fact, Aldo's was in darkness.

'Joe must have given up on any custom tonight in this dreadful weather,' I said.

Alec shook his head.

'It's hard to believe you live in Scotland sometimes, Dandy,' he said. 'No purveyor of fried fish would ever close before the pub, you know.'

'Well, maybe Thursday is his half-day,' I said. 'The man must rest sometimes.'

'Thursday?' said Alec. 'Pay-day? Never.'

'I bow to your greater knowledge,' I said. 'I hope he's all right.'

We stood looking across the harbour to the little shack for a moment, but the rain was coming down in drilling icy rods and my hat brim was beginning to droop.

'I'll go and see him tomorrow,' Alec said. 'Come inside, Dandy, before you catch a chill.' Thus cloaking his sloth in chivalry, he held open the door of the Crown and, shaking ourselves like dogs, we entered.

'What are *you* going to do tomorrow?' he said as we waited for the landlady to respond to our ringing. 'The police will take over looking for Fleur and Fleur, when she's found, will tell us at last who No. 5 is. What's left for you? A day of rest?'

'I think I'll go to Parents' Day,' I said. 'Gatecrash it, I mean. I'd dearly love to work out what's going on up there and I've got some examination papers and a letter to return to Miss Shanks. That will be my protection if she calls Sergeant Turner on me. And as for a day of rest: I'm certainly not sticking around the Crown. The convalescent widow and I have had a falling out, you know, and I can't face another round of hostilities.'

The rain had let up by the morning, but it did not leave the world new-washed and sparkling the way English rain does. Instead, the stone of the houses, harbour and cobbles was soaked and dark and the sky was a kind of exhausted grey. I looked across to Joe Aldo's shack from my window as I dressed and felt again a small flare of worry.

There was a knock at my door and I opened it, expecting Alec, but found Constable Reid standing there.

'Good morning,' I said and leaned out to call along the passageway. 'Alec? Reid's here. Come in, Constable. What news?'

'Aye, I thought ye'd like to know,' said Reid, entering and looking round with a true policeman's eye, not at all the bashful gaze of a young man in a strange woman's hotel bedroom. He would go far if his luck fell that way. 'The sarge took some convincin' and I kind of had to make your friend sound a wee bit dangerous and no' just soft, but he's agreed she might ken who our corpse is and there's no denyin' she's pinched the boat, so he's away gettin' the coast-guard and them sorted out.'

Alec gave a quick rap at the door and entered. 'Reid,' he said. 'The search is on,' I told him. 'Go on, Constable.'

'Aye, right, so,' said Reid. 'That's all.'

'And how did it go with Cissie?' I asked.

He shot me a piercing look. 'She never came to the door. She sent the cook. An' I'm askin' you again: what did you say to her?'

'Oh Dandy, for heaven's sake,' said Alec. 'What *did* you say to her? It was really none of your business, darling.'

'Nothing!' I said. 'I'm sure of it. I think it's a bit much getting her to caddy for you but I didn't say a syllable about that. And I wonder what her mother would think of these moonlight walks of yours, but I said nothing about that either. Look, if I get a chance later, I'll go to the Turners' house on some pretext or other and I'll ask Cissie, when she answers the door, what the matter is. All right? But I'm busy today. I'm hoping to crack the nut of St Columba's, and if it turns out to be a police matter, Constable, I'll give it into your hands and yours shall be the glory and the promotion; and then shall come the engagement and the orange blossom and the cottage with the roses round the door, and *then* maybe you'll stop accusing me.'

'I don't know what you're talkin' about half the time, missus,' said Reid.

'You follow as much as half?' said Alec. 'Good for you.'

I waited until I could be sure that Parents' Day was in full swing before I climbed the cliff path for what I expected would be the final time. Splashes of yellow had swarmed over the terrace and headland all morning, clearly visible from the village below, as the girls prepared the grounds for the visitors. Bunting was strung around poles and cracked smartly in the sea breeze and a flag of indeterminate design (it might have been St Columba himself) was run up the pole. From eleven o'clock onwards motorcars began to arrive, an endless rumble quite audible down the hill, and also there was the odd pair of lost parents driving along the sea front and pointing upwards to the school before executing an awkward turn at the harbour head and retracing their steps to try again. When the strains of a small pipe band (although not small enough for my liking) began to be heard drifting down from the terrace, I put the examination papers in my bag, settled my hat firmly against the gusts and ventured forth.

It was a scene of some gaiety despite the chilly greyness of the day. Long tables with coffee and cakes had been set out along the terraces and little round tables with posies of roses on them were dotted here and there on the damp grass. The hardier parents were seated, the mothers eating cakes with one hand and holding their hats on with the other, while fathers hunched against the wind and tried to light cigarettes inside their lapels. The more tender parents were forced to shelter on the terrace itself in the lee of the building, even though that kept them in full blasting proximity to the band.

'I hope to *God* luncheon is inside at least,' said a skinny mother, shivering like a greyhound, as I passed her. 'Darling, couldn't you go and petition?'

'Not my idea to come, if you remember, Ursie,' said the man she was with, who was standing poker-straight and scowling at the nearest bagpiper. I decide to attach myself to them, since I could tell from the woman's shoes, the man's tie and the drawling voices of them both that these were what Hugh calls 'our sort'. In other words, these parents were some of those I could not quite believe had a girl at Miss Shanks's peculiar little school. Perhaps if I got them talking they could explain it to me.

'One's only hope,' I said, turning towards them, 'is for a downpour proper. It would get us inside and stop that dreadful din.'

In their eyes was the flash as they recognised *their* sort and they did a bit of polite tittering.

'Do you have a girl here?' said the father. 'Excuse me! Magnus Duncan and this is my wife, Ursula.'

'Dandy Gilver,' I said. 'How do you do. I think we both know the Esslemonts, don't we?'

'Oh, how do you do,' said Mrs Duncan. 'Yes, dear Daisy.'

'I don't have a girl here,' I said. 'Yet. I'm thinking about it, though.' I crossed my fingers in hope that our acquaintance was too slight for them to remember that I had only sons. They exchanged a quick look, as husbands and wives will, but it was impenetrable to me.

'Well, St Columba's has been very good for our girl, hasn't it, Ursie?' said Mr Duncan.

'Oh, quite,' said his wife. 'Thoroughly to be recommended.' Then both of them looked down into their coffee cups and took up what promised to be a lasting silence.

'Well, that's very good to . . .' I said, staring at their partings. 'Excuse me, won't you. I see someone I have to . . .'

I did, as a matter of fact. I saw the unmistakable back view of Candide Rowe-Issing, in a lavender linen frock and an outrageous yellow hat which clashed painfully with the yellow of the St Columba's uniform. I made a bee-line for her but was waylaid before I was halfway there.

'Miss Gilver!' It was Eileen Rendall, as pretty as a picture with a yellow rose tucked behind one ear, one of the few girls not washed out by the uniform.

'Goody Goody Gilver,' said Spring, coming up behind her. 'I thought you'd gone. We were admiring ourselves for our quickest work yet, weren't we, girls?'

'Oh, I was only ever a stop-gap,' I said. 'How are you getting on with Miss Glennie?'

'Well, on the bright side,' said Spring, 'she hasn't snatched the sonnets back from us.'

'We'll always have you to thank for the sonnets, Miss Gilver,' said Katie, joining them and slinging an arm around the neck of each.

'On the other hand, she knows a choking amount of guff about Milton,' Spring finished.

'And she's a dab hand with a grammar exercise too, more's the pity,' said Katie.

'Who's this?' It was Sally Madden. 'Our Latin, French and English are all grammar exercises now. And since chemistry and algebra are grammar too, to my mind anyway, it's syntax as far as the eye can see. I love it.'

'Oh, Sally, shut up, you *can't*,' said Spring. 'And you don't love Highland Glennie. No one could love that old—'

'Girls,' I said. 'I might not be your mistress any more but that's no reason to suspend all civility around me.'

'Sorry, Miss Gilver,' said Eileen.

'Where's Stella?' I asked, accustomed to seeing them all together.

'Why do you ask?' said Stella's voice behind me. As usual, the insolence was as pronounced as it was indefinable. 'Did you want to ask—' Then her attention was caught by something behind me. 'There's Mummy at last,' she said.

'Ah,' I said, attempting the same languid tone. 'I must slope over and say hello.'

But the terrace between the lemon-yellow hat and me was stuffed with parents, rather like a church-hall jumble sale. Actually, as I looked around, a great deal like a church-hall jumble sale. Fathers in shiny suits with braces showing and mothers in patterned frocks and unfortunate hats on the backs of their heads. A mother standing very near me gave a shy smile and sidled up like a little water buffalo.

'You're one of the teachers?' she said. 'I heard those girls talking to you.'

'I'm . . .' I said. 'English mistress.' It was perhaps just vague enough not to be an out and out lie. 'Now, which girl is yours?' Of course, the chances of me having met their daughter in my one day of active service were slim and the chances of remembering her name if I had were even slimmer.

'Tilly,' said the father, giving me a toothy smile.

I opened my eyes wide. 'Tilly Simmons?'

'That's our little darling,' said the mother. 'She's good at English, isn't she?' She sidled even closer and gave me a nudge in the ribs with her plump elbow. I thought back to Clothilde Simmons's laboured and mediocre translation and gave a thin smile. I could feel the Simmons letter in my bag as though it were a hot coal.

'And is this your first visit to the school?' I said. 'I must introduce you to dear Miss Shanks.'

'Oh no, we know Miss Shanks,' said Mr Simmons. 'We're very close to Miss Shanks, aren't we, Mother?'

'You see we're not just parents,' said his wife. 'We're benefactors.'

'Or we will be soon.' Mr Simmons put his thumbs under his braces and rocked on his heels with pride. 'Just need to make up our minds between a yacht and some stables.'

'I'm sorry?' I said.

'Don't you know?' said the man, looking rather crestfallen. 'I'd have said it was worth talking about, me.'

'Father and I are going to make a bequest to the school,' said Mrs Simmons. 'Riding stables, we thought. But Miss Shanks is quite keen on a yacht to give the girls sailing lessons. Oh, Father! I hope she comes round to the stables. I'd never sleep thinking about Tilly out on them big waves.'

'We're not used to our kid being away from us yet,' Mr Simmons said. 'Never went away to school, didn't Mother and me.' I had guessed as much; everything from their hat and braces to their pancake-flat vowels announced that even though they might have a great deal of money (a very great deal if stables were on the cards) they had made it all themselves and were showering upon their daughter all the advantages they had missed. Since I am no snob (no matter what Alec says) my only concern was to help them shower it sensibly.

'Can I just ask,' I said, 'what made you decide to send Tilly to St Columba's instead of one of the bigger and better known schools?'

'Oh, we had her down for Cheltenham,' said Mrs Simmons. 'But friends of ours, well, neighbours, new neighbours, after we moved, said to us that St Columba's was the place. And their girls are to be presented at court, you know. Real young ladies.'

'I see,' I said, which was a lie. 'Well, simply lovely to have met you, Simmonses.' I gave a little bow and was amused to see them giving a real bow and curtsey in return as I left them.

'And where are all the mistresses?' said a voice as I plunged into the crowd once again. Where indeed? I thought. I had expected to feel a hand on my collar a lot quicker than this, and while in one way it was splendid to have had such a run at the parents and girls (not to mention the fact that I felt I was hearing all sorts of useful stuff from their innocent lips), looked at another way I knew that I was only ever going to solve the puzzle of St Columba's by skewering the Misses Christopher, Barclay and Shanks. Those three were at the root of it, whatever it was.

'Which mistress would you like most to talk to?' I said, turning with a smile. 'Perhaps I can take you to her or fetch her for you?'

'Miss Barclay,' said a man in a brown suit with a pipe in his mouth. 'Geography. Our Christine is going to Edinburgh University to do geography at the end of next year.' His voice had grown louder, in the hope that the bystanders nearest him would hear him and marvel.

'*Up* to Edinburgh to *read* geography, Rex,' said his wife in far softer tones.

'Rex?' said her husband. 'Who's Rex, when he's at home? I'm Reg and I always have been.' He winked at me. 'She only started the Rex lark when Christine got interviewed at the university and they said she was in!'

'You must be very proud of her,' I said, smiling with genuine pleasure for them.

'Oh well, how else would it be?' he said. 'My wife chose the school and took care of all that. I'm a plain man and happy to see the girls take after their mother.'

'You've chosen very well for your daughter, Mrs . . .' I said. 'Edinburgh University, eh?'

'She was worth it,' said the woman, curiously tight-lipped beside her beaming husband.

'And you have another daughter too?' I said.

'She's not coming here,' said the woman. She stared me straight in the eye. 'You can tell Miss Shanks that from me, whoever you are.'

At last the pipe band gave a long discordant groan and an

exhausted wheeze and were silent. A gong was struck and a voice – I thought it was Mrs Brown – announced that luncheon was served in the refectory. I turned back to the quiet woman and took hold of her arm as discreetly as I could do it.

'I need to talk to you,' I said in a low voice. 'Or rather I think you need to talk to me.'

But she brushed me off quite roughly and backed away, shaking her head.

'No, no, no,' she said. 'Not any more, not again. You can forget it.' And with that she turned and vanished into the crowd.

'My wife,' said her husband, looking after her. 'Nerves, you know. Been that way a few years now. You'll have to forgive her.'

'Of course,' I said, with a distracted smile. 'Don't mention it. I hope she's soon feeling better and please tell her I apologise if I upset her in any way.'

'Dandy?' The voice was not loud but it cut through the hubbub of jostling parents like a shard of glass. I turned and smiled.

'Candide,' I said. 'Fancy meeting you here.'

'But you have sons!' she said. 'Don't tell me Shanks is taking boys now.'

'Not as far as I know,' I said, ducking under the hat brim and clashing my cheeks against hers. 'I've just seen Stella. She's your absolute twin these days.'

'Only to look at,' said Candide in a cool murmur. 'How are your boys getting on, then? Not turning your hair white, I trust?'

'Oh well, Donald is a bit of a handful,' I said. 'Teddy hasn't set into shape yet, so who knows?' But she was not really listening and I changed the subject. 'I've seen your bathing pool,' I said. Candide's face, always quite foxy, grew positively pinched at the mention of it.

'Blasted thing,' she said. 'I had no idea that they'd put our names on it.'

'Very good of you, still,' I said. 'Given the times, especially.'

'Hah!' said Candide. 'Well, yes, that bloody pond used to be a Canaletto. There's a pale patch on the landing wall.' I stared at her and she looked off to one side, took a short sharp nip at her cigarette, almost like a little kiss, and then blew the smoke out in a long stream. 'One does what one can,' she said. 'And better a simple bequest than a lifetime's obligation worked off in testimonials.'

'Well, Stella is a fortunate girl,' I said, 'and Miss Shanks a *very* fortunate woman.' I knew I was staring harder than ever but in truth my mind was far away, sorting through all that I had heard: from the Simmonses and the Duncans, from Mr and Mrs Reg to Candide's few cryptic offerings.

'Stella,' said her mother, 'is a disappointment and a pest. I only hope she makes it all worthwhile in the end by marrying someone half-decent, that's all.' Then she threw down her cigarette, flashed me a quick smile, clashed cheeks again and swept towards the open dining-room doors, the lesser parents (and that was more or less all of them) parting like the Red Sea at her coming.

'Oh no,' I groaned for, in the space where she had been standing, there now stood Stella herself, and for once her brow was not arched and her lip not curled. She was white-faced with shock and her mouth trembled.

'What did Mummy just say?' she said, not drawling at all now.

'I didn't catch it,' I answered. Feigning unlikely deafness is such a help at so many awkward moments.

'A disappointment?' Stella said. 'A *pest*?'

'Have you quarrelled?' I asked. She had been badly enough crumpled by the unfortunate overhearing that I did not shrink from putting a friendly arm around her, as one would any child. And crumpled as she was, she submitted to it.

'No,' she said. 'The last time we quarrelled was when they said I had to come here to school instead of where I wanted.'

'Why was that, do you know?

'Friends said it was marvellous,' she replied. 'And they got a bargain, they said.'

'Well, Stella,' I said. 'You know what to do when you overhear ill of yourself, don't you?' She rallied a little.

'Of course,' she replied. 'I shall put it out of my mind.'

'Or hoard it in secret until your mother is old and infirm and then cast it up endlessly,' I whispered. 'Ask her who's a pest now, when you're wheeling her round in her bath chair. Bellow it down her ear-trumpet in revenge.'

This recovered her completely and she gave a rich chuckle and tossed her hair.

'You have a better wit than any other mistress around here,' she said. 'Why can't you stay?'

I leaned towards her.

'I'm not a mistress,' I said. 'Remember Donald Gilver who chased you out into the snow at that Christmas party at Cawdor, trying to kiss you?'

'How do you know about that?' said Stella.

'I'm his mother,' I said. I saw her eyes narrow and then widen as she recognised me. 'I spanked him with a hairbrush for frightening you and spoiling your pretty shoes.'

'So what were you doing here?' Stella said.

'I'm a private detective,' I told her and had the satisfaction of seeing her sharp little face register utter amazement. 'And I'm just about at the bottom of what's happening here. At least I might be if I could have ten minutes' solitude to think it through.'

'Can I tell the others?' she said. And a little of my short career as an English mistress was in me when I echoed Hugh and answered:

'You may.'

Where, though, was solitude to be found in St Columba's on this day of all days? I did not want to run into any of the mistresses now. After luncheon no doubt all of the dorms and classrooms would be swarming with little girls showing their beds and desks to mummies and daddies, and from the rows of seats arranged in the flat part of the grounds north of the school there was clearly some outdoor entertainment planned too. I slipped into the building by a garden door and seeing the little flower room where the mistresses' bags were stored reminded me that one room of all would be sure to be empty today. And I knew the way, thankfully. It took me only a moment to find Fleur's door, try the handle, send up a silent prayer and slip inside.

274

As the door closed softly, though, I got and gave the most tremendous shock, for Fleur's little room, cold and bare, was not empty. Betty Alder, Sabbatina Aldo, was lying full-length on the narrow bed, sobbing her heart out into the pillow, and she leapt to her feet with a shriek (matching my own) when she saw me.

'Sabbatina?' I said, recovering first. 'What's the matter, and what are you doing in here?'

She had clearly been crying for quite some time: her eyes were swollen half-shut and her nose was swollen too and reddened from blowing. Her beautiful olive skin was blotchy and her raven curls were plastered damply to her forehead and neck.

'I can't bear to be with the others today,' she said. 'My mother and father didn't come. I saw my father yesterday and I . . . told him things. I think I drove him away.'

'But you didn't want to see your father,' I reminded her. A fresh course of tears slid down her cheeks and she scrubbed at them.

'I wanted to see my mother,' she said. 'Father didn't tell me she wasn't coming. I waited and waited in the front hall until everyone else was gone and there was just me standing there.'

'But Sabbatina, my dear,' I said, sitting down beside her and rubbing her back (it seemed to be my day for comforting the daughters of uncaring mothers, today). 'Of course she didn't come. She's gone, dear. Oh, poor you! Were you pinning your hopes on her coming back?' The girl sniffed and blinked.

'Gone?' she said. 'Gone where? Coming back from where?' I think *I* might have blinked at that.

'But you knew she was gone,' I said. 'We spoke of it.'

'I didn't— Gone where, Miss Gilver? My mother? Gone where?'

I stopped rubbing her back and began instead rubbing the bridge of my own nose.

'Hang on,' I said, 'We had at least one conversation about this. And you said to me that you were going to see your father – not your mother – last Saturday.'

'Yes,' she said, nodding. 'I never see my mother on a Saturday. She goes to Dunskey House on that day. You know. Washing.'

'But who is it you're missing then?' I said. 'Who is it that's gone and left you? I feel as if I've fallen down a rabbit hole.'

'Miss Lipscott,' the child said, and her voice broke. 'Miss Lipscott, of course. She's gone. And I can't bear it.' She threw herself back down onto the bed, buried her head in the pillow and howled. I felt quite safe rolling my eyes since she could not see me, but I managed to make my voice kind and calm.

'My dear girl,' I said, 'it's quite normal to have these over-whelming feelings about one's mistresses, you know. But you shouldn't give in to them. Now, sit up and dry your eyes.'

She did sit up then.

'It's not a pash, Miss Gilver,' she said. 'It's not a crush. Miss Lipscott took care of me. I thought she was like a sister.'

'Well, that's very nice,' I said, 'but you really should—'

'You don't understand,' said Sabbatina. 'Miss Lipscott was my patron. She paid for me to be here. She even said that maybe after I was finished with school I could live with her.'

I stared at her, feeling things shift but still not knowing where they were off to.

'I was at the village school when I met her,' she said. 'She used to walk and I used to walk – on my own, because of all the teasing – and then we walked together and she brought me books and then she started coming down to the house and giving me lessons and she was like one of the family. And then I came here and she said maybe we could all live together. Only, she stopped saying that after a while. And now I don't know what to think. I don't know if she ever cared for me at all. But she said I could go up and spend the summer with her. And now she's gone, Miss Gilver, and I can't stay at St Columba's and go to university and I shall be a washerwoman like my mother and—' She stopped dead. 'My mother's *gone*?'

Inside, I groaned to have let it slip out like that.

'What am I going to do?' Sabbatina said. 'How could she go off and leave me?' And since I quite honestly did not know which one of the two women she meant, I said nothing. Anyway, I was thinking hard. She had just said something that had struck me.

'What am I going to do, Miss Gilver?' the girl whispered again. 'I did something silly and I'm sorry.'

'What?' I asked.

'I took her bags. I hid them under my bed, but it's sheets change day tomorrow and I don't know what to do.'

'You sto— You took Miss Lipscott's bags from the flower room?' I said.

'I heard you on the telephone when I came to give Miss Shanks a note,' said Sabbatina. 'You said where they were and I – I just wanted something of hers to keep. And there was a letter in her bag and I opened it – even though it wasn't for me – and now everything's spoiled. And my mother's gone too?'

'Quick,' I said, 'while they're still at luncheon. Let's go and get the bags and bring them here. I want to read this letter, to see if there's anything to tell us where she might be.'

'There isn't,' she said. 'It's just a horrible, sordid letter that spoiled everything.' She sniffed. 'Are you sure she didn't go home?' I nodded. 'Do you think she's all right? I still care, even after everything.' I gave a firm nod with nothing behind it except wishful thinking, and then together we slipped out of the room to flit up the stairs and along the passages to Sabbatina's little dorm.

'Of course, this is very wrong,' I said, somewhat belatedly, when we had got the bags back to Fleur's room again and Sabbatina had put the letter in its envelope into my hands, 'but sometimes we have to do things of which we'd ordinarily be ashamed.'

'I'm not ashamed,' she said. 'At least, I'm only ashamed for Miss Lipscott and I'm ashamed of thinking she loved me.'

'I'm sure she did,' I said. Sabbatina nodded to the envelope.

'Read it, Miss Gilver, and then tell me.' I looked down and my eyes widened. It was addressed to *Sr Giuseppe Aldo*. 'Miss Lipscott wrote a letter to my father every week,' said Sabbatina. 'I usually took it to him. I thought she was letting him know how I was getting on and all that. I put it right into his hands. Every Saturday.'

'Not to your mother and father together?' I said.

'Mother doesn't read English,' she said. 'I want to teach her but she never has time until it's late and she's tired. Maybe if I had taught her to read . . . I keep forgetting that you told me she's gone.'

I frowned a bit then, for how could any upset over a lost English mistress drown out the news that one's mother had left one? I opened the envelope and drew out the single sheet inside.

Dear Joe, it began (rather chummily, I thought, but then Joe Aldo did seem to have the knack for making chums. I was sure I had called him that myself in the course of our few short meetings). *First things first*, the letter went on. *Sabbatina's essay this week was first-rate and her grammar work is coming along wonderfully too. The other mistresses are not fulsome in their praise but I have seen her exercise books and she is near the top of the form in almost everything. I say again, as I have before, that to have such a daughter must be a great blessing and could be the foundation of a very happy life for Rosa and you if you would give up these silly notions of yours.*

Rather peppery, I thought, and read on to see to what silly notions she might be alluding. *I cannot pretend that I do not share your feelings, because you know I do and the few times you overcame my better principles were some of the sweetest moments of my life.* I looked up at Sabbatina, but she had looked away. *But I will never be responsible for coming between a husband and wife. I would not marry you if you divorced Rosa and I will not live in sin.* My head was beginning to reel. Joe Aldo the fish fryer? *I did not seek your affections and I regret not being firmer in my resistance to them in the early days when we were first friends. I am going away from St Columba's very soon, Joe. I shall continue to pay for Sabbatina's education and I shall always think fondly of you, her and Rosa and pray for your future happiness as the family, blessed by God and joined in His name, that you are. Goodbye, Fleur Lipscott.*

'He drove her away, Miss Gilver,' Sabbatina said. 'He loved her – not me – and she loved him – not me – but she wouldn't do wrong and he drove her away. And he drove my mother away too. She must have found out.'

'Sh, Sabbatina,' I said, for I was trying to think. 'Hush, now.'

Fleur was planning to run away from Joe Aldo, who would not stop pursuing her. What had happened to make her abandon the plan and flee, leaving Jeanne Beauclerc behind? I glanced down at the letter again. *I would not marry you if you divorced Rosa and I will not live in sin.*

'Oh my God,' I said. If living in sin was out and divorce was out that left only one option. And in my memory I saw Fleur bending over the faceless corpse and whispering 'Five'. 'Oh my God,' I said again. We were sure that No. 5 was not Rosa Aldo, because her own husband had told us so. But if her husband had killed her, then of course he would deny recognising the poor broken thing that his murder had made of her.

'Sabbatina,' I said, 'what "things" did you tell your father when you spoke to him yesterday? Did you tell him you'd read this letter?'

'No,' the girl said, 'but I think he guessed I had, or he guessed that I had found out about him and Miss Lipscott anyway. I told him I blamed him for making her run away.'

'Did he ask you where she had gone?' I said.

'Yes, and I told him I thought she had gone home,' Sabbatina said. 'But you told me she hasn't.'

'That's right,' I said. 'She hasn't. Wherever she is, she's safe. But you said something . . .' I was searching her face. 'You said something to me that I didn't catch hold of but I know it's important.'

'What, Miss Gilver?' she said, looking back at me with equal earnestness.

'I don't know,' I said. Then I took hold of both of her arms. Could a man who had killed his wife kill his child? If Sabbatina had told her father she knew about him and Fleur was she herself in danger now? 'I've got to go, dear,' I said. 'And I want you to lock yourself in here and wait until I or the police or . . . someone comes back before you open up.'

'A mistress?' said Sabbatina.

'If it's Miss Glennie or Miss Lovage,' I said, 'then yes. Otherwise just keep quiet until they go away.' I did not know why I did not trust the others. And I did not know whether the story of Joe and Fleur – a Juliet indeed! – was mixed up in the story of St Columba's, but I needed Alec and all my wits and I could not have the worry of this child distracting me. 'Will you be all right?' I asked her, but she had already taken some article of Fleur's clothing out of the suitcase and looked as though she were planning to curl up and mourn her lost beloved some more. 'Good girl,' I said. 'Lock the door.'

My run of luck was over: as I left the building by the same side door, I was hailed from a distance and turned to see Miss Shanks pounding towards me.

'Miss Gilver? Miss Gilver!' she cried.

'Can't stop, Miss Shanks,' I called back with a wave, and kept going. She could hardly run me down and tackle me in front of all the parents, so she slowed and stopped and I was away from her, pelting over the lawn and down the cliff steps with my mind racing faster than my feet.

Joe killed Rosa, because he thought that then Fleur would marry him. Fleur thought her refusal to marry him while his wife was alive meant that she had Rosa's blood on her hands. That much made sense. But how could Joe have thought Fleur would marry a murderer? Did he mean to make everyone believe it was suicide? Or an accident? But then why did he not say he recognised his wife when he went to see her? What happened to change his plan that terrible day when I went to the cove with Fleur and Joe went with Alec? And what of the mysterious lover who had been seen with Rosa on the cliff path?

I stopped so suddenly that I nearly tripped and fell off the cliff myself. *He was seen.* That's what changed. Alec said as much: Joe Aldo was numb with shock at the news that someone had seen his wife and 'her lover' and that the witness said she would know the man if she saw him again. After that Joe *had* to say the corpse was a stranger. And then there was the telephone call. I stopped again, but more gradually this time. How could No. 5 be Rosa Aldo when she had rung her husband on the telephone after No. 5's body had been drowned and nibbled by fishes and washed ashore again?

I came down onto the harbourside and made my way towards the Crown, but was stopped by a piercing whistle from the far harbour wall. Alec waved both his arms at me and I motioned frantically for him to come. He set off towards me at a jog but I could not wait and I sprinted to meet him. He saw me sprint and put on some speed himself so that when we met we were both blowing hard and sweating.

I had brought the letter and I thrust it into his hands.

'Bloody hell,' he said when he had finished it.

'No. 5,' I panted. 'Rosa Aldo. Fleur responsible. Joe – pass it off as suicide.'

'Until little Cissie saw them!' said Alec.

'Yes, yes, that's what I thought,' I said, recovering my breath. 'But Alec, Rosa Aldo called her husband on the telephone. I spoke to her myself. Remember?'

'Nonsense,' Alec said. 'You had never met Rosa Aldo. It's not as though you recognised her voice or anything. You spoke to someone who rang Joe. Someone who spoke a bit of Italian, such as a studious sort would pick up in a couple of years of visiting an Italian family.'

'*Fleur?*' I felt a tremor pass through me as though someone had hit an anvil with a hammer close by. 'It couldn't be.'

'Why not?' Alec said. 'I never could understand why Joe was so floored by someone supposedly seeing Rosa with her boyfriend, but it makes sense if the boyfriend was he and he was just about to shove her off the cliff top. So it can't have been Rosa on the telephone. If it wasn't Rosa, who else?'

'He must have nerves of steel,' I said. 'We were standing right there and Fleur was on the phone and he pretended it was his wife? And she pretended to *be* his wife? Why would she do that?'

'I don't know,' Alec said. 'But I'm sure she did. He told Fleur what to say and you obligingly relayed the message to him, not understanding what she said until he translated it for you.'

'I got the gist,' I said, and then another tremor made its way through my innards and this one left me cold.

'Alec,' I said. 'Cissie said she didn't understand what Rosa and the stranger were saying but she knew it was sweet-talk. I thought she didn't hear the words themselves.'

'But now you think maybe she did hear them but she didn't understand them because they were in Italian?'

'And she doesn't like fish and chips,' I said. 'So she very likely had never seen Giuseppe Aldo even if his wife was familiar to her.'

'More evidence,' said Alec. 'But Dan, what's wrong?'

'I told Joe the Turners' maid was the one who saw Rosa and friend on the cliff top. And – oh Alec! – maybe Cissie *isn't* sulking. Maybe she's missing. Maybe he got her too.'

Alec was running already and reached the police station before I had made it a yard up the street. By the time I got to the door Reid and he were on their way out again. Reid wrenched open the door of the police motorcar and Alec shoved me in and then jammed in after me. As we began to climb the hill with the engine whining, Sergeant Turner came out onto the street and stood, hands dangling at his sides, watching the three of us speed away.

Outside the Turner villa, Reid screeched to a halt and jumped down. He leapt over the garden gate, rounded the side of the house and disappeared. Alec and I scrambled after him. In the yard, the kitchen door was banging back on its hinges and Reid was in the middle of the linoleum floor with his arms wrapped round an astonished Cissie like an octopus with its prey while a thin cook looked on, a baking bowl under one arm and a wooden spoon held up like a baton.

'Cissie,' I said. 'Oh my dear girl, thank goodness!'

'Who are you?' said the cook.

'I'm a chump and this is my idiot friend,' I said to her. 'Gilver and Osborne. They were speaking Italian, Cissie, weren't they? That night on the cliff top. Rosa and the man who wasn't her uncle?'

'Lots of people speak Italian,' she said. 'Get off, Wullie.'

'Has someone been speaking Italian to you?' said Alec. Cissie blushed.

'Writing it,' she said. 'I've got a friend and admirer, Wullie Reid, and he's told me all about you!'

'What's going on?' said the cook. 'This is my kitchen, ye ken, and I'll call the mistress if you don't tell me what's to do.'

'All about me what?' said Reid.

'All lies,' said Alec, 'whatever it was. This secret admirer, Cissie – has he asked you to slip out and meet him yet?'

'He said he had to go away a wee while,' she said, 'but maybe next week, he said he'd take me a hurl in his car and we'd get some dinner.'

'Out for dinner!' said Reid. 'How am I supposed to compete wi' that on ma wages?'

'William,' I said, 'I think you're losing sight of the main point here, aren't you? Aldo only needed to keep Cissie apart from you until he was ready to shut up shop and disappear for good. He's not coming back to take her for dinner or even for a bag of chips at the harbour.'

'I don't like chips,' Cissie said. 'He promised a proper dinner.'

'Cissie, that man is a liar and a murderer,' Alec said. 'It was Giuseppe Aldo who wrote to you. He was the one you heard on the cliff path with his own wife and he killed her. He would have killed you if you had gone out to meet him too.'

'He's a very dangerous man,' I said, 'and he plays risky games. Do you realise, Reid, that he pretended his wife was on the telephone that day when really it was Fleur all the time who was in Glasgow station and . . .' I stopped and let the silence fill me.

'What is it, Dan?' Alec said.

Finally, the little pip of information which had been tickling at me was in my grasp.

'Up,' I said. 'Sabbatina Aldo said that Fleur had invited her "up" to stay for the holidays. She kept saying Fleur would go home. She couldn't believe Fleur would go anywhere else except home. But Pereford – Somerset – isn't *up* anywhere. Sabbatina meant

283

Alt-na-harrie. The Major's lodge. The place Fleur went to when her life at Pereford changed for ever all those years ago.'

'But they sold it,' Alec said.

'To an anonymous buyer,' I reminded him. 'And Fleur came into a lot of money when she was eighteen. More than she could spend on a Bugatti.' I turned to Reid.

'Constable,' I said, 'Miss Lipscott is at home in a hunting lodge near Ullapool. I'm sure of it. If you go there, you'll find her.'

'I'll never get let go all the way up there,' said Reid. 'The sarge'll be after me wi' a strap for takin' his car this far.'

'We'll hire a motorcar and you can come with us,' I said. 'It's pretty tricky to find, actually. You'd probably do better with a native guide. Meantime, Cissie, I'm sure Aldo is gone for good but until he's caught – just to be on the safe side – perhaps you'd better stay in and don't answer the door. No matter who it is calling.'

'My God, Alec,' I said as we made our way from the high road of villas to the back street where the car-hiring garage was to be found. 'Do you realise how many young ladies there currently are stashed all over this fair land? Four counting Sabbatina, who's in Fleur's room at the school, breaking her poor heart over her mother and her patron. And her no-good father as well, probably.'

'Why's she stashed?' Alec said.

'Because I wasn't thinking straight and I couldn't tell if the school was mixed up in the Aldo mess.'

'It's not, is it?' he asked, and then he rapped hard on the open garage doors at which we had arrived. 'Me again, Mr Donaldson. I'm getting to be your best customer, eh?'

'Aye, right, son,' said the man in the dark-blue cambric overall straightening up from where he was bent over an open bonnet. 'But ye're no' in luck today. The car's away.'

'Oh,' said Alec. 'Right.'

'Aye, thon Eye-tie took it yesterday. Said he'd a wee trip to go on.'

I glanced at Alec to see what he made of this.

'Has he cut and run?' I asked.

'Why on earth would he run in a hired car which would soon become a stolen car if he didn't return it?' Alec said to me.

'Eh?' said Mr Donaldson. 'Who's sayin' he's no' returnin' it? He said he had a wee bit business where there's no trains.'

'Alec!' I said, clutching at him. 'Sabbatina told me! She said she had spoken to Joe about Fleur running away. He knows where she's gone. He's gone after her to Ullapool. And he's got a day's head start on you and me.'

12

My fingers ached all the way up to my shoulders from gripping the back of the seat in front of me as the little motorcar swung around the bends and sailed up and over the bumps in the road.

'You all right back there, Dan?' said Alec, looking over his shoulder. I nodded.

'I'm too tense to be sick,' I said, 'and I haven't eaten anything since yesterday anyway.'

'Mind and not faint on us, then,' said Reid. His eyes were trained on the road ahead, peering into the small patch of light his headlamps made on this twisted lane under the trees.

We flashed past a sign for Ullapool, the white wood just gleaming enough for the black letters to show up against it.

'Not far now,' I said. 'How could anyone live all the way out here without a telephone these days?'

'And no answer to the telegram boy,' Alec reminded me.

For all our desperate efforts to get to Fleur some way – any way – quicker than chasing off in belated pursuit of Aldo had failed. Sergeant Turner stared us down to sheepish silence when we tried to tell him that the corpse was Mrs Aldo, that both the witnesses who claimed not to know it had known it perfectly well, that the lover on the headland was the husband, that the wife on the telephone was the lover, that the girl whose family sold the house had bought it . . .

'Oh aye?' he had said. 'And where does the French one in the farmhouse fit in?'

'I don't know,' I had said.

'She doesn't,' said Alec. 'That's a separate matter completely.'

'Oh aye?' said Sergeant Turner again. 'See, to my mind, when you've finished a puzzle – a jigsaw puzzle, say – you've no bits left over. That's how you know you're done.'

So he would not telephone to the nearest constabulary and have them send a man to the lodge and he would not countenance a trip in his precious police car and he would not give Reid a sudden afternoon free. He fixed the lad with his terrier-like scowl, brows down and eyes glinting, and told him to get himself round to the grocer's shop at the bottom of Main Street where a parcel of bacon had gone missing from the boy's basket and was yet to be found.

Alec and I had been waiting at the station for the next train to Stranraer and the hope of another hiring garage when Reid had hurtled up in an ancient little Mercury and summoned us with a long blast on the horn.

'Whose is this?' I asked, scrambling myself into the tight space of the spare seat behind the driver. There was no chance that Alec could fold himself into it, I knew.

'Mrs Turner's,' said Reid. 'Cissie pinched the key to the garage door for me.'

'You'll both be sacked for sure now,' I said.

'Yup,' said Reid and, turning out of the station brae, he roared off up the hill to join the road to Stranraer, Girvan and points north as if the hounds of hell – and not just Sergeant Turner and his formidable wife – might be after him.

There had been moments of calm, even passages of conversation, and in the course of bumping along the terrible Highland roads, at last the pieces of the St Columba's puzzle had fallen into place. With nothing left over, as Sergeant Turner so rightly decreed was the way of things.

'It was nothing to do with Fleur and the murders,' I told Reid and Alec. 'Not really. Except that Fleur's guilt was why she was there. She wanted to get away from men. She thinks she killed her father and two lovers, remember.'

'*Thinks* she did?' said Reid. I ignored him.

'And Miss Fielding took in waifs and strays. She took in a girl who said she'd killed her lovers and she took in the daughter of a noble French family who's done something naughty enough to be disowned. Second chances, see? The key is that the women at that school either brought money – Shanks, Lovage and Fielding – or they brought learning – Taylor, Bell and Blair. Or they were waifs and strays. That's Fleur and Jeanne. And recently Miss Glennie, too. The Lambourne Agency is obviously in on the operation, seeking out likely candidates for Miss Shanks. And the Misses Christopher and Barclay are very much her lieutenants in it all. The point wasn't that Miss Glennie used to work at Balmoral, you see. The point is that she was sacked from Balmoral. For something. Something that means she doesn't have up-to-date photographs of her mother and father even though they're still alive.'

'Disowned again?' Alec said. 'What for this time?'

'Well, she has lots of snaps of a child,' I said. 'She said it was her brother but now I think it was most likely her son.'

'That would get a governess sacked right enough,' Alec said. 'But why would it get her a job in a school?'

'Blackmail,' I said. 'Plain and simple. Barclay and Christopher are doing something for Miss Shanks that Miss Taylor and Miss Bell – scholars of depthless integrity – would never do. And something Miss Blair – as the PE mistress – couldn't do. Once Miss Glennie submits, they'll have such a hold over her that she'll work for nothing. Shanks thought Jeanne and Fleur could be persuaded to do the same but it turns out she was wrong. They were made of finer stuff; they held out as long as they could and then, when Jeanne could bear it no longer, they hatched a plan to escape from her.'

'Ah,' Alec said. 'That's why they had to go away and hide. She would have told the world of their sins if they'd just resigned.'

'Exactly,' I said.

'But what did she blackmail them into doin'?' said Reid.

'I didn't work it out until Parents' Day, today,' I said. 'They were doing various things. Or at least two different sorts of things for two different sorts of girls. And it all begins with cheating.'

'Girls cheating?' said Alec.

'No, but parents being told that girls cheat,' I said. 'Parents like the Rowe-Issings and the Duncans being told that their daughters are cheats, but that Miss Shanks will keep it quiet in return for testimonials, swimming pools and stables, that kind of thing.'

'But some of the girls are genuinely bright, aren't they?' Alec said.

'Yes, some are,' I answered. 'Sabbatina Aldo is and she's of no interest to Ivy Shanks at all. I never could work that out. Why a scholarship girl with a fine brain was not the toast of the staff-room. Now, you see, the girls who're going to university from St Columba's all come from very solid middle-class backgrounds. Those parents wouldn't drop dead at the thought of cheating as Basil and Candide would (not to a man, anyway) but they'd happily shell out for a bit of swanky advantage.'

'That's not fair, Dandy,' said Alec. 'You don't even know any middle-class people. They're the salt of the earth usually.'

'I do!' I said. 'I know Inspector Hutchinson from Perth and I know Hugh's estate factor. And I'm not saying all of them. No doubt Ivy Shanks has to go very gently to see who will be amenable and who would go to the police and daughter be damned.'

'But you're sure about the operation overall?' Alec said.

'I am. Because listen: the college-bound girls are going to read geography and history (Miss Barclay), science (Miss Christopher), and French. Hence the huge panic when Jeanne disappeared. No one is up for English – hence the huge *lack* of panic over the English mistress. Until, that is, Miss Shanks thought she had another sitting duck in me – wickedly living in an inn with a young man – and decided that Clothilde Simmons might be a whizz at English. Oh God!'

'What?' said Alec.

'I accused that dratted widow of writing a poison-pen letter to Hugh,' I said. 'But of course it was Ivy Shanks testing the waters. It was when she realised that Hugh couldn't care less and neither could I that she sacked me. Oh my God, Alec! That widow-woman must think I'm insane!'

'She'll dine out on it for years,' he said. 'So the mistresses – the crooked ones – bump up the marks?'

'Worse than that,' I said. 'I think they do the work. I never could understand why the mistresses were always burning the midnight oil while the girls were draped around like temple nymphs. Or why the mistresses were writing in black ink, and not red pencil. Or needed so many textbooks and dictionaries just for marking. Constable, if you shut down such a hotbed of blackmail and corruption, it might even offset the – um – borrowing of Mrs Turner's motorcar.'

'Depends what's waiting for us at the other end o' this,' Reid said, and all my triumph at solving the riddle of St Columba's was gone again. No one was dying there. No one was drowning. Nothing but fairness and justice was harmed. When I thought about Mrs Aldo and what might have been done to Fleur in the time Joe Aldo had had to do it, I fell silent again. My silence spread to the other two and now, in the moonlight, five miles from the lodge, all three of us were wound like watch springs, champing to be out of this rattling, fizzing little machine and dreading what we would find when we arrived.

'Corner coming, right,' I said and Reid made another of his sickening two-wheel turns. The chassis sounded like a falling load of scrap metal as the other two wheels hit the ground again. 'I take it back,' I said. 'Alec please put the hood down and let me have some air.'

'Midges,' Alec said.

'They can have me,' I groaned. 'There's a crossroads in less than a mile, William. You want the left turn and it's a sharp one.'

'How come you ken this place so well, missus?' Reid asked me.

'Shooting,' I said, through clenched teeth. 'Friends of ours used to take the next place along for the deer.' In truth, I knew the twists and reversals of the road because every time Hugh and I had travelled it I had sat in a mulish huff about the drip-ping black pines and the humpback bridges. I could not see the point of leaving Gilverton for somewhere – in my estimation – even worse.

At least it was not dripping tonight, and with the moon glaring down it was not really all that black either, but I anticipated something a great deal more hellish than dull company and a day's dreary shooting at the end of the road.

'Gates,' I said, spotting them, and we were off the road with one final twist of the steering wheel and rocketing silently on the deep cushion of pine needles which covered the drive, down and down to the lodge at the water's edge.

'He's here!' shouted Alec, seeing just before I did the motorcar pulled off the lane at the edge of the carriage sweep. 'That was Donaldson's car for sure.'

'Aye, he's here,' said Reid and for the first time I heard a shake in his voice, not only caused by the rattling up his arms of an engine under strain. We were old hands at this caper, Alec and I, but what did Reid know of chasing a murderer down in the night and capturing him?

'House is dark,' I said. The stones of the lodge were pale and glinting in the moonlight the way that granite can, but every window showed a black, blank gaze of emptiness. Reid killed the engine and the little Mercury, creaking and steaming, slowed and stopped on the gravel. We sat still and listened. The silence was absolute, a perfect endless silence with no breath of wind, no lap of waves, not so much as the call of an owl or the crack of a twig.

'Has he a gun?' said Reid and his voice, once again, was trembling.

'Shouldn't have thought so,' Alec whispered back.

'He's had plenty of time to find the guns in the house, though,' I put in and then wished I had not, for there we sat, the three of us, in a motorcar with the top down in the middle of the gravel in the bright blare of moonlight and any of those black windows could have Aldo behind them, watching.

'Let's get under cover,' said Alec and opening his door he slid out and ran, hunched over and scuttling, into the shadow of the trees. I followed him, calling softly to Reid to do the same.

'He can't be in there,' Alec said when the three of us were

huddled under the draping arm of a cedar, breathing in the sweet scent of its bark and sharp tang of its needles under our feet. 'He had a perfect shot at us then. Like wooden ducks at the fairground.'

'Now he tells us!' said Reid, with some of his old vigour. I rewarded him with a chuckle – anything to keep his courage up – and sat back against the tree.

'So what shall we do?' I said.

'If we could find the gun room . . .' said Alec.

I took a deep breath before replying. His suggestion, not quite made out loud but strongly implied, was a good one. I had never shot so much as a hare and the thought of shooting a man, even a man as conniving and evil as Giuseppe Aldo, was a monstrosity to me. William Reid too was surely too young to have been in the war and Alec's plan would change his innocent life for ever if things went that way. But what else was there for it?

'I suppose I should say that this place looks exactly the same as Corrie Dubh, up the road,' I said. 'David Bryce's best Scotch Baronial. He turned them out like muffins, you know.'

'Eh?' said Reid.

'I know where the gun room is at Corrie Dubh,' I said. 'So I think I could find it here. Of course breaking down the door will bring him running . . .' I hoped that one of them would agree and stop me, but neither did.

So, still bent double and keeping close to the trees, I led them around the side of the house to the yard door. If I was right about the floorplan, the gun room should be just along the corridor beyond it. Internal, of course, no window to smash for entry, but the yard door had a top half of glass and Alec took off his shoe in readiness.

'All right?' he said.

'Wait!' I whispered. 'Might as well . . .' I tried the handle, turned it and the door swung open.

Alec laughed softly and put his shoe on again.

We had run out of luck, though. The gun-room door, although just where I thought it would be, was locked and the key nowhere to be seen. Alec sent Reid to the corner of the corridor as a lookout and shoved me into an alcove for safety and then, taking off his coat, he put his shoulder to the door and gave it a mighty thump. It sent him staggering back a few steps without emitting anything like a crack or splinter which would hint at submission.

'Don't worry,' he said. 'That was just a tester.' I did not quite believe him, but with his next assault he took a run at the thing and made a kind of roar as he connected. With a metallic ping the lock gave way and the door burst open, sending Alec sprawling into the gun room to land heavily on his side. Reid rushed from the corner and I shooed him in like a mother hen, then followed, slammed the door and pulled a nearby cabinet in front of it.

'God damn it to hell,' said Alec, rolling on his back. 'I think I've broken something.'

'Your turn, darling,' I said, thinking of the time I had skidded down a staircase in pursuit of a murderer and smashed my ankle. 'What?'

'Rib,' Alec said, sitting up and groaning.

Reid was listening at the door.

'No sound o' nothin',' he said. 'Mind you, it's a big house.'

'Right then,' I said. 'Reid, keep listening. I'm switching on the lights, but if you hear anyone coming you hiss and I'll switch them right back off again.' I clicked the switch and blinked against the sudden brightness.

The doors of the gun cupboards were all closed and the little cabinet – for shot – which I had moved in front of the door was padlocked. I went round swiftly, rattling the handles, and peering through the grilles.

'There's nothing missing,' I said. 'I don't think he's been in here.'

'Good,' said Alec. He shuffled over to a desk which stood near where he had fallen and hauled himself to his feet. 'So he doesn't have a gun. Pity, because I'm not up to a brawl this evening. Ow! Two ribs, at least. Bloody agony, but only if you breathe, as they say.'

'So where are the keys for the guns?' I said, wondering aloud more than asking.

'Depends how fussy they are,' Alec said.

'No' very,' said Reid. 'Wi' that yard door not locked.'

'Yes,' I said. That was bothering me. I went out into the corridor again and along to where it stood open. I stepped out into the yard and crossed it. Beyond the gate a path led down to the jetty and I could see the sea loch, shining still and silver; high tide on a windless moonlit night and it was a mirror lying there. I gazed, then squinted, and then I began to run. There was a little boat out in the open and a figure in it, sitting so still that not a ripple disturbed the reflection of the moon in the water.

'Alec!' I shouted as I went. 'Reid!'

The figure had heard me and moved, I knew, for all round the boat suddenly the perfect image of the moon and trees broke and shimmered. I ran to the jetty, right to the end and peered across the water. Behind me came the pelting footsteps of the constable and then Alec, shuffling and swearing.

'Who is it?' I said. 'There's only one. Is it Aldo? Has he killed her and taken her body out there to dump it?'

'If he has, he's put her frock on,' said Reid. His young eyes had picked out more than mine. He cupped his hands around his mouth and bellowed. 'Miss Lipscott, you're all right. We—'

Fleur stood and then even I could see it was her, in her dress with her hair down her back.

'Fleur, darling,' I shouted. 'Row to shore— *No!*'

Fleur had gone. She had simply stepped over the side of the little boat and dropped into the water.

'Alec, wincing, had started taking off his waistcoat and kicking out of his shoes, but his face was shining with perspiration and his breath was ragged.

'Reid!' I said, turning to where the constable stood frozen.

'I cannae swim,' he said. I could have slapped him.

'You—You pick drowned fishermen out of the sea all the time!' I shouted. 'How can you not swim?'

'Fisherfolk never learn to swim,' Reid said. 'It's bad luck.'

I tore off my hat and coat, my dress, my shoes and my

294

petticoats too and in my chemise and stockings, before I could give myself time to think, I jumped off the jetty into the icy water.

It was so cold that my shoulders seized up around my neck and I was only paddling forward by inches, so I turned on my back, looked up and prayed for strength and courage. I prayed to Hugh, who swam in Loch Ordie every morning between May and October, to Nanny Palmer who took a cold bath until she turned ninety and had a shower machine put in, and to my old childhood self, with Pearl and Aurora and Fleur, jumping in and out of the tide at Watchet all day long.

Then I turned back over and started swimming.

I warmed a little with the exertion, or numbed perhaps, but I made it to the boat anyway and rounded it. She had not sunk and was not struggling. I could see her floating face-down with her hair fanned out and that wicked, disgusting picture of Ophelia flashed in my mind once again. I swam up and grabbed her.

'Floribunda, don't you dare, you little monkey,' I said through chattering teeth. 'Your mother will die of grief and your sisters will never smile again.'

She had reared up, spluttering, and now she flicked her hair out her eyes and splashed frantically, trying to get away from me.

'I killed him,' she said. 'I killed him.'

'You didn't kill anyone, Fleur,' I told her.

'I killed him, I killed him.'

I surged forward and grabbed her round the neck under one arm, then I turned us both onto our backs and with my free hand I made for the shore. She was limp against me and I could hear her muttering on and on, through her chattering teeth: 'I killed him. I killed him.'

'You're killing *me*,' I shouted. 'Try to swim, darling.'

I spoke lightly but I was terrified. My arm was heavier and weaker with every stroke and we were no longer on the surface but low in the water, our legs deep down into the chill. I took a breath and a mouthful of water came in with it.

'Fleur, please!' I begged, trying to shake her. She was a dead weight under my arm. I put my mouth beside her ear and yelled at her.

'Sabbatina needs you!'

She flailed then and her head rose, but it was too late.

'We're sink—' I said and the water closed over my head and I was falling.

13

My hair seemed to rip at the roots as a hand took hold of my head, then an arm was under my back, and then I was bent over the side of a boat, with my top half shivering in the air and my legs still dragging in the water. I opened my mouth and a gush of cold poured out. Alec hauled me with his one good arm until I lay on the floor of the dinghy like a load of wet washing, watching Constable Reid hang over the side with his boots wedged under the bench to keep him anchored.

Up he came, with nothing, and dragged in a tearing breath before he plunged under again, so deep that the boat lurched over until the cold water was slopping in. And up he came. And he had a foot and a leg and then her hips and her arms and her coughing, choking, head and she was in the bottom of the boat beside me and weeping there.

'We found another boat,' said Alec. 'Obviously.'

'I killed him,' Fleur whimpered. 'I killed him.'

'You killed no one,' I said, mumbling through my numb lips. 'You poor darling, you lost your father and your lover and your friend—'

'Body heat's the thing,' Alec said. 'But I can hardly move. Grab my legs, Dandy. Better than nothing.'

'Ch-charles wanted to d-drive my car,' chittered Fleur. 'And he was intoxicated. Not drink. D-drugs, Dandy, and I bought them! Leigh wanted to try something new.'

'You didn't shove them down his neck or hers,' I said.

'I f-fell out when it hit the tree,' she said. 'I tried to get them out.'

'Of course, you did, you good girl,' I said.

'I'm not a g-good girl,' she cried. 'I killed him.'

'And then you saw that wretched Elf take the coward's way out right in front of your eyes, didn't you?' She nodded, fast and shivering. 'And Giuseppe Aldo was a cold-hearted devil of a man. You told him straight, my love. I read your letter. He killed his wife, not you.'

'I know,' said Fleur. 'He m-murdered her. For me. I didn't kill anyone in a b-battle or a crash or a suicide. I know that now, because I k-k-killed *him*.'

'Aldo?' said Alec.

'I w-was in the b-boat.' She was shaking so much now that her voice was like a rattle. 'And he swam. In a r-r-rage. He swam. And I j-just j-jabbed him with the oar. J-j-jab-jab-jab. Until he was g-gone.'

'Good,' I said.

'Yes,' said Fleur, and her eyes turned upwards as she fainted away.

I hugged her close, although I was almost as cold as she was and, pushing the sodden hanks of her hair back from her face to kiss her eyes, I shuddered to remember Rosa Aldo's hair in the cable station that day, how it lay in a clump on her soaking dress, and how cold and grey her skin was above the dirty lace of her collar. Perhaps I was passing out too but all of a sudden I could feel again the water closing over my head and filling my mouth and I struggled to sit up.

'They say drowning is peaceful,' I said.

'If it is,' said Alec, 'then it was too good for him.'

'The car's dead,' said Constable Reid a few hours later. He had joined Fleur, Alec and me in the lodge kitchen, where we sat wrapped in blankets and nursing the latest in a succession of toddies.

'The Turners' car?' I asked, and he nodded.

'Donaldson's car needs to go back anyway,' said Alec. 'And you're the only one of the lot of us who's fit to drive.'

'But we're not going to Portpatrick,' I said. 'Constable Reid, you can have St Columba's on me. I expect you'll want to go and arrest Ivy Shanks and Miss Barclay and Miss Christopher. But first, can you please take me home? And Miss Lipscott too?'

Reid gave me a long cool look, which I met for a while before dropping my eyes.

'Miss Lipscott'll need to come wi' me,' he said. 'To make a statement, at least. It's up to the Fiscal if it's more.'

'Only if she saw the incident,' I said. 'Only if she witnessed Aldo's suicide, surely.'

Alec gave a low whistle.

'Constable?' said Fleur. 'I killed him and if you say I must be arrested and tried then so be it. But what about Sabbatina? She has no relations living now – not closer than Italy anyway – and I would surely be more use as her guardian than as a prisoner?'

Alec and I exchanged a glance. Fleur, we knew, would be very lucky to get away with prison. A jury, hearing of the drugs and the lovers, not to mention the telephone call covering up Aldo's crime, would more likely call to see her hanged.

'Tonight was self-defence,' said Reid. 'That I'll give ye. But here's what's stickin' in ma craw: sayin' ye didn't know who the corpse was.'

'I was frightened,' said Fleur.

'And then pretendin' to *be* her!' Reid said. 'Makin' fools o' us all.'

'It was Joe's idea,' Fleur said. 'He thought it up in a flash. He's cunning that way. And I was too frightened not to go along with it. He threatened such dreadful things.'

'But you were away out of it by then,' Reid said.

'Oh no!' said Fleur. 'You misunderstand me. I wasn't frightened for myself. It was Sabbatina. He said he would tell her about us, and tell her I never cared for her. He said he would put her in an orphanage and not even tell her why.'

'And yet you left her with him?' Alec said. 'A man like that?'

'I was going to send for her,' Fleur said. Her voice had dropped down to a whisper. 'I would have written and sent her train fare.

It was just all so confusing. Jeanne running away and me trying to pack and Ivy Shanks pecking at me like a carrion crow. Joe too. He wouldn't stop. And then Rosa's body. I just— I ran away.' She gave a tremendous sniff and then looked Alec in the eye. 'You're right, Mr Osborne,' she said. 'Running off and leaving Sabbatina there was a dreadful thing to do. A weak, thoughtless thing. Maybe I'm not fit to be her guardian after all.'

'Oh no you don't,' I said.

'I'll come with you, Constable, and take my chances,' said Fleur.

'Not this again,' I said. 'Fleur, please. You are not responsible for everything that happens in the whole wide world, you know.' And I gave both Alec and Reid a look from under my eyebrows, that told them exactly what I thought of them for torturing her. Reid shifted in his seat, but Alec is used to my looks and took this one without blinking.

'On the other hand,' said Reid, 'Sergeant Turner wouldn't like it that the story he wouldn't swallow is right enough after all. He'd no' like that one wee bit. He'd take it out on Cissie and me.'

'There's a boat out in the sea loch and a body in the water,' I said. 'What could be neater? A woman missing, a body found, her husband gone, his body found too?'

'Only how would we explain him bein' all the way up here?' said Reid.

'I could help with that perhaps,' said Fleur. 'I did offer the Aldos the chance of a summer holiday here. So he knew of the place, you see.' She gulped and swallowed hard. 'I wanted to bring Sabbatina here. I wanted to show her my home.'

'This isn't your home, darling,' I said. 'Show her Pereford. Take her down to Mamma-dearest and Batty Aunt Lilah and let Pearl and Aurora loose on her. If anything could make up for losing her parents that way, Pereford can. That's what you need, too. Go home.'

'Aye well,' said Reid. 'I can get you as far as Perthshire anyway.'

So we detoured on the way south again and reached Gilverton after sunrise, trundling up the drive towards the shuttered house, only the gardeners up and about and waving uncertainly at the unfamiliar motorcar as it passed.

'Are you looking forward to seeing Mademoiselle Beauclerc?' said Alec to Fleur. She had been quiet and deeply morose as we travelled, but now she roused herself and gave a smile.

'If she'll forgive me.'

'Of course she will. You thought she'd be safer at Low Merrick Farm than running away with you, and you were right. Aldo might have killed both of you.'

'And Jeanne had only just stopped thinking death would be welcome,' Fleur said.

'Do you know her story?' I asked her. 'Why was she open to blackmail?'

'The usual,' she replied. 'The kind of thing that would be winked at if she were a boy. And she held out for so long, but Shanks just ground away at her. She *had* to run to the Patersons', Dandy. You've no idea what Ivy Shanks is like. And she does it all with a smile on her face as if it's funny.'

Alec nodded with understanding, but when Fleur spoke of Jeanne's sins I had felt a small cold hand creep under my ribs and squeeze some organ it found there.

The car drew up and the front door opened. I steeled myself for Pallister, but it was Donald who burst out, still in his dressing gown and with a smile on his face the size of the sun.

'Mother!' he cried. 'Welcome home. What on earth are you wearing?'

'What are you doing up?' I said. 'It's . . .' I glanced at my wristwatch but of course it was ruined.

'I can't sleep,' said Donald. 'I'm too bursting with joy. Thank you, Mother, for sending her.' And with that he disappeared and his place on the doorstep was taken by Hugh.

'Dandelion,' he said.

'Oh dear,' said Alec's voice behind me in the shadows of the motorcar.

'Who's that?' Hugh said, glancing at the driver's seat.

'Constable—' was as far as I got.

301

'Brought home by the police now!' said Hugh. 'Where have you been?'

'Portpatrick,' I said. 'You knew that.'

'Nonsense,' he barked. 'I rang and rang.'

'Oh,' I said. 'Yes. And Somerset. Pereford. Hugh, look who's here. It's Fleur. Johnny Lipscott's youngest child.' I smiled my most winning smile and wiggled my eyebrows significantly too.

'Is it?' said Hugh and gave a short bow to Fleur. His manners, even when he is in a rage the size of the current one, are always civil. He leaned towards me. 'It might well be Johnny Lipscott's youngest child,' he said through gritted teeth, 'but she's too late.'

Then he spun on his heel and marched inside again.

'Off you pop then, Dan,' said Alec, struggling against a surge of laughter which would kill his broken rib. 'Constable Reid, if you'd be so good as to take me another seven miles, I think I might just as well go home. Perhaps a more restful atmosphere for my recuperation. And Miss Lipscott? If things get too hot here, you're very welcome to join me.'

'Not so fast,' I said to him. 'Reid, could you wait here, please?' I scrambled out of the motorcar. 'Or I tell you what,' I went on, turning back, 'trundle round to the kitchen door and get my good Mrs Tilling to make you each a bacon sandwich.' Then I sped off after Hugh.

He was nowhere to be seen – he can vanish like a cloaked conjuror when the mood takes him – but it was not difficult to guess where he would have gone to earth in the kind of temper he was in this morning. I rapped on his business-room door and entered without waiting, to find him sitting amongst the plans and papers which normally soothe him.

'How far can it possibly have gone?' I asked. 'Not breach of promise already surely?'

'If only!' cried Hugh.

'What?' This remark made no sense at all.

'Our son has . . .' Hugh coughed, glanced at the door, and went on in a low voice, '. . . ruined the girl.'

I let out a hefty sigh and dropped down into a chair.

'Good God, Hugh, you had me thoroughly rattled. No, he hasn't. But what do you mean, anyway?'

'Wanderings in the night,' said Hugh, so darkly that I had to try very hard not to smile. 'I caught him in the passageway and he didn't even deny it. So. Now you're home you must speak to him. And to her. And he must do the honourable thing.'

'Hugh, for heaven's sake—'

'This is no opera girl, Dandy. I can't imagine why you passed her off as a seamstress—'

'If you would open your ears and listen once in a—'

'Or a nun.'

'Donald didn't "ruin" her,' I said. 'He's years too late, for a start. Good Lord, anything less like a nun is hard to imagine.'

Hugh opened his eyes very wide so that his crow's feet showed white in his weather-beaten face.

'But she's an unmarried girl of good family,' he said, adorably. Hugh's world is a simple one.

'So if there's been ruination,' I said, 'it's she who has ruined him.'

'Well,' said Hugh, with some relief, 'he doesn't seem to have minded.'

Then he sat up very straight, shocked that his relief had led him so far as to say such a thing to me, instead of keeping it for George at the club where it belonged. I took pity on his frozen discomfiture and left him alone with his tracing paper and pencils again.

'Is that for Miss Beauclerc, Becky?' I called across the hallway, seeing one of the parlour maids just starting up the stairs with a tea tray.

'Oh! Welcome home, madam,' she said, attempting a curtsey, but with a careful eye on the milk jug. 'Yes.'

'Where is she?' I asked striding over and taking it out of her hands.

'Oh! Rose room, madam.'

'Right,' I said, grimly, taking the stairs two at a time.

'Will I fetch her bags out of the boxroom?' Becky called after me, in a hopeful voice.

'As soon as you can,' I called back.

'Oh, good, madam,' Becky said. 'Mr Pallister *will* be pleased.'

Jeanne Beauclerc was lolling against the satinwood headboard, taking the rags out of her hair and fluffing it into curls as I entered.

'Mrs Gilver!' she said. She sounded startled, but she did not sit up or stop fluffing.

'Indeed,' I replied. 'I've found Fleur for you. She's downstairs. She might be staying here or she might be staying with Mr Osborne, a friend of mine. You, as I'm sure I don't need to explain, shall not be staying here any longer.'

Mademoiselle Beauclerc blinked at that, but she did not stop smiling.

'What a pity,' she said. 'I have had a very pleasant few days.' I was speechless. 'Your son is such a sweet boy, Mrs Gilver.'

'My son is going back to school tomorrow,' I replied.

'And your husband is such a sweet man.' My speechlessness this time was of a depth and quality I had never experienced before. I simply banged down the tray and turned to go.

'But the hospitable Mr Osborne sounds very promising too,' she said in a musing voice. I hesitated, then kept on walking. Alec could take care of himself; this viper was not spending another night in my nest.

Postscript

'Frankly,' said Alec, 'I'm insulted.' We had had the carriage to ourselves since East Combe and I had finally asked him straight out if he had managed to resist the charms of Jeanne Beauclerc in the few days she had spent under his roof. 'Really, Dandy, I'm twice Donald's age with three times his experience of the world.'

'Poor Donald,' I said, not meaning it at all. 'If I'd known a broken heart would set him straight the way it has, I'd have arranged for it to be broken long before now. But it wasn't just Donald, you know. Hugh was beginning to sway in time, like a charmed snake, and I've begun to wonder why Mrs Paterson at Low Merrick Farm was so keen to get rid of such a nice quiet guest. It never struck me as likely that parents from St Columba's would really have booked up all the rooms at the farm. I reckon Jeanne was batting her eyes at Mr Paterson over the sheep pens and his wife got wind of it.'

'And what's the news from the ruins of St Columba's?' Alec said. 'Anything fresh to report?'

Constable Reid had been telephoning to me with daily updates until Miss Brown at the Portpatrick post office got sick of him monopolising 'her good kiosk' and shooed him out once and for all. Luckily, by then little bits of it had begun to leak into the press and we could follow the story as it unfolded.

'Well, of course, even before it comes to court, they've all been defrocked or lost their licences or whatever happens to school-mistresses,' I said. 'Not that Miss Ivy Shanks ever really was one. Miss Christopher and Miss Barclay, this is. I feel sorry for Miss Lovage, since she had money in the place.'

'And what's to become of the school itself?'

'Hah!' I said. 'This is priceless. You know it's called St Columba's because it was at Portpatrick that Columba landed from Ireland and tamed the heathen hordes?'

'Vaguely,' said Alec, which is his way of saying 'not at all'.

'Well, it struck a crowd of his fans as the perfect spot. And they're trying to buy it up to make a convent.'

'Oh.' Alec frowned. 'What a waste of a golf course.'

'Episcopalian nuns,' I said. 'I'm sure they play golf. Anyway, it's not decided yet. It'll probably end up as an hotel.'

We were silent for a moment.

'The ones I *really* feel sorry for are all those poor girls who thought they were marvellous scholars,' I said, after a while. 'They've had a dreadful comedown.'

'But then there are the Stellas to balance them,' said Alec.

'Oh, yes!' I said, clapping my hands. 'I had the most entertaining telephone call from Candide Rowe-Issing – furious with Ivy Shanks, of course, and quite ready to sell another Canaletto to pay a solicitor to sue her – but so delighted to find out that Stella's not a cheat after all that she almost – almost, mind – betrayed a flicker of affection for the girl.'

Alec laughed.

'Mawkishness is always unspeakable,' I went on, 'but I do think Candide has gone a little too far the other way.'

'And speaking of mawkishness,' said Alec, 'you really think the whole battalion are going to be there today?'

'Undoubtedly,' I said. 'Try not to be sick, won't you?'

Right enough, there they all were; in the garden, under the walnut tree, waving us over from the drive. Mamma-dearest rocking in her hammock, Aurora sprawled on a rug on the grass, Pearl with her feet tucked up on her wicker chair, hugging her knees, Batty Aunt Lilah pattering about with her secateurs. And coming towards us over the lawns, Fleur, in a pale green frock with her hair cut short and her arm around Sabbatina, who was as brown as a gypsy and wearing a tennis dress.

'Darling Dandy,' said Fleur, as we walked towards them, and I knew from just those two words that she was herself again.

'You're late!' shouted Pearl. 'We've had to make fresh tea twice already and the icing's melted on the big cake.'

'It's so wonderful to see you, Dan,' said Fleur. 'And you, Mr Osborne. How is that delicious little doggy of yours?'

'Where's Jeanne?' I said, and Fleur caught Sabbatina's eye and giggled.

'In the village,' she said. 'At the widowed doctor's for tea. She's made an absolute conquest of him, but it's very naughty of her to miss your visit.'

She and Sabbatina turned and started walking ahead of us back to the others.

'I'll live,' I said in a low voice to Alec.

'Doggy, indeed,' he muttered.

'Oh, darling, that's nothing,' I said. 'I did warn you about the Lipscott Delight, but you were determined to show me Dorset . . .'

'Mr Osborne,' said Mamma-dearest as we reached her. 'I have a great deal of making up to do, for what a sourpuss I was last time. Do sit beside me and let me begin. And do, of course, let me introduce you to our dear sweet precious Sabba-tinkle-tina. I had no idea you two hadn't met.'

I made sure that my chair faced Alec's and sat down to enjoy the show.

Facts & Fiction

The building that houses St Columba's is on the spot where the Portpatrick Hotel can be found, glowering down on the village. As far as I know there has never been a girls' school there and certainly St Columba's, the *institution*, is entirely fictitious.

The Crown in the novel shares a name and location with The Crown in Portpatrick, but nothing else.

I'm not absolutely sure that the tide between Port Kale and Port Mora ever goes out far enough to allow someone to walk safely along the beach between them, and so would advise even Dandy's most ardent fan not to try.

Catriona McPherson on *Dandy Gilver and a Bothersome Number of Corpses*

We're often asked . . . sometimes asked . . . somebody asked me once (to quote Flanders and Swann) where we writers get our ideas. The answer in my case is that ideas are born when one little mental pip touches against another unrelated one causing a fizzing sound and a smell of burning. When the smoke clears an idea is revealed.

One of the pips in *Dandy Gilver and A Bothersome Number of Corpses* formed when I went to a boarding school to talk to the sixth year about careers. While being shown around, I saw the plaque by the swimming pool, recording who had donated it – some grand old chap whose name I've forgotten now: let's call him The Rev. Colonel Plum-Mustard – and for some reason I started wondering about his motives.

The other pip was homesickness. This was the first story I wrote after leaving Scotland to live in California and thoughts of home and self-imposed exile were churning in me. I was also quite sternly trying to not to give in to the homesickness, so rose-tinted glasses and unreliable memories were in my thoughts also.

Fizz bang and there was the story: a boarding school, a swimming pool, an idyllic past that might be too good to be true, and a character fiercely denying herself all comforts for no good reason that anyone can see.

And of course for someone whose childhood was spent reading and re-reading Enid Blyton's *Malory Towers* and St Clare's series, imagining St Columba's College for Young Ladies was more like a return to the good old days than an expedition into the unknown. I reined myself in with sober research eventually, but boy that first draft was fun!

In fact, I might have had more honest-to-goodness fun writing this book than any before. The idea of Dandy Gilver undercover as a schoolmistress trying to teach Chaucer without being rumbled still makes me smile. I also set St Columba's in Portpatrick, a fishing village in Galloway that I know and love, allowing myself the pleasure of revisiting the harbour and hillsides and the sparkling Solway. I couldn't resist, either, having a fish and chip shop in the village where Dandy and Alec could buy battered haddock fried to perfection in good beef dripping and eat it out of newspapers, leaning against the harbour wall. Here in California, I had to console myself with a big cup of watermelon juice from my favourite taquería and tell myself it was too hot for a fish supper anyway.

The story that grew from the singed pips is pretty dark – for Dandy – and so I'm glad that the setting worked out the way it did, with charm and laughs and a good dose of the kind of food that'll stick to your ribs and see you through a winter. I hope you enjoyed your visit to Portpatrick and the puzzle of those bothersome corpses.

Catriona McPherson

The World of
Dandy Gilver

Grant's Seasonal Modes

Underclothes

Sometimes in life you get what you pay for and other times you pay for the name. With frocks and coats and bags and shoes it makes no odds. What does it matter whether you turn heads because your suit is beautiful, fits like a glove and hangs like a morning mist or because someone who knows can tell it came from Chanel, and this season too? Any lady under ninety who has not taken the veil would be happy with either.

When it comes, however, to the foundation layer – call it lingerie or call it underclothes – no one can see the drape or the name and many's the lady who will argue to save money with factory-made garments that ruin her ligne and fall to pieces in the second washing.

All in all, the old fashions were easy. A coarse cotton chemise was a punishment and an ill-fitting corset of low quality was a device of pure torture. Certain other garments, if they had lumpy seams or machine-trim, would not be worn twice either. Best silk, best lace, finest lawn, corsets that would last your life with careful laundering and an eye on your diet. The good old days.

Not but what the modern underclothes are a boon. No lady's maid mourns the passing of the binding tape and the advent of the bandeau brassiere. No lady's maid misses unpicking the stitching to take out the bones of a corset for washing and then stitching them in again. And no lady's maid ever born misses ironing fifteen rows of lace edging on a floor-length petticoat.

But things must not go too far. Ten French bandeaus; ten silk, ten wool and ten linen slips; fifteen pairs each of silk, wool and linen unmentionables. All hand-sewn with a bit of lace about them somewhere. This is the very least needed to keep the wardrobe running smoothly in all seasons. Any less than that and why have a maid at all?

Notes from Mr Pallister's Pantry

Visiting Persons

It has been necessary once already in these
annals to touch upon the matter of guests whose
social standing, whose family background, whose
very class, mounts a challenge to the usual
order in a household which is accustomed only
to entertain ladies and gentlemen.

Doctors, lawyers and other professional men
present difficulties enough, as was discussed
in my earlier writings. When it comes to female
persons who are not ladies, the challenge
is doubled. When these individuals present
themselves at times when the mistress of the
house is from home, few are the butlers in the
land who could chart such choppy waters and see
the visit through with all unharmed.

Governesses, where experience is held of
that sort of woman, will form a useful template
which can be adapted to manage gently-born
seamstresses, nurses above the rank of sister
or nuns of any kind.

In particular, the sleeping quarters offered
to such females must be nicely judged; one of the
better servants' bedrooms with its own corridor
door and a pleasant view will suffice. If none
such is available then a cadet's bedroom with no
view and on a separate floor from the family and
other guests will make an adequate alternative.

Meals should be taken in the sleeping quarters if such can be arranged, excepting breakfast where a visiting person will hardly discommode the family by joining them. Luncheon, tea, dinner and supper can be taken up on trays or the person can eat in the servants' hall before or after the general mealtime as the cook decides is convenient. If the bedroom is small or the servants' hall unsuitable, perhaps where it is combined with other purposes and an addition would interrupt these or distract lower servants from their duties, any small unused chamber on the ground floor with plain furnishings and no front view can be appointed for dining.

Needless to say, any visitor, even a visiting female of this sort, will be accorded the utmost hospitality by all.

From Mrs Tilling's Recipes

EMPRESS RICE

After a rich or heavy dinner such as will do everyone a power of good in nasty weather (for our stomachs go by the barometer and not the calendar), sliced sweet fruit or a medley of fruit done up in light syrup as a 'salad' can be acidic and unsatisfying. Far better after thick soup, then meat and potatoes, to finish off with a pudding which holds its own. What better than the favourite treat of all our childhoods – rice pudding – made even more delicious with just a little butter, cream and eggs and some candied fruits to tempt both palate and eye.

To serve four (or six if there has been a fish course too).

1 ½ oz pudding rice
1 ¼ pts good milk with cream shaken in
2 oz caster sugar
1 vanilla pod
2 fresh eggs
1 oz best butter
½ oz gelatine leaf
3 tbsp sweet dark sherry
2 tbsp apricot jam (sieved)

2 tbsp chopped glacé cherries
1 tbsp chopped angelica
2 tbsp chopped preserved stem ginger
5 fl oz double cream
To decorate
Whipped cream
6 halved glacé cherries
2 tbsp sliced preserved ginger
6 candied angelica leaves

Wash the rice and put in a bain-marie with a quarter pint of the milk, half the sugar and the vanilla pod. NB: if the cream has separated, save it until the second stage of the recipe. Cover the bain-marie and keep the water boiling under it, stirring the rice from time to time until it is tender and the milk has been taken up into it. (Mine Eyes Have Seen The Glory with all four verses and three rounds of 'Glory, glory Alleluia' between each is just right. If the rice was well-washed in warm water before beginning, there will be no need to repeat the chorus at the end, rousing though it be.)

Remove the vanilla pod, stir in the butter, which you have cut into chips with a knife, and set the rice aside to keep hot.

Now make the custard.

Beat the eggs with the rest of the sugar and milk (using every scrap of cream now). Cook the mixture very gently in a second bain-marie until it is thick enough to coat the back of a wooden spoon. If the household only possesses one bain-marie, it is perfectly acceptable to move the cooked rice into a warm bowl and leave on the back of the range, then start the custard in the same washed-out vessel as before. Such make-do and mend measures have a tendency to lead to frayed tempers and flusterment, however, and in such households as those perhaps a plainer pudding would be preferred.

In a large warmed bowl, gently the stir the hot rice and hot custard together until thoroughly mixed.

Soften the gelatine in the cold sherry for about three verses of Fight the Good Fight (Or since all four verses are equally fine, sing fast and do not stir).

Add the gelatine to the hot rice mixture, set the bowl over a third bain-marie (or one of the first two, rinsed. The rinsing can easily be done while the gelatine is melting and many well-equipped houses nevertheless do not possess three.) Stir over a low heat until the gelatine has dissolved and no dark streaks of sherry are remaining.

Now add the sieved jam, cherries, angelica and ginger, folding them in to achieve an even distribution. Pour the mixture into a basin, cover with a clean cloth and leave until lightly set. A wooden spoon banged on the side of the basin should make the mixture tremble. If it quivers or wobbles it is set too hard and must be warmed through, have a little cream added and allowed to cool again.

When a soft, trembling set is duly won whip the double cream to peaks just rightly between soft and firm and fold this into to the main body of the pudding. Spoon very gently into a mould. Do not pour as this will collapse the cream quite calamitously.

Now leave the mould in a cool larder until it is quite firm, when it can be turned out onto a plate and decorated with more whipped cream, cherries, ginger and angelica leaves. Truly a pudding worthy of Her Late Majesty's imperial stamp. (NB If too much cream was added when the first set was attempted and the second set is too soft, the resulting mess makes a fair start for a trifle.)

A FISH SUPPER

In the ordinary way of things, a fish supper is purchased at the harbourside, on the High Street or even from a street vendor, but in exile or extremis can be cooked at home.

1 haddock fillet per person
½ lb flour and a pinch of sodium bicarbonate
½ pt beer or stout (or soda water if alcohol is not permitted)
Salt and pepper
Malt vinegar
1 large floury potato per person
A large pan of good clean beef dripping.

First for the batter. Sift the flour into a bowl and whisk in the beer or soda. 2 tbsp of malt vinegar added now will make the batter even crisper. Set the bowl aside to rest for half an hour or more.

Next, the potatoes. Peel them and cut them into 'chips' the size of your pinkie. Guddle them in cold water to take off some starch and pat them dry in a tea-towel.

Heat the dripping until it is shimmering hot. Test the heat by dropping in a wee tiny bit of batter off a spoon. It should sink and immediately rise, crisp and gold. If it does not sink, your fat is too cold. If it rises brown, your fat is too hot.

Tip the chipped potatoes into the pan of fat and let them fry until they are palest gold and sparkling, then lift them out with a wire spoon and keep them near.

Now, at last, for the fish. Dip each fillet in the batter until it is coated and lower them gently one by one into the fat. Do not crowd the pan. Each fish will cook in five minutes or so. Take them out of the fat on a slotted spoon when the batter is puffed and golden. Keep the first fish hot in an oven while the later fish cook.

When all the fillets are cooked, return the potatoes to the pan to fry again while the fish is put on warm plates and the diners are called. When the chipped potatoes are golden brown, lift them out of the fat and onto the plates, shaking off a little of the dripping, but by no means all.

For more
Dandyish delights visit
• • •
www.dandygilver.com